I0702474

A Bitter Affection

RACHEL MAYS

Copyright © 2023 by Rachel Mays

All rights reserved.

No portion of this book may be reproduced in any form without written permission from the publisher or author, except as permitted by U.S. copyright law.

This book is a work of fiction. Names, characters, and places are products of the author's imagination. Any resemblance to actual persons, living or dead, events or locations is entirely coincidental.

No portion of this book was created with the use of artificial intelligence.

Cover Design by JV Arts

ISBN: 979-8-9872089-2-2

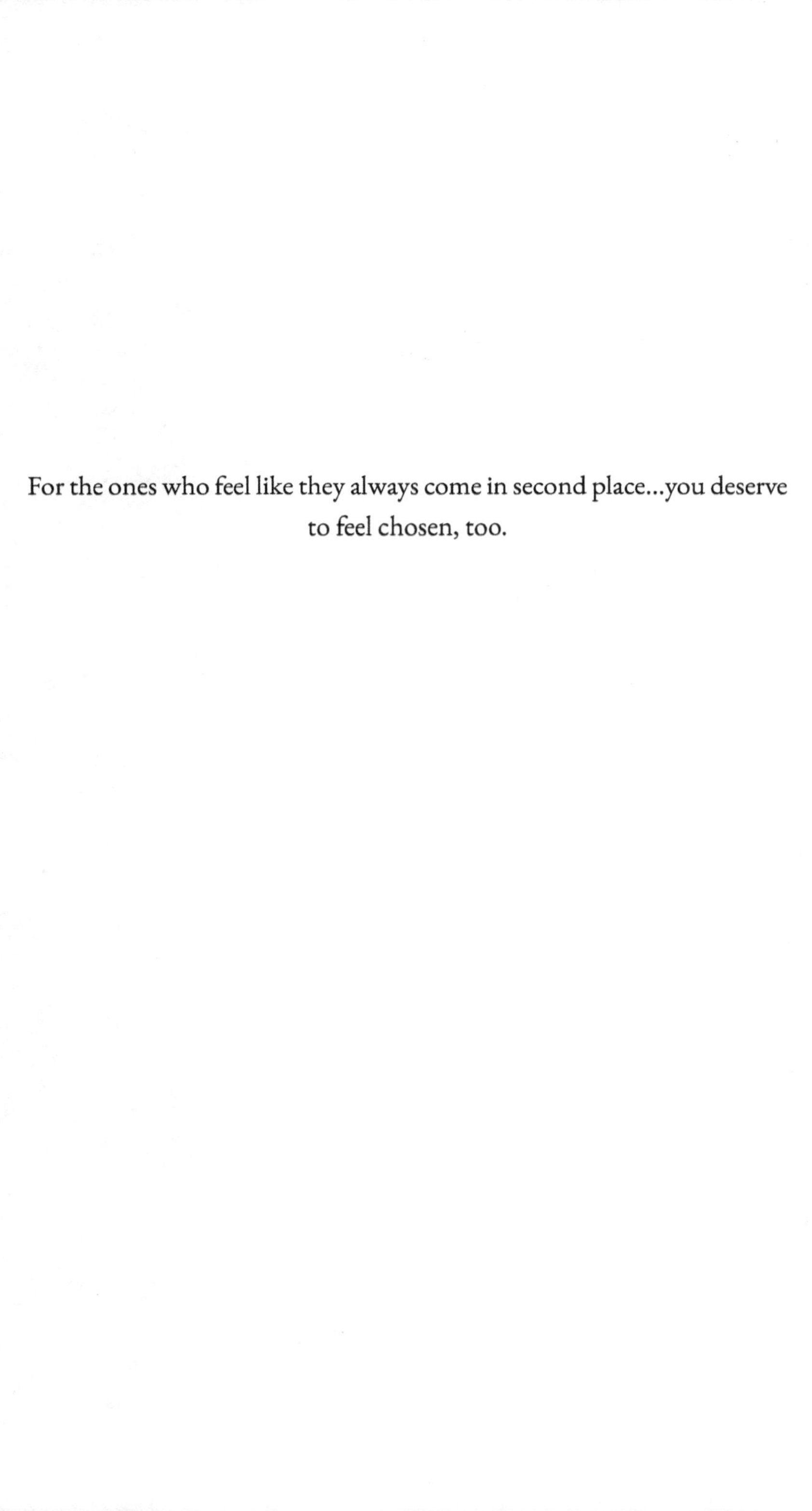

For the ones who feel like they always come in second place…you deserve to feel chosen, too.

Author's Note:

This story contains content that may not be suitable for all readers, including but not limited to, graphic depictions of and references to violence, death, depression, PTSD, and sexual assault. Please take care of your mental health!

Chapter One

ELI

ELI INHALED SHARPLY, TAKING in the acrid smell of smoke that filled his nostrils. A fire crackled nearby; the familiar scent reminded him of home. Although his senses told a tale of security, he knew it was a lie. When he opened his eyes, he'd be surrounded by strangers in a location he wouldn't recognize.

The feeling was disorienting, but all too familiar.

He opened his eyes to a bright but clouded sky. It took a moment to adjust to the daylight. The smell of rain permeated the air; there was a storm coming.

He moved his head to the side, wincing at his stiff neck. How long had he been out? Hours? Days? The surrounding forest had no distinguishing features. He could be anywhere. There was no way to tell how far they'd moved from Rysburg.

Sweat dripped from above his lip, from his forehead to his cheeks. His throat was on fire, and he couldn't force himself to swallow. A sharp pain in his side reminded him of how close he had come to death near the river.

These people...these people had attacked Rysburg. They had chased Ali and Nik and everyone else away from their home. But they'd left him alive? He wasn't sure what to make of it.

Eli let out a guttural grunt and, almost instantly, a healer appeared with a canteen in hand. She was a short woman with frizzy, dark brown hair secured in a bun. Her skin was coarse from maturity, but her eyes and lips held a youthful beauty. Her features were difficult to read, leaving her age a mystery.

"Here you go, Eli." Her voice was comforting—soft and understanding, but he flinched when she brought the canteen to his lips. He didn't know this woman. Didn't know if he could trust her.

"It's just water," she said, and for unknown reasons, he believed her.

He drank the water, the cool liquid spilling down his throat and quenching his thirst.

As she held the canteen to his lips, she hummed a little tune. It was one he didn't recognize, but even as a grown man, her motherly manner comforted him, and he lowered his guard a fraction.

"Thank you," he muttered after moistening his lips. He stared at the woman. Pity radiated from her eyes, which were warm and gentle.

"My name is Georgia. Some people call me Gigi, but if I'm being honest, I hate that nickname. It doesn't seem fitting at all for me, don't you agree?"

Eli stared at her, unblinking, still not sure what to make of her. Was she someone he could trust? Or was she as ruthless as the rest of the Coyotes?

"What do you want with me, Georgia?" Nerves began to prickle. He'd survived Rysburg only to be captured by another enemy. What sinister schemes had this group concocted for him to endure?

She raised her brows. "I want to see you healed and on your way."

Eli shook his head. He tried to shift his position, but the throbbing ache in his side was too much to bear.

"Don't do that," Georgia scolded. "You'll tear open your wound. And after I just changed the bandages."

"The wound that you gave me." The words fired off like a weapon of his own. He needed to get away. To find Ali and the others. The trees around him seemed to close in like a cage. "You and your people did this to me."

Georgia's jaw clenched. "I heard what happened to you, Eli. It was an accident."

"Like hell it was. Your men tried to kill me. Sliced a sword straight through me." He clenched his side where the blade had thankfully missed any vital organs.

"They didn't know you were one of the captives. You were dressed like a guard, and they mistook you for one. I really am sorry that you were injured."

Eli tried to sit up again and cursed the pain that shot through his right side.

"Do you need more medication?"

"No," he grunted, still agitated. He didn't want any help from Georgia or the other Coyotes.

She huffed. "Don't be like that. What happened to you was an accident, but I'm doing my best to help you now. That should count for something, shouldn't it?"

Eli counted his breaths.

One. Two. Three.

He inhaled and exhaled until the rage inside him simmered. Then he said through gritted teeth, "I will take that medicine now."

Georgia slipped away to retrieve another vial of the pain medication, and Eli once again looked around at the forest clearing. Aside from

Georgia, there were only a few others. Three men sat around the fire; the smell of smoke mixed with the sizzling of the meat on the sticks. Their faces were dirty and grim, having survived the brutal battle.

Across from him, there was a pile of sacks. A man stood to search through one, and Eli noted it was full of blankets, food rations, and a canteen, among other items. The man took out the canteen and dropped the bag back amongst the others, settling down once again by the fire.

Georgia lifted the corners of a tarp and peered at the items underneath it. She had a makeshift table set up between a large tree stump and some neighboring trees. The sound of rain tapped against the tarp as it provided a barrier between her medical supplies and the light shower of rain that was common in the spring.

When she returned, Georgia handed him the vial, and he tossed it back, allowing it to burn his throat on the way down. As if she knew the effects of the contents, Georgia once again passed him a water canteen so he could soothe his throat.

"You should try to get some rest. I imagine the rest of them will be returning shortly."

"The rest?" he asked, fidgeting on the hard ground and attempting to find a comfortable position. The medication was fast-acting; already his eyelids felt heavy. It must've been laced with some sort of sedative to force him to rest.

"Yes, we're still waiting on some—the ones who went to free the prisoners. Once they come back, we can head out."

So many questions were swarming through Eli's mind. "Will all the survivors be brought here?" he asked, daring to hope that Ali might be one of them.

She silently nodded.

"You said we're heading out. Where are we going?" He struggled to keep his eyes open. There was still so much he needed to know. So much he wanted to understand. Amidst the questions, panic started to set in. What if Ali wasn't with the other survivors? He didn't want to leave without her.

"We're taking you to Berland. It's a safe haven for the folks we rescue. You'll be well taken care of there. We'll take you most of the way, and then you'll get to meet my daughter, Genevieve. Mostly everyone calls her Genna. Anyway, she was always a bit more of a free spirit...likes to travel around with her wife, Isabel, never sticking to one place for too long. Once a month, we gather where the foothills meet the river. She provides additional supplies for our group and escorts any refugees to Berland. When she isn't helping us, she's off on her own adventures."

Georgia stared into the distance, possibly imagining her daughter and the places she may be right now.

"What if I don't want to go to Berland?"

Georgia snapped out of her daydream and eyed Eli with a frown of confusion. Like no one had ever asked this question before. Maybe no one had.

"Where would you go instead?" she asked. "With an injury like that, you won't make it very far on your own. And the Coyotes have other missions to attend to. We can't drag you with us. You need a place to rest and heal, and that is exactly what Berland can provide."

Eli considered it. Where else would he go? Andus was nothing but rubble and ash. Rysburg had likely been left in similar ruins. His family was dead. Ali was missing.

He swallowed, and it was like tiny razors gliding down his throat. He didn't want to stay with the Coyotes. They were untrustworthy and dangerous. But what other options did he have? Maybe he could stay in Berland long enough to heal and then try to find Ali on his own.

"How far is Berland?" he asked.

"It's quite a trip. It'll likely take at least a week to get there. Maybe more if there are more injured survivors."

A week?

His heart sank at the distance they'd be putting between himself and the last place he'd seen Ali. His limbs felt enormously heavy. He wanted to reach out and tell Georgia he couldn't go to Berland, but he couldn't seem to lift his arms. She had to understand—he had to make her understand—but before he could speak another word, his head lolled to the side and fatigue overtook him.

❧ ❧

The first thing Eli saw when he opened his eyes again was a man with a long scar down his face and a familiar sinister smile. He knew that man.

He bolted upright, and searing pain shot through him. Ignoring the burning agony and the spots clouding his vision, he dug his palms into the ground and pushed up, shuffling out of the clearing and away from that man.

He had watched that man nearly strangle Ali to death. The same man had pierced Eli's body and injected him with some sort of drug.

Eli bit back an anguished groan. He needed to get out of here.

"What in the hell do you think you're doing?" An angry Georgia was standing over him. Her eyes squinted as she watched him attempt to pull himself away from the group of Coyotes. "You've gone and reopened your wound."

Her words rang in Eli's ears, and he looked down at the dark red stain slowly growing on the white bandages around his lower waist.

Shit.

Georgia gently forced him to lie back down on his thin blanket so she could examine his side. "Just as I thought. I'm going to need to stitch this back up. It will not be pleasant. I told you to rest."

She stalked off to her table of supplies, clearly fuming that he had ripped open his stitches and cursing him for being so stubborn.

In the time that he'd been sleeping, more Coyotes had arrived in the clearing. There were now at least a dozen strolling about—mostly men, but a few women as well. During the commotion, several had turned their attention toward Eli, including the man with the scar.

From several feet away, he pointed at Eli. "I know you."

Eli snarled at him.

"Easy." The man put up his hands in an offering of peace. "The other guys filled me in." He nodded in the direction of the three men Eli had seen earlier, gathered around a fire. "I know you were a prisoner and not a Rysburg guard, as we had initially reckoned."

"Is that supposed to make this any better?" Eli's voice was hoarse, but he yelled at the man with everything he had. He didn't care who turned to listen now. "You tried to kill me."

The man peered around, his eyes meeting each of his crew members' as if conveying a silent command. They all returned to what they were do-ing—cooking food, setting up tents, gathering wood. They understood their leader didn't want an audience.

No one was going to help him. No one cared.

Georgia returned with fresh white strips of fabric and a small sewing kit that made his stomach turn. "Lie down," she commanded.

Eli hesitated, his eyes locked on the man who had tried to kill him.

"Oh, for god's sake. Michael, leave him be," Georgia said. The man glanced at her, and although he appeared to be the one in charge, he complied with Georgia's wishes and turned away, leaving her to tend to Eli.

"Take this," Georgia said, handing Eli a small branch no larger than the size of his hand.

"What do I do with it?" he asked.

"Bite it."

She had to be joking.

But she only stared, waiting for him to put the dirty stick in his mouth. So he did as she said and bit down on the wood. The taste of dirt coated his tongue, and he nearly gagged.

Georgia pulled back the fabric from his wound and doused it in a clear liquid that burned like hell. It seemed unfair that the pain of cleaning the gash was worse than the pain he'd felt receiving it.

"Maybe you'll think twice before you rip your stitches out again."

Georgia threaded a needle and Eli could no longer watch. He clenched his jaw and took deep breaths, his eyes squeezed shut, as he felt the needle pierce and pull at his skin.

It probably took Georgia less than ten minutes to stitch him up, but it felt like hours of torture. Once she finished, she wrapped the new bandage around him and pinned it into place.

"I'll take more of the pain medication now," Eli said. "Although you can hold off on the sedative."

He didn't want to pass out again. Not with his attacker, Michael, hanging so close by.

"Afraid not." She gave him a pitiful look. "It's likely I'll need it to treat the others coming in. Besides, it becomes habit-forming after too many doses. You'll have to try to relax on your own this time."

"The others?" he asked with a glimmer of hope. There was still a chance Ali might find her way to him.

Georgia nodded. "The rest of the group still isn't back yet."

Eli stared up at the sky until he heard footsteps approaching. He turned to find Michael standing above him with a mug in his hand.

Eli flinched and instinctively began to roll on his side, away from this predator, but Michael halted him.

"Whoa, whoa. If you tear out those stitches again, Georgia might kill us both."

Eli stilled, fighting the urge to run. He knew he couldn't even if he tried.

Michael crouched beside Eli, offering him the mug. "I'm afraid we're all out of spoons."

When Eli didn't take it, Michael chuckled. "Rest assured, it's not poisoned. I'm telling you, what happened was an accident. I would never intentionally harm someone we were supposed to be saving. Can I help you sit up?"

Eli didn't like the thought of the man putting his hands on him. Stubbornly and slowly, he pushed himself into a sitting position and rested his back against a nearby tree trunk.

Michael extended the mug once again. "It's vegetable soup. You should eat something. Georgia said you haven't eaten anything all day."

Eli thought for a second about what it might be like to toss the hot soup in the man's face. "You almost killed me," he repeated.

"And you *did* kill several of my guys. A casualty of war that I'm willing to get over. Are we going to keep rehashing this or should we leave you to starve to death while your injury prevents you from ever leaving this forest?"

Eli released a heavy sigh through his nose. He wanted so badly to beat this man to a pulp, but that would be impossible in his condition.

Michael shook his head and set the mug by Eli's feet. "Suit yourself."

Eli eyed the soup with caution and disdain. He hated accepting help from Michael, but he also couldn't remember the last time he'd eaten. Carefully, he reached forward to grab the mug, hissing at the strain it caused on his side.

The soup was watery, flavorless, and had very few vegetables floating around. But it was food, and it settled his churning stomach—a combination of medication and nerves.

After what seemed like only five sips, the bland soup was gone. Eli set the mug down beside him and slowly lowered himself back to the ground, tugging a thin blanket on top of him. His body felt heavy, though he wasn't ready to give in to sleep yet.

The rest of the camp began to settle, laying out blankets underneath tarps. Unfortunately, the only one that seemed to notice that Eli didn't have a tarp of his own was Michael. He strode over with pursed lips and a furrowed brow.

He didn't bother to say anything as he hung a tarp above Eli's makeshift bed. He silently tied it to the trees so Eli would stay dry overnight and then retrieved Eli's empty soup mug. Eli didn't say thank you. He didn't particularly feel grateful at the moment. Nothing the Coyotes did now could make up for nearly killing him.

Eli sighed heavily and winced at the pain in his side, wishing Georgia could give him one more dose before he closed his eyes.

"You should get some sleep. As soon as the others get back, we'll be heading out. It's a long hike south to the river, and you'll need your energy. It'll be a tough walk with your injuries."

The injuries you gave me, Eli thought bitterly.

He gritted his teeth but kept his retort to himself. Instead, he grunted, "I doubt I'll be getting any sleep tonight. Georgia took away my only solace."

Michael glanced around, then unzipped his coat and dipped one hand into an inner pocket, pulling out a small flask. "It's not the same as Georgia's brew, but it'll help take the edge off."

He tossed the flask, and Eli caught it with both hands. After unscrewing the cap, Eli took a cautious sniff—alcohol. He took a small sip and grimaced as it singed his throat. But even that one sip helped. It was strong and would likely help him fall asleep quickly.

"Don't go drinking it all," Michael said. "I might want some later."

Eli waited until Michael was back at his own makeshift tent before drinking half of the flask. He had half a mind to drink it all, but Michael's warning rang in his ears. The drink was plenty enough to turn his mind into a hazy fog and weigh down his eyelids. In no time at all, he was fast asleep.

Chapter Two

ELI

WHAT BEGAN AS A peaceful night turned tumultuous as the hours passed. Eli's dreams were plagued with visions of fire and smoke, ground soaked with blood. He saw his dad, a shell of the man he once was, walking toward Eli with one hand around his own throat. It was like he was trying to say something, but he couldn't speak. He needed Eli to hear what he had to say, and his eyes searched frantically, one arm outstretched toward his son.

Eli jumped back when his dad removed the hand around his neck. A wound opened up, blood flowing thick and crimson red while he stood frozen in a silent scream. Then he collapsed, and Eli never heard what he had to say.

The nightmare shook Eli from sleep. His chest ached as if someone had tried to rip it open, like his ribs were being cracked in half. He wiped tears from his eyes and began to turn, but pain rippled through his torso, forcing him to lie back down.

He gasped for air, and it suddenly felt like his own throat was constricting. Terrified, he wrapped his hand around his throat and half expected to find blood, but he only found cold flesh. Something was preventing him from breathing. If he didn't get oxygen soon, he would pass out. Already the edges of his vision were darkening blacker than the night sky.

"Eli?" A voice tore through the silent night. Shuffling feet moved closer to him. "Stop. It's okay."

Georgia was by his side in a flash, tugging at Eli's hands to bring them away from his neck.

"I can't breathe," Eli wheezed, struggling against Georgia's hold.

She quickly checked him for injuries, then shook her head. "You have to calm down, Eli. It's all in your head. Take deep breaths...in and out." She demonstrated herself with a deep inhale through her nose and a heavy exhale out of her mouth.

Eli tried to inhale, but it came in short bursts. Georgia kept her pace, grabbing his hand and placing it over her chest. As Eli focused on the rise and fall, his own breathing returned to normal. He felt his heart rate slow along with it.

Georgia gave him a warm smile. "That's better, isn't it?"

"Yeah, I was just..." Eli looked around the clearing, and the pieces began to fall into place. He wasn't in his bed at the prison. He was with the Coyotes. At least two of them had poked their heads out of their blankets to see what the commotion was about, but after seeing Georgia had it under control, they returned to their slumber.

"I think you were just having a nightmare," Georgia said with a gentle pat on his arm.

"It felt so real."

In a way, it *had* been real. He'd been there when that wound had been made—when his dad's neck had been sliced open—and he'd forever be haunted by the words left unsaid between them.

His dad had always urged him to go after things in life, to not take things for granted, and that it could all be gone in a moment. How right he had been...

"I think you might've been having a panic attack," Georgia said, a hint of worry in her voice.

"I'm fine...really."

Georgia wiped her brow and yawned. Her eyes wandered over Eli's tangled blanket and stopped when they reached a shiny flask. She picked it up and gave it a little shake. "What is this?"

The accusatory tone in her voice made Eli flinch. It didn't matter that he was a grown man. Her motherly demeanor mixed with the authority she had as his healer made him feel like a child being scolded.

Eli simply shrugged his shoulders, and she crossed her arms over her chest.

The sound of rain tapped on the tarp above them. It fell lightly, but Eli had a strong suspicion it would only get worse. He grumbled in annoyance.

"It's just a bit of rain," Georgia said. "How is your wound today?"

"Still hurts like hell." It had only been a couple days. Of course he was still in pain.

"You know I can't give you more yet." She looked around the camp and sighed. "Although if the others don't come back today, we'll have to move on without them. I suppose if no one else shows up with injuries, you'll be able to have the remaining doses of pain medication."

Georgia left him to rest while she added logs to the fire and began preparing hot water. It was impossible to fall asleep after the nightmare he'd had, and soon others began to wake.

In no time, the camp was buzzing with the excitement of a new day. A day where they'd be able to travel once again and get out of the small clearing they'd been held in for days. But there was an air of unease as well. They were still missing a few of their own and whispers of whether or not they'd show up spread around camp.

Eli sat on the outside of the mayhem, his physical presence a mirror of his internal feelings. At least in Rysburg, he had other prisoners to commiserate with. Here, he was truly alone.

Once breakfast was served—a small piece of sausage and some oatmeal—the men packed up. Eli sensed they were going slower than they were capable of, probably waiting for the rest of their group to show. He wondered how long they would wait. Whether Ali and Nik would show up with them.

Eli saw the look in the Coyotes' eyes as more time passed—the knowledge that they'd be leaving friends behind. Eli felt it too.

Georgia came to his side once she'd packed her medical supplies. "Can you stand?"

He slowly did as she asked, gritting his teeth as he took a few tentative steps. It hurt, but if he moved slowly, he could walk on his own. He stretched a little to loosen up his stiff muscles, bending his knees gently and rolling his ankles. It had been so long since he'd stood.

Shouting caused them both to turn, Eli wincing as he twisted a little too quickly.

"Georgia! Georgia," a man yelled.

Georgia rushed to the other side of camp. Eli hobbled behind her, anxious to see what the shouting was about.

Three figures emerged from the woods—two of them holding the third up by his arms. The man in the middle had his head drooped down and his legs dragged across the forest floor.

"Set him here," Georgia said calmly. She was clearly trained for this.

"What happened?" Michael asked the men as they laid their injured comrade on the ground. Another Coyote fetched a blanket to prop his head up.

"We tried to get them out," one of the men panted. "We tried to save them, but—" He swallowed hard and ran his hands through his hair.

Georgia was searching the man's body for injuries and checking for vital signs.

"Harris," Michael yelled. "Tell us what happened."

Harris had been watching Georgia, his eyes full of despair. Eli knew that look all too well. He wasn't allowing himself to hope that his friend might be okay.

"We went for the prisoners. The intel we had was old, and it took longer than we expected. By the time we got there, the guards..." Harris shook his head and then turned to the side and vomited.

"Fuck, Harris. What the hell?"

Harris spat on the ground. "The guards set the prison on fire. We could hear them screaming. The prisoners...they were still locked inside. We tried to get them out, but"—Harris shook his head again—"it was impossible. We couldn't save them. Vander tried, but it was no use. The prison started to collapse, and he was pinned underneath the beams. I couldn't leave him there. We had to get him out."

Harris looked at Georgia again, and Eli realized she'd stopped looking over Vander's body. She was kneeling with her head bowed in a silent prayer.

"You have to help him," Harris cried.

Georgia shook her head. "I'm sorry. He's gone."

Harris fell to his knees, sobbing for her to bring his friend back.

Eli couldn't watch this. He limped back to the other side of camp, but he didn't stop there. He moved through the forest with no idea of where he was going. He only knew he didn't want to be with the Coyotes anymore.

Everyone was gone. His dad was gone. Ali was gone. And now all the remaining prisoners were gone too. Gods, what kind of fucked up monsters set fire to a building with people still in it?

Eli didn't make it far before he had to pause, leaning against a tree and grasping his side. He hissed through gritted teeth. It would be harder to travel than he'd thought.

He took a minute to check his surroundings. Nothing but trees and brush as far as he could see. Nothing that looked familiar and nothing to help point him in the direction of where he'd last seen Ali.

He looked up toward the sun. At this time, it should be in the east. They hadn't crossed the river, at least not while he was conscious, so he should still be on the eastern bank. If he headed west, he could find the river and then it was a fifty-fifty chance to head either north or south and hope he ran into Ali along the way.

He began to walk away from the sun's early morning rays.

"Where the hell are you going?" Michael demanded from behind him. Eli hadn't even heard his approach.

"None of your business." Eli hobbled with his hand pressed against his side.

"You're a fucking idiot, man."

Eli rolled his eyes. He didn't have time for this, and he had no interest in hearing Michael's insults. Hadn't he done enough already?

"Where will you go?"

"Away," Eli responded.

"Very fucking clever."

Eli made it another five steps before he had to rest against a tree trunk. Sweat formed on his brow, but he gritted his teeth and took another step.

Eli couldn't hear Michael following behind, but that didn't mean he wasn't still there. He turned to look over his shoulder, and his toe caught on an exposed tree root. There was no chance to catch himself, and he hit the ground hard.

He cursed and lifted his shirt. His bandage was still white. He hadn't reopened the gash during his clumsy fall.

"Let me help," Michael said.

Eli scowled up at the man's extended hand. "I don't want your help."

So Michael stood with his arms crossed, watching as Eli struggled to get to his feet. "You are one stubborn son of a bitch. Look, I get that you don't like me. You don't trust me, and I can't blame you. I wouldn't trust me either. But you're making a terrible decision. Look at you. You're injured." He began to count on his fingers. "You've got no food. You've got no water. You don't even have anywhere to go. What will you do, Eli?"

Heat rose to Eli's face from both embarrassment and rage. He didn't want to admit that Michael was right. "I have to find her."

"Who?" When Eli didn't respond, Michael shook his head. "The girl with the blonde hair? The one who left you?"

Eli flinched, and Michael smirked in satisfaction. It made Eli's rage bubble closer to the surface.

"Ah, that's the one. She left you and you're going to risk your life for her? You won't make it longer than a few days on your own."

Eli thought about the odds of finding Ali before he starved to death. It didn't look good. A pounding in his head matched the throbbing ache in his side.

"Come with us," Michael said. His tone said he didn't care if Eli came or not, but it had to matter for some reason. Otherwise, he wouldn't have followed Eli into the woods. He wouldn't be trying to convince Eli to return to the Coyotes.

Michael took a step forward. "Please. Let us take you to Berland. You can heal there, and if you decide to look for your friends afterward, then at least you'll have provisions and full health on your side."

"Why does it matter to you? Why do you care if I die in the woods on my own?"

Michael paused to consider his answer. "I want to see a world free of corrupt filth like Rysburg, but what's the point if we don't save anyone along the way?"

"So I'm just a pawn to make you feel better about yourself?"

Michael shrugged. "Maybe. But I'm right either way. Don't die just to prove a point, Eli."

Eli scanned the forest. It was quiet. Only the sound of birds chirping, listening to the conversation unfolding between two adversaries. He couldn't explain it, but the chords dug a hollow space in his chest.

"Can I join the Coyotes instead?" he asked.

Michael chuckled, but it quickly faded when Eli didn't join him. "You're serious?"

Eli nodded.

"I'm sorry, but no. You'll only slow us down. We have other missions, and you're in no shape to help. Maybe after you heal, we can revisit the option, although once you make it to Berland I doubt you'll want to come on the road with us. For now, it's Berland or nothing, Eli. Which one will it be?"

Eli weighed his options. His heart was still blindly searching for Ali in a world with no limits. His mind, however, knew the smart decision would be to go to Berland, regain his strength, and perhaps join the Coyotes after he healed. If anyone could find Ali, it would be them. With their frequent travels and knowledge of other communities, they'd know how to track her down.

"You'll let me join you after my wound heals?" he asked.

"I'll consider it."

It was probably the best he would get out of Michael. Of course he wouldn't make empty promises to allow a stranger into their ranks. "I'll go to Berland."

"Good choice."

Chapter Three

NIK

NIK HAD NO IDEA how they were going to move Sam. He was so badly injured, and even the smallest movement caused him to squint in agony. Nik had learned a few things about tending wounds in combat, but he couldn't do much for Sam. He made a makeshift splint and attached it to his ankle, despite Sam's groans of pain.

"Are you trying to fucking kill me?" Sam hissed.

Nik shook his head. "I'm trying to make sure you don't suffer permanent damage."

Ali held Sam's hand while Nik worked. Once he was done cleaning and wrapping Sam's leg, he pulled an extra shirt out of his backpack and helped Sam out of the bloody shirt he was wearing. After searching Sam's torso and finding no large open wounds, Nik helped him into the clean shirt and tossed the soiled one into a nearby fire, still blazing from the battle.

"What now?" Sam asked. He was still wincing in pain, though he was trying his best to hide it. His face was pale, and Nik was concerned about how much blood he'd lost. They needed to move, though. There could be more Coyotes nearby, and they didn't want to be found.

"We'll carry you."

Sam nearly vomited as Nik and Ali pulled him up from the ground. Nik worried for a moment that he might pass out, but he remained conscious. The only sign he gave that he was in pain were the sharp inhales each time his body was jostled on the uneven terrain.

It was a slow trek. Sam slung his arms around Ali and Nik's shoulders. Ali was at least a foot shorter than the two of them, and it was difficult for her to lift his body, but she did her best and didn't complain.

In fact, she didn't speak at all.

Nik didn't notice it at first. He was too concentrated on moving Sam steadily and causing him the least amount of pain. But after an hour, her silence was painfully obvious. Sam was delirious and just doing his best to stay alert, but Ali...Ali was somewhere else.

Nik couldn't help but worry about her. The look on her face when Sam had told them Eli was alive had been a relief for him as well. He didn't know how she would survive losing her best friend, and he was hopeful he wouldn't have to find out. He'd do everything in his power to find Eli for her sake.

They followed the Coyotes' tracks. It was easy at first. The large group had trampled the ground; even a novice tracker would've been able to see the path. But the further they traveled, the more obscure the footprints became.

Ali's breathing was loud in the silence, and Nik knew she was struggling to support him.

"Do you need a break?" he asked.

Ali shook her head, but Sam grunted. "I do. Did you bring any food or water in those sacks of yours?"

"We did." A few loaves of bread and canned vegetables. It would hopefully last them a week—two if they rationed. When they had packed their sacks, they hadn't expected to leave Rysburg under these conditions. They'd expected a quick and easy journey south, not a long hunt for Ali's lost friend.

Now Nik had to alter his plans. He would hunt small animals that crossed their path to further extend the life of their supplies and pray the rainy climate would refill their water bottles intermittently. Hopefully that would be enough.

Ali and Nik lowered Sam to the ground and propped him up against a tree. Nik dug into his backpack, found his canteen, and passed it to Sam.

Sam pressed the opening to his lips and quenched his thirst. Then he lowered the canteen and replaced the cap. "I'm sorry to be such a burden. I know I'm slowing you both down."

"You're not a burden, Sam. What did you expect us to do? Leave you behind? We'll catch up to Eli eventually."

Nik looked across toward Ali, who leaned against a tree facing away from them. He couldn't see her face. Couldn't tell what she was thinking.

Sam lowered his voice to a whisper. "Is she going to be okay?"

Ali was strong. She'd been through so much in the short time Nik had known her. Through it all, she'd never given up hope that things would turn out all right. She was resilient, yet Nik worried this might be the moment to break her.

"I hope so," Nik said, taking the bottle of water from Sam.

He headed toward Ali and placed a gentle hand on her shoulder, sensing the tenseness there. She didn't turn to face him even as he moved beside her. Nik studied her with a concerned expression.

"Water?" he asked, lifting the canteen.

"No thanks." Her tone, cold and harsh, lashed at him like a dagger to the chest.

"You have to drink something, Ali. We've been out here all day, and carrying Sam isn't a small feat. You should eat something, too, if you want to keep up your strength."

She slowly turned to face him, and his breath caught when their eyes met. He didn't know it was possible to look into the eyes of the woman you loved and see nothing but emptiness where warmth used to be. It chilled him to the core.

Ali took a quick sip and pressed the canteen back into his hands. Then she turned on her heel and grabbed her own backpack, pulling out a small loaf of bread. Nik watched as she took a few bites, her eyes purposefully locked on his.

Good. She needed to eat, even if she did so begrudgingly.

Nik ate a portion of his loaf too. It only took a few bites to stifle his hunger, so that's all he allowed himself to consume. He washed it down with a small sip of water.

Sam groaned as Nik and Ali lifted him to continue their search. Nik wished he could ease some of his pain, but there was nothing he could do. It would take time and rest, neither of which he could give. If only he could go back in time and pack pain medicine, but it was too late now.

As the sun began to set, rain clouds moved in. Nik had spent many nights in uncomfortable sleeping arrangements during his days in the guard. He knew immediately when the first drops fell that they'd be in for a long night.

In the middle of the forest, there were few places to shelter from the storm. The best Nik could find was a tree that had toppled onto a boulder. The trunk provided enough coverage for the three of them if they huddled together.

Sam slid in first, his body most protected from the storm. Nik insisted Ali go next, and she didn't argue. Then Nik dipped below the tree trunk and scooted in as far as he could, though his backside remained exposed to the rain and wind.

They split half a loaf of bread and ate entirely in silence, wind howling and leaves rustling around them. Rain whipped against Nik's back, and he could only pray his jacket would keep out the moisture overnight.

Ali pulled a bundled sweater from her backpack and wadded it up to use as a pillow. Without a word, she turned on her side, facing away from Nik. Sam gave Nik a surprised glance before shifting and lying down beside her.

It stung. Nik knew Ali was struggling with losing Eli, but that didn't stop the ache in his heart. Nik had given up everything for her and now she was giving him the cold shoulder...literally.

He pressed his body as close to her back as he could, attempting to get out of the rain. She flinched but didn't protest. After a second, her body relaxed into his. His fingers trailed across her arm and wrapped around her waist. His breath stirred the blonde hairs that fell across her shoulder. He gently kissed the exposed skin at the nape of her neck and murmured softly, "I love you."

The silence that answered would haunt him for days to come.

Chapter Four

ALI

It had been days and the terrain all looked the same. The trees were all the same shade of green. The sky was a never-ending blanket of gray. The rare caw of a bird sounded exactly the same as the last. Ali half wondered if Nik even knew where he was going, but she knew better than to doubt his tracking skills.

They stopped frequently for Nik to examine the ground and surrounding foliage. He didn't bother to point out what he was looking for.

He tried once, and she hadn't shown any interest. Now, as she watched him, she wished she had been more engaged. She wanted to feel useful, wanted something to distract her from the misery she was drowning in.

Nik stood, satisfied with whatever he'd found. "This way. They've definitely been through here."

He sounded sure of himself, but Ali wasn't so confident.

"Do we have a plan for when we finally meet up with them? I don't think the Coyotes are going to just let us into their camp," Sam wondered aloud.

"We'll cross that bridge when we come to it," Nik responded.

Ali would walk right into their camp if that was what it took. She wouldn't abandon Eli.

Assuming he was still alive. Perhaps they'd killed him after they removed him from the shore.

If he was dead...

Ali wasn't sure she wanted to go through life without him. He was her best friend, and she'd left him there. She'd thought he was dead, but he hadn't been. He had been alive, and she had abandoned him. She couldn't live with herself if he died alone in the hands of the Coyotes when she could've saved him.

"Speaking of bridges..." Sam nudged his chin toward the open space in front of them. They'd reached another river, this one flowing wildly with the extra rain from the endless storms.

A large tree had fallen across the river in one of the narrower bends, and the flooded water was close to reaching the bottom of the tree trunk. If it had rained any harder, they would've been out of luck. It was the only way across as far as they could see.

Ali swallowed and scanned the roaring river, her eyes settling on the other shore. Her vision blurred, and she blinked once. Twice. Shadows of unknown figures swirled, and a blade sparked like lightning, striking the body on the ground. Eli's body. Images flashed faster than she could comprehend. She was going to be sick.

"Ali," Sam said, squeezing her shoulder. She was vaguely aware that her arm was still wrapped around his back, holding him up. Or was he holding her up?

Her legs wobbled, and her ears rang. This couldn't be real. She blinked again, but the shadows lingered when she opened her eyes. They spread, swallowing the light of day, and the river expanded, ready to sweep her off her feet and carry her away.

She closed her eyes and braced herself. Her heart hammered in her chest.

"Ali." Rough hands grabbed her shoulders, and she knew this was it. This was the end. "Ali, look at me."

Her eyes fluttered open to find Nik mere inches from her face.

No. She wouldn't leave Eli behind. She wouldn't let Nik convince her this time. She peered over Nik's shoulder, but the shore was empty. Something caught in her throat, and she struggled to breathe.

Ali pushed Nik to the side and heaved, expelling what little she'd had to eat that day. When she was finished, a bottle of water was thrust into her hand, and she rinsed her mouth and spat into the dirt.

Nik took her chin in his hand and turned her toward him. "Are you okay?" he asked, stroking her cheek. It took a moment to realize her skin was wet with tears.

She released a heavy sigh. "I'm fine."

Nik's eyes said he wasn't convinced. She looked away, unable to take his gaze any longer, until he took a step back and dropped his hand.

Ali wiped the remaining tears from her cheeks and concentrated on stilling her thundering heart. Yet each time she looked across the river, panic threatened to rise again. The shore was empty; she could see clearly now. But the raging river made her limbs tremble.

"How will we cross?" Sam asked, easing the moment of tension.

"I don't think we can both carry you at the same time. The tree is too narrow. I'll help you across and Ali can follow." Nik looked at her as he said her name, and Ali felt the tears forming this time.

She didn't know if she could force her legs to cross that river. She didn't know if she could take a single step. She was frozen in place, frozen in this hell.

"Or...I can come back for you?" Nik suggested. Ali nodded, and he gave her an encouraging smile. "I'll be back."

Ali watched as Nik grabbed Sam under the armpits and helped him toward the tree forming a bridge over the river. They moved slowly, Sam relying heavily on Nik. Without Ali to help, Sam was forced to put weight on his injured ankle. She felt a pang of guilt with every pained wince. She should've been helping, but her feet were still locked in place.

After lowering Sam to the ground on the other shore, Nik moved back over the tree with the grace and balance of a trained warrior, so sure of his footing.

"Ready?" he asked, reaching a hand for her.

Ali shivered and took a step back. She couldn't explain the dread she felt, but stepping near that river terrified her more than anything she'd encountered.

Nik sensed it, and his eyes softened. "Talk to me, Ali."

She didn't know how. Couldn't explain the unexplainable. The depths of her despair and fear were too much for her to process. Everything she'd been through was finally catching up to her and rendering her incapable of functioning. Losing Eli had been the last straw, the last string that tethered her to the life she'd known and the person she'd been. She was merely a shadow of herself now.

"I can carry you, if that's what you need. Is that okay?"

Ali could hardly look at him, but there was no way she could make it across on her own. She nodded, and Nik turned around with his arms outstretched.

"Hop up on my back," he commanded her.

By some miracle, Ali's feet broke free of the weights holding them down. She grabbed Nik by the shoulders and jumped up, squeezing her legs around him while he grabbed her thighs.

Nik carried her with ease back to the river, and Ali nuzzled her head against his back. She couldn't watch the water raging below them. She didn't want to hear its power, a reminder of how insignificant she was.

The edges of her vision turned dark and her grip on Nik's shoulders slackened. She felt like her very life was being drained from her.

"Keep holding on. We're almost there."

Nik dropped to the ground of the opposite shore with a loud thump that shook Ali out of her nightmare. He didn't stop there, moving farther from the water, from its loud current, until the ringing in her ears ceased.

He leaned down to set Ali on her feet before turning and taking her face in his hands. "You're all right. You're all right," he said, and kissed her temple, wrapping his arms around her.

She didn't feel all right. She felt numb. Broken.

The wind howled as Nik left her side to retrieve Sam. She felt selfish for requiring so much of Nik's help and ungrateful for shutting him out while he was being so patient with her.

A part of her blamed him for leaving Eli. She knew he hadn't done it intentionally, but if she couldn't blame him, then that only left herself. She didn't think she could take any more self-loathing.

"We'll camp here tonight. We're all exhausted, and it'll be dark soon anyway," Nik said as he dragged Sam through the trees, sweat forming on his brow.

Ali slumped to the ground next to Sam and watched Nik attempt to make something resembling a shelter out of branches and weeds. It would be another cold and wet night.

"Ali…" Sam's voice was inquisitive, and Ali turned to look at him. "You're worried about Eli."

Yes. And so much more. How had her life become so derailed?

She leaned her head back against a tree trunk and watched as the storm clouds rolled in.

"We'll find him. I believe in Nik, and I think you do too. But, Ali, when we do…when you find him again, I worry he won't find you."

She tilted her head in his direction. "What do you mean?"

Her throat protested. Days of silence made it difficult to speak. She had forgotten how it felt to form words, to hear the sound of her own voice. She cleared her throat and swallowed.

"I mean, is he going to recognize you? Don't let this break you. Be strong. If not for yourself, then for Eli." Sam patted her knee.

Ali let his words sink in. It seemed easier said than done, but she could try. She could try to find the lost fragments of herself and be the person Eli knew. Be the person Nik fell in love with.

Nik reappeared from the makeshift shelter. "It's not much, but it'll have to do."

Together, he and Ali lifted Sam and settled in for the night.

Chapter Five

ELI

Eli and Michael returned to camp. The dozen or so Coyotes were all sullen as they stood around a large fire, Vander's body atop a pyre with a blanket draped over him. Already the blanket had caught fire; his body would soon follow. They didn't stick around to watch.

Hiking with a massive laceration was as difficult as Eli had expected. He focused on his breath—in and out. He counted his footsteps, listened to the buzz of solemn whispers around him. Anything he could to take his mind off the pain in his side.

Georgia was kind enough to give him an extra dose of medication. Now that they knew no one else would be returning, she said it was okay to give him more than his fair share. No one else would need the additional rations. He was grateful but would've preferred it if the other prisoners had made it out alive.

What had started as a drizzle that morning turned into a full downpour by lunchtime. They stopped for a break and to eat under a cluster of large trees, but the water poured through the canopy. It was no use trying to stay dry.

After lunch, they carried on, only stopping when they reached a roaring river. The pouring rain had caused the stream to swell. A downed tree was placed almost perfectly over the river, forming a bridge where people began to file across one by one.

He watched them maneuver, taking slow and steady steps on slippery moss. The rain was coming down so heavy that they disappeared from his sight before they made it all the way across.

On his turn, he slowly moved sideways. Adrenaline helped him forget his pain as he focused all his attention on moving forward. It took what felt like an eternity to move from one end to the other. He ignored the white foam of rapids beneath him.

All the muscles he didn't know he'd been tensing relaxed once he hopped down to solid ground.

They didn't stop for dinner. They forged on until the sky turned dark. Eli's side began to ache again, and he knew he wouldn't be able to walk much longer. He wondered if he'd be able to get another dose of medicine or if Georgia was all out by now. Torch lights had been dispersed throughout the group and now emitted a warm glow, lighting the trail in front of him. If he focused enough on each step, he wouldn't be able to think about the throbbing pain in his side.

Between the rain, the long hike, and the rumbling stomachs, no one was in the mood to speak. So when chatter began at the front of the pack, it commanded everyone's attention.

Eli could see from the firelight that they'd made it to a city of ruins. They walked through dilapidated structures and overgrown walkways. The rubble reminded him of Andus, but these buildings were completely abandoned. It appeared that no one had bothered to rebuild here.

Eli found himself beside the man named Harris. "What is this place?" he asked.

Harris turned to Eli, surprise clear in his expression. In all the commotion of Vander's death, had the man even realized they'd saved one outsider?

Harris cleared his throat. "Don't know. There are lots of towns like this scattered throughout the Dead Lands. I suppose the residents either died from starvation or the elements. Or they abandoned their homes in search of more prosperous communities."

"What are the Dead Lands?"

Harris waved his arms at their surroundings. "Everything between the lake up north and the river in the south. There are no settlements between the two bodies of water. Only wild animals and rogue raiders, the kind of folk who aren't suited for civilian life. They'd rather live wild among the beasts of the woods, so best watch your back."

A chill ran down Eli's spine. A week, Georgia had said. A week to trek through the Dead Lands and deal with whatever nature threw their way.

They walked into one of the brick buildings and let out a collective sigh of relief. Although the windows were broken and the space was dark and cool, they finally had shelter from the rain.

Eli looked around as the Coyotes all claimed spots to lay their mats and sheets. He wasn't sure who had been carrying his pack, but Georgia set up his bed of blankets for him. He offered to help, but she swatted at his hands, telling him he wasn't allowed to bend over yet.

Eli slumped to the ground and passed out before he even had a chance to eat dinner.

The days became repetitive. Wake up, change bandages, walk endlessly, and then pass out at the next campsite. Rinse and repeat. Michael had been right about Eli's injury slowing them down. It took everything in him to keep up with the group. Their stops throughout the day became more frequent, and they ended their days earlier.

It was a grueling trip, made worse by the darkening clouds and ominous thunderstorms. The rain poured continuously as they tramped through soggy leaves and puddles. They ran out of dry firewood halfway through their week-long journey, which meant the evenings were freezing cold in addition to being wet. Some men took to sleeping naked just so they could stay dry in their sleeping arrangements and have a single moment of reprieve from their wet undergarments.

All day long, Eli's shirt and pants stuck to his body uncomfortably and blisters formed on the bottom of his feet. His shoes were full of moisture that never dried out and squished as he walked through mud and weeds. He did his best to change into dry socks as often as possible, but there was only so much he could do. There wasn't a single pleasant part of this trip.

Even poor Georgia's supplies were damp despite her attempts to keep them shielded. So far, they'd only been pelted with heavy and consistent rain, but on their last morning, thunder roared and lightning lit up the sky. Eli was thankful they were almost to the river that would be their stop for the night. They didn't want to get caught up in this weather.

It was hard to tell the time of day. He hadn't seen the sun in days and the skies were even darker today, completely blocking all the light in the sky. They guessed when it was midday based on the rumble of stomachs, and in the mornings, they relied on their internal clocks to wake them.

They were still a couple miles away from the river when Michael pointed to the skies. "Do you see it? We're almost there."

Eli searched the sky, wondering what Michael was referring to. He didn't see anything—until a strike of lightning lit up the sky.

Eli's jaw dropped. Was his mind playing tricks on him? There were buildings illuminated by the light of the storm, but these buildings were unnatural. Dozens of tall, gray rectangles stretched toward the sky and disappeared into the clouds. Their sides were reflective, and he could make out the images of clouds and lightning as it flashed across the faces of the buildings. He stopped in his tracks and marveled at the scene in front of him. How was it possible for such a thing to exist?

As they approached, he had to crane his neck to look up at them. Everything was silent except the sound of the rain and thunder that echoed off the monstrous buildings. No chatter of other humans or even animals here. The Coyotes had gone silent as well, as if they too were rendered speechless at the sight.

Grass and wildflowers grew through the asphalt, but the streets were still clearly visible. Boarded-up windows were half hidden behind monstrous objects he'd never seen before.

"What are those?" he asked Michael, who shook water out of his eyes and followed Eli's pointer finger.

"Cars. An old method of transportation."

"Seriously?" He brushed a hand over one. Rust coated his fingers. "I've heard of them, but I've never seen one. And what is that?" He pointed to a dull yellow object hanging in the sky. There were several of them in a square formation over their heads.

Michael shrugged. "Not sure. Sorry, I don't have all the answers."

Eli kept his eyes wide, unwilling to miss any tiny detail of the town they passed through. It felt like he was on another planet entirely. Everything was so unfamiliar here. They walked underneath concrete bridges and then over streets below. It was incredible the way the streets wound together like a maze of tangled vines. It was a good thing the Coyotes led the way because Eli would likely get lost without them.

At one point, they came across a small river. Based on what he had heard, this wasn't the major river they were looking for but a smaller one that fed into it. Eli could see remnants of an old bridge that had once extended across the river but had crumbled in time. The fallen concrete pieces created rapids where they jutted through the surface of the water.

A makeshift bridge had been built to replace the deteriorated one. It was a rickety old thing made with rope and wooden planks, and it looked terribly unstable.

Michael and his crew crossed the bridge without hesitation. Eli watched as one by one, they all walked over the bridge to safety. By the time it was his turn, he was satisfied he wouldn't plunge into the water below.

On the other side, the buildings began to shrink in size, and Eli took it as a sign that they'd passed the center of town. Sure enough, as they descended a hill, he could see water and on the far side, another sight he couldn't describe. It was like the ground had taken on a life of its own, climbing toward the sky until jagged edges peaked at the top. It seemed impossible.

Eli gaped. "What is that?"

Georgia chuckled from behind him, and he turned to face her. "I forget how little most people have seen of our world. Those are mountains, Eli."

Eli studied them in awe. Another word he was familiar with but had never seen himself. It was really hitting him just how big the world was and how little he had seen.

As they approached the river, they turned right, walking into an abandoned building with a red 'X' painted on the exterior wall. Michael grabbed a metal lock on the door and spun three silver dials until the lock popped open.

A bell chimed as they stepped over the threshold. It took a moment for Eli's eyes to adjust to the dark. Perhaps under normal circumstances, it would've been lit by sunlight, but with the cloud cover it was hard to see anything at all.

Eli bumped into a metal shelf and brought a hand up to steady it before items toppled off. They were standing in a large open room with tall ceilings. Some of the ceiling tiles were cracked, exposing black holes that were too dark to see into. To the left, he spotted several doors made of glass and behind them, metal racks held battered boxes with unknown contents. The right side was a mirror of the left, with more glass doors and boxes with contents Eli couldn't see. For all he knew, they could be empty.

But Eli didn't think that was the case, because between those two walls were rows and rows of wooden shelves, each stacked with jars of fruit, crates of vegetables, and piles of clean linens. Each aisle gave Eli more to discover.

"This is your supply drop-off?" he asked.

"Yes," Georgia answered.

Michael grabbed a backpack and began to fill it with fresh water, canned food, and starchy vegetables.

"Where does it all come from?"

"Berland donates a lot, but there are a few smaller towns that provide when they can. Genna and Isabel do almost all the transporting. They should be here soon."

In addition to the shelf full of supplies, there were a few cots set up in rows at the back of the room. Not enough for every traveler, but at least half of them could claim one and get some rest while they waited for Genna and Isabel.

A couple hours later, after some food and rest, the bell above the door chimed again. Two women stepped through, looking cold and wet from the storms but otherwise rather cheerful. It was hard to tell them apart in the darkness, but the first was shorter with wavy brown hair that swirled around haphazardly until the door closed behind her. She flung her arms around Georgia almost immediately. This one must be Genevieve, or

Genna, Georgia's daughter. The second had longer hair pulled back in a slick ponytail. She must be Isabel.

Several of the Coyotes swarmed them. Hugs and pats on the back were exchanged. They greeted each other like old friends. It was clear these two were very beloved by all.

The two women took their time greeting each of the Coyotes, catching up on their latest travels and filling each other in on what had happened since they last met. Frowns formed when Harris informed them of the Coyotes they'd lost in the attack, including Vander. Isabel looked like she might cry, and Genna wrapped her arm around her wife's shoulder.

The two women finally made it to Eli.

"And this is Eli. The lone survivor," Georgia said, turning to her daughter and daughter-in-law with sad eyes. "We were hopeful there would be more, but you know how these things sometimes go. As far as wounds go, he's only got a nasty laceration on his side. Bandage needs changed at least once a day, but it shouldn't be long before he can go without. Just keep an eye out for infection."

Georgia turned to Eli. "This is my daughter, Genna, and her wife Isabel. Genna will take over my healing duties. Hasn't had much training, but she knows the basics and can help with anything you might need on the remainder of your trip to Berland."

"It's nice to meet you," he said as he shook their hands. Genna gave him a warm smile. Her eyes glistened with what little light slipped in through the narrow windows sprinkled around the top perimeter of the room. They were a beautiful shade of brown, an almost identical match to Ali's. It stole his breath for a moment.

Georgia beamed with pride for her daughter. "Tell Eli where you've been. I still can't believe the places you two find yourselves." She shook her head in a mixture of admiration and disbelief.

Isabel spoke up, wrapping her arm around Genna's waist. "We just came back from the eastern coast. Met a brigade that lives aboard boats. Every night they anchor on the shores, but by day they travel up and down the beaches, only staying in one place when they need to replenish supplies on board."

"They let us stay with them for a week," Genna added. "Showed us some amazing scenery—caves that can only be accessed by water, cliffs with the most gorgeous wildflowers jutting out over the ocean, and the sands...oh, I will miss the sand between my toes." She sighed.

"We'll go back someday," Isabel assured her.

Had it not been for the mountains Eli had seen earlier that day, he would've thought they were making shit up. All the things they'd spoken of sounded like myths and legends, forgotten landscapes that had vanished at the end of the world. But mountains *did* exist. And so maybe vast oceans, hidden caves, and cliffs blanketed in flowers existed too.

"That all sounds amazing."

"Maybe they can take you along sometime," Georgia said.

Genna shot her mother a look. It seemed like a silent request not to meddle.

"I think Berland is as far as I'm willing to travel right now," Eli said, thinking of Ali and the distance he'd already put between them. It seemed impossible that they would ever be reunited, but he wasn't willing to travel even further from her.

They chatted for a few more moments before Georgia ushered her daughter away, playing the part of an overbearing mother. She pressed food and water into Genna's hands and forced Isabel to take a seat. Neither of them fought her, and it gave Eli a subtle yearning for that familial affection.

How long had it been since his own father had scolded him for coming home late? Or had served him an extra helping of eggs at breakfast? Some days, it felt like only yesterday that he had woken up in his bedroom with Ali beside him, and other days it felt so distant, like nothing more than a dream.

Michael walked around the room, checking in with each of his Coyotes and making sure their backpacks were filled with the necessary supplies for their next mission. Finally, he headed toward Eli.

"Where will you go after this?" Eli asked when Michael took a seat on the floor next to him.

"There's been some chatter about a town in the northeast. Rumors that they, uh…treat their women a little less than kind. They supposedly treat them more like property and, uh…use them for their *pleasure.*"

"That's despicable." Eli's stomach churned. The thought had crossed his mind at one point that Nik might've been taking advantage of Ali in that way, but over time it had become obvious that she was a willing partner. His heart had shattered when he'd realized it.

"You have no idea. There's a lot of sick people out there, Eli. And so many of them get away with it." Michael shook his head and clenched his jaw. "We can only do so much."

Eli had a hard time reconciling this version of the Coyotes. To him, they'd been an unwelcome catalyst, tearing down Rysburg, nearly killing him and ripping him away from Ali. They were no better than the people who had burned Andus to the ground.

And yet they had this noble mission. Somehow, they'd decided the death and destruction was worth it in the end. For the greater good.

The dim light that crept through the windows faded quickly as the storm raged on. Rain pelted the sides of the building, and Eli was thankful they had a dry place to sleep. He was growing tired of sleeping on the ground with only a tarp to keep him dry.

As he nestled into his cot in the corner of the room, Genna walked over and dropped a bag near his head. "You'll need this for tomorrow."

"What's this?" he asked, opening the top flap to peer inside.

"Your supplies. Food, clean blankets, a couple water bottles—save them. It's hard to find fresh water on the road." Genna sat on the cot next to him while Isabel claimed the one on the other side. "There's also some clothing in there. Mom told me you only have the ones on your back. They might not fit perfectly, but it's the best we can do with the limited options here. Berland should have more of a selection for you."

"Thank you," he said, tucking the items back in his pack and clasping the buckle that held it closed. "What can you tell me about Berland?"

"Mom didn't tell you?"

"She only told me it was a sort of safe haven for people like me—people without a home."

Genna nodded in agreement. "It is. It's an old community—been standing since the end of the world. And because of that, they're well equipped to handle the influx of people. You'll get your own home, there's enough food that you'll never go hungry, and I think you'll be surprised by the number of amenities they have. And the scenery...have you ever seen a waterfall, Eli?"

Waterfalls—another mythical landmark Eli never thought he'd see. "No, I haven't."

Genna laid her head on her too-thin pillow and pulled the white blanket up to her shoulders. Her tired eyes drooped closed, and she exhaled deeply. "This is a new beginning for you, Eli. You won't have to worry about the threat of violence anymore. You won't have to worry where your next meal will come from. It'll be good for you to have some stability."

Eli couldn't deny that. His life had been turned upside down in the past few months, and he yearned to have a place to call home once again.

But if Ali wasn't there, would it ever truly be home?

Chapter Six

ELI

WHEN MORNING CAME, GEORGIA gently shook Eli's shoulders until he woke.

"Let me change your bandage one more time before you go. I think you'll be able to take care of yourself after this." She worked quickly but carefully, giving him a friendly smile once she was finished. "Don't go ripping those stitches again. You won't have me with you to fix it."

"I'll do my best," he said, thankful for what Georgia had done for him, despite his early resistance. If it weren't for her, he would likely be dead.

Across the room, Michael and several other Coyotes packed their bags and threw them over their shoulders. Eli wouldn't miss them. As much as he thanked Georgia for her hospitality, he cursed Michael for requiring it in the first place.

It only took a few minutes for the group to gather their belongings and exit the building, the sound of the bell chiming as they opened the door to a cool, brisk morning. Though the storms had moved on, moisture remained in the air.

Michael replaced the lock on the door to the supply warehouse, then turned to face Genna, Isabel, and Eli. "Genna, Isabel—have a safe journey. Eli," he added with a mischievous smirk, "I hope I never see you again."

Eli snickered. "Same to you."

Then Michael and his group of renegades left, heading back north to defeat another unknown villain. Eli hoped this time they'd be more victorious...that more lives would be spared.

"Ready?" Isabel asked.

"I suppose so."

If Eli thought the first few days of their journey were difficult, it was nothing compared to the hike through the mountains. They began by crossing the river in a canoe barely large enough to fit all of them at once.

The river was calm this morning, the surface still like glass, disturbed only by the ripples from their oars. Dense fog steadily rose from the river, hindering their view. The rain had let up, but the gray skies lingered and threatened to release upon them at any moment.

Once they made it to the southern side of the river, Isabel and Genna pulled their boat ashore, hiding it between a cluster of trees. Eli would've offered to help, but his injury made it difficult to do any heavy lifting. At least walking was easier now.

Isabel led the way up a path that rose steadily through the mountains. Luckily, it wasn't too steep, and Eli was able to climb without much pain. It felt like they'd hardly made any progress at all when Isabel came to a halt.

"We'll take a break here."

Eli sighed with relief, but the rocky ground was only a tease. He was ready for the day he could sleep in a *proper* bed.

After two days, they made it to the mountain's peak, stopping for an extra hour as Eli gawked at the scenery. The sun was high in the sky and had chased away all shadows of a storm. From this vantage point, he could see the never-ending blanket of pine trees that covered the rocky terrain. It rolled on forever, reminding him of the waves on the lake back home.

"How are you feeling today?" Genna asked, her stride matching his as they meandered down the side of the mountain. His legs burned from the first two days, and he wasn't sure if it was worse going up or going down. This direction caused different muscles to flare, but it hurt just the same.

"I'm all right."

"Your side is healing okay?"

"Yeah, it looks a lot better today." He had used the last of the ointment and cloth Georgia had given him and was thankful to be so close to their final destination.

"Good. I'm glad. My mom seems to like you. I wouldn't want to inform her you died of sepsis after all this time." She smiled wide, and Eli grinned in return. The ability to cheer a person up must run in their family.

They reached a short rocky cliff and had to climb vertically up the face of the reddish-brown stone. Isabel linked her hands, offering Genna a place to step so she could reach the top and pull herself up. Eli went next and gritted through the strain as Genna helped pull him to the top. Then she easily pulled Isabel up behind him.

They paused to sip from their water bottles and catch their breath.

"It's not too much farther now. We should be there before nightfall. First thing we do when we get to Berland is get those off of you," Genna said, nodding at his wrists.

Eli looked down to where the metal bands had slipped from beneath his sleeves. He'd gotten so used to the thin silver bracelets on his wrists that marked him as the property of Rysburg. He hardly thought about them anymore.

"That would be fucking fantastic."

Late in the afternoon, they made their way to a valley nestled comfortably between two peaks. A small stream ran through the middle, and small wooden buildings lined either side, each identical to the next but decorated uniquely. Most of them had a sign hanging on the door and products displayed on the outside—flowers, fruit, clothing, and more.

The streets were filled with people. It made him nervous, once again stepping into a foreign city. At least this time, he didn't have a sack over his head.

Eli wasn't sure what he had expected from Berland. Not this quaint village with its unassuming storefronts. How could such a small place be equipped to deal with the number of refugees they welcomed? He definitely hadn't envisioned this.

"Charming, isn't it?" Genna asked.

"Genna loves it here. If we ever settle down, it will be in Berland," Isabel chimed in.

"It's…" Eli searched for the right word, one to accurately describe his feelings while maintaining politeness. Genna and Isabel clearly thought very highly of Berland, but he wasn't sold. "Cozy."

"This isn't even half of it," Isabel said.

Eli looked between buildings as they passed, expecting to see more beyond the first row of stores. "Where's the rest?"

"You'll see."

Why were they being coy? Eli didn't like surprises, especially when he was being led through a foreign town. The outside looked welcoming enough, but Berland could be a devil in disguise. Had he just agreed to let the Coyotes lead him into hell?

Blood pounded in his head as his uneasiness grew. Could Genna and Isabel sense it? Did they care that he was on edge? For a moment, he considered running, but there was still the predicament of having no place to go. So he fought his anxiety and forced himself to *trust.*

A few civilians waved and greeted Genna and Isabel; some of them even waved hello to Eli, which calmed his nerves slightly.

"Let's head here first." Genna pointed across the stream, and they took a small wooden bridge over the water, crossing a dirt path to the building she'd pointed out. "This is the town's metal worker. He'll be able to get those shackles off."

Isabel opened the door and allowed Eli and Genna to step through. An elderly man greeted them, recognizing the two women immediately.

"What can I do for you today?" he asked, wiping his dirty hands on a rag and then leaning over his wooden counter with a fatherly smile, eager to help in any way he could.

Genna pointed to Eli's wrist, and he pulled his sleeves up far enough to show the man his metal bands. "Can you get them off?" she asked.

The man stepped out from behind the counter and grasped Eli's wrist, gently turning it over to inspect it. "I can do that. Just need to grab..." His words faded as he wandered into a side room. From what Eli could see, it was a small closet full of various tools and odds and ends.

The man came back out with a long flat bar and another item that looked like the shears Ali's mother used to cut thread with, only much larger...large enough to cut metal.

"Set your arm here, boy," he said, patting a clear spot on the counter between them.

Eli propped his wrists up on the table and watched as the man wedged the flat metal tool between Eli's skin and the band. The pressure didn't last long before the other tool sliced cleanly through the shackle.

Eli's relief as soon as the band snapped was indescribable. The shame and weight of being a prisoner fell to the ground along with the metal bands, which clanged when they bounced off the table and hit the floor. "Thank you so much."

"You're welcome." The man nodded. "I don't think it ever gets easier, seeing the way people are treated on the outside."

Eli choked up. How many others had come through these doors with similar shackles? He rubbed his tender wrists and felt his unease settle just a little.

The man bade them farewell, and they continued walking down the path, which took a sharp right at the end of the shops.

Genna and Isabel paused, and Eli looked around expectantly. What were they waiting for? What did they mean to show him next?

It took a moment for Eli to realize where the gravel road led. He followed the trail with his eyes until it reached the shadows of the mountain and then disappeared. He squinted and then his jaw fell open.

The path led directly *into* the mountain. A large crevice had been cut into the side, forming a moon-shaped entrance. Though the path faded into darkness, people walked in and out, exposing the cavernous passage.

The hairs on Eli's neck and arms stood as he passed from the warm valley air into the cool, damp darkness of the mountain. He couldn't recall a time that he'd ever been *under*ground. His unease returned, and he felt like he was being buried alive. His steps faltered.

"Berland used to be a mining town," Genna explained as Eli looked up at the high ceiling. "When things started to take a turn for the worst, a lot of rich folks moved here and built underground bunkers to keep them safe from the unpredictable climate and raging fires."

"The people live *inside* the mountain?"

"Yes. As you can see, it gets a bit dark in here, so the shops and other common areas have been built outside for more natural light. But the homes have been here for centuries."

"Why didn't they build the homes outside too?" he asked, feeling more on edge the farther they traveled into the darkness. He'd rather stay above ground.

"It was easier to use the compound that had already been built and was well-equipped for habitation."

A soft buzz sounded from a nearby torch, and Eli realized it wasn't burning at all.

"Lightbulbs," she told him, grinning at his clear amazement. "They're powered with solar panels on the side of the mountain. It was too dangerous to have open fire with the natural gas in the mines, so they installed these fixtures. Now there are ventilation systems so you don't need to worry about the toxic gas, but they kept the lights."

"Not just any lights. They're on timers. You'll find more of them lit up when the sun is highest. And they begin to shut off as the sun goes down. It's supposed to help with natural sleep cycles." Isabel waved a hand like she only made sense of half of it. "The compound's original engineers concocted the idea."

He was familiar with solar power. It was how they had powered the plumbing in both Andus and Rysburg, but it was limited and often unreliable. They had rarely used it to power anything else.

"The mountain has more than just light bulbs. There are chambers built for growing crops year-round, the showers have *amazing* water pressure, and the kitchens have the most advanced appliances you can find in our world. It just made sense to keep the homes underground with all this readily available and hooked into the solar power."

Eli still wasn't sure that all those things made up for the feeling of the walls closing in on him. It had been less than ten minutes but already he missed the sunlight on his face, the breeze blowing through his hair. Down here, the air was completely still and suffocating.

The tunnel inside the mountain opened to a grand circular room with a high ceiling. All along the outer walls were open doors, revealing tunnels leading farther into the mountain. They each had a colored symbol over the top, though Eli couldn't decipher what they meant. He tried to make sense of them, but they appeared to be random.

A tall woman with long, wavy brown hair and piercing eyes stood in the center of the antechamber. While everyone else around them moved with purpose, this woman stood still, waiting for them to approach. As he grew closer, he could see those eyes were a beautiful mix of brown and green. She wore a casual black dress that hit her thighs, but she wielded the power to make it appear elegant.

She gave Eli a long look up and down. Their eyes met briefly, and Eli had to look away, feeling inferior in his dirty clothes and unwashed hair.

Genna stepped forward and embraced the woman in a warm hug. "Nice to see you again."

"You as well. Is it just the one?" the woman asked with a glance at Eli.

"Afraid so," Genna said with a frown. Then she turned to Eli. "This is where we leave you. Isabel and I need to hit up the supplies chamber, but you're in excellent hands. Till next time." She gave him a quick nod and left with Isabel through one of the many halls.

"Welcome," the new woman said. Her voice was melodic, like she was singing a song. "I know you've had a long journey, so I won't take much of your time. My name is Grace."

Chapter Seven

NIK

"HOW'S YOUR LEG?" NIK asked as Sam tentatively put his weight on it. Nik had carved a walking stick from a large branch earlier that day, and this was Sam's first attempt at using it. Hopefully it would speed up their journey. They'd already been wandering through the woods for almost two weeks and the longer they spent, the further away their goal seemed to feel.

"Totally pain free," Sam said with a forced grin.

"You're full of shit."

"It's not perfect, but it will work." Sam paced back and forth a few times.

"Let me see it," Nik said.

Sam handed the stick over, and Nik used his knife to cut off a few more inches. It was still slightly too tall for Sam's height. "Try this." He handed it back to Sam and watched as he demonstrated once again.

"Even better," Sam said with unconvincing enthusiasm. Nik had a feeling he would compliment any effort Nik made to ease his pain. He was a people pleaser; it was in his nature.

"Don't use up all your energy," Nik said as he continued to pace. "We don't have much rabbit left."

Nik had caught a couple hares in the past few days, but the wildlife here was sparse. He had no idea when he'd be able to catch another animal. They were down to their last loaf of bread and although Sam remained positive, they were all feeling the effects of starvation.

Ali still wasn't speaking, and Nik felt responsible. He was incapable of protecting her and now providing for her—just another reason for her to blame him for their situation.

He glanced in her direction now as she lay curled in a ball on the hard ground. At least she was sleeping now. Nik suspected she wasn't sleeping much at night. He'd woken a few times to find her staring wide-eyed into the night. It was killing him that he couldn't do more for her.

Sam let out a harsh breath as he dropped to the ground beside Nik. He bent over to massage his ankle. It was still slightly swollen.

"I'm sorry I couldn't do more for you," Nik said. If only he had more training in healing. He wasn't sure his splint had been enough. If Sam walked with a limp the rest of his life, it would just be another item to add to Nik's list of failures.

Sam let out a soft laugh. "You're too hard on yourself. You did what you could. If it weren't for you and Ali, I'd be dead right now. Probably half eaten by vultures."

Ali twitched violently, and they both turned to look at her. After a heavy exhale, her shoulders relaxed, and she fell into her normal rhythm of breathing. Nik shook his head. Another nightmare.

"She'll be fine," Sam said softly.

"How can you know that?"

"She put up with you chasing her and came out unscathed. She can survive anything." Sam laughed.

"Asshole," Nik murmured with a reluctant grin.

Nik strayed from camp, hoping to come across another rabbit or maybe a squirrel. Anything small and easy to kill. The rain had cleared up, but the combination of the heat and humidity left his shirt drenched. It was hell combing through the forest for their next meal.

After an hour, he returned to camp empty-handed. He'd try again tomorrow. One day at a time. That was what he'd told Ali, and what he had to tell himself.

When he made it back, Ali was awake and listening to Sam tell some children's bedtime story that Nik vaguely recognized. She sat in silence while Sam droned on and on. Even if she wasn't interested, it was the most engaged he'd seen her in days. The vacancy in her eyes wasn't as prominent. Sam always had been good at picking up on what people needed the most.

"We'll camp here another night. It's too late in the day to get very far. Might as well make use of the shelter we already have."

He was pretty certain he didn't have the motivation to move very far and then build an entirely new camp. It was better to rest and save their energy for the next day.

Nik's stomach growled, and he did his best to ignore it. He was exhausted too and lay down to take a nap of his own. The sound of Sam's voice was like a lullaby, easing him to sleep.

Before he drifted, he thought he heard a soft feminine giggle.

Something unsettling pierced through the quiet night. The sound of an injured animal or a dying creature, loud enough to startle all three of them awake.

Nik attempted to sit up but found Ali's weight against his chest. She must've fallen asleep cuddled next to him. The thought of relinquishing her touch now crushed him, but a howl belted through the air again.

"What was that?" Sam asked uneasily.

Ali sat up straight, and a chill brushed Nik's chest in her absence.

The sound rang out again, this time louder. Closer.

Nik got up from the cold, hard ground and peeked around the corner of their makeshift tent. The moon and stars were hardly enough to light their surroundings. He waited for his eyes to adjust, but another howl sent a shiver up his spine.

"We need to move."

Ali and Sam didn't need to be told twice. They collected their scattered belongings and threw them into their backpacks. Sam grabbed his walking stick and slung his bag over his shoulder. They needed to hurry, and he was ready to carry his own weight this time.

The sound of the animal echoed through the trees, but Nik was able to pinpoint its direction. He led them through the forest away from the sound, but it only seemed to grow closer. They weren't moving fast enough.

He couldn't break out in a full run the way he wanted to. Ali would keep up, but there was no way Sam could, and Nik refused to leave him behind.

They stumbled through the darkness and up an incline. The farther uphill they went, the more the moonlight broke through the canopy.

Nik didn't look back, but he knew his companions were keeping up by the sound of Sam's grunting and uneven footsteps mixed with Ali's anxious breathing.

They paused briefly at the peak of a hill, and Nik searched the perimeter for any movement. It had been a few minutes since he'd last heard the unsettling wail of the creature that followed them. The silence terrified him more than the noise. At least before, he had a sense of where the mysterious beast was.

Sam hobbled up to Nik's side. "Did we lose it?" he asked, and they shared a knowing look.

It was unlikely they'd left the animal behind. Any predator with an acute sense of hearing and smell would've been able to track them. "Let's keep going," Nik said. He'd keep moving all night if it meant they'd be safe.

They began to walk downhill through a field of tall grass that nearly came up to Nik's shoulders, Ali's head almost completely hidden by the swaying blades.

Nik's pace pushed them forward and challenged Sam, but as usual, he made no complaints. The feeling that something was watching them—stalking them—never eased.

Suddenly, the pale-green grass shifted in front of them, splitting down the middle and forming a path that snaked in their direction. Nik froze and grabbed the knife from the sheath around his waist. The animal had been silent enough to prowl within a few feet of them.

A low and deadly growl was the only warning he got before the beast sprang from the grass and hit him square in the chest, knocking the breath out of him. He felt the ground shake as Sam toppled behind him. Ali screamed.

Everything was a blur of fur and grass cloaked in night. Nik couldn't tell which direction was the sky and which was the ground. The animal's weight forced him to his back, and they rolled. Claws ripped through his shirt and skin, though adrenaline protected him from the pain. Teeth pierced his wrist, and the knife dropped from his hand as they continued to roll in the grass.

Another growl sent rancid breath his way, and he grimaced as saliva splattered his face. The wolf's thrashing teeth were only inches from his throat, ready to rip into him. He held the animal at arm's length, his muscles straining against its wild frenzy. Blood trickled down his arm where the creature had dug into his flesh.

Nik grunted and tried to force the wolf off him, but it was no use. All he could do was keep the distance between its sharp teeth and his vulnerable neck. He didn't know how long he would last under its weight.

Every muscle in his body strained, and he held on for dear life. Oxygen became scarce as he held his breath.

An object flew through the air and hit the animal in the face. The wolf whimpered and jumped away from Nik. It retreated a few steps, angered by the rock that had smacked its tender nose. It crouched and released another furious growl at its assailant.

Ali.

Her eyes reflected the moonlight, and Nik caught the look on her face before she pivoted and ran. Not terror or paralyzing fear, but courage and bravery. Like she was daring the beast to hurt her loved ones. She wouldn't allow it.

The wolf leaped over Nik and followed Ali through the rustling grass. Nik sprang from the ground and ran as quickly as he could behind them. The thought of the beast ripping into Ali's body was enough to make him nauseous. She had saved him, but at what cost?

It didn't take long for the wolf to overcome her. Nik heard a scream followed by the sound of two bodies, one human and one animal, hitting the ground. Another blood-curdling scream made his legs pump harder and faster.

"Ali!" he called for her, frantically following the sound of her agonized screams.

Nik found the beast with fangs deep in Ali's forearm. She was trying to break free, making futile attempts to throw off the wolf.

With lightning reflexes, Nik pulled a second knife from his belt and flew, landing on top of the animal. He grabbed the beast by the neck, and it yelped in surprise, releasing Ali's arm. Nik pulled its head back and sliced his knife across the beast's throat. Blood spilled out and soaked both the ground and Ali.

The wolf's last howl was a relief to Nik's ears. He let the animal's body slump to the ground beside them and scurried toward Ali, pushing his panic aside. She was cradling her arm, and he couldn't tell where the beast's blood ended and hers began.

The world fell away. Nik couldn't hear a thing, could only see the blood and mangled flesh in front of him. He ripped a piece of his shirt and wrapped it around Ali's arm, stopping the blood as best as he could. He searched her body for other injuries as the world around him spiraled out of control.

"Nik."

A whisper in the breeze.

"Nik."

She had to be okay. He should've done more. He had failed to protect her. He had failed once again.

"Nik." Ali spoke softly, but her gentle fingers caressed his face. He leaned into the palm of her hand. "I'm okay. You don't need to worry."

All he did was worry. He worried that she would never be the same. That they would never find Eli. That she would never forgive him for urging her to leave Eli that day. That he'd lost her before they had gotten the chance to enjoy just being together.

But he didn't say any of that.

He kissed her cheek, and her tears wetted his lips. "Thank you...for saving me."

In more ways than one. Although, if he did lose her...if they stayed this course, she might've damned him, too.

Ali's eyes glistened, and she opened her mouth to respond. Whatever she was about to say was cut short by the sound of Sam staggering out of the grass and falling to the ground beside them. He'd somehow carried all three of their packs with him.

By sheer luck, Sam seemed to be completely unharmed, and he surveyed their condition. Then, noting the dead wolf beside them, he muttered, "Holy shit. What happened?"

Nik was too exhausted to rehash the events, so he gave a quick summary and stood to check their surroundings. They'd veered from their path, and he wasn't certain he'd be able to find it again.

He swallowed and took deep breaths, unwilling to show any signs of worry. Extending a hand, he helped Ali to her feet. Her clothes were drenched in blood, and she shivered in the cool night air.

"We should find a place to rest for the night." Nik nodded at Ali. "And get you out of those clothes."

Chapter Eight

ALI

Ali pried the bloody shirt and jeans from her body and used a bottle of water to rinse off her skin the best she could. Flakes of dark red had dried on her skin. She would need to fully submerge to get rid of it all, but she couldn't relax while evidence of the attack still clung to her body.

Nik stood over her and wrapped a hand around her good arm. "Can I take a look?" His voice was low and soothing.

Ali nodded, then hissed when he gently turned her forearm to inspect it. He softly prodded the already bruising skin and she bit back a cry of pain. "I don't think it's broken, but it's hard to tell. How does it feel when you move it?"

"Fine."

He looked her in the eyes, and Ali avoided his gaze.

"Can you lift this?" he asked, handing her a bottle of water.

She clenched the bottle in her hand and raised it to shoulder height before lowering it again. It hurt, but it wasn't the searing pain she expected with a fracture. "It's fine," she said again.

Nik studied her again but nodded when he seemed satisfied with her answer. "Wash up. I'll start the fire."

She scrubbed at her skin until it was pink. Then she rinsed out her wound and wrapped it again in the cleanest scrap of clothing she could find. Which was difficult to do since all their clothes were dirty and sweaty. She prayed it wouldn't get infected.

Once she finished cleaning up, she returned to the warmth of the fire Nik had built. They'd stumbled upon a small cave hidden in the foothills. It was much drier than their previous campsites, something Ali was thankful for as the rain began to pour yet again.

Nik paused as she tossed her soiled clothing into the flames, but he said nothing. He only released a sorrowful sigh.

Ali could feel him slowly distancing himself, knew it was her own fault, but she couldn't help it. She wasn't ready to admit that he wasn't to blame for leaving Eli. Looking at him, speaking to him, was a painful reminder that she had chosen him over Eli. She had left Eli behind.

Sam handed her a piece of meat on a stick. At least the wolf was good for one thing. This was the best meal they'd had in days, maybe weeks. If they were lucky, Nik might be able to smoke the meat and make it last even longer. Ali was getting tired of living on berries and nuts.

"Feel better?" Sam asked, taking in her clean clothing. *Cleaner.* This outfit wasn't blood-soaked, but there was no such thing as clean in the wild.

Ali gave a non-committal shrug and dug into her dinner. Although they used no seasoning, it was the best thing she'd ever tasted. Okay, that was an exaggeration, but the meat was surprisingly tender and juicy.

Sam nodded and tore a bite from his skewer. He knew as well as Nik to choose his battles and wouldn't pressure her to open up. Instead, he looked toward the entrance of the cave. "It was good luck we found this place. I wouldn't want to be out in this storm."

As he spoke, the sky lit up with a flash of lightning and thunder boomed. The ground seemed to shake beneath their feet, and Ali could hear the pitter patter of rain hitting the side of the cave.

"Hopefully the storm moves quickly. It's not safe for us to hike in these conditions. And the rain might make it harder to track...I mean, it's already getting harder to follow the Coyotes. I...I don't know how far we were pushed off course."

Ali swallowed the lump in her throat and looked at Nik through her lashes. His gaze was apologetic. She'd known from the beginning that finding Eli wouldn't be easy, but she had allowed herself to hope. The longer it took, the less likely it became that they would ever find him.

The storm didn't pass quickly. It lasted for days.

After a week had gone by, Ali was entirely restless, knowing that the thread tying her to Eli was unraveling and washing away with the rain. It would be impossible to find him now.

The cave was damp and dark and did nothing to help her mood. She shivered and pulled on another layer of clothing.

She tried to sleep. There wasn't much else to keep her mind occupied in this cave, and she only seemed to find a reprieve while unconscious.

Where was Eli now? She hoped he was somewhere safe...and happy.

She wasn't sure how long she'd been lying on the cold, hard ground of the cave, tossing and turning, when Nik settled down beside her. Like a habit she couldn't quit, her body instantly melted into the warmth and comfort of his powerful arms. The way his chest engulfed her body like a blanket. She sighed and turned over, facing him for the first time in weeks.

He was watching her intensely. Those steely blue eyes still took her breath away, only now it was painful—oxygen forced from her lungs. The ache in her heart only grew, knowing she was the cause of the sadness in his gaze.

Her fingertips grazed the hem of his T-shirt, lifting it to feel the skin beneath, and he sucked in a sharp breath. Ali had missed this touch. She missed feeling close to him. She continued to tease, her skin just barely grazing his. He shivered, and she watched the bob of his throat as he swallowed.

Ali listened to the sound of shuffling and the tap of a walking stick. Sam was leaving for a bathroom break or some fresh air, she didn't care which.

They were alone in the cave.

With steady hands, Ali forced her palm down the front of Nik's pants and cupped him. A deep moan escaped his lips and reverberated somewhere between her legs.

His voice trembled with uncertainty and longing. "Ali?"

She didn't want to speak. Didn't want to acknowledge any of the things they'd left unsaid. So she silenced him with a soft kiss, and his lips parted obediently.

She pressed a hand to his shoulder and forced him to his back, sliding one leg across his body and straddling his lap. Her hips ground against him, rubbing that sweet spot of pleasure. It was the only pleasant sensation she'd felt in weeks, and damn it felt good.

His tongue tangled with hers, and the heat and softness made her dizzy. The taste of him was intoxicating.

Their bodies pressed together, and she felt him harden beneath her. Felt his deep and uneven breaths as he wrapped his hands around her and squeezed her ass, squeezing her against his cock. The feeling that shot through her body was divine, and she chased it eagerly.

With difficulty, Nik broke their kiss and panted, "Ali?"

She did her best to ignore him, kissing his neck, sucking on his earlobe the way she knew made his eyes roll back in his head. She knew all his sensitive spots. She rubbed a thumb over another one—the tip of his cock.

"Ali, wait," Nik said, grabbing her waist and stilling her.

Ali huffed, frustrated to be denied the blissful feeling she sought.

"Talk to me." He pushed a strand of hair behind her ear. "Please. I don't know what's going on in your head anymore."

"I don't want to talk," Ali whispered. She rolled her hips again, and his length rubbed against her center. She could feel how damp her panties were already.

Worried wrinkles formed between Nik's brows. "How am I supposed to help you if you won't talk to me?"

"I don't need you to help me," Ali snapped. It was easier to blame him for leaving Eli than it was to blame herself. "I just want to"—she leaned back and scanned the room, unwilling to look him in the eye—"*feel* something."

She was tired of being numb. Tired of trudging through the woods for weeks with nothing to show for it. Her fingers were numb. Her toes were numb. But most of all, her heart was numb. Was it so hard to believe that she just wanted a moment of *joy*, no matter how fleeting?

Nik sat up so his chest was pressed to hers once more. "You want to *feel* something?" He licked his lips and then his jaw clenched, the moment between them shifting to something more ominous. He released a small huff. "I know you're in a lot of pain, Ali, but you can't use sex to bury your feelings."

"You never had a problem with it before."

Her words hit her target. Nik flinched, anguish written all over his face. She knew his worst fear was that she didn't truly love him and had just used his vulnerability against him.

She didn't know why she said it. Perhaps she was just angry that he wouldn't satisfy her needs. Wouldn't let her have a moment of peace.

But there was some truth to the words. In retrospect, it was easy to see why she had fallen so quickly for him. He had been a source of happiness while her world was crumbling. Sure, they had grown into something more, but her initial attraction had everything to do with the mindless ecstasy he provided. It had been easy to surrender to his touch and forget how her world was crumbling around her.

It was crumbling again...and she wanted to forget.

"Is that all I am to you? A distraction?" Nik choked on his words, and Ali couldn't bring herself to confirm or deny his accusation.

She should've said something.

She should've told him she didn't mean it. She saw the agony written on his face and knew she could take it away, but the words caught in her throat.

She was angry. Angry at the world. Angry at herself. It was easy to release that anger on Nik, even while she could feel his heart fracturing beneath her palms.

She should've said something...but she didn't.

Placing his hands on her thighs, Nik forcefully removed Ali from his lap and stood, walking toward the cave entrance. Ali watched as his outline disappeared into the night.

That was it. The last good thing in Ali's life had just walked away. She was left feeling empty and cold, the broken result of her own self-destruction.

Perhaps she should've cherished the feeling of being numb.

She leaned her back against the cave wall and pulled her knees in close. The feelings she'd been keeping at bay flooded her faster than the tears that streamed down her cheeks. She cradled her face, then sobbed uncontrollably.

Chapter Nine

ELI

"I hope it's to your liking." Grace's voice broke through the silence as she followed him into the small space that would be his new home. That angelic voice made his stomach flutter. Her footsteps were so light as she glided into the room. Everything about the way she carried herself lived up to her name.

Eli glanced around his new room, taking in every detail. It was small but comfortable—and well-lit enough that for a moment, he forgot he was underground.

The main door opened into a small kitchenette with a table big enough for two and some counter space. Attached to that was a bedroom with a full-size bed, bigger than any Eli had ever owned, complete with fresh linens and a white comforter. And to the side was a door to his own private bathroom.

In the corner, next to the bed, was a dark brown dresser with several drawers. The couple outfits he'd been given from the Coyotes probably wouldn't even fill one.

The walls were painted a soft, calming blue, and a couple paintings hung on the wall across from the bed. Upon closer inspection, Eli realized the art depicted seashells. He touched the texture of the oil painting and remembered the shells he used to keep on his windowsill back in Andus. They had no way of knowing what this painting would mean to him. It was almost like this room was destined to be his.

"It's perfect," he said honestly.

"Good. The rooms are all standard, but we do our best to make them feel like home for newcomers."

"I appreciate it," he said, turning to find her staring at him with a half-smile.

The look of joy seemed to be permanently etched on her face. She hadn't let that smile falter for one moment since he'd first laid eyes on her. It was contagious, and Eli gave a small smile back.

"I brought you a few changes of clothes. I know you've been traveling through the storms, and I suspect your own are drenched and dirty. If you give me yours, I will have them washed for you."

He took the pile of clothes from her hands and set them on his dresser while she waited expectantly in his doorway.

"Oh. You mean right now?"

She nodded, and there was a hint of amusement in her big, beautiful hazel eyes. "You can shower first if you'd like. The bathroom is stocked with soaps and towels, too."

"Right." He grabbed a shirt and pants and headed into his bathroom. He showered quickly, anxious not to keep her waiting. He barely had time to register how amazing the warm water felt and how it soothed his sore muscles. He carefully washed around his wound, which was looking much better.

Once he finished showering and changing, he stepped back into the bedroom, where Grace was studying the painting on his wall.

"This is one of my favorites, I think."

"Why's that?"

"Do you see this?" Her finger traced a line of white paint. Then she moved behind him and grabbed his shoulders. Her touch was tender, but he allowed her to push him side to side, just a couple inches. "Do you see how it seems to move?"

He hadn't noticed it at first glance, but she was right. Somehow, the painting came to life.

"It's meant to imitate the tides. Like waves crashing on the shore and then drifting back out to sea," she said.

"Hmm."

"I've always wanted to see what an ocean looks like. I suppose this is as close as I'll ever get."

"You don't know that," he told her. Hadn't his life brought him far from home?

"Maybe."

Grace was still holding onto his shoulders and standing close enough he could make out the specks of green in her eyes and smell her floral scent mixed with something fruity he couldn't identify. He inhaled sharply, and she dropped her hands.

Why did he suddenly feel nervous?

He twisted his dirty clothing in his hands and felt a little awkward handing them over to her. Like he might dirty her pristine figure, but she tossed them into a basket without judgment.

"I suppose you have questions?" she asked, as if she'd done this routine a hundred times before.

Eli didn't even know where to begin. "Um, am I free to go wherever I please?"

"Of course. You're not a prisoner here."

He swallowed hard. Did she know his history?

"Everywhere outside is free for you to explore, and most of the mountain is too. There are a few chambers that are restricted, but they're all in the north wing."

"What kind of restricted areas?" he asked.

"Just things like our council chamber, research and development, farms, medical supplies...only people who work in those areas have access."

"What will I do for work? For money?"

"For now, you can just focus on getting settled. We have a fund for newcomers, so you don't need to worry about that just yet. Actually, I almost forgot," she said, digging into a bag. She pulled out a small purse and handed it to Eli.

Coins jingled as he opened it. He pulled one out and observed the silver coin. A woman's face was just barely recognizable. Years of wear had eroded the edges and made it difficult to make out her features. The only thing he could make out clearly was the dimples from her smile. They looked very similar to Grace's, and he looked up to find her watching him.

"The first Lady of Berland, our matriarch," Grace said when she noticed him studying the coin. "She was so full of herself that she created her own currency with her face plastered on them."

Eli nodded and slid the coin back into the purse.

"That should be enough to get you through the next week. After that, we can discuss open job positions."

He weighed the bag of coins in his hand and looked around his new room. It was surreal. Perhaps he had died in Rysburg and this was the afterlife.

"What now?" he asked.

Grace grinned. "Whatever you'd like. Unfortunately, I must leave you. I have other job duties to tend to today."

"What is your job?"

Somehow, her smile turned even brighter. "I'm the face of Berland."

She batted her eyelashes, and Eli chuckled. He knew she was joking, but if Berland had a face, they'd chosen the most beautiful one he'd ever seen.

She patted the basket full of his dirty clothes. "I'll bring them back tomorrow. There are a few things in your cupboard to eat if you get hungry. There's more in the supply chamber, too. Just look for the hall with a blue mark over it, off the antechamber. There's a cafeteria there as well. If you need anything else, my room is just at the end of the hall."

She pointed her finger to her left. There was an inexplicable sense of relief knowing she would be close by. She was the only person he knew in this foreign place and the only one who'd been able to settle his discomfort so far.

"Thank you."

"What's your name?" she asked. She bit her lip, and Eli's eyes were drawn to them.

"Eli."

"Eli," she repeated. His name sounded magical coming from her lips. Her beautiful eyes sparkled as she appraised him. "You're welcome, Eli."

The door clicked as it closed behind her, and Eli was left alone with his thoughts. He didn't feel up to exploring Berland yet. His mind and body were too exhausted from the journey here. Instead, he walked into his bathroom and jumped in the shower a second time. It might take a while before he felt truly clean. He took his time, drinking in every blissful moment of the hot water as it traveled down his body, scrubbing his scalp a second time and then a third.

Afterwards, he wrapped himself in a towel and grabbed something to eat from the cupboard, enough to curb his hunger, and then settled onto the bed, hoping to take a nap and maybe explore later that evening.

Without Grace's distraction or anything else to do, Eli found himself staring at the ceiling with an arm behind his head. He couldn't help but wonder where Ali was now. Was she alive? Was she still with Nik? Were they able to get away or did some of the Coyotes track them down and slaughter them? He felt like vomiting when he thought of Ali being brutally murdered. He couldn't stomach it. Refused to believe it.

No. They had survived the attack and had gotten away. And he would figure out how to find them.

Eli's arms flung wildly as he fought with an imaginary foe. His opponent swung a sword wildly, and Eli dodged it with unmatched skill. He was battling with a masked enemy, the Coyotes.

No, that couldn't be right. They weren't the bad guys.

He tossed and turned, and his heart pounded wildly in his chest as he worked to escape his tormentor.

If they weren't the bad guys, then why were they trying to kill him?

The man took a sharp jab at Eli's midsection, and he screamed in horror. Phantom pain in his side woke him with a startle. Eli struggled to move his limbs. He had tangled himself in the blanket with all his thrashing.

It was just a dream.

The lights in his room had shut off, indicating that it must be nighttime. Only the light in his bathroom remained, and it cast a soft glow over his bedroom through the crack. Enough to take in his surroundings and remind himself that he was safe now. He tore his arms free of the blanket that swaddled him.

A knock at his door sounded, and he jolted again, falling off the side of the bed and to the floor with a hard thud. He faintly heard the door open and click closed.

"Ugh," he groaned.

"Eli?" He recognized Grace's voice. Her soft footsteps moved into the room, and he met her gaze over the top of the bed.

"I'm fine. I just, uh...had a nightmare."

"I know." Her features were illuminated in the light, and her face scrunched sympathetically. "You were yelling."

"I'm so sorry. I hope I didn't wake the whole hall."

"Oh, you didn't," she assured him. "These rooms are pretty sound-proof. I was already awake and taking a stroll by your door when I heard you. Sometimes I have trouble sleeping."

"Oh...that's good. Not the not sleeping part, but the other...um, walking by thing." Why was he so flustered and struggling to speak like a normal human? As he stood, the blanket around him fell, revealing his naked body. He'd never changed back into clothes after his shower. "Oh my god."

He quickly reached down to grab the blanket, but it tangled around his ankles and tripped him, sending him flying to the floor once again.

Grace laughed softly, but Eli remained on the floor, hidden by the bed and saved from having to face her.

"Are you okay down there?"

No. He had died from humiliation.

"Eli?" she asked again, a hint of concern in her voice.

He pressed his face into his palms and his response came out muffled.

"What was that?" Her voice grew louder as she rounded the end of the bed.

"Shit." He pulled the blanket over him, this time freeing his feet from the tangled fabric. She giggled again, and even though he was completely mortified, the sound of her laughter soothed his nerves, and he longed to hear it again.

He peered up at her from his spot on the floor. She had her hair pulled back in a messy bun and wore silk shorts with a matching tank top. The thin fabric left little to the imagination. He could see the outline of her curves, of her full breasts and hardened nipples. The tank top was short enough that a sliver of skin peeked out just below her belly button. The only other woman he'd seen so much of was Ali.

Eli forced his gaze away, torn between being a gentleman and the desire to study every inch of her.

"Let me help you." She grabbed his hand and helped him up while he held onto the comforter around his waist.

"I'm so embarrassed. I didn't mean to…uh, flash you."

"It's not your fault. I'm the one who came into your room uninvited."

"Ah, yeah, I guess so." He let out a nervous breath and grabbed a pair of pants from his dresser, slipping them on while she turned away. "Still, not the best first impression."

"Technically, I think it's the second. But I'd argue you made *quite* the impression."

He stilled and tilted his head. Was she flirting?

"What were you dreaming about?"

She sat down on the end of his bed and crossed one leg casually over the other. Her large eyes reflected the light from the bathroom, staring unblinkingly at him. He didn't know how to open up to her. How to tell this innocent and bright woman the atrocities he'd lived through. And he didn't know that he wanted to. She was still a stranger, after all. A beautiful stranger with a big heart, but a stranger nonetheless.

He took a seat next to her and cleared his throat, but he couldn't form the words to respond.

"It's okay if you don't want to talk about it yet." Her voice was so comforting, and her fingers grazed his. "I'm here whenever you're ready."

The smallest weight lifted from his chest—one that he hadn't realized was there. He'd grown so accustomed to the way it felt.

"Thank you. Why can't you sleep?"

"I have a lot on my mind," she said. Her smile dimmed, and she seemed...pensive. He couldn't figure out what in Berland might be stressing her out. Was she once a newcomer, too? Did she have tales of her own that she preferred to keep secret?

"How long have you lived here?" he asked, chasing away a yawn. He knew what awaited if he laid down to rest again. He'd be haunted by more nightmares of his dad or Ali. He'd rather stay up and talk to Grace.

"All my life."

"You were born here?"

Grace nodded. "Yes. There are many of us who have been here all our lives, but there are many more like you who migrated here at some point. I'm sure it seems daunting, but just know that many have come before you and they've adjusted just fine. I'm sure you'll fit in quickly."

He could tell she was trying to reassure him, but it didn't do much good. Walking through Berland, everyone felt like a blur. He felt distant from his own body, like a ghost watching from the sidelines. He couldn't imagine a day when he'd ever fit in here.

"Well...I should probably get back to bed." She hesitated before slowly prying her fingers from Eli's. "Goodnight, Eli."

"Goodnight, Grace."

Chapter Ten

ELI

ELI WOKE THE NEXT day feeling well rested despite the midnight mishap. The lights in his kitchen had a warm glow, mimicking the morning sunrise outside. He dressed in a pair of dark jeans and a long-sleeved shirt. He checked his cupboards for something to eat, but he only found some bland crackers, fruit preserves, and some spices, none of which sounded appetizing. Recalling the cafeteria Grace had mentioned, he swiped his boots from beside the door and slid them on.

He pulled his door open and stepped into the hall. The dark gray stone was still disorienting. Everywhere he looked, the halls looked the same. Glistening uneven rock with doors spaced evenly. He wondered briefly which one belonged to Grace. She should've been more specific.

The walk through the halls felt shorter than when he had arrived. He supposed some of his apprehension was fading and he was even a little excited to see what the day had to offer him. To explore some of the town and maybe meet some other residents.

The hall opened into the large entrance bustling with activity. People were coming and going down the various halls, some of them stopping to chat with friends before going about their day. Most of them dressed casually and Eli thanked the gods that he at least didn't stand out in this way. Though no one gave him a second glance, so maybe he was already blending in.

Their voices echoed inside the chamber, making Eli's head spin. He considered taking his breakfast outside just to get some fresh air. How did they live like this?

He searched for the door Grace had described—the one with the blue symbol above it. He likely would've found it without the blue symbol as the closer he got, the stronger the aroma of food grew. He was nearly at the door when he heard his name.

"Eli!" It was Grace's voice.

He searched for her in the crowd and found her standing with two other women who looked displeased at the interruption. As he walked their way, he couldn't help but notice how most people in the room seemed to turn their attention toward Grace. He only wanted to blend in and live quietly while she was born to stand out. She was like a beacon of light that demanded everyone's gaze.

Grace waved him over, and the other ladies stared at him with curiosity. He felt their eyes on him as he closed the distance between them. "Ladies, this is Eli. He just arrived yesterday. Eli, these are my friends Heather and Amaya. We've been best friends our entire lives."

He shook their hands. "It's nice to meet you. I take it you were born here as well, then?"

"Yes, we were." The first one—Heather, he thought—grasped his hand and gave it a soft but steady shake. Amaya shadowed her and gave Eli a quick handshake with dainty, tan hands.

He could tell by the way they looked at him that they were sizing him up. Heather's eyes were big and unblinking while Amaya snuck glances between Grace and Eli. He felt like prey and these two women were predators. He shifted uneasily.

"Were you headed to the cafeteria? I'd be happy to join you," Grace said, placing a hand on his bicep. Amaya's eyes narrowed at the touch.

The prospect excited him. He certainly didn't want to eat alone, but one look at her friends made him think twice. There was something in their eyes—curious but lethal. He shook his head. "I don't want to take you from your friends."

"I can't be taken. I'm offering. No, I'm demanding," she added with a squeeze to his arm. She gave her two friends a pointed look that said it was best if they didn't argue.

Eli decided not to argue, either. Nor did he want to.

Amaya and Heather exchanged a look behind Grace's back. He couldn't decipher their nonverbal communication, though he was sure they'd have much to say once he stepped away.

Grace gave her friends a brief wave. "I'll catch up with you later."

They nodded, and Grace moved her hand to slip around Eli's arm, allowing him to escort her toward the cafeteria. The way she so comfortably invaded his space left little room for him to feel shy or awkward. She was so sure of herself; it was contagious.

As they walked, Eli noticed glances from everyone they passed. They whispered as they walked on the opposite side of the hall. A few bold individuals felt comfortable pointing in their direction. His previous invisibility was long gone.

"Do you get newcomers often?" he asked, locking eyes with one man who hastily looked the other way. Was it that obvious he didn't belong? He couldn't think of any other reason why everyone would be so invested in him.

"Hmm?"

"Why is everyone staring?" He brushed at the bristles on his chin, sweeping away invisible dirt. Maybe he had something on his face.

"I don't think anyone is staring."

She didn't elaborate, and before Eli could press the matter, they walked into a large rectangular hall full of long tables that took up the entire length of the room. Small groups of friends and families were scattered about, enjoying their breakfast, and Eli could smell the food from the kitchen. The scent was so strong that he could taste it in the air—a mix of sweet and salty that made his mouth water.

Grace led him to a buffet line, and he recognized less than half of the dishes. One that looked like a pie but not the fruit ones he was familiar with. Another tray held a white substance with various colored berries next to it. He stuck with an item he was more familiar with and piled a couple sausages on his plate. Grace didn't hesitate to toss a fluffy circular object on his plate before adding some fruit and toast to her own.

When he gave her an inquisitive look, she acted surprised. "They're pancakes. You'll love them. Trust me."

He took her word for it. They did smell heavenly.

At the end of the line, a worker waited expectantly, and Eli pulled out his bag of coins.

Grace raised her brows. "You didn't need to bring all of it. You should keep that somewhere safe." Then she helped him pick out the few coins he needed to pay for his breakfast, telling him the amount of each as she went.

She pulled out a few coins of her own and then led him to a nearby table. He took a seat across from her and she watched him, clearly waiting for him to dig in.

He smiled at how easily amused she was. Maybe he should've felt annoyed that she was watching him like he was a source of entertainment, a freak who had stumbled into her town, but her bright eyes and beautiful smile amused him equally.

Eli cut into his pancakes and prepared to give Grace her show.

"Hang on. You need some of this." Grace grabbed a metal dispenser from the center of the table and poured a thick substance over his pancakes. The aroma was sweet and enticing.

He took a bite, and his eyes rolled in the back of his head. His reaction earned a nod of approval from her. He'd acted exactly how she hoped he would.

"What is that?" he asked as he drizzled more over top of the fluffy cakes.

"Maple syrup."

"It's amazing." He took another bite. "God, I could bathe in that."

"I expect an invitation if you decide to go through with that."

Eli choked on his food. Grace was bold—bolder than any woman he'd ever known. Or than any man, for that matter. She kept rendering him speechless. It was just the sort of distraction that he needed. To keep his brain occupied with things that weren't named Ali or Andus or Rysburg. Grace was the embodiment of *fun*. There was no space for sadness when she was near.

He took a sip of water and cleared his throat. "So, what's on the agenda today?"

"I have some meetings I need to attend and a dinner later tonight with my parents. Unfortunately, I won't be able to give you a tour of the town today, but I'd recommend a stroll through the main strip. There's lots to see there. If you walk far enough, you'll find a little oxbow lake. Many people spend their free time there."

The lake sounded nice. He used to love spending summer evenings perched on the sand watching the sunset. It would be different now, without Ali by his side. "I will check it out."

Grace finished her breakfast first but waited patiently for him to finish his pancakes. He mopped up every drop of syrup with his last bite, not wanting to waste the smallest dreg of the sweet nectar.

She smiled when he wiped his bottom lip with his thumb. "I have to run, but I'll see you later?"

"I'll check my calendar."

Her smile reached her eyes, and she brushed his hand delicately as she stood to leave. "Bye, Eli."

He watched as she walked away, her hips swaying and a little pep in her step. He envied the way she moved through life with little concern. Meanwhile, it took all of his strength to keep pushing forward. It took all of his restraint not to walk out of this mountain and into the wilderness, searching for Ali.

But logically, he knew it would be better to approach it with a clear head and a plan. He just didn't know where or how to begin.

⁂

Eli took Grace's recommendation and roamed through town. There was one main dirt street that led along the river, lined with shops, cafes, and various services. Things that they would've done themselves back in Andus, but here they had the privilege of having it done for a small fee. Like the launderer or the seamstress.

He took his time browsing everything they had to offer. His favorite was a bakery. He had never realized there were so many types of bread. It was a small shop, only big enough for a couple customers at a time. Luckily, Eli was the only one waiting.

He stared at all the varieties lining the wooden counter, trying to decipher what each one was. An older man with a white beard working the counter noticed and eagerly gave him a sample of one with cheese baked on top. He said it was his best seller, and Eli could see why.

The place next door sold pressed juices, and the owner of the shop was just as excited as the last to give him samples. A red apple one, a pink one that was a mix of berries, and a yellow one that was sweet and sour at the same time. Made from lemons, the man told Eli. Eli chose the berry juice and paid the man, stepping back outdoors.

With juice in one hand and a portion of cheesy bread in the other, he headed toward the oxbow lake.

The sun had chased away the storms that had followed them from Rysburg. Trees were budding leaves, and a few flowers sprouted sporadically through the grass on the side of the dirt path.

Eli took a seat on the lake's beach. It was nothing like the one back in Andus. He was used to a lake so massive that you couldn't see the other side. This one was small enough that he could swim across. It wrapped around a small spot of land like a horseshoe, and people laid out blankets while children splashed in the shallow waters along the shore. It was peaceful, and he could see why people would hang out here.

As time passed, more people came to the sanctuary, enjoying the first nice day they'd had in weeks, according to the conversation Eli overheard. The sun was high in the sky and there wasn't a cloud in sight. He watched as children used their imaginations to make up games and play out stories. The water had to be freezing cold, but they didn't seem to mind.

A young woman caught his attention as she came between the pine trees. Her blonde hair was pulled back into a braid, and his breath caught. She sat next to a friend and her laugh carried through the air. Smiling wide, she leaned back on her elbows as she soaked in the sun. She reminded him so much of Ali. Even some of her mannerisms were similar. Eli stared far longer than was deemed polite.

When he could no longer take the heartbreak, he stood and made his way back to his room. He wasn't sure what he planned to do. Sit and wallow? He only knew he didn't want to be around anyone else right now. He didn't deserve to sit in peace on a beach while Ali was missing, most likely struggling to survive.

He was so distracted by the time he showed up at his front door that he ran straight into Grace, nearly knocking her over. She stumbled into the wall, and he wrapped a hand around her waist to stabilize them both.

"Sorry. I'm—"

"It's okay. Are you all right?"

Eli had never been good at hiding his emotions. "Of course. Did you need something?"

"I just wanted to drop this off. Freshly cleaned." She patted a small stack of clothes that Eli recognized as his own.

"Thank you."

"And I brought this as well." She held up a necklace, and the pendant glistened in the light. "The chain was broken, so I had our metal worker attach a new one."

Eli held it and felt the ridges of the purple stone set inside a rose.

Ali's necklace.

He'd grabbed it in the heat of the fight, after the Coyote who turned out to be Michael had ripped it from her neck. Eli had forgotten he even had it. It had been tucked away in a pocket; Grace must've found it in his dirty laundry.

His eyes burned, and he fought to keep the tears from spilling over. His nostrils flared as he inhaled sharply and met Grace's hazel eyes. A look of surprise met him in return.

"Eli..."

"Thank you," he choked out. Then he slipped into his room and let his grief consume him.

Chapter Eleven

NIK

Nik woke the next morning, his shoulder stiff from sleeping on the rocky terrain. The cool stone made him shiver as he sat up and rubbed the sleepiness from his eyes, then checked on his traveling companions.

Sam was lying on one end of the cave, a second shirt draped over him to help keep him warm through the night. On the other side, Ali was curled up in a ball, her back to him.

It was the first night they'd spent apart, and it tore a hole in his chest. He knew she was hurting and taking it out on him. Maybe he deserved it, maybe he didn't. But she knew how to prey on his deepest insecurity—that he wasn't worth loving. That someone as sweet as her couldn't possibly be in love with a monster like him.

He vividly recalled the day that he'd asked her why she loved him and she'd eradicated all of his doubts. That woman lying in his bed with an arm around his waist was a far cry from the version across the cave.

There was a reason he'd chosen a life of isolation. Because this...this *hurt.*

Nik stood and shook the stiffness out of his legs, then headed toward the opening of the cave. The rain had finally let up, and the sky was a clear blue with just a hint of morning fog.

Birds chirped and flew overhead as Nik turned down the path to the right, finding a tree to relieve himself. As he zipped his jeans, he was met with the sound of leaves crunching.

"Good morning," Sam said, a little too bright for this early in the day.

"Morning," Nik grumbled.

Sam stepped up to the tree, unbuttoned his pants, and propped his walking stick against the bark of the tree trunk. "So what's the plan for today?"

"Same as the day before," Nik said dryly. His fight with Ali hadn't left him in a chatty mood.

"The trail for the Coyotes is long gone by now. What are we going to do?"

"They were headed south, so we'll keep moving in that direction...see if we stumble upon them or any other civilization that might know where to find them."

It was a bleak outlook. His hope of finding Eli diminished by the day, along with his hope for seeing Ali happy again. But he refused to give up. Even if they never found Eli again, they couldn't hide in the wilderness for the rest of their lives. They needed to find a home. Someplace stable.

"Right." Sam shook himself and buttoned his pants again, grabbing his cane. "How are you going to break it to Ali?"

"I'm not. I think she knows the odds of finding him are slim." She had to know. She was smart enough to figure it out.

"You think or you know?"

Nik sighed as they walked back toward the cave. "We're not in a good place right now. She's hardly speaking to me. If I try to talk to her, I'll only make it worse. Let her hold on to whatever hope she still has left."

Sam stopped in his tracks, allowing Nik to forge ahead a few paces. "Nik," he said sternly. Like Nik was about to be reprimanded. It would've been comical under different circumstances. Though they technically were the same rank as guards, Sam had always taken a more passive role. He had never tried to give Nik orders, and now seemed like an odd time to start.

Nik turned around and waited.

"She needs you, whether she's willing to admit it or not. This is all going to catch up to her eventually. And when it does, she shouldn't have to grieve alone. You love her, right?"

"Yes." With all his heart.

"Then be there for her."

Nik's shoulders slumped. "I don't know how. I don't know what she wants from me. Everything I say and do is wrong. How am I supposed to be there for her when she wants nothing to do with me? I think...I think she hates me."

How could she not? He was the one who had told her to leave Eli behind. But in his defense, he had been certain that Eli was dead. He'd seen his body fall to the ground. If he had known that Eli was alive, he never would've pulled her away from that riverbank. Hell, he would've fought the Coyotes on his own if it meant getting her best friend back, no matter how much he disliked the man.

But he hadn't done that. He had forced Ali to leave Eli, and now she had every right to hate him.

Sam closed the few steps between them and placed a hand on Nik's shoulder. "It'll pass. She loves you, too. Just keep trying." Stepping around Nik, he moved closer to the cave. "It would be a shame if you lost her. She's the only one who's made you halfway tolerable."

Nik rolled his eyes. He would've punched Sam in the shoulder if it weren't for the injured leg that made him unsteady. He'd probably fall over.

"Sam…"

"Yes?"

"Did you lose people? We've been out here for weeks, and you've been taking it so well. I'm such an ass for never thinking to ask before. Caught up in my own bullshit. Did you leave people behind?"

Nik realized he didn't know much about Sam's family or friends. He knew that Sam's parents were both dead, but they'd never discussed any siblings or if he was seeing anyone. It was selfish that he hadn't thought to ask sooner.

"No." Sam smiled and waved a dismissive hand. "Don't get me wrong. I had many acquaintances, but I wasn't close with any of them. I don't know if you've noticed, but I've always been a bit of a loner. I'd rather spend time drawing than socializing. Making friends is exhausting."

Nik nodded. It made sense. He'd rarely seen Sam with anyone outside of work.

"I suppose you were my only friend," Sam admitted.

"I'm so sorry," Nik said, and they both laughed.

When they returned to the cave, Ali was awake and packing her bag, clearly ready to get the hell out of there. They were all ready to leave the barren lair they'd spent too many days in, trapped by thunderstorms.

Nik hesitated before telling Ali the plan. "We're going to keep moving south." Her eyes flitted toward him for a moment before returning to her busy hands. Nik ran a hand through his hair. "I think it's the most promising route."

Ali nodded silently. She knew what he meant—that it'd be useless to try to pick up where they left off before the wolf attack.

"You should eat something first." He sometimes wondered if Ali would eat at all if he didn't remind her to. The remaining wolf meat had begun to spoil, so he rummaged through his pack and found a handful of berries that miraculously hadn't been smashed. "Here."

She didn't meet his eyes but took the fruit and popped them into her mouth. She didn't bother to utter her gratitude. When she finished, she slung her backpack across her shoulders.

As they headed out, Ali took the lead, setting a furious pace. Sam cast Nik a sideways glance before chasing after her. She was obviously determined to reach their destination, wherever that might be.

Chapter Twelve

ALI

Loose stone crunched beneath Ali's feet. Her boots were so worn, it was hard to gain traction on the gravel. It made the journey long and tedious as they carefully planted each step.

Her legs burned from the uphill climb. Her body wasn't used to this elevation. She'd spent her entire life staying active and working hard to provide for her community, but this was entirely different. She was exhausted mentally and physically, but she refused to give up.

As they climbed higher and higher, she could feel the skin on her forehead burning from the sun's intense blaze. Just what she needed on top of everything else—a sunburn.

It should've worn her down, but it only made her more resilient. More determined to fight her way back to Eli. It didn't matter how hard the world tried to drag her down. Nothing would stop her.

She could hear Nik panting behind her, but he didn't ask her to slow down or take a break. After their argument in the cave, he seemed hesitant to speak to her at all. But he'd been carrying Sam for at least an hour now as the slope of the mountain grew more intense. It was too difficult for Sam, even with his walking stick.

She didn't want to slow down or take a break. Didn't want to be left alone with her thoughts. That was when things felt the most unbearable. She needed purpose, and she found it by driving forward.

The late-spring heat was brutal, and it was only a little past midday. Ali focused on her feet, testing the loose stone before shifting her weight. One wrong step could be deadly up here.

The rhythmic grind of gravel droned on. One foot in front of the other. Over and over and over. She lost herself in the routine of it.

Ali slipped but caught herself quickly.

"We should take a break," Nik muttered behind her.

She turned, and what a sore sight he was, with sweat dripping from his forehead and drenching his T-shirt. Sam looked uncomfortable hanging from Nik's back. He probably needed to stretch his legs.

She didn't want to stop, but her stomach growled. How long ago had they left the cave? Had she eaten anything since the berries? She licked her dry lips; she couldn't remember the last time she had a drink of water either.

"Fine," she conceded.

Ali sat on the ground, damp and spongy from days of rain. It didn't matter that it would get her pants wet or muddy. They'd already absorbed her sweat and there wasn't a clean patch of fabric, anyway.

She dropped her bag from her shoulder and dug around, searching for the last scraps of food. They'd need to hunt again soon, and the prospect was disheartening. This was unfamiliar terrain and who knew what wildlife even roamed up in these mountains.

"Here. I won't eat these." Sam passed her a small bag of her favorite berries.

"Thank you," she whispered, feeling guilty that she'd dragged him up the mountainside. She didn't deserve his kindness.

They ate their small lunch in silence, finding what little shade they could to get a break from the sun. Now that they'd stopped moving, Ali's muscles locked up and protested when she tried to stretch. If it weren't for the importance of her mission, she might've preferred to lie down and sleep.

But they carried on.

Hour after hour, they hiked through the forest. Their surroundings looked no different from when they had started, and Ali grew more frustrated with each step. She wanted to give up, but she wasn't living for any other purpose.

When they stopped for the night, Nik built a small fire. Though warmth radiated from the flames, Ali shivered in her sweat-soaked shirt. She rummaged through her sack and found dry clothes to change into for the night.

She headed into the trees to give herself some privacy. She was still close enough that she could hear Sam and Nik talking. It was the first breach of silence they'd had all day, and the effect on Ali was jarring.

Did they feel as though they couldn't speak because of her? Was the shadow she was casting so strong that it was darkening their day too? She would've felt guilty if she was capable of feeling anything at all.

She quickly pulled off her shirt and inspected her arm. It didn't look any better, but it also didn't look worse. A small victory. She changed into her dry clothes and headed back.

When she returned to the fire, their conversation ceased.

Nik fell asleep first. Hauling Sam up the mountain had clearly taken a toll on him. As much as Ali's muscles ached, he must be aching even more.

He looked so peaceful when he slept. Like everything between them was fine, and she was still the woman he had fallen in love with. If only they could go back in time. Then she let out a soft laugh when she realized she was wishing for a time when she was a prisoner. This must be rock bottom if captivity was more appealing.

"Are you ever going to make up?" Sam asked quietly, careful not to wake Nik.

Ali blinked. She hadn't realized she'd been staring at him. Watching each rise and fall of his chest while he slept. "What?"

Sam took a sip from his water bottle. "It breaks my heart to watch the two of you"—he nodded toward Nik—"carrying on like neither of you is dying on the inside. You're looking at him now like he's out of reach. He's not, Ali. He's right there."

Her eyes flashed back to Nik, his lips slightly parted, breathing audibly but not quite a full snore. She missed hearing the words those lips used to speak. Missed feeling them against her skin. She missed the way his eyes lit up when he smiled. When was the last time he had smiled? When was the last time *she* had smiled?

She tried to force her muscles into the expression now, but they resisted.

"You don't get it." Ali sighed. It felt impossible to fix their relationship when she was incapable of fixing herself. She was too broken.

"Explain it, then."

Ali looked at Sam, who watched her with kind eyes. He wasn't judging, only acting as a friend. She didn't know how to explain it, though. She felt like a soul-sucking void that would devour anything good around her. It was irrational, but a part of her blamed herself for what had happened in Andus to her mother and Jack. For what had happened to Eli in Rysburg and for leaving him behind. Guilt was a heavy weight pulling her below the surface. How could she reconcile with Nik and damn him to sink with her?

Her eyes burned, and she silently cursed the tear that rolled down her cheek, landing on the fabric of her pants.

"Did you know I was adopted?" Sam asked.

A clear attempt to distract her. He'd been doing it a lot lately, trying to get a smile out of her. Sometimes it worked. Most of the time it didn't.

"I didn't know."

"My birth mother was a prisoner, like you were."

Ali's mouth dropped open, and her gaze flew to Sam's.

"I know. Crazy, right?" Sam smiled faintly. "One guard took a liking to her. He visited her cell frequently, and she was in no position to decline. My adoptive parents never told me for certain, but I always got the impression she was a less-than willing participant in my conception."

Ali shivered. For a moment, she'd thought his mother's situation had been similar to hers. It made her sick to hear otherwise. "What happened to her?"

"She died during childbirth. She wouldn't have been able to keep me, anyway. Not in a prison. My birth father wanted nothing to do with me. Neither my mother nor I meant anything to him, and as far as he was concerned, I was not his child."

"I'm so sorry, Sam." She couldn't imagine not having the love of her parents. Though they were gone now, they'd always been kind and charitable, doting on their daughter at every opportunity. She'd never second guessed their love for her.

"When I was around ten, I found out who he was. My adoptive parents didn't want me to know, but I overheard them talking one night. I tracked him down in the middle of town and tried to talk to him. Told him I was his son." Sam let out a soft chuckle. "You can imagine how that went. He shoved me into a puddle of mud and told me to never speak to him again. To never *look* at him again. I'm not sure if he knew I existed…or if he did, perhaps he'd rather forget."

Ali could see the haunted look in his eyes and wondered if her own looked the same. She wanted to hug him, but that was a boundary they'd never crossed. She didn't know if he would accept it. She raised her arm to pat him on the back but decided against it.

"Anyway, my adoptive parents were great. I was in such a dark place after that happened. For years, I wondered why I was even brought into this world. They watched as I faded into the shadows, watched me fall apart. And it broke their hearts in ways I'll never understand. Somehow it hurts more watching the ones you love suffer, you know?"

Ali nodded in understanding.

"But they were there for me. I don't know if I'd still be here if it weren't for them. They stayed by my side and supported me until I was ready to come back into the light."

Ali wiped the tears from her eyes. She thought she knew where this was headed and felt defensive. "Are you going to tell me it's time to come into the light now?"

Sam shook his head. "No. Stay in the dark as long as you need, Ali. But if someone loves you enough to stand with you in the darkness, let them."

Chapter Thirteen

ALI

"I need a break." Nik was huffing and struggling to make his way down the mountain, still carrying Sam on his back down the steep path.

"We're close to the river. It's not that far off," Ali responded. She could already hear the rushing water and nothing would stop her from reaching it. Her focus and determination were at an all-time high. The more she concentrated on the path ahead, the less she worried about her own circumstances. The distraction was everything she needed right now.

"Ali, please."

Ali turned around and could see how badly he was struggling. They'd been at this for days, and he was carrying more than his fair share. They were all running low on food and drink, but Nik was suffering the most. Carrying Sam was expending his energy faster than the rest of them. She couldn't miss the dark circles under his eyes paired with the red flush of his cheeks. The heat of spring almost made her long for the cool rain again.

She didn't want to argue with him. Sam's words had stuck with her, and she was trying to be less frigid. "Okay."

Nik let out a sigh of relief, and Sam slid off his back. He immediately fell to his knees and wiped the sweat from his face with the bottom of his shirt.

Ali looked back toward the path they were on. The sound of the river was tempting. She took a few steps toward it before Nik called out to her.

"Where are you going?" He sounded exasperated.

"To the river." She shook her empty water bottle. "I can refill yours too if you'd like."

"I'm fine. Can you just wait for us? I don't want you going off on your own."

"I'll be fine. I just want a minute to myself." She took off down the path before he could stop her.

The river was further than she'd thought. The sound of the stream carried through the trees, but eventually she found the crystal-clear water weaving its way down the side of the mountain. The water was shallow, only a couple feet deep, and it rippled over brown and beige stones.

She ignored the way her heart pounded as she approached the river and stooped low to fill her bottle. If she ignored that nagging feeling of dread, maybe it would eventually disappear. After replacing the cap with trembling fingers, she dipped her hands in the water and splashed it against her face.

The coolness was unbelievably refreshing.

She contemplated removing her clothes and just lying in the water like she used to as a kid with Eli, but the pounding in her chest made her think twice. She grabbed her bag and dug around for a spare T-shirt, dunking it into the water and pulling it back out. After wringing out the excess water, she tossed it around her neck to cool her down.

Twigs snapped behind her, and she rolled her eyes. She knew it was only a matter of time before Nik followed.

"I told you, I just want a minute alone."

"Trouble in paradise?" a low and menacing voice asked from behind her.

Ali spun around. She recognized that voice. It had haunted her from that first day he'd taunted her as they left a burning Andus behind. Memories of him lashing Eli's back replayed in her mind, and she swayed on her feet. His face was covered in dirt, but she would recognize him anywhere. The menacing madness in his eyes was unforgettable.

"Hello, love," Colin said.

"Where did you come from?" Ali racked her brain for ways to escape. She considered drawing her knife, but his eyes were watching her every move. She could scream, but he'd probably attack her before Nik could reach her.

"It was the craziest thing. I was chased by an animal for days. It was toying with me. Waiting for the right moment to rip me open. Then one night, it miraculously gave up on me. Imagine my surprise when I found out someone else killed the damn beast." His sinister grin made her sick to her stomach. "I've been following you lot since you arrived at the cave. Just patiently waiting for my opportunity."

He strolled toward her, and she took a step back. She pulled back abruptly when her foot plunged into the icy stream. There was nowhere to go.

"What do you want?" she hissed.

"What I've always wanted." Colin took a few more steps in her direction, stopping only a couple feet from her. "I'm going to take my time killing you, the same way that beast would've done to me. And this time, no one is here to stop me."

Colin leaped toward her, knocking her into the stream. He landed on top of her, and her head dipped below the surface of the water momentarily before he pulled her back out by her hair.

The air was violently ripped from her lungs, and her body turned to dead weight. Not only was she battling Colin, but she was fighting with her own mind. Fighting against the panic and terror bubbling up inside her.

Ali gasped and searched for her knife. She found the handle and jabbed it into Colin's side. He let out an anguished cry before dunking her head back in the water. She had enough sense to close her mouth and hold her breath while trying to knock him off. She stabbed blindly and felt her knife strike him again, but he grabbed her wrist and twisted the knife out of her hand.

She couldn't breathe.

The river rushed around her ears. Jagged rocks dug into her back as she fought against Colin on top of her. She needed air. Despite her best efforts, she couldn't break free of his grip—couldn't get her head out of the water.

One particularly sharp rock sliced at the back of her arm, and she cried out. Water immediately spilled into her throat, suffocating her.

She was going to die.

Colin's body weight disappeared, and rough hands yanked her from the water. She hit the ground a second later and coughed over and over to clear her lungs. Then she crawled on her arms and legs, inching away from him.

"Where do you think you're going, love?"

Hands seized her ankles and twisted her until she faced the sky—faced him. She swung a fist and connected with his nose. Blood spurted, but he pinned her arms to her sides before she could get a second hit in, the weight of his body keeping her still.

He shifted so his knees were pinning her wrists, leaving his own hands free. Ali sucked in a sharp breath, ready to scream for help, but he quickly pressed a knife to her throat.

"Don't. You. Dare."

What did it matter? He would kill her either way. She didn't want to be here, pinned to the ground under his body. His repulsive breath assaulted her skin.

One of his hands slid across her stomach and up to her breast. Internally, Ali was screaming, but she stayed still and held her breath, looking for any way out of this situation.

The knife was still pressed to her throat, and the tip punctured her skin when she swallowed. Her eyes darted frantically, hoping to find something or someone to help. Would Nik come looking for her? Would it be too late?

Colin pulled her shirt from where it was tucked in her pants, revealing her belly, then further until her shirt was scrunched above her bra. He brought his knife down and dragged the tip across the skin between her breasts and down her stomach. Ali shivered and clenched her jaw from the pain of his precise slice.

For a moment, he was distracted, taking in the sight of her. His hands were everywhere, one grabbing at her chest and the other pressing the blade against her stomach until she bled.

It was now or never.

Ali reared her head back and flung it forward, headbutting his forehead. The pain was blinding, but she couldn't stop. She squirmed and tried to pry her body free from his hold, from the weight that had pinned her down.

Colin brought a hand to his head and cursed viciously. She'd caught him off guard and for a brief moment, he let his knife slip. Ali had almost ripped her body free when Colin looked her in the eyes.

"You bitch."

He grabbed her by the thighs and pulled her back toward him. Ali's body slid over the ground, branches scratching at her backside. She yelped.

"Shut your mouth," he screamed at her.

With fury in his eyes, he wrapped a hand around her throat and squeezed, trapping the air in her lungs.

Ali clawed at his fingers, and she realized something.

She wasn't ready to let go.

For weeks, she'd thought there was no point to her life. That everything she'd loved was gone. That she didn't care if she lived or died.

She was wrong...so very wrong.

She still had Nik, and even more importantly, she had her future. She was so young—*too* young to give up on herself. She didn't know what the future held, but she wanted to see it. She wanted to live. She wanted to fight.

The edges of her vision swarmed with black dots, and she reached for Colin's face—to gauge his eyes out or maim him some other way. Anything to make him let go. But he was stronger than her, and he easily leaned away from her outstretched arms.

He let out a sinister low chuckle. "You dumb bitch. You might as well give up. I'll have my way with you in the end. Why not make it easier on yourself?"

Darkness seeped into her vision. Her limbs became too heavy to lift. Even her eyelids began to close.

She couldn't give up.

A noise zipped through the air, and suddenly Colin dropped his hand from Ali's throat. Relief and oxygen filled her. She swallowed painfully and blinked the black haze from her eyes.

Colin was staring at an arrow protruding from his chest. Blood soaked his shirt, and he watched with clear confusion. He and Ali were both so surprised that neither of them heard the second arrow fly. It slammed into him just inches above the first.

Colin frowned, one hand lifting as if to touch it, and then he fell to the ground next to Ali.

"Are you okay?" a voice shouted from several feet away. Ali gasped for breath as a young boy approached. He was tall and slender, but his face was still round and full of boyish youth. He didn't yet have stubble to match his light brown hair. He couldn't be more than his early teens.

"Are you hurt?" he asked Ali again.

She struggled to speak through ragged breaths.

Her savior knelt beside her and began to inspect her, looking for signs of injury. His eyes wandered to Ali's stomach and the shallow knife marks there. Ali's limbs were heavy as she tugged her shirt back down. It was senseless to be ashamed, but she didn't want to be exposed to this young boy. How pathetic was she that she needed a child to save her?

"What's this?" He nodded at the visible wound on Ali's arm.

"An—" It was hard to speak. She coughed and swallowed painfully. "An old wound. Wolf attack."

"Attacked by a wolf and a man?" The boy shook his head at Ali's misfortune. "The Dead Lands are no joke. Are you out here by yourself?"

Had it been anyone else, she might've been wary of his questions, but something about him set her at ease. Perhaps it was because he'd just saved her life or the fact that he was so young.

"No, I'm with—"

Before Ali could finish her sentence, Nik tore through the trees, his sword drawn and ready to defend her. Ali threw her hands up, a silent plea to calm down.

The boy leapt back and drew his bow.

"Stop!" Ali said quickly. "He's with me. He's with me."

Nik's gaze scanned Ali and her disheveled state before returning to the child. His frown faltered, but he didn't lower his weapon.

"Who are you?"

Chapter Fourteen

NIK

"Easy. I don't want to hurt you." The boy lowered his bow and held up a hand as a sign of truce. It was amusing that the boy was so confident in his skills. He didn't seem to fear Nik at all.

"Who are you?" Nik asked again.

"My name is Cole," he answered. "I just stumbled upon your friend here under attack. It was clear she needed help."

Nik lowered his sword and turned to Ali, finally realizing who lay next to her, sputtering and struggling to inhale. An icy chill ran through his bones at the thought of this man's hands on Ali. "Colin? What the hell is he doing here?"

His face was dirty—a sign that he'd been struggling out in the wilderness for at least as long as they'd been. His clothes were baggy and filthy. It was impossible to tell what color they had once been. Now every item he wore was a muddy brown.

Colin grinned through bloody lips. Even at death's door, he got a kick out of tormenting others. He might've responded if he weren't choking on his own blood.

"How did he find us? Has he been following us this whole time?" Nik asked, turning to look at Ali. There was another question he didn't voice aloud, though it gnawed at him—was he alone?

"You know him?" Cole studied the man with curiosity and disgust.

"We're from the same village."

"What village might that be?"

"It doesn't matter now." Nik didn't trust the kid. What if he was like the Coyotes and had heard of Rysburg? Would he turn on them? Did he have friends or family nearby that might attack?

Leaves rustled, and twigs snapped. Sam had made his way to the clearing, wheezing as he hobbled on his injured leg. "Nik, I tried to—who is this?"

"Another friend of yours, I presume?" Cole asked.

"Yes, he's with us. Sam, this is Cole. He just—"

Nik paused when he caught a flash of light in the corner of his eye.

Turning toward Ali, he expected to find her sullen and disengaged, as she had been for weeks. But the flash had been from her blade.

She stabbed the dagger straight into Colin's chest. Colin heaved from the impact, and blood flowed freely down her hands. She yanked the knife out of his chest, tugging it free from where it'd been lodged between his ribs. Then she plunged it into him again.

Again.

Again.

Again.

Over and over, she drove the knife into him, long after his breathing stilled. Long after his eyes went dark. Like madness had taken over her.

The rest of them watched, frozen in shock.

Nik was the first to snap out of it.

"Ali," he said, grabbing her wrist as she came up for another strike. "It's done."

She shivered and let the knife fall. Her body slumped into Nik's as he fell to his knees beside her. She let him cradle her, something he'd missed terribly. Touching her. Being close to her.

He brushed his hands over her hair and whispered, "It's okay. He can't hurt you. He can't hurt anyone anymore. It's okay."

Sam and Cole stared at her in horror. Cole hadn't feared Nik, but apparently Ali's momentary breakdown had rattled him.

Nik spoke directly to Sam. "Take him back. I have more questions."

Sam looked at Cole, who shrugged like he had nothing better to do. It made Nik feel slightly better that the kid was so trusting. It was a sign that his life had been relatively calm, and he'd yet to see the terrors of the world.

He watched as Colin followed Sam toward where they'd left their bags before they'd heard raised voices and had come running to find Ali.

"It's okay," Nik whispered repeatedly against Ali's tousled and untidy braid. "It's okay."

Ali wrung her hands, smearing blood across her palms. She picked at the blood under her fingernails, but it was no use.

"Here. Let's get you cleaned up." Nik stood and pulled Ali up with him. She'd gone silent again and her guard was back up, but she allowed him to lead her toward the river's edge.

They both kneeled on the riverbank and Nik took her hands in his, lapping up water and scrubbing her skin. He rinsed between her fingers and washed her forearms. Her white T-shirt couldn't be salvaged.

"Here," he said, pulling his own shirt off. "Take mine."

Nik watched as she pried the shirt over her head. Blood had soaked through and covered her stomach. She briefly scrubbed at that too, and

Nik caught sight of the small cuts across her skin. What the hell had Colin done to her?

Ali took his shirt and covered back up. Her eyes were glassy, her skin pale.

"What happened, Ali?" he asked softly.

She didn't respond. She just stared at her hands, rubbed raw and still tinted red.

"Did he—" Nik swallowed. "Did he force himself on you?"

She still didn't look at him, but she shook her head.

Nik sighed in relief. "What did he want?"

Ali sat still, completely detached from the moment.

Nik sighed and watched the river running beside them. How had they come to this? He didn't know how much more Ali could handle—how much more *he* could handle.

At the sound of sniffling, he whipped his head back toward Ali. She was sobbing, tears streaming freely down her cheeks and falling to her lap. The agony on her face killed him.

What should he do? She'd push him away if he tried to help.

She gasped in between sobs, and it took everything in him not to hold her close.

"Ali, please..."

"You're not a distraction." The words seemed to inflict pain as she uttered them, like a poison she needed to release. Nik had known deep down that he was more than a distraction, but hearing her say it—hearing her break down—relinquished the chains holding him back.

He desperately reached around her waist and pulled her into his lap, holding her tightly while she wrapped her arms around his neck and cried on his bare shoulder.

Her body trembled as she continued to sob. "I'm so sorry."

Nik caressed her hair. "Shh. You have nothing to be sorry for."

His words only seemed to make her weep harder. "I've been horrible to you. I don't know what's wrong with me. I feel so empty and hollow, and I miss Eli, and I see you and all I can think about is that night. We left him. I left him." She said it all in one breath and inhaled deeply once she finished.

Nik's eyes burned. If he could take away her pain, he would do it in a heartbeat. "It's my fault."

"Don't be ridiculous." She sniffled and leaned back to look him in the eyes.

Nik ran a thumb over her quivering lip. "I let you down."

Ali pressed her forehead to his and cupped his face. "You didn't. There isn't anything else you could've done."

She pursed her lips together but they still trembled.

"You couldn't have done anything else either, Ali. You can't blame yourself for this."

She nodded and took a deep breath, shuddering. Her tears had slowed, though her eyes were still red and swollen.

Nik continued to hold her in his lap. He would've been content to hold her like this forever. "I love you, Ali. I love you so much it hurts sometimes."

She laced her hand through his hair and kissed his brow, then his cheek, and then his lips. "I love you too."

⁂

"What were you doing out here?"

Nik wasted no time interrogating their new companion. The boy may have saved Ali from Colin, but that didn't automatically turn him into an ally.

Cole pointed at his bow like it was obvious. He seemed mature for his age, but there was still some teenage attitude there. "Hunting. This is an excellent area for deer and small game. Though I think your brief scuffle scared most of them off today."

Ali grimaced over the *brief scuffle.* Like she was to blame for the lack of game. Nik placed his hand on the small of her back. Nothing about this was her fault.

"Where did you come from?"

"Harrodsburg. A little farm village about thirty minutes west of here."

"A farm village? How big?"

Cole shrugged. "I don't know...maybe thirty or forty so?"

Very small. No wonder they'd sent a boy out to do a man's job. He was far too young to be out on his own.

While Nik pondered this, the boy straightened. "Is it my turn now?"

Nik exchanged a look with Sam and Ali before gesturing for Cole to continue.

"What are you doing out here? Only crooks and criminals roam the Dead Lands."

"Dead Lands?" Nik questioned.

Cole nodded. "You know. The wilderness. Where no one lives."

Nik had never heard it referred to as the Dead Lands, but he supposed it made sense. So far, they'd met a handful of life-threatening events during their time there.

"You're out here. Does that make you a criminal?"

"No, but I've already told you I'm on a hunt. It's your turn to explain yourselves."

"We've been traveling," Nik said. "Looking for someone, actually."

"How long?" Cole took in their appearances—dirty, and in Ali's case, still marked with Colin's blood. Cole gave her an especially wary look. Meanwhile, Sam was favoring his right leg rather noticeably.

"Two weeks...maybe." He'd lost track of time.

Cole's next question was directed at Ali. "Are you okay?"

"She's fine," Nik answered. He was feeling particularly protective of Ali after Colin's attack.

"Does she speak for herself?"

"I'm fine," Ali confirmed.

Cole nodded and took turns studying each of them. "You're filthy. At least two of you are injured and all of you look like you haven't eaten a proper meal in weeks."

What was his point? There had been nothing pleasant about their journey so far, and having it thrown in their faces added insult to injury.

Cole peered behind him and scratched his head before looking back at Nik. He sighed and shifted his weight from one foot to the other, clearly considering what he wanted to ask next. "Would you like to come back with me?"

Nik's gut tightened. He didn't trust this kid—nothing against him, Nik just didn't trust many people at all. But one look at Ali and Sam and he could see the hope on their faces. Cole's heroics had dissipated any distrust they had.

They hadn't had a safe place to sleep in two weeks. A warm bed and fresh clothes sounded incredible right now, even to Nik. How could they turn him down?

"You would do that for us?" Ali asked, barely masking the eagerness in her voice. Maybe she was hoping Eli would be waiting for her in the village. Or that someone there had at least seen him.

"Of course. Just don't stab me in my sleep." He laughed nervously when the rest of their group cringed. "Come on. I'll lead the way."

Chapter Fifteen

ELI

Eli sulked in his room for days, refusing to answer the door when he'd heard knocking. Grace would be the only one to visit him, and he couldn't face her right now.

He couldn't face anyone right now.

He ground his teeth while he stared at the wall. His wound was healing quickly, now that he had fresh water to keep it clean and wasn't straining it so often. He'd give it a few more days and then figure out his next steps. Where he would go from here...

He hardly ate. He only showered for the sole purpose of keeping his injury clean. Most days he just lay still, willing sleep to overcome him until could summon the strength to move again. To face other humans again.

When that moment came, he showered quickly and didn't even wait for his hair to dry before heading toward the cafeteria. Now that he'd found some ambition, he feared it would disappear if he stopped moving.

Living inside a mountain made it difficult to tell what time it was. He could only guess based on whether the lamps were lit. Day or night; there was no in-between.

The black, uneven cave walls shimmered in the lamplight now. Hopefully that meant it was close to lunch or dinner time and the cafeteria would still be serving food. Eli's stomach growled at the thought.

The cafeteria was deserted when he arrived. The buffet line held empty containers and the enticing aroma from last time had been replaced with a clean citrus scent.

Eli's shoulders sagged, and he turned around. The supply chamber was supposed to be somewhere around here as well. He'd have to buy his own groceries and make something on his own.

He took a left out of the cafeteria and wandered farther into the hall, led by the noise of a crowd. Another left and he found himself at the entrance of the supply chamber. He raised his brows as he took in his latest discovery.

It was overwhelming. Rows and rows of goods lined the chamber from one end to the other. People meandered through the aisles with baskets in hand, picking out the items they needed.

Eli found a stack of baskets next to the door and grabbed one for himself. Where to begin? He wasn't used to cooking—everything in Andus and Rysburg had been prepared for him—so he'd have to stick with something simple. Rice and fish seemed simple enough. An old comfort of Andus and one of the few dishes he knew how to cook.

"Excuse me." He stopped the worker closest to him. "Where can I find the rice?"

The man pointed to Eli's right. "Three aisles down."

"And...do you have fish?" It seemed like a silly question, but he had no idea what they ate here. Most of the buffet had been unrecognizable. Maybe they didn't recognize the food he was used to either.

The man studied Eli for a moment until recognition dawned on his face. "Ah, you must be a newcomer. Have you been here long?"

Eli wasn't in the mood for small talk, but he also didn't want to make a bad impression on the local grocer. "I am. I've only been here for a few days."

The man nodded. "Well, welcome. I'm Oliver."

"Eli," he said, holding out a hand to shake.

"Nice to meet you, Eli. What did you say you were looking for?"

"Fish?" Eli asked hopefully. He wasn't sure what foods were available locally, but based on the breakfast buffet, he assumed they had a lot to offer.

"The cured meat is against the back wall. Fresh meat is only available in the mornings. That's when our fishers bring in their catch."

"Thank you."

It took Eli several minutes to track down the rice amongst the packed shelves and when he finally did, they had different sizes to choose from as well as variations of white and brown and some that were a mix. He inspected each bag and scratched his head in confusion. He wasn't sure what the differences were aside from color, so he chose the one that looked closest to what he'd always eaten back home.

The fish section was easier to spot, but like the rice, he was met with an overwhelming number of options. None of them looked close to what he'd been used to in Andus. And these were all cured, not fresh, but it would probably taste similar.

He squinted, hoping the right one would come to life and flop into his basket. But they just lay lifeless, waiting for him to make a decision.

"I'd go with that one." A delicate, tan hand appeared and pointed toward the thin, round variety in the center.

Eli followed the hand with his eyes until he turned to find Grace.

"Hello, Grace," he said a bit gruffly. He dreaded her disappointment that he'd been hiding from her, but he found no sign of anger in her features. Her eyes shone with kindness, and his nerves disappeared.

"I'm glad to see you out and about today." She folded her hands behind her back and practically danced with a mysterious joy.

Was she always this happy? It didn't seem possible.

That wasn't entirely true. He had once been as carefree as Grace, before Andus had been attacked and his life had been turned upside down. He envied her, but also hoped she'd never have someone snuff out her light the way his had been. She should be protected at all costs.

"Yeah, I suppose I couldn't stay hidden forever. My cupboards were running low." He wrapped the small fish and placed it in his basket.

Her smile was so bright, even in the dim supply chamber. Eli found it hard to swallow when he looked at her. He didn't deserve to be in the presence of such a sweet person. The darkness inside him might rub off on her.

"That makes sense." She paused, and he felt the need to explain himself to fill the uncomfortable silence.

"I'm sorry I didn't answer the door before. I've just been...having a hard time," he said, pushing his hair back with one hand.

"I figured. And how are you now?"

"I'm...better."

Grace nodded with a soft smile. "Good. I'm glad I ran into you. Would it be all right if I stopped by later?"

"I guess so."

"Just wanted to be sure you weren't going to hide from me this time."

Eli attempted to return her smile, but his face contorted unnaturally. "I won't hide."

"Promise?" Her smile widened, if that was even possible, and her eyes flickered with excitement. Her beauty was out of this world. What had Eli done to warrant her attention?

"I promise."

Shortly after Eli finished his meal, there was a knock on his door. He tossed his empty bowl into the sink and rushed to open it for Grace. After coming home and eating in solitude, he had realized just how much better her presence made him feel. Joy radiated from her and alleviated much of the pain and heartache Eli was still working through.

"Hi," he said sheepishly.

"Hi." She drew out the word in her sing-song way.

Eli held the door for her to come in, but she remained at the threshold of his apartment. "Were you...uh, were you coming in?"

"Actually, I wanted to take you somewhere. Is that okay?"

Eli nodded and grabbed his jacket off the back of his chair. He was eager to get out of the small space. The four walls suffocated him the longer he stayed there. He now recognized just how unhealthy it was to stay cooped up by himself for so long. Even if he was struggling, it was better to keep himself occupied.

As they walked through the mountain, it occurred to him that he should try to explain himself. Explain the odd behavior he'd exhibited the past few days. She must think of him as a freak. Yet here she was, extending the hand of friendship once again.

He was rubbing the bristles on his chin when she broke the silence. "What's going on in that head of yours?"

"I'm sorry if I've been avoiding you. Or avoiding everything, really." He shoved his hands in the pockets of his jacket as they exited the mountain, heading down the main strip. Flowers bloomed along the side of the path after the string of spring storms had rolled through. It was late afternoon, and the crowds were thin today, allowing them to walk in peace. No loud chatter, just the soft rustling of tall grass in the fields behind the shops.

"It's all right. You've been through a lot. If you're not ready to talk about it, I won't press you."

It meant more than he could express that she could support him without badgering him. Maybe one day he'd be able to open up.

His thumb rubbed the amethyst necklace in his pocket. Ever since Grace had given it back, he hadn't set it down. He kept it by his side, a reminder of what he'd lost and that he wouldn't stop searching until he found her.

"How often does Berland receive newcomers?" Eli asked.

"It varies. Sometimes we get a few groups in a matter of days. Other times we'll go for weeks without anyone new. Just depends. Usually the Coyotes give us a heads up before they bring people so that we're prepared. We were expecting more when you came." Her eyes dimmed ever so slightly, and he knew she understood what it meant that he had arrived alone. She had some idea of what had happened to the others even if she didn't have the gruesome details.

Eli shuddered at the thought of the burning prison, people crying as they were trapped inside. He was lucky he wasn't a pile of ashes next to them.

"Does anyone ever show up without the Coyotes?" he asked. It was highly unlikely that Ali or Nik would ever travel with the Coyotes. They'd probably kill each other first.

"Sometimes," Grace admitted. "There are a few neighborhoods within these mountains that we trade with. Occasionally, people will stumble upon one, looking for a more permanent home. The other communities aren't as well equipped as Berland to handle the growing population."

So it was a possibility, then. Ali could find one of these settlements and maybe find her way to him. Did he have it in him to sit and wait?

"Can I visit these towns?"

Grace stopped walking. "You're not a prisoner here, Eli. You're welcome to come and go as you please." She seemed to hesitate, studying him with a look of curiosity. He couldn't sense any judgment in her eyes, just concern. "Are you unhappy with your place here?"

"No, that's not it. You and the rest of Berland have been incredibly kind and gracious. I just..." Eli bit his lip and inhaled deeply. If he went down this path, there would be no turning back. Was he ready for it? "There's someone I lost in the attack on Rysburg."

Grace flinched at the description of freeing Rysburg as an *attack*. Maybe it was time for Eli to view it more as a liberation, but it was hard to do when he had been a target too, accident or not.

"I'm sorry for your loss," she said.

"Not dead," he clarified. "Or at least I don't think she is. We were separated, and I don't know how to find her or if it's even possible."

Graced nodded. She opened her mouth to say something but closed it again. "I can send a message and check if she's been seen. What's her name?"

"Ali," he said. It might not be much, but it was a step. "Thank you."

"You're welcome."

Grace pivoted down a side street he hadn't yet explored. The shops were more sparse on this street, and patches of trees and flowers filled the space between them.

They passed a group of young men who paused their conversation to stare at Grace and Eli. This was the second time he'd been stared at by the residents of Berland. He might've thought it had to do with him being a newcomer, but it only seemed to happen when he was with Grace.

Why were they so drawn to her? He knew why he was—her kindness and the way she radiated joy. And she was objectively gorgeous—long, shiny brown hair, curvy hips and big, beautiful eyes. Her reddish-pink lips were always pulled into an inviting smile.

But this felt like something more. It went beyond polite curiosity. They were *staring* unabashedly.

"Good evening, Grace," one man said as he tipped his head in respect. Grace gave a polite nod in return. This happened several more times as they passed the group of men. Grace tried to keep moving along, but they sought her attention, continuing to engage in conversation with her.

"How are you?"

"You look well."

"It's good to see you."

Grace tried to wave them off, walking backward as she responded politely to each of them.

It happened quickly. One moment he was watching as she turned to face the path again and the next her ankle was twisting, and she was falling sideways.

Eli moved fast, stretching an arm across her stomach and catching her before she hit the ground.

He wasn't the only one. Each of the men in the group had sprung forward, racing to be the first to catch Grace. The way they behaved was so bizarre. Like they were in a trance.

Grace stood straight and smoothed her disheveled top. "It's okay. I'm okay."

"Your ankle?" Eli asked, and he felt the heat of five men staring at him.

"It's okay too." She moved it in a circle, showing them all that she meant her words. No sign of pain on her face. "Thank you," she said as she pushed the many helping hands away.

She led Eli away from the men, despite their disgruntled looks. He kept checking over his shoulder until they turned back to their own conversations.

Once they were out of earshot, he looked at Grace. "Are you going to tell me what that's about?"

"What do you mean?"

He shook his head. She wasn't very forthcoming with information about herself. "You know what I mean. Everyone seems *captivated* by you."

She laughed softly. "Are you not captivated by me as well?"

A lump grew in his throat, but she spared him from answering.

"It's nothing. People are just polite here. Perhaps you're not used to that," she teased.

It was more than that, though. She was clearly hiding something, and Eli would discover what it was. He was still a stranger; maybe it wasn't fair to expect her to be completely forthcoming with him just yet.

Chapter Sixteen

ELI

The pathway opened up to a pasture nestled between two mountain peaks. A large barn stood on their right, connected to a fenced area. Grace placed two fingers in her mouth and whistled as they approached the fence. The loud noise echoed between the hills until it came to a silent halt.

Eli watched as she stared into the distance, waiting for something. After a few minutes, a dozen horses galloped toward them, their manes flowing in the wind. They slowed as they approached the fence.

Grace pulled her satchel open and handed him a mixture of apples and carrots. "Would you like to feed them?"

She showed him how to do it, keeping a piece of apple flat in her palm. He walked up to the fence with half of a carrot in his hand and brought it to the horse's mouth, flinching when it slobbered all over him. "Ugh, gross."

Grace laughed as he wiped his hand on his pants. "These stables belonged to my dad's family. Someone else manages them now—my dad is too busy with other obligations—but I still visit frequently. I love to come out here when I'm feeling down. It's peaceful, and these guys"—she patted one horse just behind its ear—"always know how to cheer me up. I thought maybe you could use some cheering up too."

The horses took turns eating fruit and vegetables from her hand, and she petted their noses.

The wind blew through her hair, and he caught her scent—apples and pine trees. As a horse took the last carrot from his palm, he conceded that this was exactly what he needed. Happiness could be found in this meadow with Grace by his side.

"Have you ever ridden a horse?" she asked suddenly.

"No." Feeding the horse with his two feet on the ground was peaceful, but the thought of climbing on top of it? His legs trembled. He couldn't imagine trusting the horse not to throw him off.

"There's a first time for everything," Grace said with a smile.

Eli took deep breaths as she strode to the barn. When she returned, she brought two horses with her, each attached to a lead. These were even larger than the ones they had fed in the meadow. Their backs fell just below his eyeline.

Grace heaved a saddle over each of their backs. Eli wrung his hands together, feeling like he should help somehow, but he was completely out of his element. She attached belts and loops with the ease of someone who'd done this a thousand times.

"So you'll just want to put one foot here in the stirrup and then swing the other over. Like this." She demonstrated on her own horse, and Eli knew right away it would not be as effortless as she made it appear. She was tall—only a head shorter than him—with lean legs, but it wasn't just her height that made it easy. The motion was second-nature for her, obviously born from years of practice.

Eli brought his left leg up to the stirrup, mimicking her movements, but he grunted and struggled to get up on the first try. He applauded her effort to keep a straight face as his right leg hit the ground again. She stifled a laugh and encouraged him to try again. He succeeded on the second attempt.

"Not so bad, right?"

Eli merely gave her a sideways glance. He listened intently as she explained the basics. It seemed easy enough to steer, move forward, and stop. Hopefully he wouldn't need any commands beyond those.

"You'll be fine. These two are brothers and will stick together."

The path up the mountain was narrow and steep, but the horses seemed to know the way. Their strides were steady and assured. The horse's massive body swayed under Eli's legs, and he squeezed to hold himself upright. It was an odd feeling. There wasn't anything he could compare it to. There was a thin leather strap attached to a contraption around the horse's face. Grace told him it was to steer, though Eli hardly had to guide his horse since it followed Grace's like a shadow.

After an hour, they finally reached the top. Grace jumped down and tied both reins around a tree, stilling Eli's horse so he could dismount too.

"What do you think?" She stood at the edge of the cliff with her hands on her hips.

"Holy shit."

If Eli hadn't known better, he would've thought they'd climbed to heaven. The air was misty and clouded the view below. The main strip of Berland was a tiny speck from this height.

A full panoramic view of the mountains stretched around them. This peak was the tallest of the range, and wind ripped at his cheeks, bringing tears to his eyes.

He retreated from the edge as his stomach turned. One wrong step would send him plummeting to his death. He grabbed Grace by the elbow and pulled her back too.

"Scared of heights?" she teased. A gust of wind rustled her hair, and she swept her brown locks behind her ear.

"Fuck yes. Any sane person would be."

She chuckled and squeezed his arm. It comforted him that she was so fearless, but her touch also sent his heart racing. "Come on. I want to show you something else."

Eli followed her back toward the horses, and for the first time, he noticed the trees they'd passed through. He'd been so focused on his horse's movements that he hadn't much noticed his surroundings on the way up. The trees all carried fruit shaped like an apple, but a deep purple color.

"What is that?" he asked as she plucked one from its branch.

"Angelfruit. Only grows at the top of these mountains. The original settlers here called it that because this is the closest to heaven you can get, and therefore this must be what the angels eat."

Eli chuckled. He didn't believe in the supernatural, but Ali would've enjoyed hearing about the folklore.

Grace grinned and tossed one of the ripe spheres to him. Eli studied it, turning it over and running his thumbs over the smooth skin.

"Eat it. It's not poisonous."

He took a bite and moaned as the juice from the fruit hit his tongue. It tasted like strawberries but sweeter, with a slight tang at the end. He wasn't religious, but if angels existed, they definitely ate this fruit.

They sat in the crook of an angelfruit tree trunk and devoured as many as they could. Even when Eli's stomach bloated, he still wanted more. Did the fruit have addictive properties? Or was it just that good?

He listened as Grace carried on about Berland traditions and history, staring out into the wide-open sky.

"You just missed our Founder's Day celebration," she said. "We celebrate the woman who opened the compound in Berland on her birthday, even though she's long gone. And on Spring Equinox, we have a festival for the arts. People play instruments, sing, dance, and make crafts. By nightfall, everyone is drunk on angelfruit wine." She laughed. "We here in Berland will take any excuse to drink and celebrate."

Eli could've listened to her talk all day. He watched her lips move as she shared all her favorite things about Berland. Her voice was soothing, and he relaxed next to her. Their shoulders pressed together, and her thigh rested against his.

"I know I said I wouldn't press, but...did that belong to someone?"

Eli hadn't realized he'd pulled Ali's necklace from his pocket, rubbing it between his fingers absentmindedly. He held his breath.

Was he ready to have this conversation?

He'd kept it together all afternoon, but if he spoke about Ali—said her name out loud—would he spiral back into misery? Or would talking about her get it off his chest and allow him to breathe?

"Yes. It belonged to Ali."

"Your friend who's missing?"

Eli nodded.

"Was she...your girlfriend?"

Eli fidgeted, cracking each of his knuckles one by one. "It's complicated."

Grace nodded and seemed to withdraw. Immediately, he missed the way her arm had pressed up against him and needed to feel that connection again.

"I mean... she was. We're not together anymore."

"Clearly," Grace said with a joking tone, and even Eli laughed. Obviously they weren't *together.* That was his entire problem.

"I mean we're not romantically together. She's with someone else." It didn't sting as much as he'd expected it to—saying those words out loud.

The corners of her mouth perked up, and he sighed with relief.

"We grew up together, and she was my best friend. We were both captured and taken to Rysburg, and that's when things got messy."

"I'm sorry." Grace looked at him with gentleness in her eyes. He could tell she meant it. It made him feel safe opening up to her.

"Things were rough in Rysburg. We had a...disagreement." Not entirely the truth, but he wasn't sure how else to explain the situation. She fell in love with the enemy and chose him over Eli. "I don't think we ever really resolved it, and now we never will. What if I never see her again?"

"For what it's worth, I think you'll find a way back to her. The way you speak about her—I can tell she still means a lot to you, even as a friend. It would be a cruel world if you were torn apart forever."

Grace was clearly sheltered in Berland. She might see second hand the atrocities that newcomers had been through, but she knew nothing of the cruelties of this world.

Grace placed a palm on Eli's upper thigh, and he ignored the way his stomach tightened at the heat of her touch. "I'm sorry for everything you've been through. Both of you."

"Sometimes I think..." Eli swallowed the lump in his throat. "Sometimes I think my life might be cursed. Like I'm not meant to have good things. Good experiences. I used up all my luck and now I'm doomed."

"I don't think you're cursed, Eli. I think you've had a rough go of things recently, but that doesn't mean this is how your life will turn out. In fact, I think your future will be better than you can imagine."

Eli covered her hand with his own. The touch sent electricity through his bones. He didn't know why, but he felt compelled to slip his fingers between hers. This connection was beyond physical, and he held his breath, waiting to see how she'd respond. She simply glanced at where their hands intertwined and gave him a small squeeze, running her thumb over the back of his hand.

Grace licked her lips, and Eli's eyes were drawn to them. His mouth went dry, and he felt a gravitational pull to her. Her scent swirled around him, sweet and floral and intoxicating. He didn't know much about Grace, but he enjoyed her company.

Eli didn't realize how close they'd gotten until a bird chirped right above them and startled them both. He leaned back, trance broken.

They sat in comfortable silence, watching birds fly over the mountains and valleys. Eventually, the sun moved behind one of the mountain peaks and shadows crept up on them. Grace's horse became restless and emitted a loud neigh that startled them both. He let their hands fall apart, and she went to check on the horses.

"Should we head back? I'm having dinner with my brother tonight and it's getting late."

"You have a brother?" Eli asked. It was uncommon to have siblings in Andus. Most couples could only manage to feed one child.

"Yes. His name is Theo. He's one of our trade liaisons, so he's frequently out of town. In fact, he's leaving again tomorrow morning, but once he's back, I'll have to introduce you to him."

"I would like that." Not only would it be nice to make another friend in Berland, but if Theo visited the other towns, he might be able to help Eli find Ali.

They stood and mounted their horses to head back down the mountain so Grace could meet her brother for dinner.

"What sort of jobs do people have here?" Eli asked. Perhaps he could get in with the trade convoys as well.

"You've been here for a week and you're already bored?" Grace batted her pretty eyelashes at him.

"No. I just…" Something stopped him from telling the truth—that he wanted to find Ali. "I want to feel useful."

"I can check for openings. What skills do you have? You look like you'd be good with your hands." She winked.

Eli felt his face flush. Her horse pranced ahead of his, and he wondered what it might be like to use his hands on her. To touch her skin and pull her body close.

He quickly shook the thought from his mind.

"I used to trap fish," he told her.

"Hmm. I don't think we have any need for another fisherman. We already have scores that go out each morning and bring in fresh fish. What did you do in Rysburg?"

"I worked in a greenhouse, but I'd rather throw myself off the side of this mountain than do that again," Eli grumbled.

Grace's shoulders shook as she laughed. "Noted. We'll find you something."

❧ ☙

Halfway back to the barn, rain sprinkled down on them. It was a refreshing reprieve from the day's sun, and Eli welcomed the cool drops on his skin. Grace prodded her horse to move faster, and Eli's horse followed.

By the time they made it back to the barn, it was pouring. Grace returned their horses to their stables and together they jogged through the woods.

Eli's feet hit the ground and mud splattered, drenching the bottom of his jeans. The puddles drenched Grace's pants all the way up to her knees. Each step he took sent more mud flying her way, but he didn't slow down.

"Eli!" She swatted at his forearm, and he grinned. He couldn't help it. The look on her face was too funny.

Until she swung her foot through a puddle and splashed muddy water all over his shirt and even his face. He wiped a hand across his cheeks and mouth, but the earthy taste lingered on his lips.

"You'll pay for that," he teased.

He placed one hand behind her back and the other behind her knees and in one swift motion she was in his arms, suspended above a large puddle. She squirmed, but it was no use against his strength. It was easy to hold her in place. And it felt *right* to have her body pressed against his chest.

Eli didn't allow himself to think about why that might be the case. It was just a compassionate touch when he'd been starved of one for so long.

"Stop. What are you doing?" She squealed and then laughed when he pretended to drop her. She threw an arm around his neck. "If I go down, I'm taking you with me."

Eli's laugh rumbled through his chest, and he felt her shiver against him.

Chapter Seventeen

ELI

THE SUN HADN'T EVEN risen yet when Eli made his way out of the mountain and down to the horse stables. Grace had told him he could claim one for himself if he took care of it. So early each day, while everyone else slept, Eli went to visit his new friend Obsidian.

Obsidian watched Eli as he cleaned the stall and filled the horse's trough. Eli brushed his long black hair and fed him a couple sugar cubes Grace had brought him from the store.

Obsidian sniffed at the white blocks in Eli's palm. He ate them, but Eli suspected he preferred the apples.

Eli rubbed the horse behind the ear and slipped a lead over his face, then strapped the saddle around his back—just like Grace had shown him.

It was a cool morning, but there wasn't a cloud in the sky as Eli and Obsidian trotted out of the stable. The horse wasn't in a rush, and neither was Eli, so they took their time heading down one of the many paths that branched out from the meadow.

Birds chirped and watched from their perch in the trees while Eli and Obsidian moved through the mountain. He stopped the horse at a small outlook, tying him to a tree and allowing him to graze on some grass.

Eli was getting used to the heights. It still terrified him to look over the ledge, but he no longer felt like his knees were going to buckle. He took a seat on the grass and watched the sun rise over the misty mountains. Shades of yellow and orange melted into the lingering navy night sky.

It was awe-inspiring, but it made Eli more homesick than ever. He thought of Ali—where she might be in this big world, so much bigger than they had ever imagined. And he thought of his dad. What would he think of such a magnificent sight?

Eli pulled his knees in close and wrapped his arms around them, sighing heavily. Obsidian could sense his rider's distress and nuzzled Eli's neck.

"I'm all right, buddy," Eli said, rubbing the animal's nose. Obsidian huffed, sending hot moisture over Eli's ear. "Ugh," he groaned, leaning away from his companion.

His eyes caught sight of something peculiar—a tree that seemed to have two trunks. Or just two smaller trees whose trunks were inter-twined. The way they had grown together, twisting up into the sky, made Eli pause.

It was incredible how nature worked. These two would be forever bound to each other—would depend on each other. For if one didn't exist, the other couldn't stand. They bent in an unnatural way that was only possible by relying on the other.

Eli took a few steps toward the entwined trees. He bent down, gath-ering a few of the rocks at the base. He stacked the largest one first and then another on top of it, and then another until there was a small tower of rocks nestled between the roots of the tree.

"This one's for you, Dad. I wish you were here to be my support right now, but know that you did a good job. You raised me so I could stand on my own."

He gathered a few more rocks and stacked them next to the one for his dad. Though he and Ali's mother had some disagreements, he knew she had only wanted what was best for her daughter. Anna had a good heart, and she deserved to be remembered too.

As he placed the smallest stone on top, he whispered, "I'm sorry I couldn't keep her safe."

There were a few more pebbles, and he slowly stacked them next to Anna's. A lump formed in his throat.

He couldn't bring himself to say the words. That this tower was for Ali. He just stared at the pebbles in varying shades of gray, clutching at his chest and the tension beneath his rib cage.

With a swift flick of his hand, he sent the last tower crumbling.

He stalked back to Obsidian, who watched with curious eyes.

There would be no stack for Ali. The living didn't need memorials.

⚜ ⚜

Grace did as she had promised, and a few days later, Eli found himself with a new job in Berland's research lab. When she'd asked him what type of position he would like, he'd had no clue. His line of work had always been chosen for him. Grace had given him a list of several open positions and this one had struck his curiosity.

The research lab. Apparently, they had an entire department dedicated to taking old inventions and technologies and working to replicate them. Her favorite was the machine that turned angelfruit into wine, but there were other more practical devices too, like the energy-efficient bulbs they used in their lamps.

Better yet, Grace had informed him the researchers were sometimes required to go to neighboring villages if they needed specific supplies. Things that only the researchers could identify. It would give him the potential to make trips to other communities and search for Ali.

Eli had stressed that he lacked the skills for a job like this, but she assured him that Luka, the head of the research lab, would bring him up to speed in no time.

The lab itself was impressive. There were dozens of worktables with papers and unknown devices scattered about. People hovered over them with intense focus. They jotted down notes on pads of paper and flipped through pages of old tomes. Occasionally, they'd turn to a coworker and discuss a question or concern. Everyone was so focused that they hardly noticed the new guy.

The walls of the lab were covered in cabinets, some without doors so Eli could see the inventions they housed. Others were covered, but Eli suspected they held materials and supplies as he watched one person open a cabinet to retrieve some metal objects.

"So, Eli, tell me about yourself. How familiar are you with research labs?" his new mentor asked. Luka was a tall, thin man with a rigid jawline and short hair streaked with gray. There was a kindness in the way he spoke. Not patronizing, like Eli might've expected from a highly educated man, but patient and respectful.

Eli bit back a laugh. As far as he knew, this lab was the only one of its kind. He sat in a chair across from Luka at one of the empty workstations. "Um, not at all."

"Ah, yes. Grace said this would all be new to you. Tell me about your education. Have you received any structured schooling?"

"No. I learned some basic reading and writing as a child, but I've never used it. I don't recall too much of it." It had never been necessary. Back in Andus, those were useless skills. Learning how to set traps or start a fire had been more pressing. Eli's cheeks heated at the admission, but Luka didn't seem fazed.

"That's all right. You're not the first person to come along without proper teaching. Dawson over there didn't know how to read or write either, but it only took a few weeks to get the fundamentals." Luka nodded toward a man on the opposite side of the lab who was bent over a desk with a studious expression on his face. "We'll get you brought up to speed."

Luka spent a few minutes showing Eli around the lab. He even had his own assigned workstation. For a few hours each day, he'd learn to read and write, and then he'd shadow Luka as they tried to replicate the most recent project.

"Where do you find these items?" Eli asked.

"The majority are brought in by the Coyotes. Stuff they find while they're out on missions—they bring more than people back. And we get most of our supplies from our trade alliances."

"Trade alliances?"

"Yes. Berland doesn't operate alone. We've made connections with other communities. We couldn't be half the city we are today if it weren't for the others."

"How often do you gather supplies from your allies?" he asked.

Luka gave him a mystified look. Eli wasn't sure if he was asking the wrong questions or what Luka was gleaning from them. "About once a month. Is there a reason you're asking?"

Eli supposed he'd been more eager than he realized. There was no reason to lie to Luka. "I was separated from someone who means a lot to me—a friend. I'm hoping I might go on some of these supply runs...maybe see if she's made it to one of the other towns."

Luka nodded. "I see. I can't make any guarantees, but if something comes up and I think you can handle it, then of course. I hope you find your friend."

In the afternoon, another worker showed him how they took notes as they disassembled their projects. Eli would be useless at that until he learned to read and write. The markings on the pages were meaningless scribbles to him.

Eli's head was buzzing by the time his first shift ended. He'd never been asked to retain so much information in one sitting. Luka sent him home with a few empty journals to practice his writing and another journal with the details of how they'd reassembled an old hand-powered washing machine to practice his reading.

He was used to physical work, but mental work was exhausting in its own way.

Eli rubbed his temples as he walked out of the lab, but he couldn't help but smile at the opportunities opening up for him. He reached into his pocket and traced his thumb over the familiar cold metal pendant he kept there.

He *would* find Ali. There was no other option.

Eli made his way to the cafeteria, hoping to find Grace. It had become their afternoon routine to go for a horse ride on the various trails through the mountain, and he had missed her company on his first day of work.

She was easy to talk to and helped take his mind off things. Plus, she had this way of making him feel *seen*. It was exciting to know someone else was thinking of him as often as he thought of her. It was a novel experience for him.

Eli spotted her almost immediately at a long table with Amaya and Heather. Amaya—or was it Heather?—shot him a look before tapping Grace on the elbow. She looked up and excitedly waved him over, her brown hair flowing over her shoulder.

"Hey, Eli. We were just talking about you."

"You were?" Eli sat across from Grace and poured a glass of water from the jug in the middle of the table. Knowing that he was on her mind made his chest swell.

As he pressed the glass to his lips, Grace said, "Yes. Amaya doesn't believe you showed me your dick the first night we met."

Eli spat out his water mid-sip.

Amaya, the one with golden brown skin and dark brown, almost black hair that barely touched her shoulders, turned to Grace. "You owe me your finest dress. I knew you were lying."

Grace held up a finger to silence Amaya. "No. Eli, tell her." She fixed him with what he imagined was supposed to be a menacing glare, but she was too sweet to pull it off.

The three ladies looked at Eli, waiting for an explanation.

"I didn't *show* her anything. She came into my room and I happened to not be wearing pants."

"Semantics," Grace said, shrugging like that settled the matter.

Amaya shook her head. "That does not count. It's not the same thing. Heather, back me up."

Heather, who looked bored with the entire conversation, brushed her strawberry blonde hair aside and rested her elbows on the table. "Technically, he did not choose to show you anything. Sounds like it was merely an accident."

"It was," Eli agreed. He couldn't believe this was the discussion he'd intruded upon.

"Fine. You win this time." Grace went back to picking at her dinner and popped a bite of mashed garlic potatoes into her mouth.

"I want that long blue one. The one with the straps on the back," Amaya said. "Don't even think about giving me the red one."

Grace made a pouty face. "Not the blue one! I wore it to the last winter ball. And I have the perfect shoes to match."

Amaya shrugged. "You can give me the shoes too, if you'd like."

"Is this what you guys normally talk about?" Eli asked.

"What else would we talk about? This is the best piece of gossip we've had in ages," Amaya said.

Grace waved her fork in Eli's direction. "You should lose your pants more often."

It took tremendous effort to keep a straight face. "Beg your pardon?"

Grace and Amaya both fell into a fit of laughter.

"Ignore them. Any bit of attention will only encourage them," Heather said. She looked like an older sister watching as her siblings goofed off.

"Noted."

"But if you wanted to put on a show, we won't stop you," Heather admitted, and Grace and Amaya burst into another round of laughter.

<hr>

"Your friends are…"

"A lot?" Grace asked. They'd headed out to the stables after dinner and were feeding the horses some leftover carrots.

"Something like that."

"I hope we didn't make you too uncomfortable." She squeezed his arm, and he couldn't help but lean into her. "They like to joke, but they're harmless. I think they like you."

For some reason, it delighted him to know that her friends approved of him. He wanted to fit in with these people. To feel like he belonged. And if he wanted to keep spending time with Grace, it was important that he get along with her friends too.

"Do they treat all your new friends like this, or am I special?"

"You're incredibly special," she teased. "I rarely make friends with the newcomers. Once they realize...well, I've said too much. Let's just say they don't stick around."

"What does that mean?"

"Nothing." Grace combed through the black stallion's mane and smiled thoughtfully. Obsidian's eyes fluttered closed at her gentle touch.

"Traitor," Eli said as he watched his horse nudge Grace and brush against her shoulder.

"He just likes me more. Don't you, beautiful boy?" Grace continued to pet Eli's horse and plant kisses on the top of Obsidian's head. "I hope you stick around, Eli."

"I plan to," he said. And he meant it. In a perfect world, he'd find Ali and they'd all be able to stay in Berland. He wouldn't have to choose one or the other. "I'm sorry I lost you a dress."

"It's okay. Maybe I'll just go naked to the next formal event." Grace shot him a wicked grin, and Eli shook his head. He couldn't stop the smile that formed on his own face.

"You are a shameless flirt, Grace."

Chapter Eighteen

ALI

ALI PANTED AS SHE struggled to carry a pole attached to two buckets back to the log cabin they'd been staying in for the past week. Ali had never been more grateful for the generosity of the Kennedy family. When Cole brought them to his home, his parents, Meredith and Alan, had graciously welcomed them. The only stipulation was that they help with chores around the farm. It was more than a fair trade.

The gentle stream where they collected fresh water was a mile away from the cabin, which didn't feel like much when the buckets were empty, but when they were full...

A piece of hair fell into her eye, and she cursed whatever gods existed. She couldn't adjust it with her hands bracing the pole on her back. It wasn't too much farther now. She could see smoke coming from the chimney up ahead. Water sloshed back and forth, and her thighs burned as she struggled to hold the pole steady.

Two young goats stumbled up beside her and watched with curiosity. They were only a few months old, and Ali had fallen in love with them from the first moment she'd explored the farm. They brushed up against her any chance they could, silently requesting head scratches, and they didn't know her history. They didn't look at her and see the scars, both visible and invisible, that she carried.

Ali was a few feet from the house when Meredith, Cole's mother, spotted her and came to help remove the buckets. "Thank you, dear. You're just in time. I was going to cook some soup for tonight's dinner."

"Isn't it a little early for dinner?" Ali asked. They had eaten lunch just a couple hours ago.

Meredith scoffed. "The three of you could use more meat on your bones."

Ali smiled. Meredith had been saying the same thing every day since their arrival. Between their blood- and dirt-stained clothes and the observable bones beneath paper-thin skin, it was no surprise that she'd welcomed them into her home immediately.

"And now Cole is going through another growth spurt. There may only be six of us, but I need to cook enough to feed an army. Best to get a head start."

"Can I help?" Ali asked.

"Could you grab a few logs for me? The stockpile inside is running low."

In the distance, Nik was chopping wood alongside Cole. He was shirtless, muscles glistening in the warm sunlight. Sam sat next to them, cutting up vegetables.

As Ali approached, Nik paused and gave her a soft smile. Things had improved between them greatly since her little breakdown. That was what she was calling it—a little breakdown. Sometimes it felt like Nik was still holding back, though. Like he wasn't sure when her next "little breakdown" would be. She supposed that was fair. It would take time to truly repair their relationship and her own wellbeing, but she was glad to have him beside her while she worked through it.

Ali grabbed a log from the pile and then a second one. Before she could grab a third, Nik was by her side. He brushed the hair out of her face and laid an affectionate hand on the small of her back.

"Can I help?" he asked.

"Yes; can you add one more?" Her hands were too full to reach down and place another log on top of the ones she was already carrying.

Nik did as she asked and then eyed her warily. "You sure you can carry all those?"

"Yes." Even as she responded, she stumbled and one log slipped from its position, threatening to tumble to the ground.

Nik caught it before it could slide off the stack, but he grabbed it along with one other. "Let me help."

"Doesn't Alan need you?"

"We were almost done. Cole can finish the rest." Nik smiled with a softness that made Ali's stomach flutter.

She nodded. "Okay then. Thanks."

"Don't mention it."

They walked back to the cabin in comfortable silence—the kind that could only be shared by two people who were completely and utterly content in each other's presence. She sensed his eyes flicking to her, only to look straight ahead when she glanced at him. She smiled and felt giddy for the first time in what felt like forever.

The front door of the cabin was hanging open to encourage a breeze throughout the house. Ali and Nik stepped inside and dropped the logs next to the fireplace.

"Do you need anything else?" Ali asked Meredith. "I'd like to freshen up before dinner."

"Go, go." She shooed the two of them away. "Just come back when you're done to help set the table."

"Do you want some company?" Nik asked as they exited the cabin. She knew that glimmer in his eyes all too well. He brushed a hand through his hair and the muscles of his stomach tightened and released, sending shivers up her spine. Her thighs clenched, and she had the urge to strip and press her hot skin against his, knowing just how good it felt to be enveloped in him.

"How can I say no?"

Nik looked at her like she was being served for dessert. His mouth parted slightly as he licked his lips.

They quickly headed toward their lodging, desperate to have some privacy. They'd been given a secondary studio home situated a few yards from the main cabin. It had previously belonged to Meredith's parents, but after they passed, it had sat empty for years. A thin layer of dust had coated the floors and furniture when they moved in.

Nik and Ali practically tumbled through the front door, laughing like they didn't have a care in the world. His hands reached to grab her by the waist, pulling her into him, when Ali gasped.

"Sam!"

Sam, who had been sorting through some clothes laid out on his cot, looked up at their loud entrance.

Ali felt Nik deflate behind her. "I didn't realize you were back," she said.

"Yep. Finished preparing for dinner and wanted to wash up and change into something less sweaty." He tossed a shirt to the side and then held up another one. Meredith had given them all a few extra sets of clothing, old items that had once belonged to Alan and herself. Most of it was too big, but at least they weren't torn or stained.

Nik quietly groaned behind her, and she knew the throbbing between her legs would have to wait. It was tough sharing a studio space with Sam, but the Kennedys only had one extra cabin, so they made the best of the situation.

"I'm going to freshen up." She turned around and gave Nik a quick peck on the cheek, staring into his disappointed eyes. She whispered, "Some other time."

The bathroom was only separated from the living quarters by a thick gray curtain attached to a rod on the ceiling. Ali stepped into the space that qualified as their bathroom and pulled the curtain shut.

She filled the tub with room temperature water and slipped in to wash the sweat and dirt from her body. Her skin broke out in goosebumps as she hurried to wash her body and hair. It beat bathing in the river, but she hopped out as soon as she could and dried off with one of the rough beige towels they'd been given.

Ali peeked out from behind the curtain. "Nik?" He turned his head from where he was resting on the bed. "Can you toss me my dress?"

He stood and opened the top drawer they shared, digging out a soft cotton sundress in pastel blue that had once belonged to Meredith. He walked the short distance to the bathroom and handed her the dress, his rough hands grazing hers as she took it from him.

His eyes lingered on her body, covered only in a towel, and the water dripping down her legs and shoulders. His throat bobbed as he swallowed, and he took a deep breath, his chest expanding as it filled with air. The tension between them was electrifying, and she wanted nothing more than to pull him into the bathroom and let him fuck her against the wall.

But Sam coughed, interrupting the moment. Ali closed the curtain again and quickly dressed.

"The bathroom is all yours," she said, and Sam grabbed a towel and his clothes, closing the curtain behind him.

Nik had returned to the bed, once again staring at her legs.

"Do you like it?" she asked, giving the short skirt a little twirl. The dress was lightweight and fell over her modest curves, making her feel feminine and desirable. Gods knew she hadn't felt sexy while they'd been traveling.

"The things I would do to you if Sam weren't here," he grumbled.

She tapped his thigh as she walked past him to the door. "But he is. Finish getting ready. I'm headed back to the house to see if Meredith needs any more help."

Ali slipped into her shoes and wandered back to the main house, which now smelled like herbs and vegetables. Meredith sang a tune to herself while she stirred the pot over the fire. Cole was busy setting the table while Alan was at the counter, cutting slices of bread.

When Cole finished, he plopped down on the bench next to Ali and pulled out some dice. They played a game he had taught her a few days ago while they waited for Nik and Sam to finish getting ready.

It didn't take long for them to appear. Before long, dishes of food and drinks filled the table. Meredith ladled soup into everyone's bowls, and they ate and talked for what felt like hours.

It was the perfect day. Aside from their chores, life here was relatively easy. They had clean clothes, a bed, warm food, and water. With each passing day, Ali felt more human again. Sam's leg was healing quickly, and so was her arm. The past week on the farm had felt like paradise.

But something lingered in the back of her mind. As another round of laughter rang through the house, she couldn't help but think of the voice that was missing from the chorus.

Eli should be here.

Chapter Nineteen

ELI

ELI SAT IN THE cafeteria with one hand around a steaming cup of tea and another propping a journal open. While it only took his coworkers an hour to read through a journal, it took him all morning—and sometimes the afternoon—to make sense of the symbols. But he was getting the hang of it, and it gave him something to occupy his time. And his mind.

He placed the journal on the table and circled a word with a pencil he'd been given. He had a running list of words to run by Luka during his next shift. Most words he could make out the meaning with some context clues, but there were a few that made no sense whatsoever. Thankfully, Luka never belittled him for his long vocabulary list.

"Are you writing me a love letter?"

Grace slid into the seat across from him and peeked at the journal. She smiled, and Eli's eyes paused on her lips, really taking them in for the first time. A deep shade of pink, almost red, and they looked as soft as clouds. His throat tightened at the thought of what those lips might feel like against his.

"No. Would you want one?" he asked with a raised brow. The idea of writing Grace a love letter excited him for some reason. Obviously, it would only be a joke.

"Of course. Maybe for my birthday."

Eli sat straighter in his chair. "When is your birthday?"

"This weekend. If you're not busy, maybe you'd like to come to my house and celebrate. There will be a nice dinner for family and friends."

Her friend. How could he say no to a friend?

"I don't know," he teased. "I might be busy."

"Liar." Her foot tapped his shin under the table.

He chuckled. "I'll be there."

"What are you actually doing?" she asked, glancing at his journal with renewed interest.

"Work stuff. I'm sure it would bore you."

"Don't let me stop you," she said, gesturing for him to continue.

Grace watched as he read from the journal. Every couple minutes, he'd look at her through his lashes to find her staring right back at him, something shimmering in those hazel eyes. It was both unnerving and invigorating. His hair stood on end when she flashed him a sweet smile, like they shared a secret. He didn't know what that secret was, but he wanted to keep it to himself. For himself.

What started as muted chatter turned into all out commotion as a young man walked through the rows of tables. Several people stood and greeted him, shaking his hand and patting him on the back. The man wore a thick coat and his face was dirty like he'd been out in the wild for a while.

Maybe a new refugee?

His smile was too big, though—a stark contrast to the hesitant frown Eli had worn while entering this new place. And the man was too familiar with the residents of Berland. He laughed animatedly while someone spoke to him from the circle now gathered around him.

Grace had turned around as well, curious about all the excitement. Suddenly, she jumped up from the table and ran to this new stranger, throwing her arms around him and landing a kiss on his dirty cheek. He held her close in a big hug that lasted long enough to make Eli squirm.

Grace grabbed the man's hand and pulled him through the small crowd and over to Eli.

"Theo, this is Eli. He just got here a couple weeks ago. Eli, this is Theo." Her grin was wider than Eli had ever seen it. He had to admit it made him a little jealous, sharing Grace's attention with another man. It was a feeling he'd only ever gotten after seeing Ali with Nik, and that thought rattled him. "My brother."

A sigh of relief.

And then nervousness again when he realized this man was important to her, and likely someone he wanted to be on good terms with.

Eli held out a hand. "It's nice to meet you."

"You as well."

Grace returned to her seat, and Theo sat down beside her.

"I didn't know you were coming back." Grace added to Eli, "Theo's been out of town. He's one of our trade liaisons, along with my father. Is Dad back too?"

"Yes. We couldn't miss your birthday." Theo raised his brows at her. "It's the big one."

"It's not that special," she responded, and her shoulders tensed.

"Not that special? You're going to be twenty, and you know what that means."

Eli had no idea what that meant. Perhaps this was an age of significance. Back in Andus, fifteen was the age that mattered most. It was when they were assigned a job and expected to contribute to society.

But that made little sense for Berland. Twenty was well past the age of responsibility. He was about to open his mouth and ask when Grace changed the subject.

"How were your travels? Any exciting stories to share?"

"Not really. It was business as usual."

Someone interrupted to bring Theo a sandwich and a drink, a token of gratitude. They gave him a quick welcome back and then left again.

"I always miss the food here. It's way better than the food we carry on our trips. Have you tried the potato soup yet, Eli? It's my favorite."

Eli had tried many dishes by now, including the soup, but his favorite had to be the pancakes with syrup Grace had introduced him to.

"The food is amazing here. My clothes fit tighter already." Eli laughed softly.

"They look good on you," Grace said, tossing him a wink.

Theo made a disgusted face. "I thought I told you not to flirt in front of me. You know how much I hate it."

Eli felt his cheeks warm. Flirting. In front of Grace's brother, of all people. It seemed so natural when it was just the two of them, but he wasn't sure how he felt about other people knowing she was openly flirting with him. His time with Grace had always felt safe and sacred.

This thing between them was playful and fun, and he wasn't ready for others to impose their expectations on them. He didn't want to think about others' opinions when he was still trying to figure out his own.

"I learned it from you," Grace retorted. "You flirted with everyone growing up. You slept with one of my best friends and then made out with my first boyfriend. I'll never forgive you for that one, by the way."

The way she said it made it obvious it had been forgiven long ago.

"Careful, Eli. He'll set his eyes on you next," she warned.

Theo laughed in a way that was contagious, and Grace joined in while Eli grinned.

"Don't worry. I'll keep my hands to myself. I promise not to touch any of your competitors in the Rite," Theo said.

Grace's eyes went wide, and the color drained from her face.

The *Rite?* Eli had no idea what that meant either.

"What is the Rite?" he asked.

Theo dropped his sandwich on his plate and looked at Grace. "You haven't told him about the Rite?"

Grace shook her head and glanced at Eli.

"What else haven't you told him?" Theo asked.

Maybe he was just suspicious because of everything he'd been through, but Eli had been fighting this odd feeling that she was keeping something from him since he'd met her. Was this proof that he was correct?

"What is the Rite?" he asked again.

Theo leaned back from the table and rubbed his forehead. "I shouldn't have said anything. This is between you and Grace." He stood. "It was nice to meet you, Eli. I hope to see you around. I'll see you later at home, Grace."

Grace waved goodbye as Theo tossed his unfinished sandwich in a bin. She looked up at Eli and found him studying her, waiting for her to explain the mystery of the Rite. He crossed his arms and sat silently...patiently.

Would he really need to ask her again?

"I'm late for a meeting," Grace blurted, and stood from the table. At his incredulous look, she said, "I'm sorry. I promise I'll tell you everything, just not right now."

Eli watched her backside as she left the cafeteria. He was stunned and confused, and despite not eating anything, he was no longer hungry.

"She's impossible to figure out, isn't she?" A man at the table next to Eli's watched Grace walk away, his hand on a spoon that rested in his bowl of soup.

How long had he been listening to their conversation?

"What do you mean?" Eli asked.

"I know you're new here, so let me fill you in. Grace is unattainable. She's always been that way and always will be. In fact, the only way you'll ever attain her is by winning the Rite."

"What is the Rite?" Eli asked for what he hoped was the last time.

The man chuckled. "It's a ceremony. The winner gets to marry Grace."

He said it so simply, as if this new information hadn't just rocked Eli's world.

Something like bile rose in Eli's throat. "I thought Berland was a sanctuary. Why would the women here be forced into marriage?"

"Oh, not all women are. Just Grace." The man had a sinister sneer and Eli narrowed his eyes at him.

"Why only Grace?"

The man raised his brows. "She didn't tell you anything, did she, boy?"

He called Eli a boy, like he himself wasn't the same age. It was calculated condescension.

"Grace is basically royalty around here. She's the next Lady of Berland and heir to all this." He gestured around the vastness of the mountain's walls.

Eli sat in disbelief as unexplainable sadness washed over him.

The man stood and slapped a hand on Eli's shoulder. "The best thing you can do for yourself is to stay away from Grace, kid. She'll only leave you heartbroken."

Chapter Twenty

ELI

Eli lay on the riverbank with his hands behind his head. Obsidian was tied to a tree behind him, nibbling on some grass. He'd spent the past two days avoiding Grace, which wasn't hard to do. He had the sense that she was avoiding him as well.

She'd promised she would explain everything, but she hadn't come to find him. After this long, he doubted she ever would. Why would she keep these things a secret? Maybe she didn't want to talk about the atrocity that was the Rite since they were still getting to know each other. But her title as the future Lady of Berland? It seemed like something even a stranger would reveal.

Eli didn't like that she kept secrets. It felt like Ali all over again. He hated being the last to know things. It made him feel like an outsider, and all he wanted was to feel like he belonged.

The sun was shining, and he soaked in the warmth of its rays, allowing his eyes to close. Despite everything on his mind, the river was a comforting lullaby and the grass was soft, beckoning him to doze.

A shadow crossed his face, but he didn't open his eyes. Probably just a cloud. It would pass in a few minutes.

Someone cleared their throat and tapped his boot.

He opened his eyes to find Grace hovering above him. He grunted, "Hello, Grace."

"I've been looking for you."

"Have you?" He didn't believe her. She could've easily found him if that were the case. He spent all of his time between home, work, or out on the trails with Obsidian. All of these were places she knew—places she'd taken him.

He sat up as she lowered to the ground next to him. "I'm sorry I didn't find you sooner. I've been thinking of what I would say to you."

"I already know everything."

Her eyes widened. "What?"

"While you've been waiting, someone else filled me in. I would've rather heard it from you, though."

"By everything, you mean..." She shifted uneasily, tucking her legs underneath her.

"All of it. The Rite. That you're meant to become the next Lady of Berland."

Concern crossed her angelic features. "Who told you?"

"It doesn't matter." It should've been her.

She frowned and played with the hem of her sleeves. "Do you have questions?"

Eli could only think of one. "Why didn't you tell me?"

She looked at him with a tentative smile and shrugged. "I liked that you didn't know who I was. People tend to treat me differently when they know I'm next in line to rule Berland. You've seen it. That's why you were suspicious from the beginning. I wanted to be just Grace to you."

"I wouldn't have treated you any differently," he said without hesitation.

"Maybe not. It's easy to say that now. But how could I have guessed how you would respond? I just wanted a chance to get to know you. Before you knew the real me."

"And who is the *real* you, Grace?" Was the real Grace so different from the one he'd spent time with for the past few weeks? How much had been real and how much a facade? He searched her eyes like he might find the truth behind them.

"The real Grace is imperfect, but she's trying her best." She gave him an apologetic smile and bit her lip in a way that most people would've taken for innocence, but Eli didn't fall for it. Grace was calculated. He wasn't sure yet if that was a good thing or a bad thing.

"You must be under a lot of pressure."

"It's not so bad yet. My mother, Lady Ellen, is still the ruler. Our council does most of the work, really. It'll be my job to oversee them. It's what I've been training for. All those meetings I have to attend."

"And how does the Rite fit into all of this?"

"The Rite is our tradition. In Berland, women are the heirs to the throne, and we're expected to...continue the bloodline. The founder of Berland was a woman. Ms. Harper. She wasn't married, but she didn't want to hand over the compound to anyone other than her own child. When men found out, they became very...competitive. So Ms. Harper did what anyone would have. She made them all compete and prove their worthiness."

Grace spilled the details like it was salacious gossip, but Eli could tell she took it very seriously. It was just a front so she wouldn't have to admit her true feelings about being treated like a prized possession.

"What kind of competition?"

"There are three rounds with people eliminated in each. They're all physical. Ms. Harper wanted a fit man, of course. That's all you men are good for, right?"

Again she joked, but Eli's concern only grew.

"The tasks are the same for every Rite. The first one is a search for a medallion in a muddy pit. There's a limited number of medallions and those who find one will move on to the second round—hand to hand combat. The winners from that round will move on to the third, which is a race. Down the mountain, retrieve a flag, and then back up. The first to make it back to the top gets the prize."

She flicked her hair off her shoulder—a prize indeed.

"And you don't get any say in this?"

"I'm privileged in a lot of ways, Eli. This just isn't one of them."

Her sad smile nearly split his heart in two. He was beginning to understand which of her smiles were real and which were forced.

"I'm surprised a place like Berland would treat you in such a way. Why do you still abide by these ancient traditions?" As an outsider, it just didn't make sense to him why they hadn't changed these archaic rules. They had created them; surely they could alter them.

"You'd be surprised how adverse people are to change, Eli. I've heard my great-great grandmother once tried to change the law, but she was immediately vetoed by the council. After that, they disagreed with her on everything, no matter how good of an idea she had, just to spite her."

"That's incredibly irrational."

"Power can make people do irrational things."

He hesitated. "You know, all this time I thought you've been flirting with me. I thought you might be, I don't know, *interested* in me. But perhaps I was wrong."

"I enjoy spending time with you, Eli."

"Me too, but in a few months, you'll be promised to someone else. I'm not sure what you expected from this. What you want from *me.*"

"You could..." she trailed off, twirling a flower stem between her fingers.

Eli shook his head. He didn't want her to finish that thought.

"You don't want to. You're not interested?"

"It's not that. I think you're beautiful and fun and cheerful and kind. Only a fool wouldn't be interested in you."

"Then what is it?"

Eli thought for a moment. He thought about just how much he wanted to divulge to her. If he was ready to discuss old wounds or if they were still too fresh.

"It's a lot, Grace." That was an understatement. The prospect of marrying someone he'd only met a couple weeks ago was more than he could wrap his head around, even if he felt bad about her predicament. And then there was Ali. His heart was still tattered, torn, and bruised. He wasn't ready to move on just yet. He wasn't capable of giving Grace the love she deserved.

"I understand," she mumbled.

"I'm really sorry, Grace. We can still be friends."

"Friends," she repeated with a smile that didn't quite reach her eyes. "Well, as my friend, I hope you'll still be coming to my birthday dinner tonight."

"I wouldn't miss it for the world."

Chapter Twenty-One

ELI

THAT EVENING, ELI PICKED out his nicest shirt and slacks for Grace's birthday celebration. She hadn't told him exactly what to expect, but given her title, he assumed it would be an elegant evening.

His stomach turned as he thought about meeting her parents. It was easy to spend time with Grace. He hadn't realized she was some kind of royalty until after he'd already gotten to know her. Now he knew her parents were the most important people in Berland and it made his palms sweaty.

Would they judge him? Question him about his background? His hometown was nothing compared to Berland. Would they see him as good enough for Grace? Good enough to be her friend, of course. He wasn't interested in anything more than that.

And yet, the idea of letting her spend her time with someone else made him sulk. He'd grown accustomed to her company and couldn't imagine taking a back seat to a future spouse.

In a few months, she likely wouldn't have much time for him.

A pang of guilt hit him in the chest. He shouldn't be thinking about the future with Grace. He should be focused on finding Ali. In a few months, it wouldn't matter what Grace was doing because he would be reunited with Ali and life would return to normal—or as close as they could get to it.

He tucked the end of his shirt into his pants and attempted to flatten a stray patch of hair. If he'd known he would spend the evening with the Lady of Berland and her consort, he would've attempted to get his hair trimmed. Now it was too late.

The patch of hair popped back up as soon as he dropped his hand, and Eli sighed. It would have to do.

As he walked down the hallway toward Grace's residence, his heart beat harder and harder. It was obvious which one belonged to her. The two guards outside hardly looked at him. They stood like statues, watching as he waited for someone to open the door. If that wasn't an ominous sign of the night to come, he didn't know what was.

The door opened, and Eli released a heavy sigh.

Grace looked gorgeous in a long green dress. It was more conservative than her usual outfits but still emphasized her curvy figure. She wore a pearl necklace over the high neck of the dress with matching earrings. Her eyes sparkled in the low light of the hallway lamps as she smiled at him.

"Come in." She opened the door wider for him to step inside.

Their home was beyond elegant. Eli shouldn't have expected anything less. The entrance was larger than his entire apartment. Two marble staircases on either side led up to a balcony. Doors flanked him on either side, though they were both closed, and in the center between the giant staircases stood a massive opening into what appeared to be a dining hall. He could see a long wooden table with a dark blue cloth covering it.

Matching chairs of sapphire velvet circled the table, and the din of voices sounded from inside.

"Your home is beautiful," he said.

"Thank you." Grace watched him take it all in with a genuine smile. He wasn't sure which was more elegant, her or her home.

"I hope I'm not late."

"Not at all. You're right on time." She touched his arm, and his heart rate instantly slowed.

Eli pulled a piece of paper from his pocket and slipped it into Grace's hand.

"For me?" she asked with a playful grin. She opened the paper and laughed as she read the words. "You wrote me a love letter?"

Calling it a love letter was generous. Eli had only written the words "love letter" inside of a heart. He'd been working hard to learn to read and write, but it was still a challenge. He had messed up three times, tossing the paper in the trash, before he finally got it right.

His cheeks burned. "It's stupid. I know. I would've bought you something, but..."

She interrupted him. "It's perfect."

"It's cheesy."

"It's original," Grace corrected him.

Eli stepped further into the home, following Grace. Heather and Amaya were already seated at the luxurious table, sipping wine and laughing. They too wore long dresses, Amaya in a lovely shade of beige that contrasted her darker skin and Heather in a pale blue. Their sense of fashion was so bizarre to him. He had only ever known practicality, but the women in Berland seemed to love the extravagant.

Theo was on the opposite side and waved to Eli when he spotted him. Eli breathed a sigh of relief when he noticed Theo's attire was more similar to his own. Theo had cleaned up and was freshly shaven, and like Eli, he wore a simple button-up shirt and slacks.

As Grace led Eli into the dining room, he found two more people sitting on the far ends of the table, previously hidden from view.

He swallowed at the sight of them. Grace's parents. Her mother peered over a wine glass and quickly set it down. There were subtle wrinkles around her mouth and eyes and though she appeared energetic, there was an air of weariness surrounding her. Was it the same forced enthusiasm that Grace always showed?

"You must be Eli. Grace has told us so much about you," the woman said. As she stood, Eli could see she wore a long gown, much like Grace, but with long sleeves and black as midnight. Eli shook her hand, noting the gold rings with green and blue gemstones that decorated her fingers.

"This is my mother, Lady Ellen, and my father Benjamin."

"Please, just call me Ellen," Grace's mother said. "And you may call him Ben."

"It's nice to meet you both," Eli said, shaking Ben's hand. He found his chair between Grace and Theo, across from Heather. Two more seats remained open, and Eli wondered who might fill them.

A servant refilled their wineglasses and provided one to Eli while they waited for the other guests to arrive. Eli took one sip and then another. With nothing else to do with his hands, he found himself drinking a little too quickly. He pushed the glass back and cleared his throat in the suffocating atmosphere. Perhaps he should undo the top button of his shirt.

"So, Eli, how are you liking Berland?" Ellen asked, thankfully breaking the silence.

"It's lovely. It's truly incredible what you've been able to do here. The way you've used and maintained the mountain is resourceful. And Grace has shown me a lot of amazing places. My old town was nothing like this. And then, of course...neither was Rysburg."

"Ah, yes. I heard about that. They said you were being kept as a prisoner and forced to work for them? I'm very sorry you had to suffer through that."

She seemed sincere, but it was hard to tell. Eli hadn't known what to expect of Ellen, and he was still struggling to figure her out. She had a smile plastered on her face, much like Grace always did, but her lips were thin and the smile didn't reach her eyes.

"Thank you. I'm happy to be in Berland. It truly is paradise."

Eli took another gulp of wine, and Grace bumped his knee with her own. A reminder to take it easy. He set his glass down with a loud clunk as Ellen continued to stare at him, sizing him up.

"I'm sure you've come across some interesting communities," Eli said to Ben. He and Theo had just come back from a trip, and Eli was curious to hear more about the other towns out there. Maybe they'd run into Ali.

Grace's father had a stern voice. It was deep and commanding. "Yes. Though none are quite like what I've heard of Rysburg. We have a standard of ethics in the communities we trade with. If we found out any of them were using slave labor...well, we'd discontinue trade and they'd be forced to conform."

Eli wanted to ask if there was any way to track someone down. If it was possible to find Ali. But he lost his chance when there was a knock at the door.

"I'll get it," Ellen said, standing to greet the other guests who had just arrived.

Voices mingled together from the other room, and Ellen returned with two men by her side. Eli recognized the first one immediately. It was the man who had told him about the Rite and about Grace's position.

The other appeared to be his father, or at least a close relative. The similarities in their appearance were striking and hard to miss. Both had dark, wiry hair and full beards covering the hard angles of their faces. Their broad shoulders and muscular limbs were evidence that these men were strong and hard-working.

"Eli, I'd like you to meet Eamon and his son Trevor. Eamon, Trevor, this is Eli, Grace's new *friend.*"

The elder man gave Eli a quick nod and a look of appraisal while Trevor pretended this was their first encounter, nodding at Eli like he'd never seen him before. He didn't make any mention of their meeting in the cafeteria, so Eli followed his lead.

Eamon took his seat first. "It's nice to meet you," he said with a quick side eye to his son. An unspoken message exchanged that had Eli narrowing his eyes. He *hated* secrets.

Trevor followed suit and took the seat across from Grace. The lingering look he gave her made Eli uneasy. He moved closer to her in his seat.

"Well, now that we're all here, I'll have the staff bring out dinner." Ellen disappeared behind the door to the kitchen, leaving them all in uncomfortable silence. Beside him, Grace took a deep breath.

"Grace, how are you adjusting?" Trevor asked, turning his attention to her. "Your mother has told me you've been taking more of her responsibilities. Preparing to fill the role."

"Yes. I've been shadowing her for some time now. It's a lot to learn, but she's a patient teacher."

"She's being modest. Grace has really taken to her role. She's very vocal in all our council meetings. Certainly has a lot of opinions...and isn't afraid to voice them. Just last week, she was arguing with several members over taxes and whether we should repair the ventilation system on the second level or use the extra funds to remodel the cafeteria," Eamon chimed in.

"And I stand by what I said, Eamon. Those funds should be used for the ventilation system. Something as frivolous as redecorating is not a priority. We should be helping the people who live on the second level. They've been dealing with a faulty system for too long. You've seen the data from the health center. It's causing permanent damage to their lungs, and it's unacceptable."

Eamon shook his head. "Small numbers. They'll live. Why should we be expected to pay for something that not all of us benefit from? Myself and many others want our tax dollars to go toward something useful. The cafeteria is for *everyone.*"

"Just because it doesn't benefit you doesn't mean it isn't useful. We don't live in a classist society, Eamon. Despite what you'd like to think." Grace spoke through gritted teeth, and Eli was surprised by the shift in her demeanor.

Eamon elbowed his son. "What did I tell you? Opinionated."

"She sure is." The look Trevor gave Grace was unsettling. Like he'd like to tame the fire within her. He'd burn if he tried.

"You're a council member, then?" Eli asked, reluctantly looking away from Trevor and toward Eamon. Someone needed to keep an eye on that man.

"Sure am. Ellen appointed me many years ago. I've been trying to get this town moving in the right direction ever since."

The way Grace shifted in her chair told Eli they didn't see eye to eye on what the *right* direction was.

These were the people she would have to work with in the future. It seemed she had her work cut out for her.

Ben must've felt some sympathy for his daughter. "Let's leave the politics for another time. This is supposed to be a cordial dinner, after all. We're here to celebrate Grace's birthday. I don't want to hear the two of you bickering all night."

"I would never." Eamon held up a hand innocently, but it was clear he'd love nothing more than to dig in and press Grace over their issues. He took a sip of wine just as Ellen returned from the kitchen, two servants behind her with trays of food.

"What did I miss?" Ellen asked as she took her seat at the head of the table.

Ben sighed, and Eamon chuckled. Eli watched Trevor as Trevor watched Grace. There was a lot being said in the room without a word being uttered. Grace's leg shook under the table—from nerves or frustration, Eli wasn't sure.

"Nothing," Ben said before anyone else could respond. "This looks delicious."

Indeed. A servant had placed a dish in front of Eli with a seared piece of brown meat and colorful vegetables smothered in herbs and oil.

"Did Trevor tell you his big news yet?" Ellen asked. "I hope I haven't missed it."

Glasses settled and utensils rattled against plates. Everyone turned to Trevor, waiting for his *news*.

"I've just told Ellen today that I intend to take part in the Rite."

An icy shiver ran down Eli's spine, and the color drained from Grace's face. He couldn't explain it, but he had the instinct to keep this man far away from her.

"Isn't that lovely, dear? Your first suitor declared. I'm sure there will be many more, but Trevor is an excellent candidate. The son of a council member. It would be a great union for you."

"Lovely. Exactly the word I'd use to describe it. Together, I think we could be quite the powerful pairing." Trevor raised a glass, but Grace left his silent salutation hanging. The smirk that crossed his face was revolting. Even Ben looked displeased. Ellen was clearly more interested in a political pairing, while Ben was more cognizant of his daughter's disinterest.

If they weren't in the middle of a formal dinner, Eli would've jumped over the table and wiped the smile off Trevor's face himself. Since that would be frowned upon, his only option was to squeeze Grace's knee beneath the table.

The fire in her eyes simmered when she looked at him, and her shoulders relaxed.

The dinner conversation continued. Trevor took every chance to display a sinister charm that made Eli clench his jaw. His words were cordial, but the malicious look in his eyes made Eli wary and made Grace squirm in her seat. Even Theo, who had been so laid back earlier that day, was now sitting tense in his seat with his eyes on Trevor. Ellen seemed to be the only one who approved of this coupling.

When the main course had finished and the birthday cake had been devoured, Grace offered to walk him out. She hesitated with her palm on the ornate door handle.

"I'm sorry," Eli said.

"For what?" Grace asked in a carefree tone. Ignoring her problems was her go-to defense.

Eli gently took hold of her arm. "It shouldn't be like this. That man..." He lowered his voice, conscious of the guests that still lingered in the connecting room. "You deserve better than this."

"Maybe. But this is how it is. How it has always been. I've known since I was old enough to talk that this would be my future. I've accepted it."

"Have you?"

It didn't matter how little she pretended this affected her. Eli could tell her entire being rebelled against it.

She opened the door and stepped out of the way, sliding out of his reach. "Don't worry about me, Eli. I'll be just fine." She avoided eye contact with him, instead staring at the tips of her shoes. "See you to-morrow?"

It was a question he had heard from her almost daily, but this was the first time he had ever heard her use that tone—almost like a plea.

A small part of him died, knowing she was hurting and there was nothing he could do except promise one thing...

"I'll see you tomorrow."

Chapter Twenty-Two

ELI

Eli woke with a start. He shivered as he looked around his pitch-black room. He couldn't remember what he'd been dreaming about, but considering his previous nightmares, he was thankful for the dreamless sleep.

It had to be the middle of the night. There was no warm glow to symbolize the sunrise. He rolled from his back onto his side and tried to fall back asleep, but it proved difficult.

After nearly an hour of tossing and turning, he threw back the comforter and placed his feet on the floor, walking the path he'd memorized to his kitchen. He flicked a light on above the sink and poured a glass of water.

His kitchen table was scattered with notebooks from work, open to pages of graphics and two-dimensional models of their latest projects. Another journal was open to his messy scrawl of writing practice. If he couldn't sleep, perhaps he should work on his writing skills.

He picked up a barely used pencil and wrote his letters, followed by a few elementary words that Luka had given him to practice. He made it through half a page before he felt restless.

Eli leaned back in his chair and sighed, rubbing his eyes. Mentally he was exhausted, but physically he was alert.

A sound rang through the hall, like something had dropped and shattered. Eli hopped up and took the three steps to his door, flinging it open to find Grace bent over and cursing as she picked up pieces of a broken ceramic bowl. Red and blue berries rolled down the hall. "Shit. Shit."

Eli laughed softly. "What are you doing?"

Grace looked up from the mess she'd made. "Oh, sorry. Did I wake you?"

"No, I've been up. Do you need some help?"

"Do you have a broom?"

Eli searched through his small entryway closet and found the wooden broom among some other basic cleaning supplies.

"Here, let me," he said, sweeping up the blue and green jagged edges of the fruit bowl. When he finished, he watched as she picked up the stray berries, gathering them to toss them away. She was wearing the same pajama set she'd worn the first night, so thin he could make out every curve of her body. And the shorts were so...short.

"You just felt like having a midnight snack?" he asked.

Grace spun around, her cheeks brighter pink than the berries in her hands. "I couldn't sleep, and no one stocked the fruit in our pantry, so I just...broke into the grocery to grab some. Don't worry, I'll pay Oliver in the morning when he opens," she added hastily when Eli frowned at her.

"Do you do that often?" The thought of the heir of Berland breaking into shops in the middle of the night was comical.

"Often enough," she said with a smile. "Oliver doesn't mind."

Eli pointed his thumb over his shoulder. "Want to come in?"

Grace nodded and quietly followed him into his home. He tossed the broken fragments into his trash can and she threw the berries on top. Then she sighed.

"What's keeping you up?" Eli asked as he straightened the blanket on his bed and gave her a place to sit. The kitchen table was too much of a disaster to clean up this late at night.

"Just thinking about dinner and my *prospects*," she said as she sat on his bed and leaned back against the headboard. She closed her eyes and crossed her arms. The vulnerability in her expression tugged at his heart. He couldn't imagine what she must be going through.

He sat next to her on the bed. "Trevor seems like a dick."

Grace huffed a laugh. "You're right about that. We actually were friends when we were younger."

Eli raised his brows in disbelief.

"I know, right? Hard to believe. He wasn't always so villainous. There was a time when he was just a normal kid who liked to ride horses and swim in the lake. Then his mom died and his dad sank his claws into him. He convinced Trevor that power was the most important thing in the world, more important than friendship. That's when I stopped feeling like his friend and more like a conquest. We grew apart pretty quickly after that. Why bother winning me over with kindness and companionship when he could just win me in the Rite?" She shrugged.

Anger bubbled in Eli's chest. Grace didn't deserve to be treated like that.

"He's not the only one. A lot of my so-called friends started treating me differently as we got older. Once they understood what my future would be. I stopped being human to them and became a status symbol. Heather and Amaya are the only ones who have stuck around."

Eli felt a lot more empathy and understanding for why she'd kept her title a secret from him. It made sense that she didn't want him to be like everyone else.

"Anyway, I guess I'll need to get over it, right? Trevor is the likely winner of the Rite. He's strong, smart, and cunning, and I can't think of many who would stand in his way. His father and his father before him have always had a lot of influence in Berland. I suppose I should get used to the idea of marrying him."

Eli felt nauseous. "It's not fair."

"Yeah, life isn't fair, though. I don't need to tell you that." She gave Eli a sad smile and repositioned until she was lying down, facing him with her hands tucked under her cheek.

Eli lay down too, facing her with his arm tucked behind his head.

"So what about you?" Grace murmured. "What's keeping you up tonight?"

"Nothing in particular. I just woke up and couldn't fall back asleep."

"No nightmares?"

Eli shook his head. "Nope."

"Good." Grace's eyes fluttered closed.

"Are you falling asleep on me?" he teased.

"Maybe. Keep talking. Your voice is soothing." Grace grinned, and Eli instinctively moved closer. The air between them felt electric, drawing him in but also exposing him to her dangerous current. He'd told himself he couldn't go there. Grace was off limits. He was still hurting over Ali, and soon Grace would be wedded to someone else.

So why was he so drawn to her curves? To her ruby lips and her sweet scent? He couldn't take his eyes off the silky tank top that was now drooping a little too low, exposing the delectable flesh of her breasts. Any lower and he'd be able to see her nipples too, already hardened underneath her top.

"Eli?" Her voice interrupted his thoughts. He'd been staring, and she knew it. There was no trace of the innocent sweetness he was so accustomed to seeing. Instead, her eyes were dark and filled with lust.

Fuck.

Grace shifted and further closed the gap between them. She was so close he could reach out and brush her lips if he wanted to.

"We shouldn't..." he trailed off.

Grace nodded, and he watched her throat bob. "I know." She licked her lips. "But what if we did?"

Eli inhaled sharply. The thought was tempting. He was lost in her trance and was having a hard time remembering his reasons for staying away. *His broken heart. The Rite.* "You're going to be married."

"I know. But I'm not yet."

"I don't think I'm ready to be with anyone."

"They say the best way to get over someone is to get under someone else."

Eli's head spun, and he laughed softly. "Who says that?"

Grace shrugged and moved even closer. Eli rolled on his back, and she slid an arm across his chest, pulling herself on top of him. He had to remember how to breathe.

"Lots of people say that," she said while her hands roamed over his shoulders and down his arms.

Fuck.

"I've never heard it before," Eli said, sliding his hands over her bare thighs. He should stop, but her skin was so soft.

"I guess you've been sheltered." Grace was fully straddling him now, and fuck if it didn't make his cock hard. It didn't matter if he wasn't mentally prepared to move on. His body had other ideas.

"And what do you get out of this? I've already told you I won't enter the Rite. This doesn't change things."

Grace pressed her breasts against his chest, and their noses gently touched. "I get to have *fun*. A little *freedom* before I'm tied down forever in a loveless marriage. Are you in, Eli? It doesn't have to mean anything."

Eli's heart roared at the mention of a loveless marriage, but it moved on quickly when Grace ran her lips across his neck.

Meaningless sex. He could do that. It didn't have to mean anything. Maybe it would help him move on from the heartbreak of losing Ali to Nik.

"Okay...I'm in."

Something in Grace snapped at those words, like she'd been holding back and only waiting for his permission. She clawed at his shirt and yanked it over his head. Her lips brushed against his, gently at first and then hungrily. She tasted just like he imagined she would—like sugar and berries. Her tongue met his, and her body melted into him.

It was exciting the way she took control. It left no time for him to second guess or hesitate as she slipped a hand beneath his waistband.

"Fuck." He let out a low groan as her fingers wrapped around him. He dug his hands into her hips and savored the weight of her body as she rocked against him.

For a fleeting moment, he thought about tossing her to the bed and climbing on top of her, but then she removed her top and his mind went blank. Grace was the most beautiful woman he'd ever seen. The sight of her soft brown hair falling over her full breasts made him suck in a sharp breath.

He lifted his hands and kneaded her flesh, and a guttural moan left his lips. "God, you're beautiful, Grace."

Her returning smile seemed to say *I know.*

And then she was sliding his underwear down. Eli lifted his body so she could pull them past his hips, then down his legs until he was fully naked for her. She paused and took in the sight of him, taking extra time as her eyes reached his hard shaft. She touched the inside of his thighs so softly that he flinched before she moved them closer to his groin.

He couldn't remember how long it had been since he'd been with someone other than his own hand. He needed her touch, needed her to stroke him—gently, roughly. He didn't care how she did it.

As if she could read his mind, she wrapped one hand around the base of his cock and tightened her grip just enough to have him gritting his teeth. His hands moved from her hips to her ass.

Why did she still have those goddamn shorts on? He pulled at the thin fabric of her pajama shorts, but the way she was sitting in his lap made it impossible to remove them.

"Grace, please." His voice was unrecognizable. So much desperation that didn't belong to him. What spell did she have him under?

She ran her hand up and down his length with a wicked smile.

"Take them off," he pleaded.

Grace shook her head. "Not yet."

He watched in confusion as she rose to her knees, picking up his discarded shirt. She twisted it until it became something like a rope. "Grab the headboard."

Eli reached behind his head, his hands gripping the wooden slats of his headboard. Grace was vibrating with excitement as she moved toward his head and wrapped the shirt around his hands and through the slats, tying it in a knot.

"Does it feel okay? Too tight?" she asked, inspecting her work. Eli was having a hard time focusing on anything other than her breasts hanging above his face.

There was an urgent need in his response. "It's perfect."

She was perfect.

Finally, Grace removed her shorts. Eli cursed the bind on his wrists because he wanted so badly to run his hands all over her. To cup the place between her thighs and see if she was as turned on as he was.

Grace moved on top of him again. This time, when she rocked her hips, he felt her wet folds slide over him. He didn't think it was possible for his dick to harden any more, but gods, that sweet sensation did it. She dragged her wet cunt over him, her brows pinched in concentration.

It didn't take long before he was throbbing and begging to be inside her. But he was at her mercy.

"You're killing me," he moaned.

She laughed wickedly. "I haven't even started."

Grace licked the first two fingers on her right hand and moved them down to her clit, swirling in a circle while her head rolled back. Eli's cock twitched, begging to be inside her. Instead, all he could do was watch...watch as she continued to build her pleasure, two fingers on her clit and her hips thrusting against his cock.

Eli clenched his jaw. If he wasn't inside her soon, he was going to come anyway, just from the staggering sensation of her pussy rubbing up and down his shaft and over the head of his cock.

"Grace..." His voice was a strained warning.

She lifted her hips and positioned herself so his cock lined with her entrance and then sank slowly onto him. Eli's eyes rolled to the back of his head.

Finally.

The sweet relief of her warmth wrapping around him, the friction of her body as she rode him without restraint. He felt it in every nerve ending, like a tidal wave flowing through him from the tips of his fingers to his heels pressing into the bed. His bound hands didn't allow him to do much other than writhe beneath her. She leaned back, giving him a full view of her pussy as she rose and lowered again on his cock, taking him deeper and deeper each time. The sight set his skin on fire, and he strained against the shirt that held him to the bed.

"I'm gonna come," he said just moments before his thighs and abdomen tensed, pleasure surging through him in a blinding bolt of energy.

Grace continued to rock her hips, slowly now, as he came down from his high. He moaned, and she rubbed her clit harder and faster until she tensed on top of him. He felt every pulse of pleasure as her delicate inner muscles fluttered around his cock.

His eyes lingered on her face and the way it scrunched in uncontrolled bliss. "So beautiful," he whispered.

Grace chuckled again and slid off of him, pulling at the shirt around his wrists to release him. She made a quick trip to the bathroom to clean up before settling next to him in bed.

Her brown hair fell over Eli's shoulder, and he relished the feeling of her body so close. He smiled when she laid her head on him, no doubt hearing his heartbeat thudding against his chest.

She looked so content. Much better than the troubled expression he'd left her with after dinner.

Grace sighed. "You and I are going to have some fun, Eli."

Chapter Twenty-Three

NIK

Nik and Sam had just finished their morning chores when Meredith called them in for lunch. As if on cue, Sam's stomach rumbled, and Nik snickered. It wasn't just Sam. Nik was starving too. Chopping wood, feeding the animals, and planting crops was hard work. Most mornings, they were up before the sun in order to get it all done.

The scent of freshly baked bread greeted them at the threshold of the Kennedy cabin. Cole and Alan were already seated at the dining table, digging into their sandwiches and salads.

"Where's Ali?" Nik asked.

"Oh, you didn't know? She wasn't feeling well this morning, so I sent her back to bed. In fact, could you take her some food? I promised to check on her, but she probably prefers your company."

Nik swallowed the panic that rose in his gut. His mind automatically jumped to the worst outcome. He pictured her lying in bed with a blank expression on her face. That she might be fading into that darkness again and he'd be helpless to guide her out of it.

He took the sandwich that Meredith had prepared and set off for their shared cabin, praying that Ali was okay and his worst fears wouldn't be on the other side of the door.

When he walked in, Ali was facing away from him, lying still under the covers. When she heard the door open, she rolled over to face him and he tried to find a trace...any hint of that dark anguish he knew too well.

He approached the bed tentatively and sat down beside her. "Meredith said you weren't feeling well. What's wrong?"

Ali sat up and took the plate from him. "It's nothing. You didn't have to bring me food."

"I'm happy to do it. Ali?"

"What?" she asked, and her mouth turned up in a grin. That was a good sign.

"Are you feeling...down again?"

Her face relaxed when she understood what he was asking. "I'm fine. It's just cramps."

It was impossible to hold back his sigh of relief. "Thank god."

"My excruciating abdomen resents that," she said playfully before biting into her sandwich.

"I'm sorry. I just...worried it was something else."

They ate their lunch together, and Nik got up to pour her a glass of water. "You're quiet today."

Ali said nothing, snuggling back into her blankets.

"Is there something else wrong?" he asked.

She played with the threads of the quilt before sighing heavily. "Do you want kids?"

Nik blinked. "Where did that come from?"

Her eyes sparkled with a strange sadness. "Do you?"

"Yes. One day, I'd like to have kids. Why do you ask?"

"Do you think it's weird that I haven't gotten pregnant? I mean...we haven't exactly been careful, and I haven't been taking anything since arriving in Rysburg. Do you think there's something wrong with me?"

Nik was completely taken aback. How long had she been having these thoughts? He supposed it had been rather foolish to not consider contraceptives before, but he'd never thought there might be something *wrong* with her...or him.

"I think you're perfect."

Ali gave a noncommittal grunt, and he knew that wasn't what she wanted to hear.

"Do you want kids?"

"Of course. Maybe not right now, but in the future, yes."

Nik spread out on the bed next to her and covered her with his weight. "You want kids with me," he teased, and she smiled.

"Yes, Nik. I want a family with you. I want it all with you." Ali traced her thumb over his lip. Though she smiled, he could still see the shadow of sorrow in her eyes.

"I don't think there's anything wrong with you, Ali. Maybe it's just stress. Maybe you're just malnourished"—he pinched her bony hip, and she rolled her eyes—"or maybe it's nothing at all and the timing is just off. We can figure it out as we go. Okay?"

Ali nodded, then linked her hands behind his neck. He leaned in for a kiss. What started as a soft peck turned slow, sensual, and passionate. He felt her stiffen, and when he pulled back, her eyes were squinted in pain.

"Cramps," she reminded him.

"You know, I hear orgasms are good for cramps. Helps alleviate the pain."

"Is that so?" Her mischievous grin matched his own.

"Mm-hmm." He nodded and slid a hand between their bodies.

Ali's head rolled back...and not in a good way. "I'm sorry. I do not feel sexy right now. The last thing I want right now is you inside me."

Nik removed his hand and chuckled. "I will try not to be offended by that statement."

Ali kissed him on the lips again in consolation, but the damage was already done. Nestled up to her body had already left him yearning for more, and his cock was heavy and hard.

"What if we just dry hump?"

Ali laughed. *Laughed.* "You're not serious."

"I'm dead serious." He moved between her legs and wiggled his hips against her just to show her how serious he was. Her eyes fluttered, and he was pretty confident he could convince her. Nik slowly kissed the outline of her jaw down to the hollow spot where her neck met her chest. He whispered against her skin, "Well?"

Her hands roamed through his hair and down his back. Her eyes drooped lazily, and her breathing turned shallow. "Can we just lay like this?" she asked, and she looked so peaceful it was impossible for him to say no, despite how badly he wanted to fool around.

A thousand moments like this would never be enough. So he rested his head on her chest, letting her brush his hair until he, too, was drowsy. He ran his hands up her thighs and waist, lulling her to sleep.

Just when he thought she was out, she said, "Nik?"

"Yes?"

"What happens next?"

He lifted his head from her chest. "What do you mean?"

"We've been here for over a week."

She paused, and he nodded, certain he knew where this was headed. No matter how good life was on the farm, she would never give up on finding Eli. But he had no idea where to go from here. There was no trail to follow, no clues that could lead them to him. "You don't want to stay here?"

"It's not that I don't want to." Her face was contorted with frustration as she looked around the room and then back to him. "I don't know if I can."

Nik found it hard to understand. He'd never had anyone that he would go to such lengths for. His mom had died while he was young, and his relationship with his father had always been strained. He'd forgotten what it was like to even have friends. Would he do all this for Sam? He hated himself a little for it, but the answer was probably not. He wasn't half the person Ali was.

Nik looked into her eyes as he made circles with his thumb over her hipbone. He'd do it for her, though. If they were separated, he'd do anything to get her back. He did know the feeling of being incapable of living without someone.

"Ali." He shook his head. "I don't know where to even begin looking for Eli. I know you want to find him, and believe it or not, I want that for you. I know how much he means to you. But there's no way to know where he is."

He bit his lip and waited for her response. It felt like an eternity passed while she played with the sleeve of his shirt and stared down, unable to make eye contact.

"You're probably right," she said, and the crack in her voice almost broke him too. He didn't want to let her down. Not again.

"I'll keep thinking of ideas." He brought her hand up to his lips and kissed her. If they ever found Eli again, he might wring his neck for all the hell he caused. Even when he wasn't around, he was still a pain in Nik's ass. Life would be easier if Eli were forgotten, but Nik wouldn't be a man worthy of Ali's love if he gave up so easily. "I'd do anything for you, Ali."

Chapter Twenty-Four

ELI

ELI QUICKLY GOT USED to the feeling of waking up next to Grace in his bed. It was comforting to open his eyes and feel her skin pressed against his after several months of isolation and neglect.

They'd agreed to keep their arrangement a secret, mostly because Grace didn't want to argue with her parents, who would surely disapprove. Or deal with the community and any future suitors who would find her behavior unladylike. Most mornings she hurried home before her parents would notice she was missing, but this weekend she had opted to sleep in with him, convinced her parents wouldn't notice for *one* morning.

He didn't have the heart to fight her on it.

"What do you have planned today?" she asked, trailing a finger over his stomach and wrapping a leg around him.

"Nothing at all. Maybe stay in bed all day? Did you have something in mind?"

"Heather and Amaya wanted to have brunch together."

"Do you need to go?" Eli wasn't sure how late it was. The last thing he wanted was to keep Grace from her friends. They were just warming up to him, and he didn't want to do anything to make them feel differently.

"Actually, I thought you might like to come too."

"Is that okay?"

Grace nodded, still playfully tracing his skin with her finger. "They said they were cool with it. Theo's invited too, so you'll have another guy there. And I promise not to talk about your dick this time."

Her humor eased some of his nerves. "Sure. I'd love to have brunch with you, Grace." He kissed her forehead and slid out of bed, leaving her with a beautiful frown.

Eli didn't know it was possible to make frowning look so good.

"What?" he asked.

"I thought we might have a little *fun* before we left."

Eli grabbed her shirt off the floor and tossed it at her. She caught it in one hand before it hit her in the face. "Not right now."

"You're no fun," she muttered, pulling the white, silky shirt over her head. She ran her fingers through her tangled brown hair and pulled it into a ponytail.

The bed squeaked as Eli leaned across it, stopping inches before Grace's face. "What if I make it up to you later?"

"How will you do that?"

A devilish light flickered in her eyes, and Eli wondered what he was getting himself into, but he yielded to her, anyway. "Whatever you like."

"Hmm." Grace tapped her index finger on her lips. "Careful, Eli. There are lots of things I'd like to do with you."

Eli's cock twitched, but they didn't have time for this. He backed away from Grace and went to the bathroom to splash cold water on his face...and think of the least sexy things he could fill his mind with.

After he freshened up, he came back to his bedroom, where Grace was slipping on her shoes. "I need to run back to my place first."

"You should just leave a few things here."

"I know, but I didn't think I'd be staying the night. You're just too irresistible."

Eli's cheeks filled with heat. She was probably only kidding, but she always made him feel ridiculously desirable.

"Meet you in the entrance hall?" she asked with one hand on the door.

"Sounds good."

Brunch was served on a small wooden platform surrounded on two edges with bushes that provided complete privacy. The patio was attached to Heather's family's salon and the back side opened up to the river, the gentle stream providing a soundtrack for their morning meal. A trellis hung over the top to provide them with shade and the sweet aroma of newly blossoming pink and white flowers.

Heather and Amaya were already waiting when Eli and Grace arrived, but Theo was running behind. Eli sat at the circular table between Grace and the empty seat meant for Theo.

"What have you two been up to this week?" Grace asked, swiping a biscuit and slathering it with angelfruit jam. She turned to Eli. "Weekend brunch is a bit of a tradition for us, especially when work gets busy and I don't get to see them as much."

That and she was seeing more of *him* lately. But he didn't voice that aloud.

Amaya spoke first. "My mom is helping me mend an old dress for the Suitors' Ball. Two of the seams have split and there are some missing hooks, but it's looking much better already. I can't wait for you both to see it."

"I'm surprised you're not wearing the one you stole from me," Grace teased.

"Won," Amaya corrected. "I won that dress fair and square."

Grace simply laughed and reached for the blue ceramic jug of juice in the center of the table.

"What's the Suitors' Ball?" Eli asked. He guessed it had something to do with the Rite, but he wanted to hear it directly from Grace.

"It's just another reason to dress up and celebrate my upcoming nuptials." The corner of her mouth rose in an imitation of a smile. "The official beginning of the Rite will be the following day. There's a gathering for suitors to declare their intent to enter the Rite, followed by more celebrating, drinking, dancing, etcetera."

"The entire summer will be one big party," Amaya said.

"For you, maybe." Grace scoffed. "I'll have to be on my best behavior while being auctioned off like a piece of art."

"A fine piece of art, at that," a new voice said.

"Theo!" Grace exclaimed, leaping up to greet her brother.

"Hey, sis." Theo hugged his sister tightly and then found his seat, greeting each person as he went. "Heather, Amaya—good to see you both. Eli, I've been looking for you."

"You have?" Eli hadn't spent much time alone with Theo. Why would he be looking for Eli, of all people?

"I just got done talking to Luka. I'm heading out on another mission tomorrow morning to pick up some supplies. He mentioned you might be interested in going with us."

Eli didn't hesitate to answer. "I am. Where are we going? What does Luka need me to get?" One question was on the tip of his tongue, but he didn't voice it. No one could know the answer.

Was there a chance that Ali would be there?

"Luka's got a list for you. Find him today and he'll fill you in on all the details. The town we're going to is called Jellico. It's at the bottom of the mountains on the southeast side. The trip will take about three days, so you should pack today as well."

Eli's head spun—mostly with the excitement of possibly running into Ali, but also at the chance to do more exploring around Berland. In the past couple weeks, it had begun to feel like home. He and Grace had quickly become close and now Luka trusted him enough to go on a supply mission. That feeling of belonging he'd been chasing was within his reach.

The rest of brunch passed at an excruciating pace. Eli couldn't wait to pack for the next three days, but it would've been rude to so hastily leave the table after Theo's news.

"Let's play a game," Amaya said once their plates had been cleared and the drinks were running low.

Eli looked at Grace, unsure of what games they were used to playing in Berland. The mischievous look in Heather's eyes made him wary.

Grace rolled her eyes. "What do you want to play, Amaya?"

"Truth or dare."

"No," Grace and Theo both protested at the same time.

Amaya slumped in her chair. "Two truths and a lie?"

"No," Theo groaned again. He apparently didn't enjoy any of Amaya's games.

"I know." Heather sat up straighter. "We should go to the tea leaf reader."

Everyone sat in silence, leaving Eli confused. "Who is the tea leaf reader?"

"She can tell your future," Heather said. "You drink a cup of tea, and she can tell what's going to happen to you based on the dregs."

"Seriously?" Eli asked. He'd never heard of someone with such abilities.

"It's not real," Amaya added. "But it is fun." Then she turned to Eli with a devilish smile. "I think the newcomer should go first."

Eli had the sense that he was walking into a wolves' den as they headed toward a small cabin off the main strip of shops. This building was less vibrant and cheerful than those that lined the riverfront street.

The exterior logs were dark gray, like they hadn't been properly treated to protect against the rain, and the windows were covered so he couldn't see inside the shop.

Grace knocked on the door three times before a woman appeared before them, dressed in all black. Her dress went all the way to the ground and a shawl hung across her shoulders.

"How can I help you, Miss Grace?" she asked. The woman gave Eli the chills, but the fact that she was on a first name basis with Grace made him a little less worried. It was just theatrics. She was a normal woman, right?

"Hello, Tessa. Eli would like to know his future," Grace said, pulling Eli to her side and then pushing him through the door.

The shop was filled with odds and ends. Some trinkets Eli had never seen before, but others looked like abandoned junk littering tables and bookshelves. It was a chaotic mess, but Tessa weaved in and out of the piles of trash until they walked through a purple drape in the back of the shop.

"Eli," she said, waving him through to a table just big enough for two.

Eli looked at Grace and pleaded with his eyes. *Come with me.*

Grace's laugh was so soft that it was imperceptible to everyone except Eli. But she followed him through the drape and stood behind him while he took a seat at the small table. She placed her hand on his shoulder, instantly slowing his heart rate.

The sound of dishes clanking and liquid pouring caught Eli's attention. Tessa was busy pouring hot tea into a small, white porcelain teacup decorated with blue flowers and a golden rim.

"Drink," she said, placing the teacup in front of him. It was still steaming hot, but Eli did as he was told, briefly blowing on the drink before taking a sip.

There wasn't anything special about the tea itself. In fact, compared to everything else he'd sampled in Berland, it was downright bland. He downed it until all that remained were soggy tea leaves at the bottom of the cup.

"Let me see," Tessa said.

She studied them for a long while, and Eli wondered if she'd forgotten that Eli and Grace were still there. Finally, she looked directly into Eli's eyes.

"You've lived a long life for such a young person." Her voice was low and gravelly, and Eli shifted uncomfortably in his seat. "You've experienced more tragedy than one person should in a hundred lifetimes. But I see a spark of hope here. Though you've seen the darkest humankind has to offer, you still choose to focus on the light. You choose to see the best in people. You choose hope over despair."

Tessa turned the cup. "Your optimism will serve you well, Eli. You'll find new joy, new friends, new love..." Tessa's eyes flickered briefly to Grace, and Eli felt her fingers dig into his shoulder ever so slightly before relaxing again.

"There's something else here." Tessa scrunched her brows. "You've lost something, but it isn't as lost as you might think."

Eli couldn't help it; the first thing he thought of was Ali. What did Tessa mean? "Can you tell where she—it—might be? The thing that is lost?"

Tessa frowned at him. "I'm afraid not, but don't stop searching. I sense that you will find it soon."

Eli's shoulders slumped. If only Tessa had been more specific.

Grace bumped his shoulder with her hip. "My turn."

Eli stood so Grace could take a seat. Tessa returned to the corner to pour another cup of tea, and Grace looked up at Eli. She whispered, "Well? What did you think?"

Eli leaned close enough to whisper in Grace's ear without Tessa hearing. "I think that was a load of horseshit."

Grace shivered at the heat of his breath in her ear and chuckled. "It's supposed to be *fun*, Eli. Don't take it so seriously."

When Tessa returned to the table, she placed a teacup in front of Grace. "Drink," she said again.

Eli watched as Grace quickly drank and passed the cup back to Tessa.

After studying it for several minutes, Tessa closed her eyes. "Your confidence is a mask."

Grace inhaled sharply.

"There are many ways in which you are sure of yourself, Grace, but there are also many insecurities. You want to please those around you, especially those with authority."

"My mother," Grace whispered.

"Hmm," Tessa agreed. Eli couldn't believe what he was watching. Tessa could've been talking about anyone. Grace supplied the answers. It was all so vague. How could anyone actually gather insight from a reading?

"What you seek will evade you, I'm afraid. But you're strong, and it won't be your downfall. In fact, it'll strengthen you, sharpen you like a blade, in the end."

Grace looked resolved. "Thank you, Tessa."

"Anytime, my dear."

Grace stepped through the curtain first, Eli following closely behind. The others were in the shop's corner, laughing and playing with some device they probably shouldn't be touching. Tessa would probably reprimand them when she emerged and push them out of her shop.

But Grace stopped and turned to Eli. "It's a shame my mother will never be proud of me." She laughed, though it wasn't funny. Clearly, Tessa had hit a vulnerable spot.

"Why wouldn't she be proud of you?" Eli looked Grace up and down. He couldn't see how anyone wouldn't be amazed by the woman standing in front of him.

"Forget it. It's just a load of horseshit, right?"

"Right."

But deep down, Eli hoped Tessa was right. He wanted to know for certain that he *would* find Ali one day soon.

Chapter Twenty-Five

ELI

THE NEXT MORNING, ELI met Theo and another man at the entrance of the mountain. It was early enough that the three of them were the only ones in the hall.

"Noah, this is Eli. He's going to accompany us on this trip on behalf of the research department."

"Nice to meet you, Eli." Noah extended his hand and Eli shook it. He was a tall man with a balding head—older, but still quite fit. How often did he go on missions to keep his muscles in that good of shape? He looked stronger than Eli and Theo combined.

"Nice to meet you as well."

"Let's get going. It'll take almost all day to reach Jellico. Do you have your list of supplies, Eli?"

"Yes," Eli said, pulling out the piece of paper Luka had given him last night. It was a short list—only three items, and on the back were illustrations of each so that Eli would know what he was looking for.

"And you?"

"Got mine too," Noah said, patting a pocket.

"Noah works in the medical field. The healers have a few supplies we'll need to grab as well," Theo explained.

After making sure everyone was prepared, Theo led the way to the stables. Theo's family always allowed the tradesmen to borrow horses for their missions, and Eli was relieved to already have some experience riding Obsidian. Otherwise it would've been a long ride down the mountain and a sore behind at the end of the day.

They saddled the horses and strapped their bags to the side, including an empty sack each for the goods they intended to retrieve. Obsidian bristled with the extra weight but soon got over his annoyance as Eli brushed through his mane.

They set off as the sun rose over the mountainside, quickly blazing through the morning dew. The path down the mountain was well traveled, much different from Eli's journey to Berland. While that trip had been full of weeds, muddy pits, and overgrown forest, this path was clear and well-kept. Like they'd taken the time to clear all the fallen branches and fill in the natural ridges with dirt to even out the surface.

The trip down the mountain was easy, pleasant even, compared to any travel Eli had experienced previously. He thought for a moment that it might be nice to be a wanderer like Genna and Isabel, but he couldn't handle it. He was desperate for a place to call home, and their life was a direct contradiction to that desire.

By lunchtime, they were more than halfway down the mountain. "It won't be much longer now," Theo told them.

"Have you been to Jellico before?" Eli asked Noah.

"A couple times, although the last time was more than a year ago. It's not my idea of a good time."

"No?" Eli asked with a furrowed brow.

"Don't get me wrong, it's a friendly village. The inn has great wine and even better women." Noah winked. "But I'm not much of a traveler these days. I'd rather stay home. Now that I've started losing my hair, the ladies don't seem to love me as much, and the wine makes an old man like me too drowsy to be much fun. You'll probably enjoy it more. A young guy like you with a face like that? The ladies will eat you up."

Eli snorted. He wasn't interested in meeting any women unless they were named Ali. But rather than seeing Ali's face, an image of Grace crossed his mind. Eli shook his head and finished the last of his fruit.

It was early afternoon when the land leveled out and they came to a wooden gate between two watchtowers. It had to be at least twenty feet tall and was attached to a wooden fence that seemed to wrap around the entire village, or at least as far as Eli could see.

The doors to the gate were propped open, making the town feel warm and welcoming before they even stepped foot into it. Just the fact that they felt safe enough to keep their borders open made Eli relax.

The inn was just inside the gates, which was good since the streets in Jellico were hardly wide enough to fit one horse, let alone three. The buildings were pressed tightly together, and they left very little room to squeeze by pedestrians.

Around the back of the inn, they tied up their horses in the shelter for the night. The innkeeper met them and handed them keys and fresh food for their hungry animals, and Theo handed over a sack of coins.

"The apothecary isn't expecting us until tomorrow, so I guess we'll start with Eli's list. Can I see it again?" Theo asked.

Eli gave it to Theo, who surveyed it. "Right. We can get the wire spools from my guy Clarence. He probably has these blades you're looking for as well. These glass panes will have to come from Talia's junk yard. Let's go there first. It will give her plenty of time to search for them before we leave in two days."

Theo handed the list back to Eli, and they navigated the narrow paths of Jellico. It made Eli feel caged in as he bumped into Noah and then Theo. They walked shoulder to shoulder for several minutes. Eli couldn't keep track of the twists and turns if he wanted to. People in worn and tattered clothing passed in every direction, not meeting his eyes. They didn't look as well off as the residents of Berland, but they seemed content with what they had.

Finally, the buildings opened up and Eli felt like he had space to breathe again. They'd made it to a chain-link fence with rusted signs hanging haphazardly. At one point in time, they might've held warnings or important information, but now they were merely decoration. They'd been painted and carved up into the shape of flower petals.

Here, too, the fence was wide open. Theo waltzed right in like he'd been here many times before and knew exactly where he was going. And he probably did, Eli supposed. This was his job, after all.

"Talia," he shouted so loudly that two black birds flew into the air and disappeared into the sky. "Talia, where are you?"

"Here," a muffled voice called from somewhere in the junkyard.

"Where?" Theo asked, looking around at all the piles of trash. Eli had no idea what any of these items were, but most looked like they hadn't been used in decades. Holes, rips, and stains marred every item he laid his eyes on.

"Over here," the voice rang out again.

"God damn it, Talia," Theo muttered under his breath.

Noah laughed. "One might think she's hiding from you. Did you do something to piss her off on your last mission?"

"Rubbish. Talia loves me. Everyone loves me," Theo said with a charming smile. Eli chuckled at how similar he was to Grace. A cool confidence that never passed the line of arrogance. The kind of character that made it impossible not to like them.

"He's awfully full of himself, isn't he?"

Eli turned to find a slim, muscular woman with long brown hair slicked back in a braid, much like the ones Ali used to wear. Eli's muscles tensed momentarily at the reminder of his missing friend.

"There she is," Theo said, wrapping the woman in a giant hug and spinning her around in a circle.

"Theo," she grunted. "Stop that."

The spinning ceased, and Theo carefully put Talia back on her feet.

"And who might these people be?" she asked, focusing her gaze on Eli and Noah.

"These are my traveling companions. Noah's visited Jellico before, but perhaps you haven't met. And this is Eli. He's new to Berland and the reason we stopped by. And to see you, of course," he added hastily.

"I suppose you're looking for something in my treasure garden?" Talia asked with a hand on her hip.

Eli looked between Theo and Noah, wondering if they were as confused as he was. So far, he had seen nothing that resembled *treasure* or any sign of living plants in the dust-filled, barren dump they'd stumbled into.

Talia laughed. "It's a joke. Haven't you ever heard the expression that one person's trash is another person's treasure?"

Eli shook his head. "I'm afraid not."

"Well, now you have. What can I help you find?"

Eli pulled out the list once again and handed it to Talia. "Theo said you might be able to help us with the glass panes."

She studied the illustration. "I might have something like this. How many do you need and how big?"

"We need four, but we'll take more if you have it. No more than two feet wide. Any larger than that will be too difficult to travel with."

Talia nodded. "I'll see what I can find." Then she turned to Theo. "How long will you be staying?"

Eli thought he noted a change in her tone. More sultry, and he felt compelled to look away. Noah, he noticed, was all too eager to eavesdrop on their private conversation.

Theo's voice lowered. "I'll be around tonight and tomorrow night, too. You know where to find me." He cleared his throat and then stepped out of Talia's clutches. "Come on, boys. That's enough work for one day. I'm ready for a drink."

The pub attached to the inn was rather full, especially considering it wasn't even dinnertime. The three men walked into the stuffy bar and found a table by the back window. Theo went to grab their drinks, and Eli searched the room.

"Scoping out the options?" Noah asked, breaking out in a playful smile.

"No. I thought maybe..." Eli hesitated. He didn't know Noah at all. Would he judge him for holding onto hope that his friend might still be alive? That somehow, in this massive maze of a world, he would find his way back to her? It seemed silly, but two pairs of eyes were better than one. "I was separated from a friend of mine. I was hoping...if there's any chance she made it here..."

Noah sighed, his smile faltering. "That's tough. I wish I could say there's a chance she's here, but I doubt it."

"I know," Eli said with a little more force than he intended. "It just...doesn't hurt to look."

Noah nodded and then fell silent. By the time Theo returned with their drinks, Eli had scanned the entire room. No sign of a blonde beauty and her grizzly companion.

They stayed for several drinks, all of which Theo paid for. When Eli and Noah offered, he said that it was a work expense and therefore they shouldn't have to pay for it from their own purses.

What few tables had been open when they arrived were now crowded as people came in for dinner and conversations with friends. Eli searched every face, disappointment growing with each that didn't resemble Ali's.

After his fourth drink, the room began to feel suffocating. "I need some air," he said, standing and moving toward the exit. He squeezed through the crowded space until he reached the door and was greeted with the humidity of the late spring evening. He leaned against the stone exterior of the pub, closed his eyes and took deep breaths.

"You all right?"

Eli opened his eyes a sliver and found the innkeeper staring at him with concern. His brows were furrowed, and he held an arm out like he thought Eli might topple over. Eli didn't know how that would help, considering the man was a foot shorter than him and at least twenty years older. Eli would probably take him to the ground with him if he passed out.

"I'm fine. I'm sorry, I didn't catch your name earlier."

"Callahan. Most people call me Cal, though."

"Can I ask you a question, Cal?"

Cal shrugged, clearly unbothered by Eli's request.

"Do you get many visitors in Jellico?"

Callahan looked at the sky and crossed his arms over his chest. He looked like he was trying to imagine every stranger that had passed through Jellico in recent days. "We get a few. Probably ten or so in the past month. Why do you ask?"

"I'm looking for someone. A woman in her early twenties, slender build, light blonde hair, brown eyes, about this tall"—he held his hand just below his shoulder—"and goes by the name of Ali or Allison. Any chance you've seen her?"

Cal squinted his eyes and again they roamed the sky like he was trying to recall a face. "That description doesn't ring a bell. But not everyone stays at my inn. There's another smaller inn down the road. Three buildings down and on the right."

"Thank you," Eli said, slightly disheartened but determined to exhaust every avenue before giving up. He strode toward the second inn.

"Good luck," Cal called after him.

Eli relayed the same description to the owner of the second inn—a woman in her sixties or seventies with gray hair twisted into a bun and weathered hands that had seen three times as many decades as Eli's had. She watched him with soft, glowing eyes.

"We had a blonde woman stop by just a few days ago," she said with a wide smile, and Eli couldn't help but return it. "I'm not sure her name, but she's still here." She pointed up toward the ceiling. "Upstairs, first room on the right. She might be out for the evening, but you might catch her."

Eli's stomach fluttered with nerves—the good kind. Could his life be turning around? Had he finally stumbled upon a streak of good luck after months of misery? It felt too easy...too good to be true, but life owed him after the hell it had put him through.

He found the rickety staircase that led to the lodging, his heart pounding with every step he took. What would he say? What would he find when he knocked on that door? Would Ali be speechless when she saw him?

He smiled at the thought of the surprise on her face and took the second half of the staircase two steps at a time with his long legs.

He didn't know how Ali had found her way here and didn't stop to question it. It was simply fate bringing her back to him. He smiled so hard his cheeks hurt.

There was a sliver of light coming through the bottom of the first door on the right—a sign of life behind the wooden frame. A shadow moved, and he heard footsteps. He thought he might be sick from the fury of butterflies moving in his stomach.

Eli stopped in front of the door with his hand held high. He inhaled, filling his lungs until there was no space left. Then he slowly let the air out and rapped his knuckles on the dark wood.

The steps inside stilled first, then moved toward him. The light under the door danced with shadows as the figure moved closer. Eli wrung his hands, wondering what he would say when she opened that door. He couldn't recall a time when he'd ever been so nervous and excited at the same time.

Eli smiled as the door creaked open. A beautiful blonde woman stared back at him, and his heart broke into pieces at the sight of the stranger's face.

"Can I help you?" she asked in a voice that was too husky—a voice that didn't belong to Ali. She placed a hand on the door frame and looked up at him with eyes that were entirely unfamiliar.

Eli choked on his words. "I... I'm sorry. I have the wrong room."

He turned and headed back down the stairs, straining to keep his despair in check and his legs from giving out.

❧❧❧❧

The next two days passed in a blur. After finding not-Ali, Eli headed back to his room and fell asleep without dinner. Theo came back to the inn looking for him late at night and Eli had ignored the pounding at his door initially, but when he realized Theo wouldn't go away unless he spoke to him, he got out of bed and told Theo to knock it off.

Judging by his red, glazed eyes, Theo and Noah had had several more drinks after Eli had left. Noah had his arm around the waist of a stumbling woman as they hobbled down the hall together, and Theo left in the opposite direction of his room, probably to find Talia.

They didn't speak of it the next day, which was perfect for Eli because he didn't feel like explaining where he'd been or why his mood had turned foul.

They made a trip to Clarence's workshop to pick up the wire and utility blades and then stopped at the apothecary so Noah could gather his supplies—some vials with a clear substance, a gauze-like fabric, and five black canisters marked with red paint. He almost dropped one as he struggled to juggle them, and Eli quickly caught it. He was delighted to find that he could read the word "flammable" without much struggle. His lessons were paying off.

"Careful, that's dangerous," Noah warned before gently putting the supplies into his sack.

All of it felt like a dream to Eli. Like he wasn't a participant but an observer. His body moved—his feet went forward, his hands reached to greet new acquaintances—but he was numb. He just wanted to go back to Berland and forget this trip had happened. It had been stupid to allow hope to take root and grow.

After returning to Talia's to pick up the glass panes, they packed up their horses and set off back to Berland. At least there was one thing Eli had to look forward to—maybe Grace would be in his room when he got home.

Chapter Twenty-Six

ALI

"How did you learn to do that?" Sam asked.

Ali stared down at the bundle of twigs and cattails in her lap. She'd spent most of the morning gathering the necessary supplies to craft a fish trap for the stream near the farm. Now Sam watched as she weaved the long green blades between a cone of perfectly arranged sticks.

"I learned when I was a kid. It was my job back in Andus. Eli and I were in charge of checking the traps, but before that we both learned to craft them on our own so we could set more and replace the ones that broke or were lost."

"Were you as bad initially as I am now?"

Ali looked up to where Sam was sitting on a horizontal tree trunk. The splintered edge let her know it had only recently fallen during one of the spring storms. Many of the branches had green buds that would never grow any larger.

Sam's trap didn't look nearly as precise as Ali's. The space between the twigs was haphazard, and they didn't form a perfect cone. She could see gaps in the woven weeds that held the trap together.

"It takes practice," she conceded.

He held up his finished product, smiling at the rubbish he'd created. "First one to catch a fish gets out of clean up duty tonight."

Ali stifled a laugh and wiped a bead of sweat from her brow. There was no chance of him winning that bet, and they both knew it. "Deal."

She stood and stretched out her legs. "What do you think Nik is doing right now?"

"Is my company insufficient?" Sam teased.

"Of course not, Sam. I always value your company." Her tone was playful, but she meant every word. Sam was a calm presence that she'd grown to rely on. Though he was only a little older than her, he always had such good advice and kept a cool head in a crisis. She admired the way he hadn't once complained as they journeyed south. If only she could be as resilient as he was.

"It's okay. Honestly, I'm not sure what they're up to, but I'm glad I got to stay back."

Alan had appeared at their cabin door before sunrise and requested Nik's help, leaving Ali and Sam on their own for the day. He hadn't said what he needed help with, just that Nik should pack a bag and he'd be gone until dinner time.

Ali didn't like the idea of Nik heading out into the wilderness—she'd seen enough to know it was an unforgiving terrain. But she trusted Alan, and Nik could take care of himself. Still, she wasn't prepared for how often her thoughts would turn to him when he wasn't near.

"You didn't want to go with them?" she asked, setting her trap aside and surveying the edge of the water for bait.

"Not at all. I'm not a fan of surprises, and an all-day trip sounds exhausting."

Something about his wearied tone made her turn to face him. "Is your leg bothering you still?"

Sam flexed and stretched his foot. "Not too bad, but it doesn't feel like the strength has fully returned. Suppose I need to work on restoring my flexibility and endurance."

Ali kneeled and grabbed two worms that wiggled in the mud, gagging as she pulled them out. This was always her least favorite part. She'd always made Eli dig for worms or insects or leeches to use as bait, but she sucked it up and did what had to be done.

Sam cleared his throat, catching her attention. "You seem to be doing better, though."

"What do you mean?"

Sam jutted his chin toward the stream. "Water doesn't seem to bother you as much."

Ali ruminated over his words. She finished setting her trap before responding. "It's not as bad as it was. I can handle little streams like this, but the thought of walking out into the middle..." Her throat closed, and she forced herself to swallow. "I know it's shallow, but I just can't get past it. It's like my mind plays tricks on me and I freeze up and lose control over my own body." She shook her head. She didn't understand why it kept happening and it frustrated her that even Sam had noticed. She didn't like being seen as weak.

"Don't beat yourself up, Ali. You've been through a lot. We all have."

"You don't seem to show it, though."

Sam shrugged and tapped his temple. "Just be glad you can't see what's going on in this head of mine."

What could he mean by that?

Before she could ask, he stood, holding up his misshapen trap. "Now, do you have some bait for this atrocity?"

⁕ ⁕ ⁕

Dinner was cold by the time Nik and Alan made it back from their adventure. Ali had just put her dishes in the metal basin at the back of the house—she had caught the first fish and therefore Sam had to wash dishes on his own tonight—when Nik and Alan dragged themselves into the soft glow of the lanterns strewn about the backyard.

Nik picked up his pace when he caught sight of her, wrapping her in a warm embrace.

"You're back late," she said.

Nik waved at Sam and pulled Ali's hand as they walked back inside the house. "Took longer than Alan guessed. One of the neighbor's roofs caved in during a bad storm. They needed all the help they could get rebuilding. We still weren't done by the time we left, but Alan wanted to get back before it got too dark out."

Neighbor was a misnomer on the farm. The way Cole had described it, Harrodsburg was a small village made up of only a dozen or so buildings, but the people lived spread out for miles and miles. In their time on the farm, Ali had seen no other neighbors, and she hadn't even seen the village itself. They were incredibly isolated from all other civilizations but it didn't bother her. It reminded her a lot of Andus.

"Was anyone hurt?" she asked.

"Miraculously, no. They had a storm cellar they were hiding in when it happened."

"That's good at least." Ali rubbed his back as he grabbed a bowl of cold vegetable soup and two slices of bread. His neck was red from the sun beating on him all day, and his muscles were tense under her fingers.

She could tell he'd worked hard today as he eagerly devoured his meal, completely unbothered that it was no longer hot.

"Oh, there's more," he said between spoonfuls of broth. He scraped the edge of the bowl, trying to get every drop. "One of the men there told us there's going to be a trade fair in town in a few days. Supposed to be lots of people coming in to exchange their goods. Alan was thrilled, but I think it'll mean extra work for the next couple days to prepare. He wants to take some of his own crops to sell, so it'll be all hands on deck around here."

Ali sucked in a sharp breath. If travelers were coming into town, there was hope of finding Eli, or at least finding someone who might know what happened to him. She tried to dampen her excitement. It was unlikely, but it was also the only glimmer of hope she'd had in weeks.

"That's great news." Her voice cracked almost imperceptibly, but Nik caught it. He focused his attention on her as he set his bowl down on the old wooden table. Then he squeezed her thigh and nodded.

"Damn right, it is."

Chapter Twenty-Seven

ELI

"Shit!" Eli hopped on one foot and looked down. "I'm so sorry."

Grace bit back an expletive of her own. "It's fine. Don't worry about it."

Grace had dragged him out of bed in the early hours of the morning and led him to a dimly lit ballroom with tables and chairs pushed to the sides to make room for a large crowd, though Grace and Eli were the only two people present. Grace had pulled out something called a phonograph, and Eli recognized it from one of his research journals. His jaw still fell open when he heard it in action.

The Suitors' Ball was still weeks away, but Grace was adamant that Eli be prepared well in advance.

They'd been practicing for hours, and it felt like Eli had made no progress. He'd never been formally trained in dance, and it was too hard to memorize the steps. He kept stepping forward with his left when he should've been stepping backward with his right.

"Why do I even need to learn this, Grace?"

She grabbed one of his hands and put it back around her waist and then clasped the other. "Because this is always the first dance for balls. It's tradition."

"Yes, you've explained that, but why do *I* need to learn this dance?" Eli was completely content to sit on the sidelines for the first dance—and all the ones that followed. He was under no obligation to participate. He wasn't even sure he wanted to attend.

In a little over a month, the dance would signal the end of their agreement. And Eli had no idea what he would do to distract himself once she was no longer sleeping in his bed at night and filling the silence during his days.

"I have to have someone to dance with," Grace said, pushing her bottom lip out in a way that made Eli want to bite it just to stop her pouting.

"I think you'll have plenty of options," he said softly.

Grace's shoulders deflated, and she sighed. "I don't want them."

Eli didn't have time to respond before Grace put on her smile and straightened, quickly masking her emotions as she was so used to doing.

"If I had known you'd be this big of a baby, I would've sent my mother to teach you. When she taught me as a young girl, she would smack my head with her shoe when I mis-stepped. She'd have you whipped into shape in no time."

"Well, I appreciate you not assaulting me, but I don't think I will ever be up to your standards."

"You just need more practice."

Eli groaned, but the music started up again and before he knew it, he was being shuffled around by Grace. They made it through three whole songs before Eli stepped on her toes again.

"I think that's enough for one day," she said, clutching her foot. "The dance isn't until the end of June, so we still have time to get the steps down."

June…

"Is it May?" Eli asked.

Grace laughed, stepped out of the heels she'd been practicing in, and pulled out a pair of flats from her bag. "Yes. When did you think it was?"

"I don't know. I just lost track of time. What day is it?"

"It's the eighteenth."

"Huh."

"What does 'huh' mean?" She sat on the ground and massaged her feet and injured toes.

"I just realized my birthday is next week."

Grace laughed again, this time more freely. "Did you forget your own birthday?"

"No, I just told you. I had no idea what month or day it was." Eli laughed along with her. It was a little funny that his birthday had almost passed without him realizing.

"What day and how old will you be?"

"I turn twenty-five on the twenty-fifth."

"I'll be sure to get you something special, then. Maybe a love note of my own."

Eli's cheeks turned pink. "You don't have to do that. It's not a big deal."

Her only response was a mischievous grin, and Eli knew he hadn't heard the last of it. He dropped to the floor next to her, pulling her foot into his lap. He rubbed her feet, applying pressure to her arches. "I really am sorry about stepping on your toes."

"I'll forgive you if you keep this up." Grace's head rolled back, and she released a soft moan. Eli's cock stiffened at the sound, and a low growl caught in his throat. He liked it when she made those noises, but it was better when she made them in his bed. If they were done practicing for the day, perhaps he could take her home and discover all the ways to draw out that sound again.

He watched her as he continued to stroke her tender soles. Her eyes were closed, and she looked so relaxed...so content. He'd happily take another dancing lesson if it meant he got to see her without the mask—not Grace, the future Lady of Berland, but *just Grace*. "Do you want to grab something to eat and head back home? I can think of a few other places I'd like to massage. It's the least I can do after breaking all your toes."

Grace chuckled and grabbed her jacket from the bag beside her. Standing, she slid her feet into the black leather flats she'd brought. "You didn't break all of them. Maybe only eight."

Eli threw his arms around her in a bear hug, and she squealed. He prodded her sides, and she laughed uncontrollably. The way her body wriggled against his chest made his heart swell. His pants were definitely fitting tighter now.

"Stop. Stop. Please," she panted.

"Promise you won't make fun of my dancing?"

"I promise. Please," she said through hysterical laughter.

Eli released her, and she spun around, grabbing the front of his shirt to steady herself. The motion flung them both against a wall. Her back hit the stone and his palms landed next to her face.

She didn't release his shirt. Instead, she bit her lip and dragged her hands down his chest.

"Grace..."

It was so difficult not to give in to her in this empty ballroom. Her touch, her laugh, her scent—it all drove him wild. He wasn't sure he could even make it back to his bedroom. Especially when she was looking at him like *that*. Like he was a drug she needed for survival. Her fingers latched onto his belt loops, and she tugged him closer.

He didn't bother to hide his arousal as he pushed his hips against her. Her eyes flicked down and then back up to his face, and he knew she'd felt him. Just in case she hadn't, he rolled his hips between her legs, and she gasped.

"Eli..." Her breaths were shallow, and he watched the curves of her breasts rise and fall with each one. She slipped her hands beneath his shirt, and he jolted at her chilled fingertips.

Eli leaned down closer, so close he could watch as her eyes darkened, filled with lust. He cupped her cheeks in his hand, closing the distance to her face...to those sultry red lips.

His heart raced, and he wondered if hers was too. He was just about to press his lips against hers when the door three feet to the right of them flew open.

Eli jumped back, dropping his hands, and Grace let go of his pants, tucking a stray strand of hair behind her ear.

"Well, well. You two look awfully cozy," Trevor said in a hushed tone.

"Hello, Trevor," Grace said. It gave Eli a jolt of triumph that she didn't use the same sultry voice on Trevor. She didn't seduce him with her eyes like she did with Eli.

His grin quickly faltered when Trevor reached for Grace and kissed the back of her hand. "And what brings you two together in this empty corridor?"

"She was teaching me to dance."

"Ah, yes, the ball is coming up." Trevor walked in a slow circle around them. His stalking left Eli feeling defensive, his heart hammering in his chest and his hands clenched into fists. He felt compelled to attack first before Trevor could.

Trevor placed a hand on Grace's arm, and Eli fought back the urge to break his fingers. "I happen to be an excellent dancer, Grace. Perhaps I could show you at the ball."

"She has a dance partner already," Eli said before he could stop himself. Until five seconds ago, he had no desire to do this wretched thing. Watching Grace dance with dozens of suitors sounded like his personal hell, but Trevor brought out the devil in him. The soft smile on Grace's lips told him she was pleased to hear his mind had changed and he *would* be escorting her to the ball.

Trevor turned to Grace. "Is that so?"

Grace pulled her arm out of Trevor's grip and moved to stand beside Eli. "I'm afraid so. You'll have to find another woman to take to the ball."

"Perhaps. But you will save me a dance. After all, it would be rude of you to only dance with one suitor"—he eyed Eli with a look of disdain, like he'd just bitten into a rotten angelfruit—"especially one so unlikely to win the Rite."

Eli didn't bother to correct Trevor. He had no intention of entering the Rite, but he also didn't want Trevor anywhere near Grace. His eyes were crazed and terrifying. There was a monster hidden within his body, just waiting for the opportunity to sink its talons into Grace.

Like hell would Eli let that happen.

"We'll see," Eli said, taking Grace by the hand and guiding her from the ballroom, leaving Trevor glaring after them.

Chapter Twenty-Eight

ALI

It was amazing what just a couple weeks of healthy eating and physical activity could do for a person. Ali was putting on weight again and returning to a healthier version of herself. The long treks to the river became easier as her muscles grew.

Even mentally, she felt better. The thought of approaching the running body of water didn't leave her paralyzed like it had at the start of their journey. It still terrified her to think of wading into a vast body of water, but she could at least carry out her duty of bringing fresh water back to the farm without having an anxiety attack.

Breakfast came and went, and Ali helped Meredith and Cole with the dishes. Meredith reminded Ali a lot of her own mother. Some days she would learn new recipes while Meredith recanted stories of her life on the farm. She had a dry sense of humor that made Ali laugh until her sides hurt. It felt good to laugh again.

After they cleaned up breakfast, it was all hands on deck as they worked to bundle various crops. All the extra produce and grains they'd accumulated in the past few days would be taken to town for the convoy coming through to do some trading. They'd head that way tonight and stay at the local inn so they could set up their cart first thing in the morning.

Alan had taught Nik how to skin some of the animals Cole hunted so their hides could be sold as well. Meredith folded them neatly and organized them in baskets based on size.

As the sun set behind the mountains, they attached the Kennedys' wagon to two of their horses. It was brimming with goods. Who would buy all this? It seemed like far too much for anyone to travel with.

Alan and Cole led the horses while the rest of their group walked beside the wagon. It was a peaceful journey to town, accompanied only by chirping crickets and the twitter of birds.

"How far is it to town?" Sam asked. Ali sensed unease in his voice, and she thought she knew why. Most days the injury to his leg seemed entirely unnoticeable, but after his confession by the stream she wondered if the long trek would be hard on him. Nik had suggested he stay back, but Sam insisted on coming along. He didn't want to miss out on seeing the town. He also didn't want to be left alone at the farm, and Ali couldn't blame him. The darkness and silence in the middle of nowhere was unsettling, even with company.

"It takes about an hour with the cart. Less if we didn't have to bring it."

"Do you go to town often?" Ali asked. This was the first time the Kennedys had made a trip since Ali and the others had arrived.

"Alan and I used to go more frequently when we were younger, but now we have so much to do on the farm. It's hard to take a day off for ourselves. Now we only go when merchants are coming through."

As the last bit of daylight faded, torches blazed in the distance. They weren't the only ones to arrive early. Ali had clearly underestimated the size of the event.

The town was made up of a dozen buildings that formed a square around the town center—a plaza that was now full of wooden carts of various shapes and sizes. Some of them had tarps thrown over them so she couldn't see what was inside. Others were open and had taken the risk that rain might damage their wares.

She peered into one and noticed vegetables of every shade of green one could possibly imagine. Another had tan wool blankets folded and stacked high, held down by leather straps attached to either side of the cart.

There were no other roads besides the ones leading in and out of town. Harrodsburg was entirely comprised of the small town square they now stood in.

There was only one inn, and at least a dozen other carts were already scattered around the back side of the building, spilling out from the town square where there was no longer room to park.

A man with a gray beard and a straw hat greeted them before handing Alan a key. Apparently, he'd been expecting the Kennedys and already had a room reserved for them.

"It's a full house," the man said in a gruff but friendly voice. "You've got the last room. The family suite, just like you requested."

"Thank you, Sully."

The first-floor pub was rowdy and full of energy, something Ali sorely lacked. It was so crowded that most people stood around tables littered with tankards of lager and half eaten bowls of soup. The air was hot and took Ali's breath away. None of them had the energy to hang out with the rambunctious crowd, so they made their way to the staircase leading up to the suites.

Their room was on the second floor, third door on the right. It looked like it could've been a small apartment at one time over the bar below. One room had a full-size bed, which Meredith and Alan took. The other room had two twin beds. When Cole tried to claim one, Meredith scolded, "You can sleep on the couch."

That left one bed for Sam and the other for Nik and Ali to share. The only way to fit comfortably was to sleep on their sides with Nik hugging her waist. Despite the noise from downstairs, she dozed off faster than expected, safe and secure in Nik's arms.

Ali woke the next morning to the smell of breakfast cooking in the kitchens below—sausage with a hint of bitter coffee.

Sully and his employees had cooked an entire buffet of eggs, grilled sausage and ham, vegetables, and potatoes for all the incoming travelers. They ate a quick meal and then followed Alan to the cart to set up shop.

In the morning light, Ali could see the rest of the small village. The town itself wasn't much to see. There was a small fountain in the center of a cobblestone square. The fountain was dried up, but the marble statue was still picturesque—an angel with intricate wings staring down at the town with a wistful look. A gown fell over her shoulders and swept into the basin, where water would have flowed once upon a time.

"The town's protector," Meredith said when she caught Ali staring.

"It's beautiful."

"She's said to bring about prosperity. Rather pertinent considering our business here." Meredith gestured to the carts and crowds gathered in the town square. Indeed, it was odd that such a small town had assembled such a large trade fair.

"She's doing her job well." Ali smiled.

Around the town square were a handful of small log buildings with wooden tables set up outside. Each table displayed an assortment of goods for trade or purchase. The wool blankets she'd seen the night before were now hanging on a line, displaying the dyed patterns for all to see. Next door, a florist was trimming stems and arranging flowers in a blue and purple vase. Beside him, a woman had a vat of hot wax that she dipped string in, creating soft white candlesticks. Everywhere Ali looked, her senses were overwhelmed with the fair's sounds and smells.

People who didn't have a permanent shop for selling, like the Kennedys, simply parked their carts around the outskirts of the town square and chatted with other villagers as they made their way around the square.

"Go on. Go explore." Meredith slipped a small bag of coins into Nik's hand.

He looked at her with surprise. "You don't have to—"

"Nonsense. You've been helping on the farm for the past two weeks now. Go spoil yourselves."

They stood there, still uncertain about taking money from the woman who was already giving them a home.

"Don't get used to it. I can't afford to give you much, but this is a special occasion. It's your first time in town; you should enjoy yourselves."

"Thank you," Nik said, and Ali and Sam murmured their gratitude.

The first few stops next to the Kennedys cart were full of more produce. They quickly passed those by and moved on to a shop with rainbows of fabric on display. Blankets, scarfs, sweaters and more were woven together with vibrant threads.

Ali was picking through the many options when Sam gasped and shuffled to the next stand.

"Well, we all know what Sam wants," Nik commented.

A paper supply shop was set up. They had minimal offerings, but Sam was already admiring a small notebook. Nik didn't think twice before pulling a few coins from the bag and handing them to Sam. "You heard Meredith. Spoil yourself."

Sam's excitement over holding a new notebook was contagious. They jumped around from shop to shop, trying to find the perfect items. Nik found a small leather sheath for his hunting knife. His old one was wearing thin.

Ali had a harder time choosing. She was holding up a nightgown in a gorgeous shade of blue when Nik came up behind her. "I don't think so."

She inspected the piece again. "Why not?"

His hands wrapped around her waist, and he pressed into her backside. "Because *that* is incredibly thin and if you wear that in front of me, Sam will never forgive me for fucking you on every inch of that little old house."

Ali snickered and put the nightgown back on the hanger. "You're probably right."

She continued to browse the clothing items while Nik and Sam moved on to the next cart. Everything was so beautiful and expertly crafted. She couldn't picture herself wearing any of it. Her clothing was all so practical.

Eventually, she gave up and moved on to find Nik and Sam chatting with the cart owner. As she got closer, she noticed Nik holding a small wooden box in his hands.

"What did you find?"

He turned to her, and she studied the box, carefully crafted with metal hinges and a hand carved design on top. When Nik opened it, she felt hot tears prick her eyes. Ten spools of thread organized in a rainbow lined the bottom of the box and on top, slots were created intentionally to hold a dozen needles.

It looked so similar to the one her mother had once owned. She could easily recall the way her mother would sit at the kitchen table, mending the shirts and that Ali ripped carelessly while playing as a child or working when she was older. Ali had never had much patience for such a talent, but now she wished she'd spent more time at the table with her mother, sewing her own clothes. She'd never get that time back.

A tear fell, and she quickly wiped it away. "It's perfect."

"I didn't mean to make you cry," Nik said, clearly alarmed. He rubbed her shoulder and tilted his head to look down into her eyes. "Are you all right?"

Ali nodded. "Yes, I'm just...overwhelmed. I'm sorry. It just reminds me so much of my mother."

Nik's mouth parted. "I didn't know."

She'd never told him why she'd picked up sewing and embroidery back in Rysburg. To him it was just a hobby, but to her it meant so much more.

He closed the small box. "We don't have to get—"

"No!" She grabbed for the box. "It's perfect."

Their next stop was a bakery. Vanilla, cinnamon and nutmeg permeated the air before they even approached the cart. A young woman was busy taking care of all the guests that had stopped by her cart. It was easily one of the busiest stops in the courtyard.

"We don't have to—" Ali started to say, knowing it would be a while before the woman could help them.

Nik grabbed her by the wrist. "We're getting something. I know you're dying to try something sweet."

He winked, and Ali was reminded of one of their earliest encounters with chocolate cake. It was hard to say no to that. Sam didn't notice their exchange, too keen on browsing the remaining items. It looked like half the cart had already been sold.

It didn't take long for Ali to choose between the many breads, pies, scones, cookies, and more. A vanilla cupcake with a light buttercream frosting called her name. Nik chose the same while Sam grabbed a chocolate chip cookie.

They found a spot on the ground under an oak tree on the outskirts of town to sit and take a break from the crowd.

"His birthday is coming up," Ali said suddenly.

Nik and Sam exchanged a look before turning to her expectantly.

"Eli. His birthday is in a few days. My mom used to help me bake a cake each year for his birthday. I wonder how he's celebrating this year...or *if* he even is."

She tried not to consider that he might be dead. She refused to believe in that outcome. Until she was proven wrong, she was sure Eli was alive somewhere, celebrating his birthday with new friends in a safe place—just like they'd found on the farm.

Again, Nik and Sam exchanged a troubled look. Nik placed his cupcake in his lap and ran his hand up her back, pausing to caress the back of her neck. "I'm sorry you can't be with him to celebrate. I'm sure he's thinking of you, too."

Ali looked into his eyes and found nothing but sincerity. Sometimes his love caught her completely off guard. That he would put aside his feelings toward Eli? His love was unhesitating.

She scooted closer to him and kissed his cheek and then his lips, tasting the lingering frosting. "Thank you."

As the evening wore on, most of the villagers and merchants made their way toward a bonfire behind the inn with scattered tables surrounding it. The place was packed. Sam spotted a few seats left at a table, but they'd be forced to share it with two other women.

As they walked up beside the table, Sam asked, "Is it okay if we sit here?"

"Of course," the woman on the right said with a welcoming smile. Her partner remained silent but gave a nod of approval before taking a swig from a bottle.

Ali and Sam took a seat while Nik went to grab them some drinks.

"You don't look familiar. Are you from around here?" the woman on the right asked.

"Um, no. We wound up here a couple weeks ago. I'm Ali and this is Sam. My boyfriend, Nik, is the one who went to get drinks. Are you two from here, then?"

The woman on the left finally spoke. "We're just passing through."

Her friend tsked. "Don't mind my wife Isabel. She gets grumpy when she's tired. It's nice to meet you, Ali. Sam. I'm Genna."

Nik returned just in time to catch her name. He sat their bottles down on the table and slid onto the bench next to Ali. "What did I miss?"

"We were just getting to know Genna and Isabel." Ali gestured toward their new acquaintances. "If you're not from here, I'm guessing you came to trade?"

Genna was the one to answer. Clearly Isabel wasn't very talkative. "We stop by pretty frequently. It's a convenient place to trade while we travel."

"Do you travel a lot?" Sam asked.

"All the time. We don't really have a permanent residence, but we like it that way." Genna turned to Isabel and gave her a loving peck on the cheek. Isabel looked on the verge of rolling her eyes, but she refrained for her wife's sake.

"So you are just...constantly on the move?" Ali asked. It sounded exhausting. She'd only experienced that for a few weeks and had hated every second. How did they go without a bed? Or a kitchen?

"Yes. There's so much of this world to explore. We also assist in trading with some of the surrounding towns, so that keeps us busy. The locals are always happy to give us a place to stay and freshen up, plus a hearty meal."

"And what about you?" Isabel asked. "Where are you from?"

"Nowhere near here," Ali said with a sigh. Thinking about home or even Rysburg put her in a bad mood. She sipped from her drink and listened as Sam asked more questions and Genna eagerly told stories about their life in the wilderness. Ali looked around at the crowd gathered around the fire. So far she hadn't seen anyone that even remotely resembled Eli. She should've known better than to get her hopes up. Finding him here had always been a long shot.

After an hour, Cole came to find them. It was time to head back to the cabin.

"It was nice chatting with you," Genna said. "We should get going too."

She turned to Isabel and said, "We have to travel to the meeting point bright and early tomorrow morning. The Coyotes are expecting us the day after next."

Ali turned her head so quickly, she thought she felt her neck crack. Surely she had misheard. "I'm sorry. What did you just say?"

"What? About the Coyotes?" Genna shook her head in amusement. "Not like the animals. It's a group of people. That's just what they call themselves."

Ali couldn't swallow. It was like she forgot how. She just stood there staring at Genna and Isabel while her heart exploded into a million pieces. Nik's hand touched the small of her back, and she inhaled sharply.

Genna could tell something was off. "Do you know them?"

Since Ali had forgotten how to form sentences, Nik spoke for her. "We know of them. We have reason to believe a friend of ours is with them."

Isabel shifted in her seat. "Are you refugees?"

"Something like that," Nik lied. If these were friends of the Coyotes, then it was probably best they didn't know that Sam and Nik were from Rysburg.

Genna accepted his answer. "Any refugees would've been taken to Berland."

"Berland? Where is that?" Ali choked out. Sam stepped closer to her and placed a hand on her arm. If it weren't for Sam and Nik, her legs might give out.

Genna exchanged a look with Isabel, who seemed to give her a disapproving one in return. A silent conversation was exchanged between them before Genna spoke again. "We can take you there. We can't miss this meeting with the Coyotes, but after that we can come back and lead you there. It's only a three-day trip."

Ali's lips were dry. Her tongue felt swollen in her mouth.

"You would do that for us?" Nik asked.

"Sure. We're due to head south of Berland next week, so it's not too far out of the way to swing by here. We'll meet you here in a week."

"Thank you so much." Ali expressed her gratitude, but it didn't feel like enough. "Our friend...can you tell me if you know him? If you took him there?"

Genna nodded.

"His name is Eli. He's tall—"

"Eli?" Genna interrupted before Ali could fully describe him. She nudged Isabel with an elbow. "We know him. We took him to Berland about a month ago."

Ali clasped her hands to her mouth. Her entire world had been thrown off its axis. Just when she thought all hope was lost, two strangers had come along like an answered prayer. She sobbed into her hands.

"Thank you. Thank you." She wasn't sure if she was thanking the two women or the gods above, but either way, she would see Eli again.

Chapter Twenty-Nine

ELI

"I TOLD YOU THIS wasn't necessary," Eli moaned.

Grace had shown up at his door early in the morning before he'd even woken up. The banging on his door had startled him awake, and she'd pushed her way into his home before he could get a word out.

He should've known when she hadn't stayed the night on the eve of his birthday that she was up to something.

When she set a cake on his dining table, he laughed at her sense of urgency. Grace had sprung into party planning mode the second he'd let it slip that his birthday was coming up.

Step one—wake Eli up at the crack of dawn and overload him with sugar.

Grace searched for a knife in his kitchen drawers. "I know, I know. But you can't *not* celebrate your birthday, Eli."

She sliced into the cake and served him a piece. It was only when her eyes ran up and down his body that he realized he wasn't wearing a shirt and the shorts he slept in were thin and left little to the imagination.

It occurred to Eli at that moment that he was still semi-hard from a rather pleasant dream he'd been having before Grace had interrupted. A dream about Grace...

"Perhaps I could give you something else first?" she asked, suggestively eyeing his erection.

Eli let out a low hum. Honestly, he wasn't craving cake. Grace's lips, however...

He backed up until his knees hit the bed and sat down, leaning back on his hands.

Grace's eyes glittered with excitement. Blow jobs were hot, but it was even more of a turn on that Grace seemed to enjoy it as much as he did. Grace seemed to enjoy doing a lot of things to Eli, treating him like her sex toy, but he didn't mind in the slightest. She was *exactly* what he'd been needing to mend his broken heart.

She dropped the serving utensil on the table and abandoned the cake, wasting no time grabbing his shorts by the hem and pulling them down past his knees and to the floor.

She knelt between his legs and practically salivated at the sight of his thick cock, a drop of arousal already present at the tip. Her tongue darted out to taste him, and his head rolled back.

Grace left a long, sweet kiss on his head, pulling back to whisper, "One."

One what?

She kissed his dick again, swirling her tongue around him and dragging it up the underside. "Two."

His cock ached for her touch. For more of her and less of this teasing.

"Grace," he pleaded.

She covered him with her mouth, taking just a couple of his many inches. The heat of her made his balls tighten and his thighs tense.

More. More.

His cock left her mouth with a pop. "Three."

She gave him a wicked smile and continued to tease and taunt him with kisses of varying length and pressure. Some gentle, some that had him hitting the back of her throat. On and on until she reached twenty-four and Eli was struggling to breathe and fighting the urge to flip her on the bed and bury his cock inside her.

He needed twenty-five. Twenty-five kisses for his twenty-fifth birthday.

As if she could read his mind, she took as much of his length as she could and wrapped her hand around what remained, twisting her palm and dragging her mouth up and down his shaft. Her other hand cradled his balls, and Eli knew he wouldn't last much longer.

He twisted a hand in her hair, guiding her at the pace he needed while she sucked and licked and rubbed like she only lived to please him.

Eli rocked his hips, relentlessly fucking her mouth until she moaned. The vibration sent him over the edge, and he spent everything he had into her mouth. She swallowed as he pulled back, wiping her chin with the back of her hand.

"Happy birthday, Eli. I don't think the cake will taste nearly as good as you."

He cleared his throat and grabbed Grace by the forearms, pulling her up off the floor and into his lap. "Can I return the favor?"

She ran a hand through his hair, and he leaned into her palm. "Afraid not. We've got plans and we're already late. You should get dressed."

Eli didn't protest. As much as he'd love to lay Grace on his bed and spread her legs wide and run his tongue over her slit, he knew whatever she had planned would be worth it. Grace was thoughtful in everything she did.

Once he was fully clothed in jeans and a forest green T-shirt, he sat at the table and dug into his cake. It was ridiculously sweet to be eating first thing in the morning, but Grace had also brought two cups of black coffee to dampen the effects of the sugar. "Did you make this yourself?"

"Would you love it less if I said no?"

Eli shook his head. Grace didn't pretend to be an expert in the kitchen. Perks of growing up with personal chefs.

"It's the thought that counts," he replied. "What else is on the agenda today?"

"I told everyone to meet us at the entrance of the mountain. I have a surprise planned for you."

Eli raised a brow. He wasn't sure he liked the idea of a surprise, but Grace's excitement was contagious. He trusted that she knew the kinds of things he would like to do on his birthday. She'd already crossed off one.

She boxed up the remaining cake once he finished his slice and packed it in a bag, presumably to take along on their excursion. "Bring extra clothes."

Eli frowned. "What in the hell does that mean?"

Grace's smile was mischievous. "Don't look at me like that. I promise it'll be fun. You are wearing underwear, right?"

"What?"

She didn't answer and instead headed for the door. Eli rushed to grab a bag with an extra set of clothes, thankful he was in fact wearing underwear, and followed her out into the hall.

Theo, Heather, and Amaya were waiting for them in the grand entrance, looking exhausted but excited for whatever Grace had planned. Theo had a large bag and Heather was carrying a basket. Eli could only guess what was in either of those.

"Did you force everyone to wake up at the crack of dawn?" Eli asked.

"No," she said with a shrug. "I simply asked them to be here bright and early."

Eli waited. He sensed there was more to it than that.

"And then I told them if they weren't here, I would break their fingers."

Eli laughed. Grace might appear innocent and friendly on the outside, but she was not one to be messed with. He had no doubt that her friends had taken her warning seriously.

As he approached the group, there was a rumble of birthday wishes. It was a pleasant realization that this group had gathered to celebrate him. That over the course of a couple weeks, they had become his friends too.

"Ready?" Grace asked with too much pep. Eli swore she never slept and yet somehow had more energy than all of them combined.

Grace led the way, and the rest trudged behind her. There was a bite of cold in the air as the sun struggled to make it over the tops of the mountains. They didn't come across a single person as they walked through town. Even the shops still had their doors closed this early in the morning.

"Happy birthday," Theo said with a pat on Eli's back.

"Thanks. Do you have any idea where we're going?"

"Yep."

"How is that fair?"

Theo shrugged. "Grace wanted to surprise you, and I have no intention of getting on her bad side. My sister seems nice, but it's always the nice ones you have to look out for."

Eli thought of broken fingers and couldn't hold back his smile. "You're probably right."

They came across a section of the river Eli was familiar with. A light breeze rustled the tall grass on the edges of the water and a frog leapt into the stream as they passed. He'd spent a lot of time alone here with Grace, but she didn't stop there. She led them onto the trail that ascended higher into the mountain. It went past the waterfall she'd taken him to on one of their first horse rides and deeper into the trees. Their trunks grew taller and thicker, leaving Eli feeling disoriented. He could no longer tell which way led back to the mountain.

Where in the hell was she taking him?

They were in no rush. They leisurely weaved their way through the forest and up the mountain, laughing at Theo and Grace's familial banter and listening to Amaya hum a tune. The trees began to thin and the sun broke through, warming Eli's skin and reflecting off the nearby stream.

When Grace finally stopped, Eli found himself standing in front of a small pool of water, where a handful of waterfalls no taller than five feet fed into it. It seemed they had reached the springs that fed the river. The mist from the waterfalls reflected a rainbow, and the pool itself was a crystal clear aqua. It was the most majestic thing he'd ever seen, and he'd seen a lot of things since coming to Berland.

"Do you like it?" Grace asked, beaming with delight. The trees were scarce around the pool and the sun had risen, casting a warm glow on her skin. She somehow shimmered more than the water.

"It's beautiful," he said without taking his eyes off her. Had she really planned this just for him? It didn't seem real that someone would go to such lengths to make him happy. He'd known Grace was beautiful from the moment he laid eyes on her, but the more time he spent with her, the more he realized how beautiful she was on the inside as well.

Theo unpacked his bag. He pulled out towels, one for each of them, and then he tossed his clothes on the ground and ran to the edge of the pool, jumping into the air and pulling his legs in tight. He hit the surface with a splash, and Amaya and Heather followed shortly after.

When Grace began to remove her sundress, Eli felt an impulse to look away, but one look at her red thong left him immobile. She slid her dress over her head to reveal a matching bra and Eli's mouth went dry. Her ass was so squeezable and although he appreciated her effort to surprise him, he desperately wanted to take her back home so he could cup those ass cheeks in his palms and bury his face between her breasts.

She stood there while he gawked at her like a fool. Her confidence was astounding and mesmerizing too.

Grace pulled her hair back into a ponytail and gave him that wicked smirk of hers. "Are you just going to stand there watching? Or are you getting in too?"

She turned and took three long steps toward the pool before jumping in. When her head came back up, she faced Eli with a look that said *come and get me.*

Eli grabbed the back of his shirt and pulled it over his head. He threw it toward the bundle of towels and tried not to think too much as he stripped down to his briefs and tossed his pants aside as well. The need for underwear made more sense now. He jumped into the water with a huge splash, and Grace was there to greet him when he resurfaced.

She flicked water in his face and then wrapped an arm around his neck. The water was shallow enough that Eli could stand and hold on to her waist while she playfully clung to his body. He was close enough to see the water droplets glistening on her eyelashes and feel her breasts pressed against his chest. He stared into her eyes, admiring the way they blended from green to caramel. Standing with her in his arms, they were the only two people that existed.

At least, until her brother climbed out of the pool just so he could jump off the rocky edge again. He landed in the water beside them, sending a wave over their heads. They both laughed it off and swam in circles around the small, private pool.

By the time lunchtime arrived, Eli's cheeks were turning pink. They laid out a blanket, and he found out what was in the basket Heather had brought—a picnic consisting of sandwiches, mixed fruit, and wine. It appeared Heather had packed at least a bottle per person.

Amaya unscrewed the top of one bottle and took a sip straight from the container. Guess they didn't think glasses were necessary.

The sound of suction rang out as Amaya lowered the bottle. She wiped her lips with the back of her hand and passed the bottle to Grace. Then she turned her attention to Grace's brother. "So, Theo…who are you taking to the ball?"

Theo was just about to bite into his sandwich but paused. "Why do you ask?"

"Just curious," Amaya said.

Grace laughed and reached into the basket to grab her sandwich. "They have a bet."

"What kind of bet?" Theo asked with sincere curiosity.

"About which one of them you're going to ask to go with you."

Amaya and Heather both shot daggers at Grace before exchanging a scheming look.

"Who wins if I ask both of you?"

Eli felt a bit sorry for Theo. He had the looks of a heartthrob, but he didn't seem interested in either of Grace's friends. He may have been a flirt, but it was obvious nothing serious would ever happen between him and Amaya or Heather. Maybe he was still thinking about Talia, although Eli didn't get the feeling he was serious about her either.

Heather deflated. "That's cheating, Theo."

"Sorry, ladies. I'm afraid I can't take either of you. I'll be out of town."

"Liar. Mom would never send you on a mission during a festival. Especially not this one," Grace said.

"This festival season is going to last months. We can't just stop doing business because you've got to find a spouse. Besides, maybe I'm not traveling for business. Maybe it's for pleasure."

Grace tossed a berry at Theo's head, but he swatted it away. "Fine. You're right. I will be here, and I will be at your silly dance. But I plan to go alone. Sorry, ladies."

After lunch, Theo, Amaya, and Heather returned to the water. They chased him around the pool, and he playfully dunked their heads under the surface while they tried their best to drag him underneath. Eli remained on the shore with Grace.

"Tell me about this," Grace said, pointing to the tattoo on his rib cage. She was lying on a blanket next to him, propped up on one elbow while he sat facing the pool. He shivered as her fingertips traced the lines of ink.

Eli shrugged. "It's just a bird. I thought it looked cool, so I got it." He smiled at the man he'd been back then. Life had been so simple and carefree. Marking his skin with art had been just a way to pass the time.

"And these?" she asked.

Eli looked down at his chest. "These are my mom and dad's birthdays. These are waves. I got them because they looked like the lake back home and then the sun is setting on the horizon here. See?" He pointed as he described each one.

He got to the moon under his collarbone and felt the weight on his chest. He didn't much feel like explaining that was the one he'd gotten with Ali. Eli simply told her, "This is the moon."

Grace rolled closer to him. "What about these?" she asked, looking at his back.

"That's just...a mess," he said with a sad smile. There had once been intricate designs inked into his skin, but now they were mangled with scarred flesh. They didn't resemble anything anymore.

Grace seemed to note the change in his demeanor. "I didn't mean to pry," she said, moving to sit up next to him.

"Don't worry about it." He laid his hand on her knee and traced the inside of her thigh with his fingers. Her skin was so soft and velvety. Eli quickly glanced at the pool where the other three were still preoccupied, then placed a gentle kiss on her neck, just below her ear. "Thank you for this, Grace. I couldn't imagine a better birthday."

She tossed her hair over her shoulder, and he caught her sweet scent. "I still have one more surprise for you."

Her eyes raked over his body, and Eli immediately knew she had something devious planned. Her devilish behavior must've been wearing off because surprisingly, he was ready for whatever it was.

Chapter Thirty

ELI

Grace tugged on Eli's hand. He had assumed they would spend the evening in bed with his wrists tied to the posts again. Or maybe she'd let him tie her up this time. So he was surprised when she had shown up at his door wearing a thin black garment that was tied in the front and handed him a mask.

"What is this for?" he asked.

"You'll see."

Then she urged him to follow her out of the mountain. Where was she leading him this time? What more did this town have to offer that he hadn't seen yet?

The sky was already dark when Grace led him toward the edge of town, to a fork in the path. The left would've taken them to the oxbow lake, but Grace went to the right. As they headed further down the path, the light from town faded and they walked in darkness.

"Are you bringing me out here to kill me?" Eli joked. A bird chose that moment to caw, adding to the chilling atmosphere.

"Of course not."

Eli followed Grace for several more minutes. He was just beginning to wonder how far they were going when he spotted a warm light in the distance. It grew as they got closer, and he made out the windows of a brick building.

The building had no name or sign, no indication of what lay beyond the front door. The light came from the windows on the first floor, but curtains covered the windows on the second floor. Music and chatter came from inside the building.

"Is this a bar?"

"Something like that. Put it on." She pulled out her own mask and placed it over her face. The black mask matched her cloak but had speckles of gold scattered around the eyes.

"Why do I need this?" Eli asked again as he examined the face covering. Grace didn't answer him.

"Turn around," she said, and he did as she requested. "You'll have to squat. I can hardly reach you."

Eli bent down so Grace could tie the mask around his face. It covered his eyes and part of his nose but left his mouth bare. He stood once she was finished and turned back to find her eyeing him with a wide smile.

Somehow the mask made her eyes and red lips stand out even more. In the dull light, her eyes were the only thing that sparkled. And those lips…Those lips were a temptation Eli could never resist.

Grace opened the door, and a woman met the two of them, wearing what appeared to be a silky black robe. Eli couldn't help but notice the way it dipped between her breasts, showing far more skin than most women were comfortable with in public.

He cleared his throat and looked to Grace for answers. She avoided eye contact and waited for the woman to speak.

"Welcome to Azalea's," she said with a voice like a siren, light and alluring.

The woman greeted the two of them with an unusual familiarity. It didn't matter that they wore masks. The woman acted as if she could see right through them, and that Grace and Eli were two of her most important patrons.

They followed the woman from the entry through a dimly lit parlor, passing a few small alcoves half covered in purple velvet drapes and up a small staircase. The dark plush carpet turned to hardwood as she directed them to their own private table. As Eli sat, he looked around at the other patrons seated at small tables lit only by candlelight. They were all unrecognizable behind masks of varying shades and styles. Another woman came by to take their drink orders.

Eli nearly choked on his own spit when his eyes caught on the black lingerie the woman was wearing. The only thing she was wearing.

"A glass of wine for the lady?" she asked as if Grace were a regular and knew exactly what she'd want.

"Yes, please. And he'll take one too."

When she turned to retrieve their drinks, Eli stared at Grace.

She let out a soft laugh. "What?"

"What was that? What is this place?"

"It's part two of your birthday present, Eli."

He leaned in close and whispered so no one could hear. "She wasn't wearing any clothes, Grace."

Grace further closed the distance between them and whispered against Eli's ear, "I know."

At that point, Grace untied the belt around her long black coat. It fell open, revealing a skin-tight dress that barely covered Grace's ass. It was as if the black lace was stuck directly to her skin, but upon closer inspection, it was attached to a nude fabric, giving the dress a see-through effect. It was *nothing* like any of the other gowns Eli had seen Grace wear. But there was one thing he knew with absolute clarity—this one was his favorite.

He suddenly became aware of music playing as two women appeared on a raised platform in the center of the room. They wore elaborate costumes of fuchsia, turquoise, and gold and matching masks. Costumes that left very little to the imagination. But they sparkled and the entire room was mesmerized as they began to dance to the music.

Grace swayed to the melody and every so often watched Eli, smiling as if to make sure he was enjoying himself too.

"Are you allowed to be here?" he asked. "I'm surprised the future Lady of Berland is comfortable being seen in such a place."

"I'm *allowed* to do whatever I want."

He tilted his head to the side, and she brushed him off. This didn't seem like the place for proper people to spend their free time. He almost laughed at the thought of Ellen or Ben visiting Azalea's. He somehow doubted they would be okay with this.

"Relax. Even if someone recognized us with the masks, everyone here is very tight-lipped. No one will admit to seeing a single soul here because that would mean admitting they were here, too. It's a code of honor"—she grinned—"or dishonor that we all keep very sacred."

Their waitress brought back their drinks and Grace stood momentarily and sat back down in Eli's lap, her side to his chest and her legs crossed and draped over his right knee. He wrapped his arm around her waist and rested his palm on her thigh. Every movement made him painfully aware of how short her dress was and how plump her ass felt. Was it abnormally hot in this bar or was it just the heat he felt at the touch of her skin?

She wrapped her arm around his neck and toyed with the neckline of his black shirt.

"What are you doing?" he asked as she nestled into his lap. He didn't think it was a coincidence that she kept rubbing against him.

"Getting comfortable." She sipped on her wine and kept her eyes on the stage. The two women carried on with their choreographed routine and were eventually joined by a few more dancers in sparkling lingerie.

Grace wiggled in his lap again, and Eli's hips jerked. He gripped her hips and held her in place. "Stop doing that," he growled.

"Doing what?"

He couldn't recall the last time he'd gotten a boner in public. Probably when he was a young teen. If she didn't knock it off...

Grace shifted again, and there was no mistaking the erection she'd nudged with her ass. Her smile widened; she'd gotten exactly what she'd wanted.

"Grace," he rasped.

"Yes, Eli?" She ran a finger over his jawline and then brushed her thumb over his lip. His hold on her hips tightened.

"What are you doing?"

"Do you want me to stop?" She leaned into him, and he glanced down. Something lodged in his throat. He could see straight into her dress...could see her perfect breasts and instantly wanted to pull the fabric down to reveal them in their entirety. His cock stirred again against his will.

He struggled to speak. "I didn't say that."

Her hand was now traveling down his abs. He shuddered when her cold fingers slid past the waistband of his pants. She was dangerously close to touching his hard length. And he was dangerously close to letting her.

Becoming incredibly self-conscious of their behavior, Eli looked around the room. He spotted one man with his hand up his partner's shirt, playing with her breasts as she kissed his neck. On the other side of the room, a man was on his knees before his partner. Her skirt kept certain things hidden, but there was no mistaking what was happening as she moaned and squeezed her eyes closed.

Holy fuck.

Grace stared at him with an inquisitive look. It was as if she could read his mind and was waiting for permission to continue. He shouldn't be doing this, *especially* not with Grace. What if people recognized them? By now, Theo, Heather, and Amaya knew there was something going on. It was hard to hide from their closest friends, but the rest of Berland was in the dark about their secret affair. What if they found out, and it ruined her prospects for the Rite?

The sickening feeling rumbled in the pit of his stomach. It happened every time he thought of the Rite, but he chalked it up to not wanting Grace to end up with an asshole like Trevor. He felt protective of her, even if she would never belong to him.

Grace was still looking at him, patiently waiting for a reaction. If she didn't care about people watching them, then neither did he. He slid a tentative hand between her thighs. He only made it a few inches before she grabbed him by the wrist and shook her head.

He gave her a questioning look. The music had grown louder and some of the dancers were now mingling in the crowd. Grace's voice was warm against his ear. "It's your birthday. This is for you."

Grace adjusted once again. This time she turned around to face him, straddling his lap with just enough space to unzip his pants. Her skirt rolled up to her hips, and he stifled a moan at the sight of her matching lacy underwear. He didn't think she could hear him over the sound of the music.

Eli jumped and looked around the room again when Grace gently tugged at his jeans. Everyone was too busy doing their own thing to notice the tent in his briefs. Too entertained to watch as Grace rubbed his dick over the cotton of his underwear.

He groaned as she cupped his balls in the palm of her hand, massaging him gently. He couldn't believe this was happening.

Grace nodded to someone behind him, and he turned to look over his shoulder. Two of the dancers were eyeing them with curiosity. He wasn't sure what silent command Grace had given them until one produced a black leather bind and held his hands together behind the chair.

His eyes were wide as he turned back to Grace, and her shoulders shook with a small laugh. "Is this okay?" Her question was sincere, and it calmed his pounding heart. Until her fingers slid up and down the outline of his shaft and he inhaled sharply again, pulling on his newly bound wrists.

"Better than okay."

He could sense the two women behind him moving. One hand lightly touched his neck, sending shivers up his spine. She began to pepper kisses near the collar of his shirt. Two seconds later, the other's lips were hot on the shell of his ear while her hand drifted down over his pec. His cock was aching to be released from his underwear now. He was throbbing in anticipation of Grace's fingers wrapping around his length.

The surrounding air smelled like vanilla and alcohol. It left him feeling lightheaded and weightless. There were so many hands on him...so many mouths...but he was only focused on one woman.

Grace pulled the front of his briefs down enough for his cock to spring free. Rather than immediately grip him, she took her time touching and teasing his thighs and the lower part of his stomach. Anywhere—every-where—but the place that needed her attention most.

Eli let out a frustrated groan. Grace really enjoyed torturing him. He rocked his hips, hoping to make contact, but she continued to evade him.

It wasn't lost on him that he was being pleasured by three women with his dick hard and exposed in a room full of strangers. Eli had never envisioned this in his wildest dreams and yet he'd never been more turned on.

At last, Grace trailed her index finger down the side of his cock. It took everything in him not to explode from her simple touch. There were still mouths sucking on his earlobe, his throat, his shoulder. All of that pleasure seemed to concentrate in one area—the tip of his cock where Grace was rubbing her thumb.

She leaned forward, and he felt the soft lace of her underwear brush against him, eliciting a sense of bliss he'd never experienced before. He was so close—so close to being deep inside her.

His mind was empty of all other thoughts. It didn't matter that there were people watching. It didn't matter that they shouldn't be doing this in public. What mattered was Grace's hand sliding the pre-cum over the tip of his cock. What mattered was Grace's pussy and the thin piece of fabric that kept him from feeling it for himself. That kept him from sliding into her.

Eli strained against the chair, and the leather restraint dug into his wrists. It should've hurt, but all he felt was bliss.

Grace was stroking him lazily with a wicked grin. One of the women leaned in to kiss his collarbone and he jerked out of the way. He didn't want her to obstruct his view. He wanted to watch Grace and the way she delighted in touching him.

Her cheeks were tinged with pink, and she squeezed her left breast with a free hand. One of the women stepped toward Grace and sucked on her neck, too. If Eli didn't know better, he would've thought she was enjoying this as much as he was. He didn't know if he should be turned on or jealous that the woman got to taste Grace's skin while he was held back.

Their eyes locked, and she tugged him harder and harder. Faster and faster until every muscle in his lower half was tensed. He could hardly breathe and as she squeezed him tighter, it was like she was squeezing the breath out of his lungs.

Eli's legs began to shake, and his jaw trembled. He clenched it and tried to keep his composure, but Grace was relentless. Moments later he was gasping for breath as he came undone in her hands.

Her eyes were lit with fire as she watched him explode. She was a devilish woman.

The two dancers backed away and left him stunned, breathing heavily with Grace perched in his lap. She wore a victorious grin, and he couldn't help but grin back at her.

⁕⁕⁕⁕⁕ ⁕⁕⁕⁕⁕

The night presented itself with many more drinks and even more voyeuristic opportunities. He'd tried to slip his hand between her thighs once more while she watched another couple strip down to nothing. He'd tried to move his hands over her breasts as they watched two dancers combine their bodies in a position he'd never seen before. Grace refused all of his advances even after almost a whole bottle of wine.

She reiterated, "This is *your* birthday, Eli."

"Well, if it's *my* birthday, then I think I should call the shots," he slurred back.

"What's your next birthday wish, then?"

He'd never been so sloppy drunk in his life, but Grace made him feel safe and free to be entirely himself. "I wish to suck on your nipples." His head lolled between her breasts, and he kissed her warm skin.

Grace laughed and propped his head up. "I think it's time for bed, Eli."

"Mm-hmm," he agreed.

"Not *that* kind of bed. You need sleep...and some water."

Standing outside of his home, he fumbled for the key in his jacket pocket.

"Are you sure you don't want to stay?" he asked, tucking a stray curl behind her ear. She was fucking gorgeous. Her dark hair and beautiful eyes, more brown than green in this light, were mesmerizing.

"Not tonight."

"Right." There was a tightening in his chest as he turned the doorknob. "Might as well get used to sleeping alone again."

He didn't know why he'd said it. It slipped out before he could stop it. Curse that angelfruit wine. He felt like an absolute idiot and when her ever-present smile faltered, he wanted to kick himself. He immediately wanted to take it back.

She played with the tie of her cloak nervously. When she spoke, it was little more than a whisper. "For what it's worth...if I could choose..." She hesitated while he leaned against the door frame. "I would've chosen you."

Eli watched her walk away, down the hall to her own home. Then he flopped down on his bed, waiting for the room to stop spinning. His skin was hot as he pulled off his shirt and stripped out of his pants. He was so angry with himself for ruining the moment. Grace had planned the perfect day, and he'd fucked it up.

He nestled into his blankets and then a smile appeared on his face. *She would've chosen him.* He'd only begun sleeping with Grace as a way to get over Ali, to move on from someone who hadn't chosen him. He realized with a twinge of guilt that he hadn't thought of Ali since the trip to Jellico.

But Grace was beautiful, smart, funny, kind...and crazy in the best way. It was impossible to think of anyone else when he was with her.

And she would've chosen him.

Chapter Thirty-One

ELI

IT TOOK SEVERAL DAYS for Eli's pounding headache to subside and even longer for his cheeks to stop turning crimson every time he ran into Grace. Just thinking about their time at Azalea's made his dick hard. He didn't have any regrets about their public indecency. In fact, he very much wanted to return and experience more new things with Grace.

Neither of them had brought up the moment before she'd left him in a drunken stupor. It was easier for both of them to pretend he was too drunk to remember. He wasn't ready to stop seeing her, and he supposed she must've felt the same way. So they continued on as if nothing had been said.

Eli flipped back a page. He was supposed to be reading notes on his latest project for work, which was already difficult enough, but his mind was elsewhere. He hadn't digested a single thing written on the last ten pages.

After attempting to read the description under an illustration five more times, he finally decided to call it a day. Maybe he'd give studying another try later. He snapped the book shut and laid it on the table next to his bed.

Needing something else to do to keep him distracted, he grabbed his jacket and headed out toward town. There were still so many shops he hadn't visited yet, but he hoped to run into Grace.

Eli made a quick stop at the supply chamber on his way out. He grabbed a bundle of apples so he could feed Obsidian and the other horses. It had been a few days since he'd last visited them.

He stopped by the stables first and once the fruit was devoured, he took a few minutes to comb through Obsidian's black mane. Obsidian eyed him with a surly expression.

"I'm sorry," he said. "I know it's been too long since I've visited. Why don't I come back later tonight and we can go to the twisted tree, just you and me? How does that sound?"

It had been a while since Eli had visited his father's memorial, and he suddenly felt the urge to sit and tell his dad about the last few weeks and all about Grace. Well...maybe not *all* about her. Some things were not meant to be shared with a parent.

He was so confused. Grace was supposed to be a meaningless fling, but she felt far from it. She also was off limits. They had less than a month now until the Rite began and he lost her forever. He wished his dad was here to give him some of his famous guidance.

Obsidian huffed and stomped at the ground. Eli wasn't sure if that was a good sign or a bad one, but he patted the horse's back and he trotted off into the meadow.

His next stop was the bakery. He craved some of that cheesy bread he'd gotten on his first day in Berland and was delighted to see a fresh batch had just been set out. In addition to the bread, the owner convinced him to purchase a roll filled with cinnamon and sugar. It smelled amazing, so it was impossible to turn him down.

Next, he headed to the juice shop. There were a handful of people in line to order, so he had to wait his turn. While he was standing at the counter inspecting the various pitchers of juice, the door opened and a tiny bell chimed.

"Buy me a drink?"

Eli didn't have to turn around to recognize Grace's voice. "Sure. You choose, though. I can't decide between the apple or the citrus."

She came up behind him and peered over his shoulder, examining the colorful beverages on the counter. Her vanilla scent enticed him, and he was suddenly thirsty for something other than juice. He leaned into her, his cheek brushing against hers.

"Definitely the citrus," she said.

Once Eli paid for their drinks, they found a bench that faced the river where they could sit and enjoy their refreshments. He reluctantly shared his baked goods with her after some persuasion and pouty eyes that he couldn't resist.

"You make it really hard to say no," he told her.

"I know." She smiled and sipped from her cup, and Eli was drawn to her lips. Full and bright red. She licked the remains of her beverage from her upper lip and Eli was drawn to that too.

"Are we still on for dance lessons tomorrow?" she asked, pulling a bite from his loaf of bread. She popped it in her mouth and made a pleasured moan that had Eli blushing again.

He cleared his throat. "I wouldn't miss it. How many days until the big ball?"

Nineteen. He'd been counting the days himself, though he wouldn't admit it to her.

"A few more weeks." She tossed a crumb into the river and a fish popped up to nibble at it. A few more swam up beside it and tried to steal what little they could. A heavy sigh came from beside him.

"What's wrong?" Eli asked.

"Just thinking about how much my life is going to change. I always knew it would, but now that it's almost here—I don't know." She shook her head. "I just wish things were different."

Eli knew what she meant. Their lives couldn't be more different, but this wasn't how he'd expected his life to go either. There were a lot of things he would change if he could.

For starters, his dad would still be here. Ali would still be here. But maybe some changes were for the better. He never would've met Grace or realized just how big the world was if he'd never been dragged from Andus. He'd still be with Ali, and the vision didn't appeal to him as much as it once had.

Grace interrupted his thoughts. "It's not all bad, I guess."

Her tone suggested she was trying to convince herself more than him.

"I am excited to play a bigger role in leading Berland. I have a lot of ideas for our future. This place has been known as a safe haven, a sanctuary, and I have every intention of keeping it that way. I want to see my people prosper."

"What kinds of ideas?" Eli was genuinely curious about the things that excited Grace.

Her eyes lit up and not in that mischievous way like they did when she was trying to have things her way. It was a look of determination and pride in her abilities. "Did you know there are even more layers to Berland? We currently only occupy the first and second levels, but the compound runs deeper. The tunnels through the original mines are endless. Some of our researchers have said the resources down there are valuable and could be used for new discoveries or to replicate old inventions."

"That's amazing. Why haven't you?"

"The older council members don't think it should be a priority. They say it's too much work and not worth the risk. Before I was born, one of the tunnels collapsed on an exploration team and they've been abandoned ever since."

"But you think it's worth it?"

"I do. There's growing dissent that we can't keep growing at this pace. We're taking in too many people without the resources to provide everything they need. I think this would be a good solution to give people jobs and expand trade. Plus, we could extend the housing for more newcomers."

"Sounds like you've got it all planned out."

"Planning and doing are two different things. I need the council to respect me and take me seriously in order to accomplish anything. Some council members don't think my mother or I should be in charge at all. Eamon has done a great job of sewing discord."

"Why would he do that?"

She tilted her head and donned an irritated expression. "I don't think he likes women very much. But it's more than that too. Eamon believes that he is owed power. Many, many years ago and several generations back, Eamon's ancestor married a Lady of Berland. Together they had a son, but they never had a daughter. So when she passed away, her sister became the next Lady and Eamon's ancestors felt slighted by this. They felt the son should've become the next ruler, but that's not how things work here."

"So he thinks he has some sort of claim?"

"He does. And unfortunately, there are some people who would rather see a man in control. He's a smooth talker and does an excellent job at selling himself as the solution to all the problems we have in Berland, even if half of them are imaginary issues."

"How could anyone fall for his deception?"

Grace shrugged. "Berland may be a sanctuary, but we still have our own struggles. And it's easy to place that blame on a woman in charge. They see me and my mother as pacifists while Eamon boasts of strength and ambition. We look weak with our empathy for others where Eamon promises wealth and prosperity. He'd never be able to deliver, but they don't realize that."

"I hate that guy so much," Eli grunted.

Smiling, Grace responded, "Me too. But it doesn't matter. When my mother passes, I will be the next Lady of Berland, and Eamon can't do anything to stop it."

"But Trevor…"

"Trevor thinks he can control me, that a marriage will be their second chance at securing power, but he will find out just how wrong he is too."

The thought did little to calm Eli's nerves, but if anyone could handle herself, it was Grace. He smiled at her. "I think you'll be perfect for the job. You're the kindest, most compassionate person I've ever met. The people are lucky to have you."

Grace sipped from her cup and shot him a glance. Her cheeks turned pink when she realized he was watching her. "Why are you staring at me, Eli?"

He shrugged. Because she was stunning. Because he wanted to memorize her—every lash, every freckle across her nose, every sparkle of green in her brown eyes—before he lost her. "No reason."

Grace rolled her eyes, but she didn't question him again as they sat in silence—her watching the river float by and him watching her.

"What is that smell?" Grace's nose crinkled, and it would've been one of the cutest things Eli had seen, but the scent in the air burned his nostrils. It was familiar. Like a campfire, but too ashy.

Grace's eyes went wide. "Oh my God."

Before Eli could respond, Grace rushed past him, and he spun to see where she was headed in such a hurry. His stomach dropped as he watched a pillar of black smoke billow toward the sky in the distance.

He sprinted behind Grace, dodging between groups of people who had lined the street to point and gawk at the black cloud. A large crowd had already gathered in the town square, and shouts of confusion and chaos rang in the air. Grace and Eli pushed their way through the barrier of people until they were at the front of the crowd and could see what was happening.

Eli watched as one man entered the burning building and another man exited, bracing a woman around the waist while she coughed. Her face was black with soot and her clothing was singed.

"Clear the way! Clear the way!" An elderly woman waved at people to make room. Three more men came sprinting with buckets of water, but there was no way they could extinguish the fire with such little man-power. Eli watched as they soaked the ground and walls of the nearby buildings. They weren't trying to stop the fire, merely prevent it from spreading to the tightly spaced shops in town. Over and over again, they carried water from the nearby river.

He ran up to one of them. "How can I help?"

The man wiped sweat from his brow. "We haven't got any more buckets. There's nothing you can do here."

That didn't sit well with Eli. He couldn't just stand by and do nothing. He watched as another man jogged into the burning building and ran after him, Grace shouting his name as he disappeared into the darkness.

Smoke filled the entryway, and he could hardly see anything but the man in front of him. He covered his mouth and nose with his sleeve and squinted, following the man who seemed to know where he was going.

Eli had no idea what room they were in as he clumsily made his way over broken tables and chairs. A vase was smashed on the floor, singed petals scattered around it. Parts of the ceiling had already collapsed, and he looked up, wary of the blazing wood that could rain down on him at any moment.

A weak voice coughed. "Help! I'm here. Help!"

The man raced in the direction of the voice, Eli right on his heels.

There was a woman trapped in the corner of the room. A broken wooden beam was lodged across her left shoulder, and she was pushing against it with all her might, struggling as she inhaled more smoke. "Help!"

Eli's eyes widened when he realized who it was—Ellen. They needed to hurry and free Grace's mother before the entire building went up in flames.

"Grab that end," he told the man. The beam was heavy, and Eli strained to lift it. He held his breath to prevent more smoke from filling his lungs. The beam shifted enough that Ellen could crawl out of the way, and Eli let it drop. He and the other man helped her to stand.

They didn't linger to watch the room turn to ashes. They rushed out of the building with Ellen dangling between them. As they exited the dark building, the sunlight blinded Eli and he coughed, trying to suck in more fresh air. Every breath was like swallowing sand. He fell to his knees.

"Mom!" Grace bolted forward, catching her mother under the arm where Eli had just released her.

Another man pulled Eli off the ground and dragged him away from the burning building and the crowd of observers, far enough that he could breathe and collapse on the ground. The man gave him a bottle of water. Eli struggled to open it before the man took it back and removed the cap. "Drink," he said, putting it to Eli's lips.

"Are you okay?" Grace asked. She was kneeling next to her mother, who had her own bottle of water. Someone handed her a wet cloth to wipe the ash from her face. Several strands of her hair were singed along with her clothing. It was a good thing they had gotten to her when they did.

Eli coughed again before he was able to speak. "I'm all right."

"What happened?" Grace asked, looking back and forth between her mother and Eli.

"I don't know. I was meeting with a few council members, Nelson and Violet, for tea. We'd only been here for five minutes when there was an explosion and the roof fell on top of us." Ellen whipped her head back toward the building. "Is everyone else safe? Did they make it out?"

"I'm not sure, but I can check," Grace reassured her mother, who looked like she was about to sprint back into the crowd and check for herself. As stoic as Ellen seemed to be, it was evident she cared for her people.

Ellen tried to stand. "I need to talk to Nelson and Violet. I need to see if the owner of the shop made it out. There will be damage, and we need to organize reconstruction efforts. What about the buildings next door? Is the fire contained?"

She rattled off question after question, her concerns mounting one by one. She was in leader mode even though she had just barely escaped death herself.

"I can take care of it, Mom." Grace looked at her mother with a softness Eli hadn't seen from her yet. "It'll be good practice to play Lady of Berland for a day."

"Perhaps you're right."

Eli knocked on Grace's door as his eyes flitted between the guards that stood on either side. They didn't acknowledge him, but he greeted them anyway.

Grace quietly pulled the door ajar. She looked exhausted, tendrils of hair falling out of her loose bun. She hadn't changed out of her clothes from earlier that day, and they were stained with ash and soot. "Eli. I wasn't expecting you. Come in."

"Sorry for showing up unannounced. I just wanted to check on you and see how your mother is doing."

"She's okay. She's resting now. She had some minor burns and her shoulder was dislocated, but the doctor fixed her right up. You should've heard her screaming at him. I've never heard so many curse words come from my mother's mouth." Grace laughed quietly. "He gave her some pain medication and sleeping aids, so she'll be out for a while."

Grace's eyes were red and swollen. She looked more than exhausted; she looked devastated.

"There's something else," he said, waiting for her to fill him in.

"Nelson is dead. He succumbed to his injuries shortly after he made it to the medical chamber. My mother doesn't know yet." A tear rolled down her cheek.

Eli closed the distance between them and wrapped her in a warm embrace. "I'm so sorry, Grace."

Her hands clutched his back, and she buried her face in his shoulder. Her whole body seemed to relax into him. He rubbed her back while she softly sobbed. The day had clearly taken a toll on her.

"Will you stay with me?" she whispered.

"Where's your dad? Theo?" Why was no one here to help Grace? To help care for Ellen?

"They're out on a mission. They won't be back for a few more days."

"Of course I'll stay." Eli held her hand as they ascended the main staircase and ventured into her room. He hadn't been inside before, and he paused for a moment to take it all in. Her bedroom was larger than his entire apartment. It might've been bigger than his home back in Andus as well.

The beige carpet had swirls of burgundy and emerald green, and the wallpaper that covered the top half of her walls was equally intricate. The bottom half was lined with planks of dark brown walnut.

Her bed was fit for a queen—large enough for both of them and two more people if they felt so inclined. It stood high off the ground, so Grace had to hop into it. Eli lay next to her, tucking her in tight so her back was pressed against his chest.

She was quiet for so long, Eli thought she had fallen asleep. He closed his eyes.

"It wasn't an accident," she said quietly.

Eli raised his head off the pillow. "What?"

Grace turned in the bed to face him. "One of the council members stopped by earlier. He told me they found some flammable materials on the rear side of the building." She shook her head like she didn't completely understand it. "Like someone had drenched the side of the building in some sort of dark liquid. It wasn't hard to send the whole building up in flames with that."

"Who would do that?" He thought of Ellen and the others who had been in the building. "They killed Nelson on purpose?"

Grace shook her head, and more tears filled her eyes. "I don't think Nelson was the target."

"Your mother?" he asked in disbelief. When she nodded, his stomach flipped. "You don't think Eamon…"

"I don't know," she said softly. "I don't think he would be so bold, but maybe he's already making plans in case Trevor doesn't win the Rite. Maybe it's part of his larger plan to make my mother seem incompetent."

"I am scared for you." If they would attack the Lady of Berland without hesitation, then they could attack Grace, too. How was she so calm when her life could be in danger?

Her fingers reached up and trailed the scruff along his jawline. "They won't come after me."

"How can you be certain?"

"Because they need me. They could seize power by force, but even with the support they have, it wouldn't be enough to control everyone in Berland. The people wouldn't accept them unless they go through the proper channels."

"The Rite…"

"Exactly. I'm safe." She winked at him, but her lips were pressed tightly together. She didn't want to go forward with the Rite any more than he did. He squeezed her closer, and she wrapped a leg around his waist.

In less than a month, these moments would come to an end.

Eli stared at the woman wrapped in his arms. Her chest rose and fell with every shallow breath, and her eyes glistened in the dim light of her bedroom. He slipped his hand up her shirt, and she gasped at his delicate touch. He rubbed his thumb over her skin until she relaxed into him again.

He'd always known that Grace's temporary distraction would come to an end. She'd served her purpose in helping him get over Ali, but he had a hard time picturing life without her, without being able to touch her or hold her. The idea of another man touching her made his skin crawl.

"I hate this," he whispered, more to himself than to her.

Grace's light breathing was her only response. She'd already fallen asleep.

Eli kissed her forehead and brushed the hair from her face, watching her sleep peacefully.

"What am I going to do without you, Grace?"

Chapter Thirty-Two

ELI

THE NEXT DAY, GRACE woke with a renewed energy. It was more than Eli could keep up with. It always astonished him how she could carry on like nothing ever bothered her. She was so good at masking her feelings, a skill Eli had never mastered.

She got dressed in casual clothes—jeans and a tank top with sandals—and dragged Eli out of bed.

"What are you doing?" he mumbled, still half asleep.

"We have work to do," she said, picking up his jeans from the floor and tossing them at him. They hit his head when he didn't even bother to hold out his hand to catch them.

"Five more minutes," he said. He'd slept horribly. His nightmares had returned, but instead of Ali or his dad being murdered or tortured, it was Grace. He envisioned her held between two men as they took turns hitting her and threatening to do worse. It made his stomach churn, and he lifted his head to look at her, just to make sure she was here...and safe.

Grace smacked his ass, and he jumped.

"What was that for?" he asked, more alert now.

"If you don't get out of this bed, I will do it again."

"Fine, I'm moving." He stumbled out of bed and dressed in his clothes from the day before. He'd showered before he visited Grace, but somehow his clothes still smelled of smoke. "Have you checked on your mom today?"

She nodded. "I took her breakfast first thing. I told her about Nelson." Grace paused and fiddled with the silver ring she wore on her finger.

"How did she take it?"

"She blames herself."

"How is it her fault?"

"It's not. But it's the weight of being a leader. She feels responsible for everything that happens in this town. She called the meeting, and she was likely the target. Therefore..." Grace shrugged. "Anyway, the evidence has been moved to the council chamber. Do you want to come with me and see if there's anything that could implicate Eamon or Trevor?"

"Do you think I'll be any help? I don't know what I'm looking for."

She shrugged again. "Can't hurt. Plus, you can keep me company." Her familiar smile returned, and it was hard to turn her down.

"All right then. Lead the way."

⁂

The council chamber was in a section of the mountain Eli hadn't yet been to. The ground sloped downward as they walked the halls, which were completely deserted.

"Am I allowed to be down here?"

"You're with me. You can go wherever I go," Grace responded, continuing down the dark hall. Unlike the residential sectors, this hall had no doors. No openings to supply chambers or dining halls with loud chatter.

It seemed like it had been forgotten entirely except for one door at the very bottom of the slope. A large metal frame with a rectangle box was fixed to the wall next to the door. Grace pressed a few buttons, and he heard a small click.

Grace pushed open the heavy door and they entered the council chamber. Already, several lamps around the exterior were lit, illuminating the regal, circular room. In the center was a large wooden table and eleven chairs placed around it. One was elegant, like a throne with sapphire velvet and matching jewels embedded in the frame, while the other ten were less exquisite.

"Is this where you sit?" he asked, running a finger along the arm of the head chair.

"No, my mother sits there. One day I will, though." She pointed behind Eli. "That's where I sit."

To the side of the room was an additional chair meant for observing and not participating. Agitation pricked at him. He had a bone to pick with those old snobs. She didn't even get a seat at the table?

Grace noticed his disgruntled expression. "It doesn't bother me. It's just the way it is."

He turned back to find her browsing a floor to ceiling shelf that covered more than half of the room. An endless number of boxes and stacks of papers filled the shelves. Some of the boxes were labeled, and some were not.

"What are we looking for?" he asked as he came to stand beside her. There was something rather adorable about her look of concentration as she scanned the box labels.

"It should be...ah. Here it is." She pointed at one that was slightly above her head.

Eli nudged her with his hip. "Let me." It was easier for him to reach the box and safely pull it down, taking it to the table where they could go through its contents.

Grace began to carefully pull items out. Eli didn't recognize most of it; a lot was burned beyond repair. He wasn't sure why half the items had even been saved.

Grace stalled as she pulled out a clear bag of jewelry—a ring, a watch, and what looked like a locket. "Nelson's belongings."

Eli recognized the ring as a gold wedding band. "Did he have a wife?"

"She passed away a few years ago." Grace placed the bag back in the box. No one would retrieve Nelson's items. The thought made Eli simultaneously feel alone, knowing he had no family left, and surprisingly grateful. If he died tomorrow, Grace would never allow him to become a forgotten bag of trinkets locked away in a box somewhere in the dark.

Even if they would never be married or grow old together, Grace was his person.

The next item she pulled out was a charred canister. It was a little larger than the size of Eli's hand. The exterior was black, but there were flecks of red that still stood out on the burnt container.

"Let me see that," he said, reaching for the canister in Grace's hand. She held it out, and he turned it in a circle. "I recognize this."

"You do?" Her voice was full of surprise. They both knew she had only invited him to keep her company. Neither had expected that he'd actually be able to contribute.

"Yes. These canisters...they came from Jellico. I was on the trip when Noah brought them back."

"Noah? The one who works in the medical chamber?" Her eyebrows furrowed, and she stared at the container in his hands. "Why would he bring this back?"

Eli shook his head. "I don't know. I didn't think much of it at the time. My head was...elsewhere." He'd been distracted by his search for Ali and the blonde woman who had crushed his hopes of finding her. It hadn't seemed odd at all that a medical unit might have use for a flammable substance. He had no clue what it was for.

"Noah doesn't seem like the type to set fire to a building with people in it." Eli pictured the man from the trip to Jellico. He couldn't imagine that he would harm a fly.

"Maybe not, but I think we should pay him a visit."

Eli helped Grace pack the evidence back into the box and placed it on the shelf. They left the council chamber as if they'd never been there, Grace meticulously ensuring everything was in its rightful spot. Eli half wondered if they were supposed to be in there at all as she scooted one chair half an inch to the right.

When she was done, she turned to him. "Let's go."

Eli had only been to the medical chamber on one occasion. Shortly after he'd made it to Berland, he'd visited to have someone check on his wound and clear him for infections. Thankfully, he hadn't had any reason to return.

The hall leading up to the medical chamber was much busier than the one they'd walked to the council chamber. There were several children accompanied by their parents with sniffling noses and scraped knees. One woman was cradling a newborn baby and rocking the child back and forth.

Grace immediately headed to the counter where a woman with choppy black hair was waiting with a notepad and pen. The woman glanced down and back at Grace. "Did you have an appointment? I didn't think you were coming in for another few weeks."

It still seemed odd to Eli that everyone recognized Grace wherever she went. He never saw her as the royal figure she was. To him, she was just Grace—his friend and confidante.

"I'm not here for my appointment. I need to speak with Noah. Is he in?"

"He just stepped out for lunch, but I can let him know you stopped by. Do you want me to give him a message?"

"No need. We'll just wait in his office." Grace grabbed Eli by the hand and left a stunned receptionist staring slack-jawed as they headed in the direction of Noah's office. She probably wasn't used to being so blatantly dismissed, but she couldn't exactly tell Grace what to do.

Grace appeared to know precisely which door belonged to Noah, as if she'd been here many times before. She twisted the doorknob and Eli found himself in a small office just big enough for a desk with a chair on either side—one for Noah and one for patients. A small counter lined the back wall with cabinets on top. Their clear glass doors allowed him to see various vials and containers of different shapes and sizes, all of which were locked up.

Grace peered through the glass panels, as if she might find another of the flammable canisters, but she crossed her arms after only a few moments searching.

"Find anything?" he asked.

Grace glared at her reflection in the glass panes. "No, nothing."

"Guess we'll just wait for him to come back from lunch," Eli said, taking a seat in the chair closest to the back wall. "The woman at the front desk mentioned an appointment."

Grace leaned against the desk, facing Eli. She picked up an apple that had been sitting on the edge and tossed it from one hand to the other. "She did."

Eli's eyes trailed along Grace's long legs extended beside him. She was wearing those tight leggings he liked. They were soft and felt like clouds, and they also accentuated her thighs and ass.

"Is there something wrong?" he asked.

"Isn't that kind of personal?" she countered, taking a bite from the apple.

Eli blushed. "You're right. I'm sorry. Forget I asked."

Grace chuckled. "It's fine, Eli. It's just a routine check-up so I can get my birth control tonic." She laughed again when his eyebrows rose. "You didn't think I would sleep with you without it, did you?"

Eli suddenly felt incredibly stupid. He hadn't even considered it. Ali had always been the responsible one, taking the necessary precautions. He never had to think about it. "Oh. Makes sense."

Grace grinned at his obvious discomfort, centering herself on the desk and placing her feet in his lap. There was something about the way she sat on the desk, peering down at him, that made his heart flutter and his cock twitch.

She bit her lip, and Eli leaned in, grabbing her by the ankles. "What are you doing, Grace?"

Who knew the act of biting a lip could be so sexy? But Eli was entranced by the sight of her pink bottom lip pressed under her white tooth. It made him want to bite her bottom lip too, pull it into his mouth and suck until she moaned and arched her back, pressing her hips into him.

"Nothing," Grace said, feigning innocence. She was the furthest thing from innocence Eli had ever encountered.

He stood, pulling her by the ankles to wrap around his waist, and leaned over her. He whispered in her ear, "Liar."

She exhaled, and the heat of her breath brushed over his ear, traveled down his spine, and settled somewhere in his abdomen. She ran her hand over his chest, leaving a trail of fire in its wake. She shivered when he released a low rumble of pleasure. He needed to be closer...needed to have her.

A noise from the hall forced them to stop. Eli abruptly pulled himself away from Grace, and she spun around and looked toward the door.

Eli could make out the voices, and unfortunately, he recognized them both. The first belonged to Noah, and the second belonged to Trevor.

"Shit," Grace said quietly, scrambling from the desk. She shot a panicked look around the room and spotted a coat closet. Before Eli could question her, she yanked the door open and beckoned him inside. He had to hunch over just to fit, and she squeezed in beside him. Her elbow jabbed into his side. She shifted, trying to make more room, but she only wound up with her hip pressed against his groin.

Her eyes flitted down and back to his face. Eli shrugged. Of course he was hard. She'd just had her hands all over him.

They didn't have time to speak before the office door opened and the two voices became clearer.

Noah spoke in hushed tones. "I told you not to visit me at work."

"You've been avoiding me. You didn't leave me with much of an option."

"I upheld my end of the bargain. As far as I'm concerned, we're done. We have nothing else to discuss."

"We'll be done when I say we're done, Noah. Or have you forgotten our deal?"

Eli looked down at Grace, and she just shook her head. *What deal?*

Noah sounded more outraged when he spoke next. "I haven't forgotten shit. I did exactly what you asked of me. I got you your fire starters, and don't think I haven't figured out exactly what you needed them for. You *killed* someone," Noah hissed. "I'm not doing anything else for you."

"We'll see about that. Just remember, Noah—I can let your daughter in on our little secret anytime I want to. Wonder how she'll feel knowing that you're not her real daddy. That her mom was nothing more than a whore."

There was a sound of scuffling and a gargled noise, presumably from Noah. "You wouldn't dare."

Something, or someone, slammed against the wall. "I would. And I will. Remember that. I'm honestly surprised she hasn't figured it out by now. She looks nothing like you. Ain't that a good thing? Your wife probably died of embarrassment just looking at your ugly mug on a daily basis." A sinister laugh. "I'll stop by next week to pick up those supplies. Don't disappoint me, Noah."

A door slammed shut, and then there was another slam, like fists against the wall or perhaps the desk.

Grace stared at the closet ceiling, shaking her head, and Eli's shoulders slumped. Trevor was blackmailing Noah. It suddenly made much more sense. Noah wasn't the type to harm anyone, but he would if it meant keeping secrets that could harm his family. If his wife had passed away, then his daughter was all he had left. Eli understood the desire to protect your family, blood-related or not, more than anyone.

Noah didn't stay in his office long. The door opened and closed again only fifteen minutes after Trevor left. Eli didn't hesitate to pull Grace out of the closet and through the office door. He had no idea how long Noah would be gone, and he'd be damned if they had to spend all afternoon in that tiny space.

There was no sign of Noah when they entered the hall back to the receptionist's desk. She peered at them momentarily over the top of her paperwork as they walked by but said nothing.

Eli didn't breathe a sigh of relief until they were back in the entry chamber, filled with noise and commotion as people weaved in and out of the mountain and toward various halls. He stopped to catch his breath and settle his racing heart directly in the center of the room. People took small steps around them but otherwise paid them no mind.

Grace ground her teeth and stared toward the mountain's exit. She shook her head, and her pained look had Eli grabbing her by the shoulders, massaging her arms and trying to comfort her. For once, he didn't care if people saw them together. He didn't care if anyone knew how close they'd become. It was unsettling to see Grace unhappy, and he only cared about bringing that contagious smile back.

"Grace?"

She faced him with a renewed fire in her eyes. "He won't get away with this."

Chapter Thirty-Three

ELI

ELI SAT IMPATIENTLY IN a stiff chair, staring at his own reflection in the cracked mirror in front of him. Heather worked her fingers through his hair, snipping little bits every so often with a concentrated expression on her face. It turned out that her family's hair salon was the only one in Berland and busy as hell. He'd tried to make an appointment after their first brunch on the backyard patio, but this had been the first opening.

He knew his hair was unruly, but Heather was polite and didn't comment. Amaya, on the other hand, gave him a hard time every time he saw her in the cafeteria or in the halls on his way to work. It was kind of like having two younger sisters.

Grace never commented on his appearance, and it made him a little nervous. Eli had never been self-conscious before, but now he took more time choosing his clothes each morning. He spent more time in the shower, scrubbing the dirt from his body, and applied a citrus oil on his skin. He hadn't told Grace about his hair appointment; would she like the change in style?

"Sit still," Heather chided.

"I'm late. I told Grace I'd meet her half an hour ago. Are you almost done?"

"Ask me that one more time and I'll slice off your ear." He saw her grin in the mirror as she continued to work.

"You'd better listen. Heather is a cold-blooded killer," Amaya said from the chair in the corner. She was flipping through a book, waiting for her turn to get her hair trimmed.

Heather rolled her eyes. "If you sit still, no harm will come to you."

Eli did his best to imitate a statue. The last thing he needed was a chunk of hair missing or worse—an ear. He scrutinized Heather's work in the mirror. So far, no bald spots could be seen.

"I'm surprised you're still spending so much time together," Heather commented.

"Hmm?" Eli asked distractedly.

"Well, it's just that Grace told us that you have no intention of entering the Rite. Don't you think you're getting her hopes up?"

"We're just friends."

"Oh, please," Amaya said, taking her eyes off her book. "Grace is our best friend. She tells us everything."

"And she means *everything*." Heather made eye contact with Eli in the mirror.

Was it getting warm in here?

Eli cleared his throat and almost fidgeted in his seat until he remembered Heather's shears. "If you know everything, then you know it's not serious. Grace just wants to have some fun before settling down. It doesn't mean anything."

Heather's shoulders shook, and Amaya returned to reading her book with a shake of her head. "Men are so stupid."

"What does that mean?" He couldn't get a good read on Amaya's expression. She was too far out of his line of sight, and he didn't dare turn toward her.

"It means that Grace is clearly into you, Eli. And I may not know you as well as I know her, but I think the feeling is mutual."

Eli gave her his best side eye.

That wasn't true. It couldn't be true. Grace was just his friend, and the start of the Rite was only two weeks away now. Soon she'd be married to someone else, and he would move on with his life—without her.

The thought was depressing, but not because he had *feelings* for her. No, she was just a friend.

Heather finished, and he took a final look at his fresh cut in the mirror, delighted with what he saw. It rattled him that his first thought was how much Grace would like it.

He stood from his chair and took out his coin purse.

Heather waved him off. "It's on the house. We don't charge friends here."

"Are you sure?"

She nodded. "I'm sure."

"Thanks. I appreciate it." Eli headed for the door. "I'll see you around."

"Eli." Heather's voice stopped him, and he turned back. Amaya had set her book down again and was looking between them. "You should reconsider."

He gave her an inquisitive look.

"The Rite. You should reconsider entering." Heather gave him a soft and understanding smile while Amaya eyed him with hope. He knew they only wanted the best for their friend, but he couldn't be that guy.

Eli found it hard to swallow. He'd been so adamant that his fling with Grace meant nothing. She was only a means to get over Ali. If he allowed himself to fantasize about entering the Rite...the possibility of getting hurt again terrified him. He couldn't do it, even if he felt more than friendship for Grace.

He just waved as he exited the salon.

⁂

Eli walked quickly to meet Grace at her home. Hopefully she wouldn't be too angry about his tardiness.

What would it be like to enter the Rite? Was that what Grace wanted?

If he entered, was he even capable of winning? The three tasks required physical strength, speed, and agility. He wasn't exactly in his prime, but with a bit of training he could get back to the athletic man he'd once been growing up in Andus.

He knew with absolute certainty that he didn't want Trevor to win. Who, then? Who would be good enough for Grace?

Eli was so lost in his own thoughts that he barely heard the voices coming from around the corner of the hall leading to Grace's place. They were coming toward him slowly, and after a moment, they seemed to halt altogether. He stalled when he recognized one as Trevor's.

There was nowhere to hide, so Eli pressed against the wall, hoping the shadows would protect him long enough to hear a fraction of their conversation. His heart pounded with anticipation. He shouldn't be eavesdropping, but he couldn't help himself. What if Trevor spilled something that could incriminate him further? Or plans for a future attack that they could prevent?

"This will be good for us, Trevor. We need a voice like yours on the inside. And at the top, no less. You must come out of the Rite a winner. We're relying on you."

Eli didn't recognize the second voice. It wasn't Noah or Eamon, Trevor's father.

Who was 'we?' How many people were involved in this rebellion?

"It's almost guaranteed I will. I haven't heard of any real contenders," Trevor said. "I heard that Steven, the baker's son, is planning to compete, but that guy's afraid of his own shadow. Nate was going to enter but reconsidered after I threatened to take his sister to bed." Trevor laughed.

"Don't be so sure of yourself. Don't let your guard down. That's when people surprise you."

Trevor's voice lowered to little more than a whisper, and Eli scooted closer. He peered around the corner to see the two men huddled closely together. Trevor twisted his head to make sure they were alone, and Eli darted back into the shadows.

"I can promise you that I *will* be the winner. And when I marry that girl, I'll make sure things change around here. She won't know what hit her."

"I hear she's hard-headed. Will you be able to control her?"

Eli furrowed his brow and cracked his knuckles. He was one insult away from breaking Trevor's nose. Grace wasn't a woman to be controlled.

"You underestimate both my physical skills and intelligence. A girl like that is easy to manipulate. All women are the same. They just want to be fed compliments and showered with gifts. And if that doesn't work, I'll use a more *hands-on* approach, if you know what I mean."

Eli fumed at the thought of Trevor laying a hand on Grace. She was too smart to fall for his manipulations, but he was strong and bigger than she was. Could she protect herself if he tried to physically harm her?

He was still reeling over Trevor's comments when Trevor and the other man rounded the corner, startling him and causing him to jump.

"Eli. Didn't expect to see you here."

"Likewise," he snarled.

Trevor's haggard-looking companion stared at Eli with suspicion and disdain. He raised his hand and scratched his short beard, peering through squinted eyes. He was probably wondering how long Eli had been listening to their conversation, but Eli couldn't care less.

He attempted to step around Trevor, who was giving him an equally uncivil glare.

"Watch yourself, Eli. Wouldn't want people to think you're snooping where you don't belong." Trevor flashed a menacing grin, his white teeth sparkling in the low light of the tunnel. His eyes had a maniacal flare to them.

"I think I'm right where I belong."

⁂

"You don't need to worry about me," Grace told Eli later. They were sitting on the cliff that overlooked the waterfall. It had become one of their favorite places to hang out. She picked at the yellow flowers in the grass and pulled petals from their stems one by one.

"Why aren't you more upset about this?" Eli demanded. His gut still churned from the conversation he'd overheard, but she was acting like Trevor had merely been discussing the weather. He had *threatened* her. And they both knew he was capable of murder. Sometimes the brave face she put on was maddening.

"Because Trevor won't win the Rite. We'll stop him before he can even enter. Once we find some concrete proof, it'll implicate him. I'll talk to my mother, and he'll be exiled."

She tossed aside an empty stem and pulled another flower from the ground.

"We can't rely on that. Plus, he's not alone. The other guy specifically said *they* were counting on him. How many are in on this? If we stop Trevor, there are still others out there. They're plotting something big, Grace."

"I hear you, Eli. I do. But I think for now it's best if we focus on Eamon and Trevor. They seem to be the leaders in this thing. Their claim to power is the only thing giving this rebellion any sort of legitimacy. Without them, the rebellion dies."

"Any ideas on how we can get our hands on some proof?"

"Still working on it." She tossed another empty stem at him. It fell into his lap. He could feel her gaze on him and when he looked up, she didn't look away.

"What are you staring at?"

Grace reached up and ran a hand through his hair. "It looks good...but I think I liked it better before."

"You liked it when it was a scraggly mess?"

She nodded and continued to run her hand through his hair.

Eli closed his eyes and swallowed hard. It was a relaxing touch. It felt *right*. He recalled his earlier conversation with Heather and Amaya, and his stomach fluttered.

He opened his eyes again, and Grace's expression was filled with longing. Her eyes sparkled like the glistening river and her lips were parted, enticing him to have a taste. His chest constricted in longing of his own. It was unexpected but not unwelcome.

The moment seemed to last forever, and Eli reached up to cup her cheek. She leaned in closer, and the scent of angelfruit and honey and vanilla filled his nose.

Her hand traveled down his face, past his neck, and rested on his chest. His heart raced in response.

"I can feel your heart, Eli," she said softly, her voice like an alluring melody. She looked at him through her long lashes.

His heart pounded even harder.

Eli leaned in until their lips were mere inches apart. She licked her lips, and he couldn't think or speak. All he wanted was to place his lips on hers and press his body against hers. He wanted to be tangled in her until he forgot the threat of a rebellion. She had the ability to command his thoughts and chase his worst fears away.

Something echoed through the woods, and Eli froze. "Did you hear that?"

Grace stared past his shoulder into the trees. She squinted, trying to make out where the noise had come from.

It happened again.

"It sounds like voices," she said.

Eli furrowed his brow. The conversation he'd overheard had him on edge. He couldn't tell if he was hearing voices or if it was all in his head. He strained to listen closer, to see if he could make out words or if it was just a bird or other wild animal.

Grace rose, moving toward the beaten path and into the brush.

"What are you doing?" he asked in a hushed voice.

Grace summoned him with a wave of her hand. "Come on. Let's go see what it is."

He didn't like it, but what choice did he have? Stay on the cliff and wait to be found? Or go see what the noise was and hope it was only a squirrel?

Grace closed the gap between them, placing a hand on his arm. She squeezed him and pulled him closer. "Trust me."

Trusting her was easier than he thought it would be. It was hard to explain, but she made him feel safe. Like nothing bad could happen as long as he had her.

Grace slid her hand down his arm and laced her fingers with his, and his shoulders relaxed. She stepped back into the forest, pulling him along. "Ready?"

He nodded and traced the back of her hand with his thumb, following her toward the voices.

Closer.

Closer.

Until they finally reached a small group of people. One woman leaned against a tree, chatting with a man who sat on the ground. Another man hunched over a sack, looking for something. And two more women who were swapping a canteen.

The first woman turned to find Eli and Grace watching them. Her eyes widened.

"Holy shit."

Chapter Thirty-Four

ALI

"WE'RE GOING TO MISS your help around here," Alan grumbled as they ate one last breakfast with the family who'd been hosting them. "This one can't chop wood half as fast as you."

Cole rolled his eyes when his father nudged him in the side. It was only a joke; he more than carried his weight around the farm. That much had been clear from day one when their paths had crossed while he was hunting on his own.

"We'll miss you too." Ali smiled when Meredith wrapped her in a matronly hug. It was true she would miss them—they'd become part of their small family—but her excitement over seeing Eli again was hard to contain.

They finished their breakfast and helped clean up before heading to their cabin. Most of their bags were already packed. Meredith had given them a whole sack of food and water to take with them, and Ali was incredibly grateful. She didn't expect this trip to be anything like their first few weeks in the woods. The likelihood of running out of supplies or getting lost was low since Genna and Isabel would be guiding them, but she still wouldn't turn down extra supplies. She never wanted to wonder where her next meal would come from ever again.

"What do you think Berland is like?" Ali asked as she folded the last of her clothes. She'd already asked the Kennedys, but none of them had ever been there.

"I haven't really thought about it," Nik replied.

"You haven't?"

Nik shrugged. "It doesn't matter to me where we go, Ali. As long as you're happy, I'll be right by your side."

"You seemed to like living here on the farm." Ali tightened the strands of her sack and clasped the metal buckle on the front, then looked around the room to make sure she hadn't forgotten anything.

"I liked not wandering through the woods. I can make a home anywhere, but I never want to be homeless again."

She could understand that. Rysburg had never felt like a home to her either, though she didn't tell him that. He had to know already that it had never felt right to her. The farm had reminded her a lot of Andus, and she hoped Berland would be the same.

"I think it'll be paradise. Blue skies year-round. Never rains. The beds will be the softest you've ever felt," Sam joked.

Ali grinned at his ridiculous prediction, and even Nik chuckled. He'd been a little withdrawn since they'd found out Eli was in Berland. Ali wasn't an idiot. She knew Nik and Eli were far from being best friends and he would've been content to never see Eli again. But he'd put aside his own feelings for her, and she loved him for it. It would be an adjustment for all of them once they were reunited.

"Well, let's get going then," she said, slinging her bag over her shoulder. Her hair was pulled tight into a single braid, and she felt ready to take on the world. Nik and Sam both pulled their backpacks on, and Nik paused to brush her bangs behind her ear. He stared long enough for her cheeks to flush. "What?"

Nik shook his head. "Nothing. I'm just happy that you're so happy."

Leaving the farm was a stark difference from when they'd arrived. She'd come here tattered and unraveled and was leaving as a new ribbon tied in a bow. She took Nik's hand.

"If you two are done ogling each other, I think it's time to head out."

Nik and Ali grinned. They set off on the path toward town, closing the door to the cabin behind them.

"You know what I'm most looking forward to?" Sam asked.

"What's that?"

"Not sharing a room with you two anymore."

Laughter burst from Nik, and he wrapped an arm around Ali's waist. Warmth spread through her body. "You and me both, brother."

❧❧❧❧❧ ❧❧❧❧❧

Genna and Isabel were waiting for them in town, just like they had said they would. Genna sat atop one of the picnic tables perched around the fire pit, although its flames were long gone. Isabel stood in front of her with her hands twisted in Genna's hair.

Ali thought her vision must be going bad when Isabel smiled. She seemed so serious, but perhaps she had a softer side that she reserved only for her wife. She quickly turned stoic again when she saw them approaching.

"You made it," Genna said, hopping down from the table.

"Have you been waiting long?" Ali tried not to bounce on her toes.

"Not at all. Ready to get going?" Genna's gaze swept over them and their large sacks, satisfied that they were prepared. "Follow me."

Birds were chirping in the early morning hours when Ali woke. For a moment, she forgot where she was. She blinked and cleared the sleepiness from her eyes, looking around at the clearing in the woods. She flinched, thinking the farm had only been a dream, but it all came back when she spotted Genna dozing with her arms around Isabel.

They were halfway to Berland.

The first part of their trek had been uneventful. Time had passed slowly, refusing to appease Ali's enthusiasm and impatience to step foot in Berland. They'd hiked all day before stopping for the night, hanging two tarps between the tall trees and lying on the rough ground.

Ali's back hurt from the hard forest floor, but at least she was warm and comfortably pressed against Nik's side. Since no one else seemed to be awake, she resigned to nestling further into the crook of his arm and watching his chest rise and fall. His mouth was slightly parted, and she listened to his heavy breathing with a smile on her face.

She was lucky to have him.

He flinched when she slipped a cool hand under his shirt. "Your hands are freezing," he grumbled, still half-asleep. She liked his hoarse voice when he first woke in the mornings.

"Sorry."

He pulled her tight against his side, and she felt the familiar longing of wanting his body between her thighs. She pressed her lips to his, and his untamed beard tickled her chin. When she slid a hand in his pants, he moaned and eased her lips apart, gliding his tongue across hers. He was hard, and knowing they had an audience was torture. They needed some alone time.

Across the clearing, Genna and Isabel were sleeping peacefully and beyond them, Sam's eyes were closed with one arm behind his head.

She shifted out of Nik's hold, and he grumbled again. "Where are you going?"

"To the river. I want to wash up before we start moving again," she whispered.

Nik covered his eyes with one arm, blocking the light of the rising sun.

"You can come with me if you'd like," Ali teased.

Nik tossed his blanket to the side and sat up straight, the length of him still visible through his pants. "I'm up."

They grabbed their backpacks and headed down to the river. Nik chose a spot where the water was crystal clear. Ali dipped her hand in; it was warm compared to the cool morning air.

Nik stripped down to nothing and hopped into the river. The water came up to his stomach, hiding the more exciting bits of his body. Still, the hard lines of his abs were a sight to behold.

He followed her gaze and raised a brow. "Are you coming in?"

Ali removed her shirt and pants and tossed them on top of his clothes. She took a step into the water and then another before her body froze up. She bit her lip and watched as the water ran downstream. It sent chills up her spine and made her vision go hazy.

She'd been doing so well. She thought she'd be able to handle stepping into the shallow water since time had passed and they were on their way to see Eli. But the memories still rushed in like a dam had broken upstream, flooding her mind and leaving her struggling to breathe.

She covered her face with her hands, driving away the visions that still haunted her. Her heart rate sped up. Her hands were clammy. The buzzing in her ears prevented her from noticing Nik walking her way, treading through the water.

"Here. Take my hand." Warm fingers closed around her hands, and he pulled her step by step into the water. "Don't look down. Just look at me."

She locked eyes with him, inhaling sharply as the water reached her stomach. She fought back the urge to close her eyes and focused on his touch. His gaze.

When they made it to the deepest part of the stream, he pulled her closer and wrapped his arms around her waist. "Is this okay?"

Ali sighed heavily and tore her eyes from him long enough to take in their surroundings. The water still flowed freely around them, but it felt more like a gentle current than the surging nightmare she'd expected. She allowed herself to surrender to his embrace. "Yes. Thank you."

It was hard to swallow, but she concentrated on his skin, smooth under her fingertips. She trailed them down his wet chest below the water to his cock, eliciting a smile from him.

Nik reached around her back to unhook her bra and eased the straps from her shoulders. He threw it back to shore, where it landed a foot from their other discarded clothing.

He grabbed her legs under the water, wrapping them around his waist, and she rocked her hips. The feeling of him was familiar but sorely missed.

She began to pepper his neck with tender kisses, tasting the freshwater mixed with his salty skin. She felt his throat bob as he swallowed and sighed against her ear.

Nik slid one hand down her stomach to the hem of her underwear. She rolled her hips again, desperate for him to touch her, but he gathered the fabric in his hands and yanked, ripping her flimsy underwear at the seams.

"Nik!" She smacked his arm. "I don't have many pairs left."

Nik laughed, his lips grazing her neck. "You don't need them."

Ali conjured a mental image of her backpack and tried to count the number of undergarments she had left, but she was interrupted when Nik gently bit her collarbone.

He pressed her core against him, and she felt his hardness against her stomach. She ground her hips into him, his cock gliding over her clit under the sparkling water.

Nik's movements were slow and calculated. His mouth moved down from her clavicle to the top of her breast, kissing and sucking as he went, leaving Ali feeling lightheaded. He swirled his tongue over her nipple and took the bud between his teeth, causing her to jolt in a mix of pain and pleasure.

Ali reached down, wrapping a hand around his length, and he groaned into her skin. He rocked his hips, and his cock slid in and out of her palm at a controlled pace.

She wanted more—needed more. This restraint was no good. She wanted to unleash the carnal beast in him.

Hands wrapped around her thighs, he positioned her so the tip of his cock was at her entrance. Then he filled her with one hard thrust.

"God, Nik," she moaned, and crashed into his shoulder. Her whole body felt weightless and radiant. The world around them fell away, and it was just them. Time stopped. They were alone in this moment.

He grabbed her ass and squeezed so hard, she was sure she'd have bruises on her cheeks. She clawed at his back, relishing the way his muscles tensed under her fingertips.

Nik rocked back and forth, and each motion had Ali begging for more. Squeezing him between her legs tighter. Clawing at his shoulders harder. Kissing his neck and earlobe in a frenzy.

She leaned back and peered down to where they were connected beneath the current, releasing a frustrated whimper as he drove into her again and again. It had been so long since she'd had relief.

Oh, God, just the sight of him pulling out and then sliding back in was going to make her come.

"You like to watch, don't you?"

She nodded and rolled her hips to meet each of his advances.

He began to walk back to the shore of the river, fighting against the current. Ali continued to grind into him, driving him wild. His shaky breaths puffed against her ear, and his body trembled beneath her.

Nik held her tight as they came out of the water and barely made it two steps on wobbly legs before dropping to his knees. He cradled Ali and laid her on her back. Leaves and dirt stuck to her skin the moment she touched the ground, but she didn't care.

Ali shivered as a light breeze crossed her wet body. She watched as Nik kneeled before her and grabbed her by the hips, thrusting into her again. Her head rolled to the side, and she bit her fist to stifle a moan.

"Look at me. You wanted to see, Ali? Watch me fuck you."

Ali turned to face him again as he pulled almost all the way out. His eyes were dark with lust as he drove back into her, lifting her hips off the ground. Ali's walls tensed, and she dug her nails into the damp dirt beside her.

His eyes melted every fiber of her being. He ran his hands up her stomach and massaged her breasts, running his thumbs over her nipples. Ali grabbed him by the wrists and circled her hips into him furiously.

"I'm going to come, Nik."

Nik pulled her off the ground to sit in his lap. She bounced on top of him, chasing that high until her whole body shook in ecstasy. Losing all control, she clenched around him and bit his shoulder while waves of pleasure crashed over her again and again.

Nik slipped in and out of her throbbing pussy several more times before coming undone himself. He grabbed her face and claimed her lips, prying them apart with his tongue and dipping in to taste her.

Ali met him with equal passion. It seemed impossible to ever have enough of him. His touch. His taste. His smell. She wanted to be surrounded by *him* forever and always.

He relaxed his pace and gently sucked on her bottom lip, tugging at it with his teeth. He swirled circles over her back and sighed into her neck. "Do you know how much I love you?"

"Almost as much as I love you."

He chuckled, and the rush of air tickled her skin.

"Impossible."

Chapter Thirty-Five

NIK

"We can set up camp here tonight," Genna said from the top of a hill.

When Nik made it to the top, he eyed the sizable piece of flat land with a spectacular view of the valleys below. It was a vast sea of green trees and the occasional glisten of a flowing river. Small streams covered the mountains like veins and from this height, he could see how they all connected.

"How close are we now?" Ali asked. She'd been asking that almost every hour, but it didn't seem to bother Genna.

"We'll be there tomorrow afternoon at the latest," she replied, tossing her bag to the ground.

Nik got straight to work scrounging for firewood. The days were rather warm, but the nights brought freezing temperatures, so it was best to have plenty stockpiled before nightfall.

Ali came to help him carry smaller branches for kindling. He could've done it himself, but she liked feeling useful and he liked her company. As she was reaching down for another twig, she squealed in delight, sending a couple birds flying into the distance.

"What? What did you find?"

Ali held up some long gray strands of foliage. When he didn't recognize them, she rolled her eyes. "I suppose you're too *sophisticated* to know what it is. It's gray grass." Her smile was wide and filled with joy. What a drastic difference a few days and a piece of good news could make.

"Gray grass? Isn't that what barbarians use to get drunk?" he teased.

"Barbarians," she huffed. "Do you think you're better than the rest of us? Still think of me as your prisoner?"

"We can pretend if you'd like." He was only joking, but her cheeks instantly flushed and suddenly he envisioned bending her over a table again. He raised a brow. His pants felt too tight and, by the way Ali's eyes traveled down his body, she was aware of it too.

Ali gathered the gray grass on top of the tinder she'd accumulated. She stopped next to him on the way back to the others. "I know what you're thinking." He looked up from where he was kneeling to pick up another log. "I'm thinking about it too. Your hands on my ass while I beg for mercy. But you won't let up. You just keep teasing and tormenting until I'm too weak to stand."

Nik's mouth was too dry to speak. Whatever leash she had him on had strangled the words right out of him.

She bit her lip and her face turned rosy again, shy from her sudden burst of cheekiness. He loved that about her.

"If that's what you want," he managed in a husky voice. He brushed his hand up the back of her leg, squeezing once he got to her ass.

She nodded and cupped the side of his face.

Dropping the logs he'd gathered, he crawled forward on his knees and wrapped his arms behind her thighs. He looked up at her and was ready to pull her to the ground with him when she chuckled.

"Not here, Nik."

Nik groaned, and his arms fell. She was going to leave him hard and hurting. His gaze fixed on her behind as she walked away. He had to blink multiple times to get the image out of his mind.

When he returned to the rest of the group, Sam was already mixing vegetables in a pot Isabel had provided while Ali crumbled gray grass into tiny pieces. Nik built a small fire and moved the pot over the flames.

It didn't take long for dinner to be ready. Little bowls of soup were passed out, and Ali rinsed out the pot and replaced it with water to boil for their tea. She bent down to place the pot back on the flames, and Nik was certain she positioned herself to give him the best view of her ass.

Such a tease...

The pot of water began to bubble. Ali grabbed it by the handle, serving cups of gray grass tea to everyone. Isabel and Genna were familiar with the contents and happily drank theirs. Sam took a tentative sniff before raising the cup to his lips. Ali watched Nik expectantly, waiting for him to take the first sip of this "barbarian" drink.

So he took a gulp while she stared at him, then grimaced. "That's vile."

She laughed and took a seat next to him. "It does the job. Eli always loved this stuff."

He snorted and had to compose himself. Of course Eli would enjoy the earthy filth. "That explains so much."

She wasn't wrong about its potency. After his third cup of gray grass tea, he was feeling its effects. Ali felt it even more. She laughed hysterically at the smallest jokes and swayed next to him. His tingling fingers wrapped around her waist and pulled her into his side.

Her eyes were droopy when she turned to look at him and like glass in the light of the fire. Her beauty was unmatched by anyone he'd ever seen, and he leaned forward to kiss her lips.

Her tongue slid into his mouth, and he sucked on it, pulling her body closer.

"Easy, you two," Sam called out.

Ali broke their kiss and laughed again. She was so carefree. And so fucking beautiful.

"Poor Sam. I don't know how he made it all this time with the two of you," Genna said.

If she only knew. They'd been a lot to handle, but not in the way Genna thought. These intimate moments had been lost for so long, Nik wasn't sure if they'd ever return. For a while, he wasn't sure if Ali would ever look at him the same. But something had snapped that day Colin attacked. The fire inside her had been reignited, and he was thankful to see it return, though he hated that Colin's attack had been the catalyst. Her days at the farm had only further improved her mental state.

It finally felt like things were returning to normal between them. Better than normal. Their love had been tested and they'd survived.

"It's getting late," Isabel said, dumping the soggy grass from her mug. "We should call it a night."

Ali jokingly pouted before downing the remainder of her drink. She stumbled to her backpack and struggled to pull out a blanket. Nik had to help her when it got stuck in the opening.

She pushed her disheveled bangs out of her face and smiled at him. "What would I do without you?" She pressed her pointer finger into his chest and moved it downward to the button on his jeans.

Nik glanced at their companions, who were occupied with their own sleeping arrangements. "What happened to 'not here?'"

"I changed my mind," she said. She undid his button and rubbed a hand over the top of his jeans.

Not again. This was not happening tonight, and he wouldn't let her get him aroused again only to be left with blue balls. He grabbed her hand and laced his fingers between hers, gently kissing the back.

"Not tonight, Ali," he whispered.

"I can be quiet."

No, she couldn't.

"I can't."

She pouted for a moment, then tore off her jacket and laid down beside him when he lowered to the ground. He tossed the blanket over their bodies. He assumed he'd have to fight off her frisky hands, but within minutes, Ali was breathing softly with her head on his chest.

⚘ ⚘

Nik woke to the scent of a fire burning. He rolled over to find Ali already awake and sitting next to Sam, who was stoking the fire. She held a mug of steaming water in her lap. Without any tea leaves or coffee grounds, they were forced to drink hot water instead. It was either that or gray grass, and it would probably be best if she didn't get drunk first thing in the morning.

Nik shifted and tossed the blanket to the side. He stretched his arms high above his head and heard a few cracks.

"Good morning," he said to Ali and Sam as he took a seat around the fire.

"Good morning," Ali returned. She was joyous this morning, no doubt thinking of reuniting with Eli later today. Nik prayed that nothing would go wrong on the last leg of their trip. It would kill him if that smile ever left her face again.

Sam tossed a small loaf of bread and Nik caught it, breaking off half before handing the rest to Ali.

"I already miss Meredith's cooking," Sam said as he tore a piece from his own loaf. It was bland and dry.

Isabel appeared with a blanket around her shoulders. "I don't think I've ever heard so much complaining. You lot would never make it out here."

Sam chuckled. "I wouldn't want to."

Isabel rolled her eyes, unimpressed with their group's affinity for the wilderness. "Finish your breakfast and pack up. We need to get moving."

Nik felt as though his shoulders had permanent imprints where the straps of his bag had settled in. He couldn't wait to reach their destination and drop the bags for good. Perhaps he could convince Ali to give him a nice, long massage. He'd be happy to return the favor...

They spent most of the morning following the river upstream. Nik kept looking toward Ali, uncertain of how she'd feel next to the raging stream. Anybody else may not have noticed the way she held her breath. Or the way she stared straight ahead, refusing to look at the glistening water beside them. She did a good job hiding her distress, but Nik noticed. He took her hand and slid his fingers between hers, and she gave him an appreciative nod. A silent acknowledgment that she would be okay.

By midday, the sun was beating down on their backs. Sam's leg was almost healed now, but he wasn't used to long hikes. They still needed to stop frequently so he could take breaks. Ali appeared to grow a little more impatient with each one, but she tried to reign it in, knowing Sam couldn't help it.

She leaned against a tree while Sam sat down on a broken tree trunk. "Sorry," he told her.

"Don't be. I know your leg must be killing you. We'll get there eventually."

Nik opened his backpack to find his water bottle, buried somewhere beneath the clothes and blanket he had hastily packed that morning. He finally found it and pulled open the cap when a sound in the woods had them all turning their heads.

"Holy shit," a familiar voice uttered.

Chapter Thirty-Six

ELI

Eli could hardly believe his eyes. He blinked several times, but the figures before him remained clear as day. Almost too clear. He could only focus on one—the blonde with a smile that grew by the second.

Ali pushed off the tree and took two tentative steps toward him before breaking into a full sprint. She squealed in delight, a tone he hadn't heard from her since they were kids playing hide and seek in the woods.

She bounded across the opening and flung her arms around his neck. Her legs wrapped around his waist, and he nearly fell over with the weight of her body. Even with her weight and warmth, he still had a hard time grasping that this was real.

Ali was real.

Eli grabbed the back of her head and felt a single tear of joy trickle down his cheek and into her hair. "Ali?"

Ali's legs dropped back to the ground, but she kept her arms around his shoulders, clinging to him tightly. He felt her shake with either a sob or laughter; it was hard to tell.

How? How was she here?

"I thought I'd never see you again," she said, leaning back to look him in the eye at last. Her eyes were glistening with tears and he took in the rest of her. She hardly looked any different than when he last saw her, perhaps a little thinner and more tan, but her smile and sparkling eyes were the same as he'd remembered them.

"Me too. How is this possible?"

Ali looked behind her, and Eli followed her gaze. Nik gave him a look that was only slightly disgruntled, his lips pressed together tightly.

Still a dick.

Sam was sitting on the ground, massaging his lower leg and ankle. He gave Eli a quick wave and Eli returned the gesture. And then he recognized the other two faces—Genna and Isabel.

"We've been looking for you for weeks," Ali admitted. "It was by accident that we ran into Genna and Isabel. A miracle that they knew who you were and *where* you were."

She smiled, and it nearly cut him in half. How heartbreakingly beautiful that smile was. He still couldn't believe she was here, touching him. Breathing the same air as him. It felt as though his heart had stopped beating. Time stood still.

He wrapped her in another hug just to be sure she existed.

A throat cleared, and he reluctantly let her go.

Grace stepped out from behind him. "Hi. I'm Grace," she said, reaching out a hand to Ali. Eli's heartbeat came back with full force. In all the time he'd imagined reuniting with Ali, he hadn't considered what it would be like to introduce her to Grace.

Ali took it and gave Grace a friendly grin. "I'm Ali. It's nice to meet you."

"Ali?" Grace glanced at Eli before sizing Ali up with a beaming smile. He tensed for a moment while two of the most important people in his life came face to face. Eli knew Grace well enough to know her cordial interest in Ali was sincere. "Eli has told me about you. I'm so glad you've made it to Berland."

Eli looked between the two of them—one woman who'd held his heart for nearly his entire life before tossing it aside, and the other who had helped him dust it off. He didn't know where to look, what to say.

"And thank you for bringing them," Grace said to Genna and Isabel.

The women had walked up behind Ali, Nik and Sam not far behind them. Grace shook their hands as she introduced herself.

Genna gave her a dismissive wave. "It was no problem at all."

"Will you be staying a while? My brother is home. I'm sure he'd love to see you both."

"Afraid we can't," Isabel answered. "This has set us back a few days on our latest adventure."

Genna rolled her eyes. "She's being dramatic. Our anniversary is coming up, and she has some big gesture planned. She thinks she's being sneaky but I'm onto her."

Isabel, whose eyes had widened, conceded, "Fine. We can stay *one* night."

"Here, let me," Eli offered, reaching a hand to carry Ali's bag, before she was whisked away by Grace.

She took Ali by the arm and led them ahead, treating Ali like another one of her girlfriends. Eli shook his head but admired the way she fiercely cared for people. Grace would go out of her way to make Ali and the others feel welcome, just like she had with him.

The two of them couldn't be more different. Grace with her bouncy brown curls and her bubbly, outgoing personality stood a few inches taller than Ali, who spoke quietly and timidly and fiddled with her blonde braid when she got nervous.

Nik fell into step beside Eli. His voice was scratchy when he spoke. "I thought you were dead."

Eli turned, prepared to meet Nik with a snarky response, but the pain in Nik's eyes caught him off guard. "I thought I was, too."

"I'm glad you're not," Nik said, and Eli actually believed him.

The pair walked the rest of the journey back to the mountain in silence while Grace pointed out buildings to Ali. Ali's head was on a swivel, taking it all in.

The newcomers stopped in their tracks when the entrance of the mountain came into view. Eli laughed softly when Nik's jaw dropped. He'd forgotten what it had been like when he first stepped into the shadows of the mountain and viewed the grand entrance. It had been a shock to him too.

Now it was his home.

Grace moved to lead them through the arch carved into the mountain, but Eli flung his hand out, wrapping it around Ali's wrist.

Several heads turned in his direction, but he paid them no mind. "Can I take you somewhere first? Just us?"

Ali nodded.

Grace removed her arm that was looped through Ali's and gave him a warm smile—a smile that said she trusted him. "I'll take these guys to their new homes. Take your time."

Nik gave Ali a look that said he'd rather accompany them, but he gave her a curt nod before fixing his gaze on Eli. Eli resisted the urge to roll his eyes. Nik was pretty possessive for someone who'd known Ali less than a year.

Eli had a fleeting desire to slide his arm around Ali's waist just to see the steam come out of Nik's ears, but Grace was here. As much fun as it would be to antagonize Nik, he had no desire to do anything that would hurt her.

So he turned on his heel, and Ali followed.

"What is this place?" Ali asked.

"I've named it the Twisted Tree," Eli said. He'd forgone the horses today, thinking Ali might not be ready to ride one. Instead, they'd hiked up to one of his favorite outlooks—the Twisted Tree, where he'd built a memorial for his father...and for her mother.

"Very original," she teased, running a hand over the rough bark of the larger tree, following it as it intertwined with the smaller one.

She paused upon seeing the unusual rock formation. "What is this?"

Eli swallowed and sighed. "I guess you could call it a headstone. Although I don't think it technically is if there's no body buried there. Memorial is probably a more accurate description."

Ali looked at him inquisitively.

"I made it for Dad...and for Anna."

Tears formed in her eyes before she could turn from him. "Eli, this is...I don't know what to say." She kneeled beside him and covered her face.

He wrapped an arm around her shoulders. "Shh. It's okay."

When her tears finally subsided, she stared with red eyes at the two memorials side by side. "Do you think they'd be proud of us now?"

"Absolutely," he said without hesitation. "I come up here sometimes just to talk to him. I like to think his soul is resting somewhere, keeping a watch on you and me. If I know my dad, he's probably having a large cup of gray grass right now to celebrate us finding each other again."

Ali laughed. "You're right, although I think he'd be devastated to know we're still not married."

They both fell silent.

Eli covered the back of her hand with his own. It felt so foreign. Like they no longer fit together. The electric warmth he used to feel had disappeared. "You don't need to worry about me, Ali. I'm okay."

He didn't have to say it. She knew he was talking about Nik and the fact that she'd chosen him over Eli. But he *was* okay.

Ali studied his face. Whatever she saw there must've set her at ease. "You are, aren't you?"

Eli nodded. "I get it now," he said. He understood what it was like to develop feelings for someone unintentionally. He understood now how it just happened without even realizing until it was too late. One day a person walks into your life and before you know what's happening, you're forever intertwined with them.

He pictured Grace and the way her hair flowed over her shoulder first thing in the morning, before her eyes opened and the weight of Berland fell on her shoulders. So at peace and entirely his.

It didn't feel like there was one specific moment in which he had fallen for her. It had been all the small moments. The soft touches. The sly grins. Her boisterous laughter. And the way she *chose* to spend her time with him. He never felt like he had to compete for her affection.

Ironic since the only way to win her heart was to enter the Rite, something he hadn't allowed himself to consider. The day she'd told him about the Rite, it had been so easy to say he wasn't interested. But now...things had changed. Could he really give her up? Was he ready to take on that level of commitment to both her and Berland? The weight of such a large decision made his stomach turn.

Ali pulled her legs in and wrapped her arms around them. "So tell me about this place. What have you been up to? Tell me more about Grace."

His heart skipped a beat at her name. Surely, Ali hadn't meant any-thing by it. She couldn't read his thoughts, after all. No, Grace was just the only person she'd met so far. He tilted his head, cracked his neck, and dove in to the tale of everything that had happened to him in Berland so far.

Chapter Thirty-Seven

NIK

Nik watched as Ali moved about their noticeably empty new room. It had the distinct air of being uninhabited for a long time. The air was stiff and there wasn't a single trinket in sight to give any indication of what the previous residents might've been like. The walls were stark white, the concrete floor pristine, with a beige circular rug placed under the bed.

Ali inspected every barren surface, running her fingers along the threads of the olive comforter on the bed. *Their bed*. It didn't feel real to him. This was the new beginning that they'd been wishing for even before Rysburg had been attacked. They'd wanted a fresh start, but something didn't seem quite right.

"It's rather empty, isn't it?" Ali asked, as if reading his mind. "Like we're just visiting."

"It'll fill with bits and pieces of us soon enough."

She nodded and took the few belongings she owned out of her bag, placing them in the chest in the corner of the room. Her possessions hardly filled half of the top drawer.

"Leave some room for me, will you?" he joked, and she flashed him an amused grin.

"I'm going to shower before dinner."

Ali walked into the bathroom, leaving the door open behind her. He heard the water turn on and a minute later, a shirt flew through the air and fell to the floor.

He chuckled.

A second later, her pants landed on the floor next to her shirt.

Nik bit his lip at the thought of her naked body standing under the hot stream of water. He peered into the bathroom, but the glass door of the shower was already foggy. He could only make out the blurry outline of her figure.

Nik knocked on the shower door and she opened it an inch, her eyes sparkling with mischief and her cheeks flushed from the water and the heat building between them.

"Yes?" she asked before taking her bottom lip between her teeth. He wanted to take a bite himself.

"Would you like some company?" His words were laced with seduction as he tried to peek beyond the inch of open space. His face pressed closer to hers, but she stopped him with the touch of a finger. Using her pointer finger, she pushed his lips away.

"I have to wash my hair, Nik. Can't I have one minute to myself?" Her tone suggested she'd rather have anything *but* a moment to herself. Ali started to close the door to the shower, but Nik caught it, forcing it open. The door rattled, and Ali pressed her back to the wall of the shower, her entire body bared to Nik, dripping and hot.

"Nik!" she yelled and then laughed, splashing water at him. The spray landed on Nik's face and splattered his shirt.

He tsked. "You shouldn't do that, Ali."

"What are you going to do? Punish me?" Her eyes issued a challenge, and he watched as she felt her way down her neck and to her breasts, playing with her nipples before reaching between her legs.

Watching Ali get herself off was one of his favorite things to do, but right now he wanted to slide his fingers between her folds and pump into her until she trembled and moaned his name.

She licked her finger and brought it down to her clit, her chest heaving as tension built.

Holy fuck.

Ali watched him impatiently as he kicked off his shoes and removed his shirt and jeans. She stepped forward before he could remove his briefs, gripping him over the fabric.

Nik grabbed her wrists and pressed her back into the shower, stepping in behind her and letting the hot water wash over him. She stared at the outline of his shaft through his wet underwear and pushed her hips forward, desperate for contact. He hardened to know how needy she was for him.

His voice dropped an octave. "Turn around."

He loosened his grip on her wrists just enough for her to spin and face the wall, then pinned them with one of his hands. Ali writhed and pressed her backside against him, grinding her ass into his cock.

"Uh-uh," he admonished. He used his other hand to wrap around her waist and between her thighs. He used all his strength to still her against him, and she whimpered at the harsh pressure of his hand over her clit.

She tried to buck several times into his palm before realizing his hold was too strong. She was at his mercy.

"If I let go, will you be a good girl for me?"

She hesitated before nodding.

Nik released her pussy and slid his hand up her stomach to cup her breast, her back against his chest. Ali jolted again, rubbing her ass against him.

"What did I say, Ali?"

She laughed and continued to grind against him.

"Do you want to be punished?"

Her shoulders tensed, and Nik watched them relax as he ran a hand down her spine. If she wanted this...she'd have to tell him.

She stayed quiet a moment too long. Maybe she was having second thoughts.

"You're safe with me, Ali. I won't do anything you don't want me to do."

Ali tilted her head back, and Nik leaned forward to kiss along the edge of her jaw. She was already breathing heavily. He wanted to give her everything she desired—whatever that may be.

"Nik?" she asked uneasily.

Fuck. That primal want in her voice made him want to bury himself inside her cunt and drive into her until she cried his name over and over again. He wanted to feel her pussy gripping him so tightly that he saw stars.

"Yes?" he whispered into her neck.

He felt her jaw tremble beneath his lips. Ali had always been a little timid when it came to voicing her needs aloud. Sometimes she needed some encouragement. "Do you want me to spank you, Ali?"

She swallowed and then nodded. Nik let out a soft laugh, and she shivered. "Fuck, Ali, you're going to drive me crazy."

He released her wrists and took a step back, grabbing her by the waist to steady her. She clawed at the tile of the shower and hung her head, waiting for his palm to make contact with her skin.

Nik pulled a hand back, but before he could bring it down, she flinched. "Wait."

He brought his hand down and slid it between her thighs, rubbing her wet pussy and calming her nerves. "Just say the word and I'll stop. Okay?"

Ali took a deep breath and nodded. "Okay. I'm ready."

Nik drew his hand back once more. He brought his palm down against her flesh and a smack rang out through the bathroom. It sounded worse than it was. He didn't want to hurt her. Ali jumped, but then she rolled her hips with a needy pleasure. Nik knew if he placed his hand between her thighs, he would find her dripping wet—and not from the shower.

"Harder," she said.

Nik never would've imagined this was what Ali craved. He had never met anyone like her. As he brought his hand down a second time, the strike of her flesh stung his palm. She hissed, then let out a shaky breath.

"Still doing okay?" he asked.

"Yes," she responded irritably. "I will tell you if it's too—"

He interrupted her with another slap. She gasped with surprise and then gasped again when he slid his fingers between her folds. Nik used his fingers to spread her wide, teasing every inch of her while she squirmed and rolled her hips.

He pressed one finger inside and she dropped her head, her entire body shaking. She moved one hand to the apex of her thighs, but Nik grabbed her by the wrist.

"Did I say you could touch yourself?"

She shook her head and muttered, "No."

"Put your hand back on the wall." He released her wrist, and she did as he commanded.

"Such a good girl," he muttered, pulling his finger out and sliding it along her entrance, teasing her slick center until her knees began to tremble.

Nik pressed his finger inside again and again, slowly building her up to a devastating end. He sucked in a sharp breath when she squeezed around his finger, hungry to be filled by more of him. Then he slowly eased a second finger inside, and she threw her head back with a satisfied moan.

"Do you like the way that feels, Ali?"

She struggled to form complete sentences. "Yes. Yes...fuck, Nik. Please."

He slid his fingers in and out of her at an agonizing pace, and she clamped her thighs around his hand.

"Stop teasing," she begged.

Nik stifled a laugh. He forced his knee between her thighs and spread her legs back open wide, continuing to thrust his fingers inside her. Then he placed his other hand on her lower back, pushing her hard against the wall of the shower. She gasped as her stomach met the cool, smooth tile. Nik used all his force to keep her pinned to the wall and drove into her vigorously with his fingers.

A cry of pleasure ripped from Ali's throat, and her walls squeezed around him. He edged his fingers along the inside of her pussy, appreciating the way she hung onto him for dear life. He pushed in and out. In and out. In and out until she couldn't handle it anymore.

Ali released a torrent of rapid, shallow breaths as her body seized in ecstasy. Her knees buckled, and Nik wrapped a powerful arm around her waist, holding her against him as he continued to finger her through her orgasm.

He finally pulled out of her when her breathing returned to normal and her head rolled back onto his shoulder. He watched drops of water run down her face. His tongue traced the trail of water, drinking from her skin before sucking on the juncture of her jaw and neck. Her body shuddered when he sucked on her earlobe while massaging her breasts.

He wasn't done with her yet.

Ali reached behind her and pulled on his hair. Nik could still feel the way her arm quivered next to his cheek, too weak to hold up on her own. His hands roamed her body, circling around her clit and then up to her breast. He ran his thumb over her nipple and then pawed at her side, up her arm until his fingers intertwined with hers in his hair.

Ali's other hand drove a wedge between their bodies until she was cupping him over the fabric of his briefs. He was hard in her palm, and her light touch sent shivers up his spine. He hummed his approval in her ear as she began to stroke him.

Nik was forced to release the arm around her waist when she wiggled out of his grip and turned to face him. Without so much as a second's hesitation, she dropped to her knees, and he wanted to shatter at the sight.

As she tugged at the top of his briefs, she bit her lip and looked up at him through long lashes.

Fucking hell...

He braced his hands on the wall of the shower as Ali pulled his underwear down his legs and he stepped out of them. She left them lying on the bottom of the shower as she ran her fingers back up his ankles. His calves. The sensitive spot behind his knees.

"That fucking tickles, Ali." Even as he said the words, his cock twitched.

She gave him an evil grin in response before continuing to run her fingers over his thighs, gripping his ass as she leaned forward.

Nik banged a fist against the wall when she wrapped her fingers around his shaft, slowly pumping him in retaliation for the way he'd teased her. She let the tip of her tongue graze the underside of his cock, from the base all the way to the tip, glistening with arousal. Then she pulled back and licked her lips like he was the best dessert she'd ever tasted.

Ali locked eyes with him before covering the head of his cock and wrapping him with her tongue. He shuddered as she flicked her tongue over him and took him deeper.

Water dripped down his face, and he wiped it away with the back of his hand, not wanting to miss a second of this. He watched as she bobbed her head, using her palm to twist him gently at the base and the other to massage his balls.

He let out a strangled string of words of admiration and affection.

"So fucking beautiful."

"Love your lips on my cock."

"You feel so good."

Each word of praise had Ali sucking him harder and faster. His eyelids fluttered, but he forced them open again to watch her work him. Her eyes watered as he nudged the back of her throat, and he felt her swallow around him.

The ground beneath his feet was about to give out.

He made shallow pulses, pressing forward as deep as she could take him. The pressure built in his core and worked its way lower. He hissed shaky breaths through his teeth and wrapped a hand in her wet hair, cupping the back of her head. She could barely move as she stared up at him, licking and sucking as she worked to unravel him.

"So fucking pretty with my cock in your mouth."

She smiled, and her lips stretched over him. It was as if she was enjoying this as much as he was. She probably was. He knew her well enough to know that look in her eyes.

Ali whimpered, and it was like electricity shooting through his body. He pulled her by the hair, and she released his hard length, saliva dripping off her chin. Nik gave himself one...two...three hard strokes, and he erupted, spilling onto her breasts.

The devilish gleam in her eyes returned, and she swiped a finger through his cum and swirled it around her nipple.

That was the moment his legs gave out.

Nik dropped to his knees, and she climbed into his lap. He could still feel the slickness between her thighs as she wrapped her legs around him. She tenderly rubbed his back while he rested his head on her shoulder, his hands sliding over her wet skin.

"I love you, Nik."

Her hand made lazy strokes through his hair, and Nik felt as though he could fall asleep in her arms.

But the water turned lukewarm. They must've used their allotted hot water.

As he pulled back from Ali, she shivered and gave a small laugh. "I really do need to wash my hair."

Chapter Thirty-Eight

NIK

Nik reluctantly left Ali to finish cleaning up. He wrapped a gray towel around his waist that was surprisingly soft. Nothing like anything he'd ever owned. While searching the drawers, he stumbled across a few new outfits for each of them.

He held up a pair of jeans and a blue long-sleeve shirt, the latter of which was a bit large for him, but it was better than putting on his sweaty, dirty clothes again. He'd love nothing more than to set those vile clothes on fire.

As Nik slipped into the pants, there was a firm knock on the door. He hurried to pull the shirt over his head and tossed his towel over the back of a chair before he pried the door open.

Eli stood at the threshold. He looked beyond Nik's shoulders into the room, his face scrunched in confusion. "You were supposed to be in the dungeons."

Nik rolled his eyes and gave a mocking laugh. He stepped back and made way for Eli to enter the room.

"Where's Ali?" he asked as he sat a dark glass bottle on the round table in the kitchenette. He searched the cabinets for glasses as if it were his home, not Ali and Nik's.

"In the shower. She should be out in a minute. Do you need something?"

It hadn't been that long since Ali had returned from her private conversation with Eli. They'd been gone for quite some time, but Nik had done his best not to pry despite the curiosity that rippled through his veins. Just like he tried not to be too irritated that Eli was standing in their kitchen after he'd already spent most of the afternoon with Ali. He had to remind himself they hadn't seen each other in almost two months.

"Just to bring a housewarming gift. And to let you know Grace wants to invite you to dinner at her home."

Nik took a seat across from Eli, who had opened the bottle and poured a light pink liquid into two glasses.

"What is this?" Nik asked, taking the glass from Eli. He took a sniff, reminded of the last time someone had served him a mysterious drink. At least it looked and smelled better than gray grass tea.

"It's angelfruit wine."

Nik had never been one for wine, but after arriving in Berland and finally getting a chance to relax, he felt like taking the edge off.

He took a sip and was assaulted with a sugary sweetness that lingered on his taste buds. The slight burning sensation of alcohol tickled his throat, and he grimaced.

Eli laughed as he sipped from his own glass. "Not your taste?"

Nik shook his head. "I don't think so."

Awkward silence hung in the air. Eli shifted in his seat and cleared his throat after each sip of his drink, like he was about to say something but decided against it. They'd never been anything remotely close to friends, and it seemed the small talk ended with wine.

As if he suddenly remembered something, Eli reached into the pocket of his jacket and pulled out a glistening chain. It swung in his hand and when it stopped moving, Nik recognized the amethyst stone pendant hanging in front of him.

An inexplicable sense of relief ran through him. It was only a simple piece of jewelry, but it represented so much more. It represented his love for Ali and everything they'd been through. He recalled with perfect clarity the day he'd picked it out for her winter solstice gift...and their first time together after he'd given it to her at the New Year's Banquet.

"Where did you find that?" he asked as he reached for Ali's necklace.

"I grabbed it that night during the attack. I saw it on the ground somewhere between setting a forest on fire and bursting into a run. I thought you might want it back."

Something tugged at Nik's heart, reminding him of that day and what they'd lost. Weeks filled only with bad days and memories that would haunt him for the rest of his life. He rubbed his eyes and tried to erase the mental image that had appeared—the empty look in Ali's eyes staring back at him whenever he'd been brave enough to look into them.

"Are you okay?" Eli raised a brow and took another sip from his drink. "Do I even want to know what went on out there?"

Nik swirled the drink in his glass and brought it to his lips before remembering the sickly-sweet taste and setting it back down. "Ali didn't tell you?"

Eli shrugged his shoulders. "She was very *factual* in her recounting. I could tell something wasn't right, but she didn't tell me much aside from where you've been and how you came to be here."

Nik rubbed the hair on his chin. It didn't feel like it was his place to tell Eli what Ali had gone through. She would tell him in her own time, if she chose to.

"Is she okay?" Eli asked.

It was frustrating how much Eli cared for her. It would be so much easier to hate the guy if he wasn't a good person. But Eli was like a fucking parasite. There was no getting rid of him.

"She's doing better now," Nik answered truthfully.

The sound of the shower ceased, and seconds later, Ali popped her head out of the bathroom door. "Oh. I didn't know you were here, Eli."

Nik turned around and was thankful she was at least wearing a towel. He sighed heavily, wishing she would cover up further. When he turned back to Eli, he found him facing the table, staring intently at his hands. *Good.*

Eli cleared his throat. "Just came by to check in and make sure you were situated."

"He brought wine." Nik made a ceremonious show of swirling his glass.

"Thank you. I'll just change and be right back out."

Nik pointed to their shared dresser. "There are fresh clothes in the second drawer from the top."

Ali slid the drawer open and grabbed a few items before returning to the bathroom. When she emerged, she was wearing a black T-shirt with light jeans that squeezed her ass in all the right places. Despite nearly starving for weeks on end, she'd managed to gain a little weight in their brief stint on the farm. Even the healthy glow was returning to her cheeks.

There were only two chairs around their small table, so Nik pulled her by the wrist until she was sitting in his lap. Eli didn't so much as flinch. He must've come to terms with Nik and Ali's relationship. That or he was so happy to be reunited with her that he didn't want to cause trouble.

Ali took a sip from Nik's glass, not bothering to pour her own. "Oh, this is delicious."

Nik chuckled. "You would enjoy that sickly sweet concoction."

Ali did a little shimmy that she sometimes did when she was satisfied. He noticed it most frequently when she got her hands on dessert. Which made sense since angelfruit wine was sweeter than cake. She shimmied again, and he had to shift in his chair and think about anything other than her ass rubbing against him.

"So what did we miss here? You've just been living in luxury this whole time?" Nik asked.

"I wouldn't call it luxury, but it's certainly better than that hell you call home."

Ali sighed heavily, and she didn't have to say a word for Nik to know her thoughts. She didn't want to be put in the middle of them. So he bit his tongue. Hard enough to draw blood.

"Sorry," Eli said without prompting. But it wasn't an apology to Nik. It was to Ali. He stared at her long enough to make Nik's eye twitch, then shook his head. "I can't believe you're sitting here in front of me. I missed you so much."

Nik's hand on her waist tightened involuntarily. Before he could taunt Eli or throw another insult, there was another knock on the door and Ali stood up. She turned the knob and opened the door, allowing Grace to step through.

Grace gave them a bright and cheery grin. "Dinner is ready."

Nik got the impression that she was always cheerful, which was a bit annoying, but she seemed too nice to hold it against her.

"Hope you all are hungry."

Eli drained the rest of his glass in one gulp and then Nik's glass too before grabbing the half-empty bottle. "Let's go."

Chapter Thirty-Nine

ALI

THE HALLS OF BERLAND'S mountain were like a maze. Being underground was disorienting, and the walls and never-ending line of doors all looked the same to Ali. It didn't help that the halls lacked any distinguishing features.

They reached the large entrance hall again, and this time Grace led them toward a different tunnel.

"How big is this place?" Ali asked Eli, who was walking next to her with a familiar pep in his step.

From his other side, Grace responded, "We have nearly two thousand rooms between this floor and the lower level. And, of course, a few common areas as well like the infirmary and cafeteria. You'll get used to it. See the symbols above the halls?" Grace pointed above the one they were entering now. A golden crown. "They'll help you make sense of it all."

They'd almost made it to the end of the hall when she pointed out a door. "That's Eli's place. I'm sure you'll want to make a note of that."

Eli had mentioned that Grace was his closest friend here, and that she knew all about Ali and their past. It was obvious he'd grown close to her in the time he'd spent in Berland. Ali ignored the twinge of jealousy that someone might've replaced her as Eli's best friend. It wasn't fair to keep him all to herself when she had Nik.

Eli deserved to be happy too. She was glad he had other friends now.

"Yes. Thank you."

"And here's my place." They had stopped in front of a grand door, twice the size of the ones they'd seen before, with ornate details. Two guards stood outside. They did not acknowledge the group accompanying Grace; one simply opened the door for her, and she led them inside.

The interior was like nothing Ali had ever seen before. The high ceilings made it feel cavernous but extravagant, and two staircases spiraled along either side of the entry. The attention to detail had withstood the test of time, and Ali could make out unique designs along the staircase railing as well as the crown molding.

"I live with my parents, but they won't be joining us tonight." Grace rushed toward the dining room they could see through a curved archway.

Ali gave Eli a questioning look.

He leaned in close enough to whisper, "Grace is royalty around here, but she doesn't like to talk about it. She just wants to be normal like the rest of us."

Ali simply nodded, though she didn't understand why someone would choose normalcy over *this*.

They moved into the dining room where the table was set for ten people. White ceramic plates with a blue floral pattern and silver utensils lay on top of matching blue tablecloths. Matching silverware, which was a far cry from the scrambled collection of utensils Ali had growing up. Even the forks and knives had intricate designs carved into the handles.

Two of the seats were already occupied by a woman with dark brown hair and tan skin and another with wavy, light red hair and freckles strewn across her cheeks.

"These are my friends, Amaya and Heather," Grace said, pointing to each of her friends. "Ladies, this is Ali and Nik."

"Where's Sam?" Eli asked. "I thought he'd be meeting us here as well."

"I sent Theo to retrieve him," Grace answered. Then she addressed Nik and Ali. "Theo is my brother. Genna and Isabel are with him as well. They should be here any minute."

They all took a seat at the table. Grace sat next to her two friends, and Ali sat with Nik on one side and Eli on the other. It felt like a divide of sorts. Old friends on one half and new acquaintances across from them.

Ali felt the need to initiate conversation, but it was as if all thoughts had escaped her brain. She'd never had to make friends before. Aside from Nik and Sam, everyone in her life had just always been there. Thankfully, Eli was chatty and alleviated some of the pressure.

He told them all about his experience so far in Berland and that they would love it here. He talked about a lake and then briefly mentioned his job in the research lab.

"It's incredible. They have all these artifacts that are centuries old. It's our job to try to recreate them. You should see some of the stuff they have here, Ali. It'll blow your mind."

Ali smiled as he carried on discussing his new job, though she had a hard time comprehending much of it. It sounded like he was speaking a foreign language. He was learning to read and write, too. His eyes lit up as he explained his latest project.

"Luka says you're the fastest learning apprentice he's had in his entire tenure," Grace said, winking at Eli. "Eli's going to be one of the best researchers to come out of the lab, mark my words."

She beamed at him, and Eli's cheeks turned pink.

Ali blinked a few times to make sure she was seeing properly. Then she turned to Nik to see if he had caught that too. He raised his brows, and she knew he had. Was there more than just friendship between them?

Eventually the others arrived, escorted by Theo. Theo was just as flawless as his sister, with beautiful blue eyes and dirty blonde hair that looked soft to the touch. It was an interesting contrast from Grace's dark hair and hazel eyes. If it weren't for their similar bone structure, it would've been hard to tell they were siblings.

Theo was quite the gentleman. He pulled Sam's chair out and offered to pour a glass of water while he pushed his chair in. He did the same for Genna, but Isabel insisted she did not need his help.

Once everyone was settled, a pair of servants came out with hot meals and placed them in front of each guest. Steam rolled off the sautéed vegetables and charred fish. There was more wine on the table, and Eli poured a glass for himself, Ali, and—to her surprise—one for Nik as well.

Of course when Nik grimaced after a sip, she realized it wasn't a thoughtful gesture but a well-placed snub. Eli grinned as he swirled his glass of wine.

Men.

"So what have you lot been doing while Eli was here?" Theo asked.

The space around Ali seemed to tighten, like the walls of the dining room were closing in and suffocating her. She cleared her throat, but Nik spoke first.

"We were just doing a little exploration."

A round of laughter for his dry humor.

"How long were you out there on your own?" Heather asked between sips of wine.

"A couple months, I guess. You sort of lose track of time after a while. But we weren't on our own the whole time. We came across a family who took us in, and it was while we were with them that we ran into Genna and Isabel."

"Very lucky of you," Theo said. "These two are angels."

Isabel rolled her eyes, and Genna laughed. "He's exaggerating. We did what anyone would have done. Our job, first and foremost, is to help people. How could we not help you after we realized you were looking for Eli? It would've gone against everything we stand for."

Ali watched them all interact. It was comforting to be surrounded by a group of friends. It reminded her so much of Andus and how close they had been as a community. These people had that, and she wanted it too.

"So before that, you were sleeping on the ground? What did you eat?" Heather had so many questions. Ali knew on some level that she was just curious. She had probably always had the shelter and safety that Berland provided. But her questions felt invasive.

"It was hard," Ali said. "We didn't really have any clue where we were going and there were times I wasn't sure we'd survive."

If *she* would survive.

The rest of the group seemed to understand that it wasn't something they wanted to talk about, and Heather quickly abandoned her line of questioning.

Eli gave her an encouraging nod and straightened in his seat. "Well, you're here now," he said, raising his glass. "A toast. To new friends and old."

They all raised their glasses and drank their wine, even Nik.

Ali tried to shove the memories of the past few weeks into a mental box, forcing the lid closed and tossing the key into the river that was always raging in her mind. She was here now with Eli and Nik. She was alive. There was no need to relive her nightmares.

They ate through lighthearted conversations and friendly banter. Even Nik and Eli got along for most of the night. When Heather offered to *fix* Ali's hair, Eli helpfully suggested that she *fix* Nik's beard first.

He wasn't wrong. It was out of control. Nik lifted a glass in his direction as if to say touché.

Grace offered seconds when Nik and Eli devoured their main course. Ali lost track of the number of bottles of wine that flooded the table. The entire evening felt extravagant, fit for a princess.

By the time dessert was passed around, Ali couldn't handle any more. Which was a shame because she really did love cake. Instead, she watched as Eli helped himself to the biggest slice. He looked much healthier now. His cheekbones were less pronounced and his muscular arms had regained their form.

Out of the corner of her eye, she watched as Theo wiped frosting from Sam's cheek, a moment that no one else seemed to notice. Maybe she had drank too much wine. She shook her head and sipped from her water glass.

Then the evening came to a close. She had no idea how it had gotten so late, but it was well past midnight. Nik helped her out of her chair. That angelfruit wine was stronger than she'd thought.

As they said their goodbyes, Ali watched as Grace gave Eli a hug that lasted a few seconds too long. Again, she shook her head, certain that she was seeing things. Must've been the wine.

Ali wrapped an arm around Nik's waist. "I hope you remember the way home, because I sure as hell don't."

He chuckled and planted a chaste kiss on her temple. "I've got you."

Chapter Forty

ALI

It was easy for Ali to fall into place in Berland. It felt like they'd walked through the desert and found themselves at an oasis. Everything was simple here.

And yet, she found herself waiting for the other shoe to drop.

Nothing could be this perfect.

She and Nik made their way to the cafeteria one morning—a cafeteria that served food to the newcomers for free while they settled in. This place was a utopia.

Nik grabbed them something to eat while she saved a seat at a table in the far corner. She liked sitting on the edge of the large room so she could watch everyone else come and go. She was slowly learning names and understanding the ins and outs of Berland. In just a few days, she had already learned so much.

There was a group of elderly ladies that came by every morning, gossiping as they grabbed their breakfast. This morning they were discussing the latest scandal—some woman by the name of Katherine had slept with a man that wasn't her husband. They hunched over and attempted their version of whispering, but their hearing must've been diminishing because their gossip was loud enough for everyone to hear.

Ali laughed and scanned the crowd for more entertainment. While she was surveying the breakfast crowd, Eli came walking through the tables looking bright and cheerful. It was reminiscent of the way he used to look before their workdays in Andus. He had always been too energetic in the mornings and had a contagious level of optimism. It was nice to see it returned.

Eli did a double take when he saw her sitting alone and headed straight toward her. "Good morning. Why are you sitting here alone?"

"Nik just went to get our food. Shouldn't you be at work? How's the project coming along?"

She still didn't understand all the details of how they recreated objects, but Eli was obsessed with his work and that was enough to make her happy for him.

"We hit a snag. We're waiting on a few materials to come in on the next load of imports. I have the day off, so I thought I'd show you around town if you'd like."

"That sounds amazing."

"What sounds amazing?" Nik asked as he took a seat next to Eli. He handed Ali a plate with toast, eggs, and fresh fruit while he dug into his oatmeal.

"Eli offered to give us a tour of the town."

Eli gave Ali a look that said he'd rather it just be the two of them, and Nik caught on immediately. He cleared his throat. "Actually, I told Sam I'd hang out with him today."

Nik was clearly lying. Just last night, he'd said he wanted to do some exploring today.

Ali didn't miss the small grin on Eli's face at Nik's proclamation. It would just be the two of them today. Quite honestly, it was something she was looking forward to as well. It had only been a couple months, but she felt like they'd been apart for years. She had a hard time letting him out of her sight. She could explore with Nik another day.

"Great," Eli said a little too cheerfully. "I'm going to grab a coffee and I'll be ready. Finish up your breakfast."

Once he had left Ali and Nik alone, Ali brushed Nik's hand. "You could've come with us."

"It's fine. I don't want to intrude. Besides, Eli wants my company as much as I want his."

He wasn't wrong, so Ali didn't argue.

"What will you and Sam do today?"

"Braid each other's hair. Talk about our feelings. The usual."

Ali laughed and rubbed Nik's back. "I don't think your hair is long enough for braids, sweetie." She twisted her fingers through his strands, only two or three inches long.

They finished their breakfast and then Nik left to find Sam while Eli and Ali headed toward the mountain's exit.

Ali squinted when they were greeted with the abrasive sunlight. It was such a stark contrast from the darkness of the mountain, but she welcomed the warmth on her skin.

"Why do they live in a hole in the ground? Wouldn't it be better to live outside?" she asked, gesturing at the beautiful weather.

"The homes under the mountain are from before the fall of civilization. The people were paranoid about an apocalypse, so they built homes underground to stay safe. Guess they had good reason to be paranoid," Eli said with a shrug. "Anyway, the infrastructure is all under the mountain. It would've been a pain in the ass to build new homes and tie them into the electrical grid. Easier to just use what's already there."

"I guess so." She still missed the natural light pouring through her window in the morning. The lamps that mimicked the day and night were a shoddy substitute. "Tell me more about this place. What are all these buildings out here if not homes?"

Eli gave her a brief history of the town, told her about their trade network and neighboring allies. They passed small shop after shop and he pointed out each one, describing what goods they sold or what services they offered. He led her inside one and eagerly shoved a loaf of bread in her hands that was covered with melted cheese.

"This one is my favorite," he said.

She couldn't help but notice the change in him. In Rysburg, he'd been completely shattered, a mere shadow of himself. She felt like her insides could burst seeing him so happy now. And she didn't think it was solely because of the town's amenities.

"Tell me about Grace," she said.

"What about her?"

He skillfully avoided her gaze, and she gave him a look that she hoped conveyed her annoyance. She hadn't imagined that moment at the dinner party. Nik had seen it too. "She's pretty."

"She is…"

"You've spent a lot of time with her?"

"I guess you could say that. She was my first friend here, and she's done a lot for me."

Ali nodded, partly to herself.

Eli noticed her knowing smile almost immediately. "What is that look for?"

She feigned innocence. "Nothing."

"I know you better than anyone, Ali. Don't lie to me."

"Do you have feelings for her?"

Eli stopped abruptly in his tracks, a look of horror on his face. "Why would you ask that?"

His reaction was almost comical, but she didn't think it would be wise to laugh. Did he really think it wasn't obvious? "I couldn't help but notice how close you two are. And then at dinner…"

"There's nothing between Grace and me. And there never will be." He deflated a little but continued their walk, the sound of gravel crunching beneath their feet. They passed a woman sitting on a stool outside of her shop, carefully weaving a basket. Beside her, finished baskets were stacked in rows for easy perusal. The woman tipped her head in greeting as they walked by.

Ali smiled. "Never say never, Eli."

Men could be so oblivious sometimes. There was *definitely* something going on between them, whether he was ready to admit it or not.

Eli heaved a sigh. "Grace is…unavailable. Even if I did like her like that, we could never be…anything."

"Why?"

Eli choked on his words, and Ali wondered if she'd asked the wrong thing. "Grace is special."

Ali smiled. Now they were getting somewhere.

"Stop that," Eli said, pointing at the dimples in her cheeks.

She put her hands up in defense. "Stop what?"

"I told you Grace is like royalty around here."

Ali raised her brows but didn't interrupt. It was clearly difficult for him to talk about this, even though they'd never had any trouble communicating before.

"Her mother is the Lady of Berland—the ruler of this community. And Grace is next in line to take her title."

Ali nodded. "And that's a problem because…?"

Eli began to pace, and Ali raised her brows. She couldn't remember ever seeing him this worked up. "There's this ceremony—the Rite. It's a competition—three rounds of physical contests with eliminations in each. The winner...the winner gets to marry Grace and rule beside her."

"Like an arranged marriage?" Ali had heard fables of other civilizations who forced couples to be together. She'd always assumed those were myths. "That hardly seems fair. She doesn't get a say?"

Eli plopped down on the ground. They'd made their way to the small lake, shimmering in the late morning sun. He ran a frustrated hand through his hair as she sat down next to him. "Unfortunately not. She seems resigned to her fate. And I don't think her mother would let her out of it even if she wanted to. Grace is incredibly loyal to Berland and its traditions."

"Well, why don't you enter, then?" Eli was naturally fit. Whatever these physical challenges were, Ali had no doubt he could win if he wanted to.

"I'm not entering."

"Why not?"

He grew irritated. "Ali..."

"I'm just saying that she seems like a nice girl. I don't see why you wouldn't—"

"Because I'm not you. I don't fall head over heels with the first person that comes my way."

Ali flinched. She had forgotten for a moment the Nik-sized wedge between them. She'd been stupid to think they were past it. All she could do was stare at the ripples on the surface of the lake and try to fight back tears.

Eli pinched the bridge of his nose. "Ali, I'm sorry. I didn't mean that."

"No, you did." She turned away from him, but he heard the break in her voice and wrapped an arm around her waist to hug her close. She wiped a stray tear from her cheek and leaned into him. "I just want to see you happy, Eli."

"I am happy."

She wasn't sure she entirely believed him but decided not to press him any further. The last thing she wanted was to upset him after she had just gotten him back.

Instead, she would have to trust him.

Chapter Forty-One

ELI

ELI SAT AT THE edge of Grace's bed as she flung clothes from a closet the size of his entire home. Another dress flew through the air and landed on a pile that was already up to Eli's knees. "What are you looking for?" he asked for the third time.

Her voice was muffled from the closet. "I told you. There's a white dress that I *need* for the dance."

"Why don't you just wear one of these other white dresses?" There were already at least four in the pile in front of him. He didn't understand why she could only settle for one specific dress. He pulled one from the pile in front of him, and his fingers were suddenly covered in glitter that he couldn't brush off.

The dress had to be ancient. How in the hell it had maintained its sparkle was beyond Eli's comprehension. He brushed his hands against his jeans, but that only made it worse. Now his pants had a shimmer about them.

Her face appeared in the doorway, looking frazzled. He'd never seen her look so unkept, and it made him laugh a little. "Because, Eli"—she huffed, irritated by his idiocy—"the one I'm looking for is sparkly."

"Like this?" He held up the culprit of the glitter contamination.

"No. That's beige. I need *white.*"

Ah, of course. How could he be so silly? Obviously there was a difference between beige and white.

An excited squeal erupted from the closet. "Found it!"

A moment later, Grace appeared wearing a shimmering white dress that accentuated every one of her curves. Eli had seen her in several stunning gowns, but this one surpassed them all. It had thin straps that crisscrossed down her back and a long slit in the front that he could spot her tan leg through. And the sparkles—he understood what she meant now. The whole thing reflected light in such a way that it seemed like she was the sun itself. She was an ethereal goddess sent from heaven.

Eli snapped his jaw shut after another minute of staring at her. "Wow."

"See? I told you. What do you think?" She spun in a circle so he could take in the whole look.

"I've never seen anything more beautiful."

"I know, right?" She stood in front of a mirror in the corner of her bedroom and adjusted bits and pieces of the dress until it lay exactly how she wanted it.

Eli hadn't been talking about the dress, but she didn't seem to notice. He watched her from behind, his eyes studying the intricate way the straps twisted down her spine leading all the way to her lower back. Any lower and she'd be showing off some very intimate bits of her body. Curves that he was used to seeing as he bent her over his bed and...

When he brought his eyes up again, he found her watching his reflection in the mirror with a raised brow. "See something you like?"

A nonsensical noise escaped his throat, and his cheeks were on fire.

Grace slipped a finger under the strap over her right shoulder, bringing it down to her bicep. She repeated the motion on her left shoulder and shimmied out of the dress.

Eli quickly looked to the floor as the dress fell to her feet and then back up, up her long legs and squeezable hips, up to her generous breasts.

Grace snickered at his tortured moan. She slowly inched toward the bed where he sat, then pressed a finger to his chin. His eyes briefly flitted over her bare body once more as she lifted his gaze to meet hers. He swallowed hard and maintained eye contact.

Her knees knocked against his. He reached out, feeling the bare skin of her legs, and she shivered as he ran his fingertips over the backs of her knees. He felt his way up her thighs and to her waist, pulling her in to kiss her stomach.

Her head rolled back, and she brushed a palm over his scalp. When she looked back down at him, it was like she was staring into his soul. Like she could read his thoughts, could see how badly he wanted her.

They were playing a dangerous game, and he wasn't sure he'd be able to forfeit in the end.

Just as her hands wrapped around his neck, voices sounded downstairs.

Grace stepped back into the closet, and Eli released an exaggerated breath. When she returned, she was wearing a tank top and leggings, her hair pulled back in a messy bun. Somehow, she still looked as gorgeous as she had in the dress.

Someone knocked on her door, and Grace hurried to unlock and open it. Eli folded his hands in his lap to hide his erection.

"Grace, I needed—" Her mother walked into the room. "Oh, Eli. I wasn't expecting you. Why was this door locked?"

Grace crossed her arms over her chest, looking guilty. "Am I not allowed to have some privacy?"

Ellen cocked her head. "Of course you are. I would just prefer if your privacy didn't include other men when the Rite is just around the corner. No offense, Eli."

"None taken," he murmured, but he didn't think Ellen heard him. She continued to ramble.

"I've told you before it's improper to be alone with men right now." She sighed with one hand on her hip and the other massaging her temple. This was the first Eli had heard of Ellen's warning. Grace hadn't mentioned that her mother didn't approve of them spending time alone together.

Ellen carried on. "I'm sorry. We can talk about this another time. I came here to tell you the results of the investigation into the fire."

Eli sat straight, his attention fully on Ellen now. She gave him a look of contemplation and sighed. "I suppose you know everything Grace does, so you're welcome to listen."

She assumed correctly. Eli had been with Grace when she broke into Noah's office and already knew what she had told her mother.

"Gabriel was arrested this morning—"

"Gabriel?" Grace interrupted.

Eli looked between mother and daughter, waiting for an explanation. He hadn't met a Gabriel and had no idea how this man was connected to the rebellion.

"Yes, Grace." Ellen's eyes closed to slits, displeased with her daughter's outburst. "They found empty canisters like you described in his home."

"There must be a mistake." Grace's voice had become frantic.

Eli still had no idea what was happening. "Who is Gabriel?"

Grace began to pace in circles with her hands on her hips. "Gabriel is a member of the council. He's been a member for decades and he loves this town. He would never do something like this. He would never attack *you*," she said, pointing at her mother.

"There was evidence in his home, Grace. How can we dispute that?"

"It was planted," she shouted. "What about Trevor?"

"What about him?"

Eli frowned, still trying to wrap his head around what was happening.

"I told you he was the one who threatened Noah. He's the one behind this. I'm sure of it. Eli heard it too."

Ellen's mouth curved into a disapproving frown. If she hadn't known for certain that Eli had been with Grace when they were doing their own investigation, she did now.

"It's true," he interjected. "Trevor was blackmailing Noah. Did you investigate him?"

"We didn't have to. We received a tip about the evidence at Gabriel's before we had a chance to question Trevor," Ellen said.

"A tip? From who?" Grace asked.

Ellen hesitated. "It doesn't matter."

"*From who?*" Grace asked again, more forcefully.

Ellen sighed, knowing her daughter wouldn't let it go. "From Eamon."

"Eamon?" Grace was fuming. "What reason could Eamon *possibly* have to lead you away from Trevor?"

It didn't take too long for Eli to place the name though he'd only met him once. Trevor's father. Of course he would point them away from his son.

"You've got the wrong person," Eli said just as Grace chuckled in a disbelieving manner.

"That's enough." Ellen's tone was harsh and commanding. The voice of a leader, no longer the voice of a concerned mother. It was enough to silence both Grace and Eli. "The investigation is closed. Eamon is an upstanding member of this community and I trust him, despite what you think of his son. You must've misheard him. Perhaps your feelings toward him are tainted by the upcoming Rite."

Grace snarled at the accusation. Trevor was vile whether he competed in the Rite or not.

"Let it go, Grace. You have other things you should be focusing on." Ellen moved to leave Grace's bedroom but stopped at the doorway. "Eli, I think it's time for you to go home."

Grace huffed beside him but didn't interject. He wanted to stay, to comfort Grace. She looked heartbroken that Ellen didn't believe her. He knew how much her approval meant to Grace.

"I'll see you tomorrow," he said, then he followed Ellen out of the room and down the stairs.

When he reached the bottom step, Ellen abruptly turned to face him, a cold and indifferent expression on her face. "Do you intend to enter the Rite, Eli?"

Straight to the point. Her candidness caught him off guard. "I...um..."

"If you care about my daughter, it's time for you to let her go. She has a future she needs to start embracing. The sooner she comes to terms with that, the less painful it will be."

Eli shook his head, speechless.

Ellen raised a finger. "Don't insult my intelligence. I know what the two of you have been up to. You better hope the rest of Berland hasn't figured it out. You'll make a fool of her. People need to take her seriously and that'll never happen as long as she's sneaking around like a child. It's time to put an end to this juvenile behavior."

Eli did care about her. The last thing he wanted was to be the reason the people of Berland didn't take her seriously. Grace would be a kind and generous leader, the kind that people revered for years long after she was gone. But something like ice sliced at his heart...

"What if I did enter the Rite?"

Ellen's eyes went wide, and her jaw slackened before she caught herself. "Don't."

"Why not?" He needed a reason. His own no longer seemed valid.

Ellen stepped closer, and though she was several inches shorter than him, he still felt miniscule under her shadow.

She pointed a finger toward the door. "Because there are things about Berland that you know nothing about. Leading a community of this size while trying to keep everyone happy is a delicate balance. The last thing Grace needs is for someone to come along and disrupt that balance. The people here don't know you, and they aren't going to trust you anytime soon. So let her go. Let her be with someone that has spent their entire life here and has the advantage of familiarity."

"Someone like Trevor you mean?"

"Yes, someone like Trevor. You may not like him but he doesn't need your approval. He's spent much of his life seeking the approval of this community unlike you. And if Grace doesn't want to rock the boat, he's exactly the kind of suitor she should wind up with. Let her go. Do you understand me?"

Eli didn't know what to tell her. The last thing he wanted to do was make Grace's position more difficult. It was hard to believe that marrying him would cause such chaos, but perhaps Ellen had a better grasp on the stability of Berland than he did. Still, he couldn't deny his growing desire to enter the Rite. So he lied.

"Understood."

Chapter Forty-Two

ALI

THERE WAS SOMETHING INCREDIBLY intimate about dancing. Being only an inch away from Nik's face had an inexplicable effect on Ali's body. Every bone in her body stood at attention, and she was laser focused on the way their bodies connected. She was so close, she could stand on her toes and kiss his lips if she wanted to, but they had an audience.

Ali and Nik were standing in the middle of an empty ballroom, doing their best to follow Grace's instructions while Eli sat against the wall, watching until it was his turn. Apparently, he'd already had a few lessons, so he got to sit this round out.

It was hard to hear Grace's commands when Nik's eyes were scorching her skin. There was a vague mention of a beat or step count. It was all hazy compared to the electricity coursing through her veins, originating from where their hands entwined.

His other hand dug into her waist and pulled her body flush against him. The way he was looking at her took her breath away. Such softness in his eyes and a slight tilt in his head. When she bit her lip, he smirked in return. One of her hands rested on his shoulder and she rubbed her thumb over his neck, pleased at the way he leaned into her palm.

He made a sound that could only be described as a purr, and she continued to rub his neck as he rumbled.

"You're moving too slow," Grace said in an exasperated tone.

Nik's shoulders slumped, and he released Ali. "We can't all be natural dancers like you."

"Nonsense. This isn't natural talent. It's the result of practice and perseverance. Here, let me." She glided between Ali and Nik and forcefully put one of his hands on her hip and held the other with her hand. There was nothing romantic about it. Grace was simply a teacher instructing her student. Ali giggled as Nik stood straighter after being admonished. He was certainly paying attention now.

Ali walked to the edge of the room and sat on the floor next to Eli. His long legs extended in front of him made her legs seem exceedingly short.

Eli's eyes were set on Grace as she forced Nik around the room, correcting his steps and fixing his posture. "And I thought I was a terrible dancer."

Ali smacked him in the chest, and he laughed.

"Tell me I'm wrong." His shoulders shook from laughing so hard.

Ali started to say something but then stopped, grinning widely. "You're not wrong."

"You remember that one goose that used to live by the lake? The one with a maimed foot?" Eli asked through fits of laughter.

"Stop. Don't you dare." Ali couldn't hold back her grin.

"That's what Nik looks like." Eli wobbled back and forth, imitating Nik's lack of elegance.

Ali burst out laughing and clutched her side as she struggled to breathe. "Oh my god, you're right."

"If you two have nothing better to do, you could practice too, you know," Grace called out over the music and their hysterical giggling.

Nik threw them a look of irritation, and Ali forced herself to take deep breaths while Eli stifled his own snickering. Neither of them got up to practice, preferring instead to watch Nik and Grace waltz around the room.

"How are you adjusting?" he asked.

"Good. I wasn't sure what to expect coming here, but it's been better than I could've imagined." That was an understatement. Two weeks had already passed and Ali had never felt so relaxed in her life. As newcomers, they were pampered beyond belief. Someone had come by earlier that day to drop off freshly laundered clothes. Their next-door neighbor had baked them muffins. And while Grace had promised to help them find jobs, they'd yet to find the right position, so Ali divided her time equally between the sunny shore of the lake and playing in bed with Nik.

"Better than where you spent the past few weeks?"

Ali still hadn't told him everything that had happened between Rysburg and Berland. She felt ashamed of how she'd broken down without him and embarrassed by how she had treated Nik and even Sam at some times. She'd only given him the bare minimum details—that they had stayed at a farm for a little while. How they had run into Colin, though she didn't elaborate how he'd put his hands on her. Some details weren't necessary. Her heart sank at the memories.

Eli sighed. "You're my best friend, Ali. After everything we've been through, I hope you know you can trust me. You can tell me anything."

"I know," she said softly. "It was...hard. And it's equally hard to relive. After losing Mom and Jack, you were the last thing I had tying me to the life I once had. And then I thought you had died."

Eli flinched.

"Yeah. We saw you go down and at the time, I thought that was it. Until we found Sam and he told us you were still alive. But even then, I was so far gone. I spiraled into a horrible place. We were struggling every day to survive, but I was struggling for a reason to survive, too." She ignored the stinging in her eyes as she tried to explain what she had felt during that time. "It was all my fault. You were gone, and I had no one to blame but myself. I felt like I was being punished for the choices I've made."

"It wasn't your fault, Ali."

Ali looked down at her lap and nodded solemnly, swiping the back of her hand across her cheek to erase the tears. She spoke softly. "I know that now."

Eli placed his hand on her thigh, squeezing it encouragingly. "Things will be different now. We're together again and we're both safe. That's all that matters."

She liked his optimism. It was something she had always admired about him. That feeling like her world was about to come crashing down still lingered like a shadow that she couldn't shake, but it was easier to ignore now. She only had to remind herself that Berland was a sanctuary, and she was safe and secure with her family.

Across the room, Nik and Grace were arguing. Grace pointed out all his mistakes while Nik insisted he was doing it *exactly* as she had shown him. Grace then took a deep breath and repeated the motions more patiently this time.

"She's something special, isn't she? I would've given up by now," Ali said as she watched them twirl around the room. Still no improvement, and Grace gritted her teeth when Nik stepped on her foot for the tenth time.

"She is."

Something in his voice made her turn to look at him. She watched, and it was clear just how special he thought Grace was. Eli had looked at Ali a lot growing up. He'd looked at her with joy and respect and sometimes playful annoyance. But he'd never looked at Ali the way he was currently looking at Grace—full of longing and infatuation. The hungry desire was practically radiating from his body.

He spoke without looking at her. "I can feel you staring at me."

Ali returned to watching the dance lesson. "Are you sure—"

Eli snapped his head toward her so quickly that she swallowed the rest of her words. She wasn't interested in starting another fight with him, even if she thought he was being an idiot for not going after what he so clearly wanted.

When he was satisfied that she wouldn't nag him, he returned his gaze to Grace and Nik.

"He's not so bad," he said so softly she almost didn't hear him.

Ali had never thought she'd see the day when Eli might accept Nik. It felt like a small victory. She smiled and squeezed his arm while Eli rolled his eyes.

Chapter Forty-Three

ALI

ALI SAT ON A plush stool in Grace's grand bedroom. The room was unlike any she'd ever seen. It was bigger than her entire home back in Andus. Ornate designs covered the walls from floor to ceiling, and Grace's bed was big enough for three people to sleep in comfortably. Her floor was covered in a soft beige carpet and the walls were covered with shelves of trinkets, signs of a life well-lived.

The ladies had gathered in Grace's room to prepare for the Suitors' Ball that night. Amaya and Grace were chatting excitedly and running around grabbing clothes, hair styling tools, jewelry, and shoes. The room looked like a windstorm had ripped through it and left behind complete chaos.

Ali tried to keep her eyes on Grace and Amaya as they walked around the room, holding up various gowns and muttering their approval or disdain. Heather pushed Ali's head forward while she continued to style her hair in an elegant up-do. She used pins with pearls attached to keep her hair in place.

"If you don't stay still, I'm going to stab you again," Heather told her.

Ali had kept her head on a swivel and because of that, she'd been jabbed with several pins already. She exhaled and forced herself to sit still. "How much longer?"

"I'm almost done. Your hair is so long. Have you considered getting a cut? Maybe shoulder-length? It would look so good on you."

Ali fidgeted. She was fond of her long blonde hair and signature braid. "I don't know..."

"Well, if you change your mind, you know where to find my family's shop."

Ali enjoyed the company of the three women. Like Grace, they had welcomed her easily, and she was grateful for their friendship. Having girl friends was different. She snickered at what it would be like to do her hair and dress up with Eli.

"What about this one?" Grace held up a light pink dress that cinched at the waist and the tulle bottom would hit around Ali's knees. She gave it a twirl, and the bottom caught on the breeze and lifted elegantly.

"That'll wash her out," Heather told her.

They were searching for the perfect dress for Ali to wear to the ball. The other girls had picked their gowns weeks ago, but since Ali had nothing fancy enough for such an extravagant event, Grace had volunteered to lend her one.

"This one is pretty." Ali did her best to swivel in the chair with Heather's hands in her hair, but she could barely make out the dress that Amaya was holding up now.

Heather's hands stopped moving. "I'm wearing green."

"So?" Amaya asked with a hint of annoyance.

"So..." Heather let out a scandalized huff.

"It's fine," Ali said before Heather could argue. "I don't like green."

Fashion had never been a priority in Andus, but Ali knew one thing for certain—never compete with another woman. It was clear that the color green belonged to Heather tonight. It would look far better on her anyway, with her stunning red hair and freckles.

After a few more minutes, Heather released Ali from her seat. "All done."

Ali moved to the edge of the bedroom. She stared, mesmerized by her reflection in Grace's mirror. She hardly recognized herself between the hairstyle and the rouge Grace had insisted she try. Her pink cheeks gave her a sultry look while her eyes were lined in dark kohl that made them pop. She'd never had much of a reason to pay attention to her looks, but it occurred to her for the first time that she was quite beautiful.

"Thank you. It looks amazing."

"Don't worry about it."

She turned her head slightly to the left so she could admire the loose curls, one side swooped back and held with a bejeweled pin. "How did you get so good at this?"

"It started when I was a kid. The barber shop has been in our family for generations. My mother taught me a lot of the basics but as I got older, I liked to experiment on my own hair."

"Now she's the biggest trend setter," Grace gushed over her friend.

"Oh, stop. It's not that big of a deal." But Heather turned to hide a smile from her friend's praise.

"She's just being modest." Grace leaped over the piles of clothing scattered around her floor. Standing next to Ali, she held up two bracelets—one with crystal beads and the other a silver bangle. "Which one?"

"For me?" Ali asked.

"No. For the foot stool. Yes, for you." She alternated raising the bracelets and letting the light hit them while Ali considered them.

"You don't have to do this. You've already given me so much."

"I know. I want to. Any friend of Eli's is a friend of mine."

Ali noticed the way Grace smiled when she said Eli's name. It both delighted her to know that someone cared for Eli the way he deserved and also saddened her because he wouldn't do anything about it. Maybe she would try to talk to him one more time at the ball. "I guess the one on the left."

Grace handed her the crystal bracelet and slipped the silver bangle on her own wrist. "Perfect. This one goes better with my dress."

Ali quietly slid the jewelry onto her left arm, then watched as Heather and Amaya left to change into their gowns. "I'm glad he had you."

Grace gave her a questioning tilt of the head.

"Eli. I'm glad he wasn't alone. I was so scared for him, that he was out in the world by himself, injured or scared or both, missing his family and feeling abandoned. But all along, he had you."

There was something more authentic about the smile on Grace's face now. It was less forced than the usual facade she wore. Grace took Ali's hand and gave it a small squeeze, a small acknowledgment that Eli had been in good hands all along.

"Can I be honest?" Grace asked, and Ali nodded. "I think I needed him as much as he needed me. It was nice to have someone who listened when I spoke. Most men around here only see me for my title. They see a chance to have their opinions heard and couldn't care less about mine. Eli is the most kind and considerate man I've ever met. And not bad to look at either." Grace winked.

"Do you love him?" Ali asked. She regretted it almost immediately. She wasn't supposed to be interfering with Eli's relationship or not-re-lationship. But she was so curious. Maybe she wanted to absolve herself of some of her guilt, but she also truly wanted Eli to have what she had. To find his person.

Grace dropped Ali's hand, but her smile remained steadfast. "What's not to love?"

There was a flicker of pain hidden beneath her wide smile, and Ali knew it had to do with the fact that Eli wasn't entering the Rite. Grace would have to settle for one of those men who only wanted her influence, and it made Ali feel even more agitated with the entire situation.

Love was a gift that wasn't meant to be taken for granted. It didn't come by often. To be lucky enough to experience it and turn the other way? She couldn't grasp it.

Grace suddenly gasped, looking at something behind Ali. Ali turned to see what the distraction was. Amaya had returned to the room, holding up a maroon piece of fabric.

"Oh, *that* is the one."

Chapter Forty-Four

NIK

NIK STOOD AWKWARDLY WITH Sam, Theo, and Eli, fidgeting with the buttons on his long-sleeved dress shirt. He hated dressing up, but he hadn't had much of a choice. Grace had made it clear that the suitors' ball was a formal event. He grinned though as Eli tugged at his too-tight collar. At least he wasn't the only one who appeared uncomfortable.

Nik searched the ballroom. It had been transformed from the dark and dismal hall in which they'd practiced dancing into an ornate and exquisite ballroom fit for a princess, which Nik had to remind himself, Grace practically was.

The walls, once nothing more than black stone, were now covered in floor to ceiling drapes of ivory. The tables that had been stored in a dark corner were now spread across the room with matching tablecloths and floral arrangements of lilacs and pink hydrangeas.

He looked around the room again, peering over the tops of heads and in between clusters of bodies. There had to be at least a hundred people present already, but he couldn't see Ali nor tonight's guest of honor anywhere.

That morning, Grace had come by their home and practically ripped Ali from his arms. They had just barely woken up when Grace had barreled through the front door.

They really needed to get locks on their door.

Grace had insisted they were having a "girls' day" and that Ali would see him tonight.

That had been twelve hours ago.

Nik had been left to get ready for the ball on his own, wondering what the hell Grace was doing with his girlfriend. Of course, Ali was probably enjoying herself. She was more social than Nik and had grown closer with all the girls. Nik wasn't jealous, though. It was good for her to have friends...specifically friends that weren't named Eli.

Nik, on the other hand, didn't enjoy socializing. Spending an entire day hanging out with the "boys" was the equivalent of torture for him. He'd rather be training or doing something productive. He wasn't good at sitting around and doing nothing.

He shifted uncomfortably on his feet, very conscious of the lack of conversation amongst their group. The soft harmony of the string band was hardly enough to cut the unease.

Sam broke the silence with a heavy sigh. "I'm going to grab a drink."

"I'll show you to the bar," Theo offered.

Before Nik could object, they both scurried away through the thickening crowd, leaving him alone with Eli.

"So..." he started, before realizing he had nothing to follow it up with.

"So," Eli responded with a mocking grin. Fucking prick.

"You know what? I think I'm going to go get a drink as well."

Nik stepped in the direction that Sam and Theo had disappeared to, but Eli grabbed him by the arm. When Nik looked back with a scowl, Eli nodded at the entrance of the hall.

"My god," Nik whispered when he saw her.

Everything else fell away. Eli. The ballroom. The strangers. The other women who had linked arms with Ali.

When she found him staring at her, Ali beamed. She was naturally beautiful, but whatever they had done to her hair and cheeks just accentuated that beauty.

And that dress...

Nik didn't know if he should memorize the way it clung to her body or take her back to their room and shred it to pieces. Deep red strips of fabric wrapped from her shoulders down her chest, crisscrossing and wrapping behind her back. The effect somehow pushed her breasts together in a way that left Nik weak in the knees. Her ribs were left exposed, as was her right leg where a slit in the dress rose all the way to her hip.

Fuck, she was so beautiful.

"Do you need a tissue?" Eli asked.

"What?" Nik was still staring at Ali. He couldn't take her eyes off her as the group of women walked their way.

"For that drool."

"Fuck off."

It was a good thing the women were close now, or Nik might've punched Eli in the gut. Instead, he gave Ali his most charming grin. Her chest turned pink and Nik loved that he had that effect on her.

So responsive...

Nik hardly noticed Eli as he asked Grace to join him. "May I have this dance?"

"Absolutely." Grace took his hand and together they headed to the center of the ballroom. Their two friends, Heather and Amaya, left to search for drinks and eligible partners to dance with.

Left alone with Ali, Nik said, "You look..." He couldn't think of the words to describe her. Every adjective that came to mind failed to live up to how breathtaking she was.

Did she know how beautiful she was? She couldn't possibly or she never would've chosen to be with Nik. He didn't feel worthy of her.

Ali blushed and swept a stray strand of hair behind her ear. "Are you going to ask me to dance?"

Nik let out a soft laugh. "You want me to? Didn't you see the bruises on Grace's feet after our lesson?"

"I think it's worth the risk."

"Then yes, Ali. I would love to dance with you. But first, I have something for you."

Ali's eyes brightened as he reached into his pocket, pulling out a silver chain with a purple rose pendant.

Ali reached out with a look of shock. "My necklace? How did you...where?" She ran her fingers over the newly repaired chain.

"It's a long story. Here, let me help you." Nik took the necklace back and gestured for her to turn around. She pulled her hair off her neck, and Nik carefully clasped the chain and let the necklace fall into place.

Ali turned back to him, looking down at her necklace with a reminiscent grin on her face.

"It looks perfect," Nik said. "You look perfect."

Nik took her hand and together they walked to the dance floor. The string band was playing just loud enough to hear over the dull roar of the crowd. Ali linked her hands behind his neck, and he took her by the waist.

Dancing with Ali was absolutely worth the risk of a broken toe. As Ali nuzzled her face into Nik's chest, he wrapped an arm around her waist and held her tightly. So much of their lives had been changed, ripped apart, but this...this embrace held him together. She inhaled a deep breath and looked up at him, and he wondered if she felt the same.

Nik lost track of the number of dances they shared. He managed not to step on Ali's feet, but they did bump into an unhappy couple at one point.

An hour after the dance had started, a booming voice rang out, and the music paused. Next to the band, Grace's father was readying for a speech.

"Welcome. Welcome, everyone. Thank you so much for coming tonight. I just wanted to take a moment to express my gratitude to everyone for attending. It means the world to me to see my beautiful daughter, Grace, being celebrated with such magnitude."

Grace stood next to the stage and gave a small wave to the crowd as they turned to her. She didn't look the slightest bit uncomfortable at the attention she was receiving and her father's words of praise.

"Today is an important day for me as a father. I love my daughter very dearly and for the past twenty years, I have watched her grow into the kind and thoughtful woman she is today. She has brightened every single one of my days, and I've enjoyed accompanying her through each step of life. Now it is time to make way for another man who will no doubt enjoy walking through this next phase of life with you." He raised his glass in Grace's direction, speaking directly to her now. "I love you, Grace, and I am so very proud of you."

The crowd clapped and cheered while Ben stepped down from the stage and hugged his daughter.

Then Ellen had her turn.

"Not only is this an important day for my family, but it is also an important day for Berland. Our history is rooted in unity and striving for excellence, something the Rite represents so perfectly. I still remember my Rite like it was yesterday. You don't have to remind me it wasn't." The crowd chuckled at her well-rehearsed joke. "Seeing the people of Berland step up to a challenge is truly something to be proud of."

Ellen carried on about duty and tradition and a lot of other buzzwords that were meant to convey the importance of the Rite, but her speech reminded Nik of the ones the Head Commander used to give in Rysburg. Insincere and only meant to persuade the people of one opinion or another. He wondered what Ellen truly thought of the Rite. Did she really believe it was the best way to unify Berland or was it just easier to carry on with traditions, even the ones they'd outgrown?

Ellen closed out her speech with a few parting words of admiration for her daughter and a toast. "To Grace."

Those with drinks in their hands raised them in the air while the rest of the crowd repeated, "To Grace."

Ali and Nik sat at one of the unoccupied tables in the corner. Most of the chairs had been moved around as people took what they needed and dragged them to other tables. Only one remained, so Ali sat sideways on Nik's lap with her right side against his chest.

Nik wrapped his hands around her waist, taking a moment to admire the cut-out sections of her dress that displayed her sides. He ran his thumb over her smooth skin and smirked as she sat up straighter.

Ali cocked her head to the side. Her eyes glimmered in a way that hypnotized Nik, making him forget they were in a crowded room rather than their alone in their apartment. He continued to brush long strokes along her side, smiling mischievously. How many soft touches would it take to get her wet?

Not one to be outdone, Ali traced her finger along his collar, slyly undoing the top button of his shirt. Nik raised a brow when she dragged her finger down his chest. How many buttons did she intend to get away with?

"God, you two are insufferable." Eli placed his hands on his hips and shook his head like an older brother who had just caught someone feeling up his sister.

Nik rolled his eyes at Eli's impeccable timing but was thankful he'd at least moved on from the jealous ex-boyfriend behavior.

"Don't you have somewhere—anywhere—else to be?" Nik asked.

Ali gently smacked his chest where she had just been toying with his shirt. "Be nice."

An impossible task when it came to Eli. Tolerance was the best he could offer.

After removing his hand from her waist, Ali stood and straightened her dress. Nik missed the warmth of her body immediately. "Ready for another dance?"

Nik didn't need to glance down to know his pants were tighter than usual. Playing with the soft skin below Ali's breast had that effect. "I think I need a couple minutes."

"Fine. Eli?" She turned expectantly toward her friend.

"Sure." He held out an arm for Ali to hold, and Nik considered what it might be like to break that arm. But Ali gave him a warning look, so he resisted the urge.

Chapter Forty-Five

ELI

"ARE YOU TRYING TO make him a raging, jealous lunatic?" Ali asked when Eli asked for one more dance after three songs had already played. She'd left Nik alone at the table and so far, he hadn't come to interrupt them.

"I don't know what you mean." Eli looked anywhere but down at her, a devious grin spreading across his face. "Okay, fine. Maybe a little."

They both laughed, and she pinched his shoulder.

"Do you think it's working?" he asked.

Ali searched to find Nik sitting in the corner where they'd left him. He was leaning forward with his elbows on his knees and watching them closely.

Eli smirked, and Ali shook her head. "I think so. You're terrible."

"Oh, come on. Let me have this. It's too easy to get under his skin. Look at the way his brows are scrunched up. He looks like he wants to kill me."

"Why are you two like this?" She shook her head.

At least Eli could joke about it now. There was a time when the thought of her and Nik together was enough to kill him. Now he could tease her without pain searing through his chest.

They fell into a comfortable silence and danced slowly around the room. Each time Eli found himself with his back toward the stage, he saw Grace flitting between tables, greeting people and talking to men he didn't know. There was a jealous monster threatening to rise out of him, but there was nothing he could do about it. He'd have to learn to live with it.

Ali hissed, and he looked down. "If you squeeze me any tighter, you're going to leave bruises."

He loosened his grasp on her waist. "Sorry."

Ali turned to see what he'd been looking at and her face fell when she saw Grace with another man, her palm in his as he planted a kiss on the back of her hand.

"Eli..."

He had a feeling he knew what she was about to ask, and he wasn't sure if he could have this conversation again. Every time he was forced to face the idea of entering the Rite, he found himself gravitating toward saying yes.

But Ellen's warning still echoed in his mind. If he entered, he'd be setting Grace up for failure. Ellen had chosen the words of her speech wisely.

Tradition.

Eli was untraditional. He was a newcomer, and being with him would put a strain on Grace's leadership. She was better off without him.

"Yes?" he asked with a weary sigh.

"Have you given any more thought into entering the Rite?"

"Are we going to do this again?"

Ali bit her cheek, and he could tell she was fighting the urge to argue with him, maybe as much as he was fighting the urge to change his own mind. She lasted all of sixty seconds before she broke the silence again. "It's just that...she really seems to make you happy, and I don't want you to regret not at least *trying*. What's the harm in trying, Eli?"

His feet stopped moving in the small circles they'd be drawing on the floor for several songs. He dropped his hold on her waist altogether. "I can't, Ali."

"Can't what?"

Eli felt like ripping his hair out, and Ali sensed his frustration. After all the years they'd spent together, it was easy for her to pick up on his body language. The way he stiffened and retreated a few steps.

"I didn't mean to upset you, Eli. I just think...I think that you'll regret it if you don't go after what you want. Will you be able to live with yourself if you choose not to fight for her?"

Something caught in Eli's throat. No matter how hard he tried to swallow, it stayed, strangling him. He clawed at the collar of his shirt again.

He was over this entire night. He was done with Ali's interrogation, and he wanted to close his eyes and stop the questions that were rolling around in his mind. He was more confused now than ever before. He needed more time to figure things out. It was all happening too quickly.

Eli looked up to find the person he needed to talk to most. In the corner of the room, near the double doors leading to the hall, Grace was being escorted from the ballroom, Trevor's hand on her back as she reluctantly walked with him. She looked back over her shoulder and caught Eli staring. Her eyes said everything he needed to hear.

Eli didn't hesitate as he rushed toward the door, Ali following right behind him. The worst possible thoughts rushed through his mind. Had

Trevor found out they'd overheard him in Noah's office? Was he going to threaten her or worse, hurt her?

They rushed into the hall, and they weren't far behind Grace and Trevor, whose hold on Grace's arm made Eli fume. Eli closed in on them with lightning speed.

"Wait!" he heard Ali yell, but before she could stop him, he was grabbing Trevor by the collar of his jacket and slamming him against a wall.

Grace let out a surprised yelp and covered her mouth.

"What do you think you're—"

Eli's fist connected with Trevor's nose before he could finish his sentence. "Don't *ever* touch her again."

Trevor laughed even as blood trickled from his nose. There was something sinister in his smile that sent chills up Eli's spine, and he pulled his fist back for another punch that landed across Trevor's upper lip. Multiple streams of red were flowing now, but he still gave Eli an evil grin as he licked the blood from his lips.

"A few months from now and I'll be able to touch her whenever and wherever I want, kid."

Out of the corner of his eye, Eli saw Ali move closer to Grace and hold her hand, comforting her as Eli terrorized Trevor.

Eli pulled his fist back again, this time aiming for Trevor's left eye. He acted quickly, though, and dodged Eli's punch. Eli yelped when he hit the hard stone wall. Something crunched in his knuckles. He bent over in pain, and Trevor used the opportunity to knee him in the stomach. Then he drove an elbow into the back of Eli's head.

"Trevor!" Grace screamed.

Eli wouldn't go down so easy. He stood up and wrapped Trevor in his arms, throwing them both to the floor. He swung once at Trevor's face and then a second time but Trevor blocked it.

Eli and Trevor were a tangled mess of limbs and bodies until Nik ran up from behind and grabbed Eli by his torso. Nik struggled to pull him off of Trevor and had to dodge a few stray punches, but eventually Eli was restrained and Theo got a hold of Trevor.

Grace approached, frantically searching Eli's face for wounds and inspecting his scrapes and rapidly forming bruises, but Eli had a hard time focusing on anything other than Trevor. He wanted to *kill* him.

Trevor's sneer was as wicked as ever. "Enjoy your time with her now, Eli. Once I win the Rite, the bitch is mine."

Eli might've enjoyed another punch to Trevor's face, but Nik beat him to it. There was a loud crack and Trevor fell back a few steps, hit the wall, and then sank to the floor. Nik flexed his hand a few times and then turned to face them.

Grace and Eli both studied him with a mix of surprise and gratitude.

Nik shrugged. "Sorry, but no one should speak about you like that."

Grace smiled with appreciation before grabbing Eli by the arm. "Are you okay?"

He winced as she brushed his cheekbone. "I'm fine. Are you okay?"

Eli watched as Grace wrapped his knuckles in a clean white fabric. Scrapes covered his right hand, and every movement made his joints scream in protest.

"That was stupid," Grace whispered as she continued to work.

"He had it coming. If he ever puts his hands on you, I'll kill him."

"You're being ridiculous."

Eli used his free left hand to twist her arm around. Bruises in the shape of a hand were already forming where Trevor had gripped her in the hallway.

She hastily hid the marks from sight.

"What did you want me to do? Stand back and do nothing?"

Her expression had been clear before leaving the ballroom. She had looked scared and wanted his help.

"No. I'm glad you came. I just didn't expect you to get into a fistfight."

"He's dangerous, Grace."

She sighed. "I know that. But... Eli, there's a high likelihood that Trevor will win this thing. I don't know what I'll do if he does. I'm afraid this might've made things worse."

Eli swallowed the bile rising in his throat. He hadn't thought it was possible to make the situation worse. "Your mother is fine with this?"

"She truly doesn't believe that Trevor has done anything wrong. She still sees him as the innocent kid he used to be. Back when the worst thing he did was hide a fish under his friends' beds as a prank." She laughed, though it was humorless.

"Why doesn't she believe you?"

Grace wrapped his wrist in silence. When she finished, she sat back in the chair that she had borrowed from Eli's dining table. He sat patiently on the end of his bed, waiting for her to answer his questions.

"My mother doesn't take me seriously. Or rather, she thinks I don't take this job seriously. As much as she still sees Trevor as a harmless child, she still sees me as an irresponsible teen—boy crazy and with a head full of air."

Grace's head hung, and he used his pointer finger to tilt her chin up. "You are not stupid, Grace. Your devotion to your city is admirable and selfless. You go above and beyond to care for your friends. You are smart and your ideas are insightful. Your mother is blind if she doesn't see how amazing you are."

Her eyes glistened, and he didn't like the way her shoulders slumped in defeat. Grace's light was a beacon of hope, and he hadn't realized how strongly he held onto it until it was diminished. "Grace?"

"I think it's time for us to go our separate ways. Tomorrow is the official start of the Rite, and I just think it would be better if we said our goodbyes now."

It felt like a punch to his gut. She said it so matter-of-factly, making it clear she didn't think this was up for debate. Something was stuck in his throat, simultaneously making it hard to breathe and even harder to respond.

Grace picked at a stray thread of her dress, looking down so Eli couldn't see her face. He leaned forward on his bed and again tilted her chin up, brushing his thumb over her bottom lip. "Grace?"

"It's too hard, Eli." She inhaled sharply with a new resolve. "I can't marry someone else while I'm still thinking of you. I think...I think I could've loved you. I know this thing between us was just supposed to be careless and fun, but somewhere along the way..."

Eli was speechless. Her words so perfectly captured his own emotions. He should've been elated. Instead, he felt like he'd stumbled upon an overflowing river during a drought, only to find out it was just a mirage.

He leaned forward, and her forehead touched his, and he listened to her shaky breathing. He clung to her trembling hands and tilted his head forward, his nose bumping into hers.

"Grace," he whispered against her skin, so close he could practically taste her. He felt the moisture of her tears as they fell down her cheeks.

Just a little closer...he needed her closer.

Their knees pressed together, and she was looking at him through dark tear-soaked lashes.

And then...her lips were on his. Tender and all-consuming. His entire body was electrified.

Her lips trembled, and he wanted to break the kiss. He wanted to tell her that he felt the same. But then she whimpered, and her body melted further into his.

Eli grabbed her by the waist and pulled her into his lap, rolling his hips and devouring her. He traced her lips with the tip of his tongue until she parted them and then he could taste her—feel her hammering pulse.

Her hands traveled up his arms and into his hair, pulling him close, and he could hardly breathe but didn't dare break the kiss. If he died of suffocation, then it would be the greatest death of all time.

Grace ground into him, and then it was his turn to moan. God, she felt so perfect in his hands. He clung to her curves while she dragged her hands down his chest.

And then it was over.

She broke the kiss and stood from his lap with a sob. The pain on her face crushed him. She looked completely wrecked. "I'm sorry. I just...it never meant anything." She rushed through his door and closed it before he could respond.

Lies.

Lies she had told herself to survive.

It had *always* meant something. For both of them.

Chapter Forty-Six

ELI

THERE COULDN'T HAVE BEEN a better day for the opening ceremony. The sun was shining bright and there wasn't a single cloud in the sky. In fact, the only gloom seemed to be emanating from Eli.

He felt sick to his stomach.

He couldn't get Ellen's warning out of his head, but he also couldn't stop thinking of Grace's face as she'd left the night before, telling him it hadn't meant anything.

She was wrong. But what he had to do to prove it to her...

Could he?

All morning, he had been lost in thought. The dark expression on his face had been enough to keep Ali from asking any questions, though he could tell she wanted to. She had encouraged him to accompany them to the opening ceremony, and he had accepted. It likely would have been easier to stay home and hide in bed, but he couldn't bring himself to take the coward's way out.

It seemed as though everyone in Berland was headed toward the empty field to witness the opening ceremony. The path was packed with people walking shoulder to shoulder and chatting excitedly. Something this big hadn't happened since—well, since Grace's mother had gone through the process.

Their excitement was contagious, and Ali practically danced as she walked down the crowded street, beaming with a radiance that ended abruptly in Eli's shadows. Along with the opening ceremony, there would be celebrations all day long with food and drinks and all the merriment a person could dream of.

If Eli survived this day, he'd drink his fair share of wine.

Each of the shops they passed had bright flowers displayed. Banners hung across the path and streamers had been thrown haphazardly over every possible surface. All the shop owners were prepared for the crowd that would infiltrate town after the big announcement.

It wasn't just the shops that were dressed up. Everywhere he looked, people were sporting fresh haircuts, clean trousers, and posh blouses. Many of the women wore airy summer dresses, including Ali.

They reached the last of the shops on the main strip and wandered into more open terrain. Fields and trees lined the path as they made their way to a wide opening settled in the valley. One structure appeared out of place—a building with shuttered windows and a closed door.

Azalea's.

Eli grinned before he could stop himself, thinking of his birthday night there with Grace. But that was in the past.

Forget butterflies. A violent monster was growing in his stomach, gnawing and clawing its way out. He was going to be sick.

"Are you okay?" Ali asked as she fell into step beside him.

"Fine." He spoke curtly, afraid that if he opened his mouth much more, his breakfast might spill out.

"I wonder what that place is," Ali said as she tried to peer into the clouded window of Azalea's.

"It looks like it's permanently closed," said Sam.

"It's not," Eli responded.

She turned to look at him, and he could feel his cheeks turn red. He should've kept his mouth shut.

"Then what is it?" she asked.

Eli cleared his throat and adjusted the collar of his shirt. "It's a bar of sorts."

That caught Nik's attention. "A bar? Why didn't you say so? We could check it out after the—"

"No," Eli said firmly.

"Why not?" Ali pressed on.

"It's...not for you," Eli said.

"Why does it feel like you're hiding something, Eli?" Ali asked with a raised eyebrow.

He ran a hand through his hair. "It's...provocative."

Nik and Ali shared a look that made Eli want to pummel him. Nik was the perfect person to take out his frustrations on today. The last thing he wanted was to be teased by that asshole.

Eli resumed his walk, picking up his pace to get some distance between them.

Ali quickly caught up to him. "So you've been there?"

"Yes, Ali. I've been there."

"With Grace?"

He flinched but quickly replaced his irritation with a blank expression. "Yes. Are you done with the interrogation?"

"Fine." She held her hands up in surrender. "I won't ask any more questions."

The once-empty field was set up with a temporary stage covered in a tent-like structure. Three elegant navy and gold chairs were in the center—one each for Grace and her parents.

Benches formed a half circle facing the stage, leaving enough space in the center for the contestants to stand. It was empty now. They wouldn't be called forward until later—after Grace's mother gave an opening speech.

"There's Theo," Sam said, pointing to one of the benches closest to the stage. As they got closer, Sam teased, "The brother of the bride doesn't even get a seat on stage?"

"No. I'm just the spare." He smiled good-naturedly and patted the seat next to him.

Sam sat down beside Theo. Nik slid onto the bench next, then Ali, leaving Eli on the end. Eli's leg bounced uncontrollably, and he wrung his hands together. His mind was full of a buzzing static he couldn't shake. Somehow both bursting with whirling thoughts yet devoid of any sense.

"Are you okay?" Ali asked him.

"Yeah. Why wouldn't I be?"

Ali's eyes roamed to his shaky knees and back up to his face a few times.

Eli stilled. "Right."

The noise around the makeshift stadium grew into a roaring commotion as more people filed into the open field. The benches were packed tight with bodies and eventually people were forced to stand in the back. Every single person in Berland was surely present today.

Eli could hardly focus. Beside him, Ali and the others were lost in conversation. She'd already given him several concerned looks, but he didn't have it in him to tell her what was going through his mind. He could hardly put it into words the way he was being torn in half.

He should've made up his mind by now. No, he had made up his mind. He wasn't entering. He'd told Grace that and he'd told her mother that. He'd told himself that a thousand times.

So why did he still feel conflicted?

He rubbed his sweaty palms together and stared at the empty chair that Grace would soon occupy. He felt the lump in his throat growing and clawed at the invisible obstruction. Sweat dripped down his neck, and he cursed the blazing sun.

"You're fidgeting," Ali reminded him.

Eli grumbled but couldn't argue. There was no way to shake his nerves. He rolled his shoulders and then cracked his neck. He searched the crowd, his eyes stalling on each person he came across that appeared single and a reasonable age for marriage. It pissed him off that these people had nothing holding them back.

"Are you—"

"Please, Ali. I'm just trying to get through this."

At last, Ellen and Benjamin walked onto the platform hand-in-hand, both dressed in matching royal blue. Ellen's dress was sleeveless and flowy, perfect for the summer day, and Benjamin wore matching slacks with a white dress shirt. They waved at the roaring crowd and as they reached the center of the stage, Grace made her grand entrance.

Next to her parents' dark attire, Grace's white gown illuminated the stage, her face so pale it almost matched her dress. The top hugged her curves while the bottom fell loosely at her sides. Her heels clicked as she walked across the stage.

The muscles in Grace's face twitched as she did her best to feign a smile. It was hard not to compare it to the sweet look of bliss she always had first thing in the morning when she woke up next to him.

Eli didn't think it was possible for the lump in his throat to grow any larger, but now he was surely suffocating.

Grace took her spot between her parents, and Ellen raised her hands to quiet the assembly of civilians. She began a prepared speech about her beautiful and charming daughter.

Eli didn't hear much past the first sentence. His eyes were locked on Grace, who seemed to be consciously avoiding looking in his direction. She looked all around at the crowd but before she found Eli, she quickly darted her eyes down toward her feet.

It might've been a coincidence, but after she repeated this routine a fourth time, Eli knew it was intentional. She couldn't—or wouldn't—look at him. And he felt sick over it.

"So," Ellen continued, disrupting Eli's thoughts, "with that being said, let's begin the declarations."

Eli understood what that meant. Grace had told him once how this day would go. Each person would come forward individually to the clearing and make it known that they wanted to participate in the Rite with the intent to marry Grace.

All eyes turned to the space at the front of the stage that had been left open.

A man who appeared to be in his late thirties, a short buzz-cut and sun damaged skin was the first to walk into the opening. He cleared his throat and said with a booming voice, "My name is Charles, and I wish to compete for Lady Grace's hand in marriage."

The man gave a slight nod to Grace, and she smiled politely in return.

A second man came forward and repeated the same line as Charles, followed by another and then another.

One by one, the line of men grew until there were at least twenty standing before the platform. More time passed between each one and it seemed the declaration of participants was coming to an end.

Trevor, never missing the opportunity to garner attention, had waited until the last minute to come forward. He probably wanted to make a scene, to make it known that *he* was the contender they needed to beat.

He stood with his chin held high and gave a slimy wink to Grace. She did her best to hide her distaste, but Eli noticed the uptick of the corner of her mouth. "My name is Trevor, and I wish to compete for Lady Grace's hand in marriage."

The words left a bitter taste in Eli's mouth. Trevor's voice was more snake-like than human. Everything about the man was foul and untrustworthy.

Eli couldn't handle it.

"Is there anyone else—" Ellen's voice was a fuzzy static in Eli's ears. His limbs were trembling.

He looked to the stage where Ellen was now scanning the crowd for any movement that might indicate another person was on their way forward. Eli looked at Grace. She was frozen—the epitome of regal. She hated this, but she still put on a smile and would carry the weight of the world for her people. For stability. So her people would respect her and know they could rely on her.

The second her eyes met Eli's, he saw through all of the bullshit. He saw the shadows already threatening to dim her light. Yet there was resilience there. A dare to the universe to try to break her. She would prevail...and he would help her.

Then Eli was on his feet. He cleared his throat as he stepped into the space next to Trevor.

"My name is Eli, and I wish to compete for Lady Grace's hand in marriage."

Chapter Forty-Seven

GRACE

Grace was vaguely aware of the roaring crowd as she focused on her breathing. Her cheeks flushed and her corset felt too tight. Sweat formed under the weight of her gown. The shade of the stage didn't do much to shield her from the hot summer day.

But none of it mattered.

Eli was standing there, on the far end of the row of suitors, squinting against the rays of the sun as he declared his intention to enter the Rite.

She'd never felt more alive.

She hadn't expected it. She'd been sure he had made up his mind long ago that he wouldn't enter. And then leaving his room last night...he hadn't argued. Hadn't told her that she was wrong and that he had grown to care for her after all.

It had been mortifying admitting to her feelings while he fell silent. She thought she had read him wrong.

But here he was.

She watched as he side-eyed Trevor with a look of vitriol and then turned to face her again. He returned her beaming smile and even snuck a wink in her direction.

The air felt lighter somehow. Less suffocating.

She was so lost in her own thoughts that she didn't even hear her mother dismiss the crowd and mark the end of the ceremony. People began to move toward the path that led back to town where they could begin drinking and celebrating the beginning of the Rite and the official start of summer. But the men—her suitors—lingered near the stage.

It was her turn for another speech.

She stepped toward the edge of the stage, and the men listened intently, including Eli who she found herself gazing at more than the others. She couldn't help it. She shouldn't play favorites, but there was no denying he held her heart already.

"I just want to thank each of you for being here. Your devotion to Berland...and to me...is greatly appreciated. The first round will be one month from today. As you all know, the first round is a competition of speed and perseverance. Since there are sixteen of you, you'll be racing to find eight medallions in a pit of mud. Those who find one will move on to the next round, while those without will be eliminated. Any questions?"

The men shook their heads. The first round was pretty simple, so she didn't expect there to be much confusion.

"Great. Then you are all dismissed. I look forward to our next meeting."

She watched as most of them turned to head back toward town. A few lingered, hoping they might have a private moment with her, but she was only interested in speaking with one of them.

Grace followed her parents to the edge of the stage, noticing her mother's pursed lips and flared nostrils. Grace didn't know what had set her mother off this time but frankly, she was tired of trying to please her. No matter what Grace did or who she tried to be, none of it was ever enough.

From here on out, she would only try to live up to her own expectations, her mother be damned.

Meanwhile, her father was congratulating her, but she was too busy peering over his shoulder. A couple more of the men had disappeared now, realizing she was busy with her parents and that they wouldn't get that private moment any time soon.

Only Eli and Charles, the first man, remained.

Her father gave her a hug while her mother gave her the cold shoulder, only muttering a quick "good luck." Grace didn't ask what was wrong. She'd find out soon enough. Her mother never lost a chance to tell her she needed to grow up or take her position more seriously.

Grace watched her parents walk hand-in-hand from the field, and then she approached Eli and Charles.

Charles spoke first, eager to cut off Eli. "Miss Grace, could I have a moment?"

Grace smiled, and she found it easy to be sincere. She was *happy*. Recklessly happy for the first time in what felt like forever. "I'm sorry, Charles. I actually need to speak with Eli for a moment. Why don't I find you back in town and you can buy me a drink?"

The poor man looked delighted at the prospect, and he tipped his head before walking off in the opposite direction.

Grace waited until he was out of sight. Then she lunged and wrapped her arms around Eli's neck, planting a passionate kiss on his lips. He froze in shock but quickly wrapped his arms around her waist, lifting her slightly off the ground. She broke the kiss long enough to say, "I thought you weren't going to enter?"

"Me too," he said before devouring her lips again.

She leaned back and ran her fingers through his hair. "What changed?"

"I fell in love with you."

Acknowledgements

I have to start out by saying this book was *brutal* to write. So to my fellow author friends, thank you for putting up with my constant complaining about this story, its pacing, and for encouraging me even after I deleted and rewrote the whole thing multiple times. It was a journey to get here but I'm so happy to have you by my side.

Thank you to my alpha readers and beta readers! Anna, Chloe, Sam and Shelby – I appreciate your words of wisdom and your support means the world to me!

To my best friends – thank you for being the ultimate hype squad! Without your encouragement, I never would've published one book, let alone two.

Last but not least, thanks to anyone reading this book. I love sharing stories but they would mean very little without anyone to read them.

For a list of titles by Rachel Mays, please visit
www.authorrachelmays.com

www.ingramcontent.com/pod-product-compliance
Lightning Source LLC
Chambersburg PA
CBHW030917300726
48970CB00001B/206